"One Might Almost Fancy You Were Glad to See Me, Milady. . . ."

She could feel the fury crashing from him, sense the enormous control that kept him from reaching for her throat.

His eyes narrowed. "You look so pale, Phaedra. Has my return astonished you that much? What did you think they were going to do to me, Armande de LeCroix, the most noble Marquis de Varnais?"

"I don't know. I only thought to—" She faltered. If she but breathed she would brush up against him.

"To have me hanged?"

"I wanted protection! Did you think I was going to wait to see what malicious plot you next had in store for me?" Phaedra cried.

To her astonishment, he smiled. "You are a very impulsive woman, Phaedra Grantham." He traced her jaw, making her pulse run riot. "I wish the mistrust between us could end. . . ."

SERENA RICHARDS

Masquerade

BERKLEY BOOKS, NEW YORK

MASQUERADE

A Berkley Book / published by arrangement with
the author

PRINTING HISTORY
Berkley edition / January 1990

ISBN: 0-425-11740-5

A BERKLEY BOOK® TM 757,375
Berkley Books are published by The Berkley Publishing Group,
200 Madison Avenue, New York, New York 10016.
The name "BERKLEY" and the "B" logo
are trademarks belonging to Berkley Publishing Corporation.

PRINTED IN THE UNITED STATES OF AMERICA

10 9 8 7 6 5 4 3 2 1

Chapter One

THE IRON BARS ACROSS THE WINDOW CAST THEIR SHADOWS UPON Lady Phaedra Grantham's face as she paced the confines of her cell. She raked her fingers through tangled masses of red-gold hair, her dark-fringed green eyes darting from the grate in the heavy oak door to the window far above her head.

The distance between the dingy plaster walls seemed to grow smaller each day, and the room closed in on her like the jaws of a trap. She knew it was all a trick of her imagination, the result of staring too long at the black beetles as they scuttled through the cracks to freedom—a freedom she might never know again.

Phaedra shivered, rubbing her arms. 'Twas so cold in this place. She pulled the ragged remains of a blanket over her lawn nightshirt as her bare feet trod ceaselessly back and forth on the wooden floor. The thin cloth afforded small protection against the wind that blew through the broken glass beyond the bars.

Had the gnarled branches of the trees shed the last of their brittle leaves? She had no way of knowing. She had lost track of the days. All she could see of the world beyond was a patch of October sky, a pale wintry blue—the same color as *his* eyes. The man she had known as Armande de LeCroix, the Marquis de Varnais.

Her adversary, she reminded herself fiercely. The one person on earth who could have brought her to such a pass. The thought of him made her breath come quicker, and she clenched her fists.

Something stirred inside of her, like tiny wings fluttering deep within her womb. Phaedra stopped and leaned against the thick door. Cradling her hands across the slight swell of her abdomen, she forced herself to relax. She must not upset herself again. She must remain calm—if not for her own sake, then for the sake of the child.

This resolution was forgotten when she heard the scratching sound on the other side of the door. A blood-soaked arm shot through the small opening of the grate. Phaedra bit back her scream as she shrank away from the sticky red fingers pawing at the air.

A shrill laugh trickled along her spine like the icy blade of a knife. "Have you forgotten me so soon, my dear?" a voice crooned. "I came to tell you I've escaped."

Phaedra lowered her trembling hands from her mouth. Through the grate, violet eyes gleamed at her. She saw a thicket of blond tresses framing a young girl's face—a face that once perhaps had been beautiful, but now was gaunt, ravaged by such horrors as Phaedra refused to contemplate. She whispered, "Marie? Is that you? Dear God! What have you done to your wrists?"

The woman giggled behind her hand like a child hiding a secret. "I told you these Russians could not hold an Austrian princess captive. My bones are too delicate for their clumsy shackles. I wriggled free. And when I tell my brother . . . "

The violet eyes clouded. "My brother," she repeated as if searching for some elusive remembrance. An expression of haunting sadness crossed her features, only to be quickly replaced with her familiar, childlike smile.

"Yes, I've told my brother, the Emperor Franz Joseph, all about you—"

She broke off as Phaedra heard a rough voice shout, "There she is. Seize her."

With another hysterical laugh, the woman disappeared from view, followed by the sound of running feet. As Phaedra buried her face in her hands she heard a heavy thud, and then a series of shrieks.

What were they doing to the poor creature? Since the first day of her imprisonment, Phaedra had refused to look through the grate into the main gallery beyond. She knew too well what horrifying scenes waited on the other side of that door.

But as the woman's screams were choked off, Phaedra could

bear ignorance no longer. She had to know what was happening. She flung herself at the grillwork, clutching the rusted iron.

The woman Phaedra knew only as Marie Antoinette jerked spasmodically on the straw-covered floor as a burly guard lashed her hands behind her.

"Stop it," Phaedra cried. "Leave her alone, you fool! Can you not see she needs a doctor?"

"Shut your mouth. Or you'll need one yourself!" The guard grabbed Marie by the ankles and hauled her away, heedless of the blond head banging against the floor. "Scrawny little bitch. I told them we needed smaller manacles."

"The poor thing is mad, damn you!" Phaedra's fist smashed against the grate, scraping the skin from her knuckles while tears of anger burned her eyes. "Have you no pity?"

"Have you no pity? No pity! No pity!" Her words were taken up by other voices, until they echoed around the hall, swelling into an indistinguishable howl. Against her will, she stared at the occupants of the large chamber. What Phaedra saw was like a scene from Dante's *Inferno*—twisted limbs writhing against their chains, mouths issuing forth sounds unheard of outside the regions of hell. Scores of vacant eyes stared at her, empty reflections of the beings whose souls had been stolen from them ages ago.

All hope abandon, ye who enter here. The poet's verse pounded through her brain. How had Dante, writing centuries ago, imagined a place like St. Mary of Bethlehem Hospital in London? The poet had been expressing his visions of hell. Hell . . . Bedlam. They were one and the same. How long before Phaedra's captors reduced her to the same broken state as those poor wretches on the other side of the door? How long before she became as mad as her captors claimed?

"Someone will help me," she whispered, dashing aside her tears. Jonathan? No, he was her longtime friend, but he was too weak, incapable. But if Jonathan could find her cousin. Only Gilly was bold enough to find some way to save her. Where was he?

He should have returned to London by now—unless his Irish temper had gotten the better of him, and he had challenged the man known as Armande de LeCroix. She shuddered as the image of that aquiline face forced its way into her memory. The thin lips twisted into a cruel smile as his rapier cut through the air, the sable-brown hair flowing back from his brow. In his hands, the blade became an extension of Armande's own lithe and ruthless strength.

Surely Gilly would not be so foolish as to fight with the Marquis. No, Gilly was too clever for that, Phaedra reassured herself. As she started to withdraw farther into her cell, a flash of movement in the gallery caught her eye. Peering through the grate, she saw figures grotesquely out of place in the ragged company of lunatics. The pink satin of the fop's knee breeches and waistcoat stood out as brightly as the purple silks of his lady friend. As they progressed lazily through the hall, Phaedra sensed that they were headed toward the door to her cell.

"Dear God, not again," she murmured. Retreating to her cot, she sat down, gripping the edge of the mattress, hoping she might be spared the humiliation just this once. But her prayers went unanswered. The key chinked in the lock and she heard the false syrupy tones that her gaoler, Belda, adopted for visitors.

"And in here, m'lord, m'lady, is the treat I promised your worships. One of the finest spectacles Bedlam has to offer."

Belda's bewhiskered face appeared in the doorway, sneering at Phaedra as she entered, balancing a tray of food against her drooping bosom—one of the few features of Belda's bulky person that indicated her sex.

"Come in, come in," she called over her shoulder to the visitors as she set the tray down on the stool. "There's naught to fear."

The dandy stepped inside, his long nose sniffing the air with distaste as he leveled his quizzing glass at Phaedra. His lady clung close to him, shaking out the polonaise loops of her gown, ducking her head so that her powdery mountain of frizzed hair did not brush against the doorframe.

"Oh, Danny," the creature wailed, blanching beneath the layers of rouge. "This one's not even chained."

"Perfectly all right, miss." Belda grinned. "She's quiet most of the time, though she's been known to get wild. But I'm here to see she behaves herself, ain't that right, dearie?"

The matron prodded Phaedra's arm with one pudgy finger. "Say good morning to the nice lady and gentleman."

"Go to perdition," Phaedra said, her fingers clamping down harder upon the mattress.

"Naughty, naughty." Belda pinched Phaedra's chin until her eyes watered. "Mind your manners. We wouldn't want to have another session in Dr. Crowley's tranquilizing chair, would we?"

No, *we* wouldn't, Phaedra thought as she yanked her head aside. She would not let Belda goad her into a display of temper this time. Too often, she had provided the spectacle visitors craved, throwing herself forward to beg for help or railing at them for their heartlessness in coming to gawk at the unfortunate inmates. It was worse when she recognized her visitors, as she did now. The foppish man was Lord Arthur Danby.

He and the lady stood just inside the door, looking her over as if she were one of the animals in the Royal Menagerie. Her tray of food was within reach. How would those two white-powdered heads look with some of Bedlam's gray stew dripping down into their ears?

Out of the corner of her eye, Phaedra caught Belda's malicious grin. No, that was just the excuse the matron was looking for. Phaedra grit her teeth and forced her hands to lie folded in her lap.

Lord Arthur Danby swung his quizzing glass by its string. "Well, she's hardly worth having paid an extra shilling to see." His companion pouted her agreement, unfurling a painted chicken-skin parchment fan before her face.

"I liked that skinny man downstairs much better."

"The one who kept exposing his privates? Charmelle, you nasty gel." They both went off into a fit of giggling which Belda interrupted by seizing Phaedra's hair and forcing her head back.

"But look. This one is a famous noblewoman, Lady Phaedra Grantham. The demented thing tried to take her own life. Threw herself into the river."

Phaedra pursed her lips to keep from crying out. *Tis a lie. I was pushed. Someone tried to kill me.* Such statements only ended with her being bound and gagged until the "mad humour" had left her.

"Phaedra Grantham?" Danby stepped forward for a closer inspection.

"Oh, Danny, do be careful," Charmelle cooed. "Her green eyes look so wild."

Lord Arthur scratched at his neck beneath the edge of his bag-wig. "But stap me, Charmelle. I believe I've met this woman somewhere before."

Of course you did, you fool, Phaedra thought as she glared up into Danby's vapid face. The cloying reek of his orange flower-water scent made her stomach churn. *You passed out on the floor of the Gold Room the night I first suspected Armande de LeCroix of trying to destroy me, using you as his tool. But I daresay you were too drunk to remember.*

Danby scowled as if she had spoken the words aloud, then shrugged as if the effort of memory was too great for him. "Bedlam is full of attempted suicides. I still see nothing so interesting about this one."

Belda released Phaedra's hair and rolled her eyes piously heavenward. "Ah, but her wickedness goes beyond trying to throw her own life away." The matron tugged Phaedra's gown tight against her frame, revealing the slight swell of her stomach. "She tried to kill her poor babe, too."

Phaedra wrenched her shift out of Belda's grasp, the heat of anger flooding into her cheeks. Belda's large breasts shook with her chuckle. "Aye, a babe—and this fine lady's husband long in his grave. So you know the child be none of his getting, unless her high-and-mightiness found some way of lying with a corpse."

Charmelle shook her head behind her fan. "Tsk, tsk."

"Get out of here. Get out of my room, you old hag, and take these dolts with you." Phaedra leaped to her feet, her hands balling into fists.

Belda tapped a finger significantly to her temple. "Thinks she's still back at her estate, playing grand lady of the manor."

All three of them stared at her, waiting as if for the curtain to go up on the farce at Drury Lane. She heard Belda snickering under her breath. The laugh reminded Phaedra of her grandfather, Sawyer Weylin.

"Your passions will be the ruin of you, girl," the old man had been wont to tell Phaedra. "The flame of your hair burns clean through your scalp, setting your brain afire."

No, not this time, Grandfather. She could almost see the old man nod his head in approval. So strange to think that she would probably never see him again. Phaedra sank back onto the cot, closing her eyes tight, wrapping her arms around herself until she felt the anger receding. A disappointed sigh escaped Charmelle while Danby yawned.

"Mayhap you should refund their money," Phaedra said to Belda. The matron jerked back her arm to deliver a blow, then lowered it in frustration. Straightening her shoulders, Phaedra sat more erect, suppressing her triumphant smile. Never since entering this place had she felt so much in control.

Lord Arthur stepped aside to examine her food tray. When he

raised the cover from the bowl, the odor of rancid gruel permeated the room; he hurriedly pressed a lace handkerchief to his nose.

"Faugh! What is this stuff? Boiled rats?"

"No, indeed." Belda bustled over to him, stirring a spoon through the thickened, grayish lumps. "'Tis a most nourishing stew. I prepared it myself."

While the two of them had their backs to her, Phaedra turned her attention to Charmelle, who lingered by the doorway. The temptation was too great to resist. Phaedra squinted up one eye and bared her teeth, mouthing the words, "I'll tear your heart out and eat it."

Charmelle's painted mouth hung open for a moment before she screeched, "Owww, Danny, save me." She whirled in a rustle of purple skirts and petticoats, blundering into the door. Amidst a cloud of powder, she fled the room.

"Charmelle! What the deuce!" Lord Arthur spluttered, running after her and slamming the door behind him. Belda eyed Phaedra with suspicion, but Phaedra sat with her hands folded across her lap, gazing vacantly at the wall.

Banging the lid back down over the soup bowl, Belda scowled, "You'd best not be up to any more of your tricks, m'girl. Eat your dinner, or I swear I'll come back and stuff it down your throat. We want no more of your starving nonsense."

Phaedra continued to stare as if she heard nothing.

Belda paused just outside the door to peek one last time through the grate. "You don't fool me none with those saintly airs. You'll end up buried at the crossroads with a stake through your heart yet—you mark my words."

With this grim prediction, the matron stalked away. Phaedra waited until she heard the heavy feet retreating before she permitted her lips to twitch into a smile. As she thought of Charmelle bleating like a terrified sheep, the smile became a chuckle, the chuckle a laugh which shook her entire frame. She rocked to and fro with her mirth until the tears stung her eyes. Abruptly she stopped, ramming her hand into her mouth. Heaven help her! She was starting to sound like Marie.

Drawing in fortifying breaths, she calmed herself. No, they would not make her mad. Even if no one came to help her, she would find some way to save herself and her child—despite Belda, despite the throngs of insensitive visitors. Despite Armande.

She had barely time to dry her tears when she heard the scrape of the key. Not Belda again so soon. She had controlled her emotions as much as she was capable of in one morning. She could not bear any more torment in silence. She half-rose, tempted to fling herself at the door and keep the old witch out, when she heard a familiar, gravelly voice.

"Phaedra, it's me."

A slender man of medium height stepped into the room, his dark eyes anxiously seeking out hers, the sensitive mouth twitching into a semblance of a melancholy smile.

"Jonathan!" Phaedra hurled herself into his arms, burying her face against the plain brown poplin of his waistcoat, reveling in the cold, fresh scent of autumn that still clung to his greatcoat. His thin hands tangled in her hair.

"Oh, Phaedra, Phaedra. My . . . dear one."

"Take care, sir," Belda growled a warning from the threshold. "Her hands'll be around your waist one moment, your throat the next."

"Be gone, old woman. Leave us in peace."

Enfolded in the comfortable security of her friend's embrace, Phaedra heard with surprise the authoritative note in Jonathan's voice. Equally surprising was the manner in which Belda meekly obeyed, although she did grumble as she locked the door behind her, "Damned fool. Serve him right if he gets his eyes clawed out."

Phaedra raised her head, eagerly scanning Jonathan's careworn face, unable to still the hope that flared to life. "You have done it, then? You have secured my release?"

The dark eyes filled with tears. "My dear, I would give anything if I could . . . Alas, no, I am not yet able to bring you home."

One crystal droplet overflowed, trickling down his face. Phaedra swallowed her own disappointment for his sake. She caressed away the tear, her fingers trailing over his rough cheek, pitted from the bout with smallpox that had almost cost him his life.

"Do not distress yourself," she said, easing herself out of his arms. "I—I am sure you will find a way to help me very soon."

Dear, loyal, ineffectual Jonathan. She sank back down onto the cot with a sigh. Where was Gilly when she so desperately needed him?

She did not realize she had voiced the question aloud until

Jonathan replied, "I am sorry, my dear. I can find no trace of your cousin. I have written to Ireland, but . . ." Jonathan spread his hands wide in a helpless gesture. "He seems to have vanished from the face of the earth."

Phaedra's heart grew numb. Gilly vanished? No, nothing could have happened to him.

"And Grandfather?" she asked softly.

"Sawyer is—is mending somewhat." But Jonathan's smile was too forced to deceive Phaedra.

Her grandfather was dying, she thought sadly. Her relationship with the old man had been stormy at the best of times, and yet she would fain have seen him one last time before he . . . Phaedra suppressed the thought, her heart already overburdened with despair.

She started to inquire after Armande, then stopped herself. No, she need not imagine that he was ever coming back. The Marquis de Varnais had accomplished what he'd set out to do.

Jonathan hovered over her. "My dear, you look so pale. Have you not been eating?"

She gave a tiny shrug, the hopelessness of her situation beginning to weigh heavy upon her. "What does it matter?"

"It matters a great deal to me." Jonathan turned to peek inside the contents of her soup bowl. He pulled a face. "I know the food here is not the most palatable, but you must keep up your strength."

When she made no response, he clasped one of her hands between his own. "Please, Phaedra. For me."

She returned his reassuring squeeze, favored him with a quavering smile. "Very well, Jonathan. For you, I will try not to lose heart. I believe you are the only living soul who cares in the least what has become of me."

Instantly, she regretted her words when he dropped to one knee beside her, the severe angles of his face softened by the glow of his eyes. He pressed a kiss into her palm. His voice thickened as he said, "You know I would do anything to bring you happiness."

Phaedra squirmed; even under these dire circumstances, she was discomfited by Jonathan's expressions of devotion. She carefully disengaged her hand. "Just get me away from this place. That is all that you can do for me."

He bowed his head, concealing whatever hurt her blunt statement may have given him. Phaedra tried to take the sting from her words by stroking aside the strands of graying hair that drooped over his brow. He rose awkwardly to his feet.

"I know what you must be suffering," he said, "but when you are free, I shall make you forget all this ever happened. If you could but keep your courage awhile longer . . ."

Jonathan gave a nervous cough. "One thought did occur to me. I wondered if the—the father of your child might be a man of enough influence to counteract—that is . . . I do not wish to pry but, if you would trust me enough to tell me the name . . ."

Phaedra broke into a mirthless peal of laughter. "You think I should appeal to the father of my child?"

"Please, Phaedra. I am sorry. I did not mean to make you overwrought. Please don't laugh like that. It frightens me."

"That is only because you do not know. Mayhap I should tell you his name. Then you could share my amusement."

Jonathan drew back with a flurried gesture. "No, don't. I regret that I asked. The name is of no consequence. He—"

"His name," Phaedra grated, "is Armande, the most noble Marquis de Varnais." She watched with grim satisfaction as the color drained from Jonathan's face; but she felt relief that someone else should at last share the burden of her dreadful secret.

"Varnais," Jonathan said hoarsely. "I feared it . . . but I never thought it possible. He seems so dispassionate, so cold."

"Aye, as cold as a drift of snow." But even as she spoke, Phaedra envisioned a pair of icy blue eyes, burning with the blazing intensity of the blue core in the midst of flames. She saw sternly set lips that could be tender; his hard-muscled limbs that, when devoid of their cool satin, were bronzed like a sun god's, his passion just as warm.

"And you!" Jonathan's tone was vaguely accusing. "I always believed you hated him."

Phaedra shook her head to dispel the sensation of Armande's presence that was all too real, all too vivid in the midst of this frozen hell where she now resided. "I do," she shrieked. "I loathe him with all my being. I do! I do!" She punctuated each word by pounding her fists against the cot, tears suddenly splashing down her lashes. No matter how hard she tried, she could not stop the tears from coming. She flung herself down, no longer fighting her despair, allowing it to burst forth in a storm of weeping. Ah, but she had always thought hate such a fiery emotion—until she met

Armande. Now she knew that it was a chilling, numbing thing. She felt so cold, so empty.

Jonathan clumsily patted her shoulder, mumbling some words of comfort, adjuring her to rest, to eat. All would turn out for the best. Then he was gone. She sat up slowly, feeling as if she had lost her last contact with the world of sanity.

Drained from her bout of weeping, Phaedra reached listlessly for the bowl of unappetizing stew. One thought alone sustained her: the child inside her. She would let nothing else matter. Damn Armande and his quest for vengeance. Let him destroy himself in his vast wasteland of hate. Such an emotion would never touch her life or her babe's. It had been love that had driven her into Armande's embrace, love that would now sustain her and the child. She would love enough for both of them.

Holding fast to that thought, she raised the spoon to her lips, averting her eyes from the grayish lumps of meat. She managed to swallow a few quick bites before she gagged. Belda's cooking was worse than ever. For the sake of her child, Phaedra choked down half the contents of the bowl before setting the spoon aside. One more mouthful, and she feared she would be sick.

Burrowing deep into the thin cot, she pulled the ragged blanket tightly over her arms, seeking whatever warmth and rest she could find. She had scarce closed her eyes when the first pain struck.

Her mouth flew open in a startled gasp at the intensity of it. She had no time to recover before the next one struck and the next, like waves of a storm-tossed winter sea washing over her, shards of ice in the water piercing her. She flung her arms over her stomach as if she could somehow protect herself from this unseen assailant.

The pain intensified, waves no longer, but a steady agony, a knife twisting and turning inside her. Her body jerked in a series of bone-wrenching spasms as she tumbled off the cot, clawing at the floor, her hand clattering against the food tray, sending clumps of stew flying against the walls. Even through the mists of her pain, the terrifying thought penetrated her consciousness. Poison! She had been poisoned! Then she was lost in the sound of her own screams.

An eternity passed before distant figures bent over her, shrouded by her pain-filled gaze . . . Belda's gap-toothed grin, a leering goblin amidst this nightmare of agony . . . the ghost-white face of the doctor . . . hands wrenching her from the floor. *No, dear God, no. Don't touch me!*

Ahead of her loomed the blessed darkness, if she could only reach it. But her limbs shook so. The darkness came and receded before the glaring white light of pain. How cold she was! But at least the cold dulled the merciless ache inside of her. She was freezing to death, and she did not care. 'Twas such a relief to be done with the pain.

Eventually even the cold ceased to bother her. She felt her eyelids growing heavy, so heavy as the frigid chill of her cell faded. For the first time in weeks, she felt warm. It was no longer autumn, but the last days of spring. Phaedra's eyes fluttered closed, allowing herself to be enveloped by the heat, the glowing lights of the ballroom. It was spring again, and she was seeing Armande de LeCroix for the first time . . .

Chapter Two

THE HEAT OF LADY PORTERFIELD'S BALLROOM ASSAULTED PHAEDRA'S senses in one great wave. Through the slits of her velvet mask, she stared up at her ladyship's famed chandelier, tier upon tier of crystalline ice set ablaze by no fewer than five hundred candles. For a moment, her eyes were so bedazzled that the ballroom became a blur of color, an array of silk-clad forms that flashed with diamonds and other gemstones.

She blinked, accustoming herself to the brilliant scene. A sea of white-powdered heads inclined toward where she had paused beneath the archway. Even the profusion of spangled masks could not disguise the malicious speculation in the eyes that had turned her way. Above the scrape of violins, Phaedra heard the whispers. "Phaedra Grantham. I thought she was still in Bath. Imagine! Attending a masked ball unescorted! Who would bring her, my dear? Her husband?" Titters of laughter, then indignation. "Shocking, I call it. Not so much as black ribbon on her petti-coats, and the poor man not dead a year."

Phaedra moved her hand upward to adjust her own mask. Of course, she need not wonder how her identity had been so easily guessed. Self-consciously, she touched one of the shining red curls that gleamed against the gold-figured silk domino she wore over her gown. As always, she wore her locks unpowdered, in defiance of fashion—or perhaps only in defiance of her grand-father, who claimed he detested red hair.

As she tried to meet the room full of hostile stares, she felt as though time had reversed itself. Suddenly she was seventeen again, stepping into this same ballroom for the very first time, only not alone. Then her husband had stood by her side, and the strange faces had surged nearer for a closer inspection of Lord Ewan Grantham's bride. She remembered clinging to Ewan's elbow and being ruthlessly shaken off. Trembling, she had forced a smile to her lips, wanting so badly to make a good impression, wanting to make Ewan proud of her. But her husband's well-modulated voice had cut through whatever self-possession she had maintained. "Ah, Lady Porterfield, this is my bride, Phaedra, fresh from the wilds of Donegal. You must excuse her appearance. I had not thought it necessary to tell her hoops were always worn for evening functions. One would have imagined that even in Ireland . . . Ah, well. Phaedra, make your curtsy."

She felt his hand in the small of her back, shoving her off-balance. "And don't mumble, dearest. Her ladyship will think you unacquainted with English, and I assure you no one here speaks Gaelic any more than they do Hindi." Ewan had joined in the laughter at his own wit. Her eyes brimming with tears, Phaedra had stared at her handsome husband as if seeing him for the first time. Cruel, petty, mean-spirited, he would never love her. She had realized, more painfully still, that she did not love him; she had realized this in a room full of heartless, uncaring strangers. The knowledge left her soul stripped bare. She felt set adrift, alone.

Alone . . . even as she was tonight. Phaedra shook out her skirts, dispelling the hurtful images of the past. She was no longer seventeen, but six and twenty, no longer a bride, but a widow. Ewan was dead. These people, his shallow friends, no longer had the power to wound her, nor could they force her to observe the hypocrisy of a mourning she did not feel. Lifting her chin, she placed one silk-shod foot after the other, stepping with measured tread into the ballroom, her fingers tightening around the ivory handle of her fan.

Phaedra had not gone far when she was accosted by a set of wide hoops swirling under the rustle of a blue silk domino. The lady's rows of white-dusted curls were adorned with ostrich feathers, the outline of her mask emphasizing the pert tilt of her chin and the black silk patch expertly placed at the corner of her pouting red lips.

"My dearest Phaedra," the young woman trilled. "So unexpected a pleasure."

"Good evening, Muriel," Phaedra said.

The woman started, apparently disconcerted to have her disguise so easily penetrated. But Miss Muriel Porterfield's high-pitched voice was easily as distinctive as Phaedra's red hair.

"I simply never dreamed to find you returned to London, let alone as a guest at my ball. And so charmingly late, as usual."

Phaedra gave her a brittle smile. "You are looking well, Muriel. But if you will excuse me, I believe I must offer my respects to your esteemed mother." She gestured toward where a formidable dame stood, her hollow cheeks puffed out with cork plumpers. She held court amidst a circle of clucking dowagers, all of them unmasked, all of them haughtily aloof from the ball's proceedings.

Muriel caught Phaedra firmly by the elbow, steering her in the opposite direction. "Most unwise. Dearest Mama is already in a high tweak. She disapproves of masked balls. It took endless coaxing to persuade her to allow me to have this one. And now your arrival!" Muriel rolled her eyes. "Frankly, she is less than enchanted. So old-fashioned, you know, in her notions of propriety, especially with regard to widows—being such a notable one herself. She still wears weepers upon her sleeves, and Papa has been dead an age."

Phaedra attempted to disengage her arm. "I did not come here to be intimidated and skulk around as if—"

"But she is, at this very moment, attempting to decide if she should have you discreetly evicted. Far better to avoid Mama until she has time to reflect upon the rashness of such a decision." Muriel smiled demurely until the patch placed by her dimple quivered. "I have always found it so."

Phaedra hesitated, risking one more look at Lady Porterfield. Both overplump cheeks shook with outrage. Phaedra opted for the better part of valor. It was no part of her plan to find herself escorted to the door before she had achieved her purpose in coming here this evening. She hoped that would not take long. The heat was oppressive. Already she could feel beads of moisture gathering upon her brow beneath the mask.

"Very well," she conceded, allowing Muriel to lead her through the press of guests.

"Is it not the most infamous crush?" Muriel sighed. "My ball shall be acclaimed a roaring success, though I was most distressed earlier. Parliament sat so late, we were dreadfully thin of masculine company. All the men are such selfish beasts these days. They talk of nothing but the American war and that scurrilous rogue writing those horrid pamphlets. I wish they might hang this tiresome Robin Goodfellow and be done with it."

"They would have to discover who he *is* first." Phaedra's lips tilted into a smile that she quickly suppressed. It would not do to look as though she knew more than she ought.

But Muriel appeared too taken up with enumerating the triumphs of her ball to take notice of much else. "Three young women have swooned from the heat already. We've done far better than Lady Hartford's rout. She can boast but two casualties."

"You may have a fourth victim upon your hands if I do not soon get a breath of air." Phaedra fanned herself more vigorously, an unpleasant thrumming starting inside her head in tempo with the scrape of the bows against the violin strings. The sensation grew worse as the crowd surged backward to make room for the dancers in the center of the marbled floor. But Muriel found them a spot near one of the massive white pillars that supported the cherub-bedecked ceiling of the ballroom, and sent one of the liveried footmen to procure Phaedra a glass of lemonade.

Phaedra sipped at the tepid liquid, studying the brilliant blur of dancers as they promenaded before her. All the men looked so much alike in their white-powdered wigs, their features obscured by the strips of velvet tied about their eyes. Why of all things did this affair tonight have to be a masquerade? It made the task of locating one particular man nigh hopeless. She had not even any notion what the Marquis de Varnais looked like. Doubtless the fellow would be possessed of a long, thin nose, perfectly sized to be poked into other people's affairs. Her temper threatened to get the better of her all over again when she thought of her grandfather's last letter.

You can cease importuning me, my girl, Sawyer Weylin had written. *I absolutely refuse to send my carriage to fetch you as long as my new friend, the Marquis de Varnais, advises against it. Armande believes that Bath is the perfect place for widows.*

If the marquis fancied that, Phaedra thought, clenching her jaw, then it was obvious he had never been there. Bath was no longer fit for anyone but invalids and gout-ridden old men. How could her grandfather listen to such tripe? Beneath her anger lurked her old fear that Sawyer Weylin meant to abandon her before she found some other means of independence. Her grandfather had made clear his displeasure that she had not borne a child to Ewan. But that would have been a near-miraculous feat, considering how rarely her husband had ever touched her.

Phaedra suppressed that old bitterness, concentrating upon her anger with this Armande person. When she found him, she would give him a blistering set-down he was unlikely to forget. The Marquis de Varnais would think twice before ever attempting to interfere in the life of Lady Phaedra Grantham again.

Intent upon scanning the crowded room, Phaedra paid but halfhearted attention to the steady stream of gossip Muriel poured into her ears.

". . . and Lady Lizzie Devon is rumored to be already with child. You can be certain all the old tabbies will be counting the months backward when that babe is born. And did you hear about poor Tony Aackerly? He was caught stealing a gold watch from a jewelry shop, and was flung into Newgate like a common thief. Only fancy! That some shabby shopkeeper could have a gentleman treated thus—"

"Never mind all that," Phaedra cut her off. Although she was loath to do so, she saw that she would have no choice but to enlist Muriel's aid. "Answer me one question. I am looking for a man. I heard that he was to be present at your ball tonight."

"Dear me." Muriel simpered. "For one so recently widowed, you seem in a powerful hurry. Though perhaps marriage is not what you have in mind?"

"What a shocking suggestion from a young *unmarried* female!" Phaedra said. "But I shall resist the temptation to carry tales to your mama if you point out for me Armande de LeCroix, the Marquis de Varnais."

"Aha!" Muriel's eyes danced. "You always were a sly one. Not nicknamed the Lady Vixen for nothing! I might have known that even buried in a dreary place like Bath, you would manage to hear about our mysterious marquis."

"Mysterious?" Phaedra frowned. "Why mysterious?"

"My dear, he simply seemed to spring up in our midsts out of nowhere. No one had ever heard of the man before."

Phaedra found this intriguing. "But surely the French ambassador would know all the noblemen from his own country."

"It scarce matters. Lord Varnais is absolutely the sensation of the season. Now if you will excuse me. Mama is scowling at me. I really must pay more heed to the *invited* guests."

"But I want you to introduce me to the marquis."

Muriel's bow-shaped lips puckered into an expression of smug satisfaction. "He is not here yet. Like you, le cher marquis adores making a grand entrance." Lifting her skirts, she prepared to glide away.

"But how shall I recognize him?" Phaedra asked.

Muriel shrugged. "When Armande de LeCroix puts in his appearance, even if he is masked, you will know him."

Phaedra reluctantly let Muriel go. The young woman's casually dropped remarks had changed Phaedra's entire estimation of the man she had come to confront.

Mysterious . . . never heard of before. But her grandfather trusted few men and liked even fewer—and reserved a special antipathy for foreigners. His sudden friendship with this marquis seemed all the more puzzling. The rogue must be possessed of a great deal of charm; she could scarcely contain her impatience to meet him. But, tired from a day's hard journeying, she was in no humor to wait much longer. Thanks to her grandfather's refusal to send his carriage, Phaedra had been obliged to travel upon the common stage, squashed between a fat farmer's wife and a shopkeeper smelling of fish. Her widow's jointure was small, and the cost of her fare had made a considerable dent in her meager savings. This fact only added to the grudge she harbored against the unknown marquis.

Her irritation increased with her growing discomfort in the stuffy ballroom. Despite the fact it was too early for the unmasking, she removed the velvet, which had begun to chafe the sensitive skin beneath her eyes, and stuffed the mask in her knotted purse.

Refusing several invitations to dance, Phaedra kept her eyes fixed on the doorway. She studied the few late arrivals, one masquer, a portly gentleman whose garters peeked out beneath his breeches, the other a gangly youth who'd affected the style of the Macaronis, his hair a mountain of powdered frizz.

Damn Muriel. Why must she play at these games? Phaedra would never be able to guess which man might be the marquis. Thrusting aside another hopeful dance partner, she moved forward, determined to end this nonsense by making blunt inquiry.

The next instant she froze where she stood. Another man strode in behind the other two. Sweeping off a great cloak of black silk lined with scarlet, he flung it to a footman, the candlelight playing over a broad pair of shoulders covered by a cream-colored satin coat in the first mode of elegance. His white-powdered hair was pulled back in severe style, tied in a queue at the nape of his neck. He wore no domino, his only effort at disguise the silver mask concealing the upper portion of his face. Why then, Phaedra wondered, did he possess such an aura of intrigue?

Perhaps it was the way he moved. He stepped forward into the room, somehow conveying an impression of aloofness, of isolation even in the midst of the crowd.

Phaedra jumped as the bone sticks of a fan rapped her on the shoulder. She tore her gaze from the man to confront Muriel's glinting eyes. "Well, my dear, may I not present you to the marquis? It is a meeting I would not miss for worlds, I assure you."

Phaedra nodded, her heart giving a sudden thud. She followed Muriel, scarcely watching where she was going, her eyes drawn to the man who was as yet oblivious to her existence.

He must be handsome, she decided from what she could see of his features, but in a cold sort of way. His lips were frozen in an expression of hauteur; his jawline was perfectly chiseled, as though carved from granite.

"My dear Marquis," Muriel said, propelling Phaedra forward. "You have arrived at last."

"Bon soir, mademoiselle." As he turned from greeting Muriel to encompass Phaedra in his bow, she saw the eyes that glittered behind his mask, narrow slivers of ice-blue that chilled her to the soul. Try as she would to suppress it, a shiver swept through her.

"My lord, you must allow me to present a dear friend of mine," Muriel began, but the marquis interrupted her.

"Introductions at a masked ball, mademoiselle?" he mocked. "You will destroy all the evening's mystery."

Muriel giggled. "Alas, sir, I fear my friend is far too eager for your acquaintance to await the unmasking. Lady Grantham, may I present Armande de LeCroix, the Marquis de Varnais. My lord, the Lady Phaedra Grantham."

"Enchanté, madam." His voice was low and seductive, steel sheathed in velvet.

Phaedra saw no sign that he even recognized her name. Yet he must, since he had obviously felt it his duty to keep her in exile from London.

Phaedra felt herself blushing. "I trust my name is not unknown to you, monsieur." What had come over her? Her speech held none of the haughtiness she had rehearsed during the coach ride from Bath.

Brushing aside the lace at his wrist, the marquis produced an enameled snuffbox from his waistcoat pocket, flicking it open with a careless gesture. Phaedra watched him, her eyes riveted on every graceful movement. As he raised a pinch to one finely chiseled nostril, his mouth tipped into a slight frown.

"Grantham? Now, where have I heard . . . Ah, yes." He snapped the snuffbox closed, his eyes returning to Phaedra. As he studied her with cold assessment, a chill tingled along her spine. "You are Ewan Grantham's—er, how do you English put it—Lord Ewan Grantham's relict?"

The words broke the spell of his fascination as effectively as a slap in the face. A surge of heat rushed through her. How dare he treat her as if her entire life and being were summed up by her marriage to Ewan?

"No, my lord," she snapped. "That is not how I would put it at all. I think perhaps you might know me better as Sawyer Weylin's granddaughter from Bath."

"Indeed?" he asked, his attention wandering past her to the ballroom.

"I trust you have no difficulty in recalling his name. It would seem that my grandfather sets great store by your advice. A fact I find most astonishing."

"It always pleases me to be a source of astonishment to a lady." He favored her with a brief nod, the king dismissing a peasant girl. "Your pardon, madam. Another recent acquaintance beckons me." He walked away, leaving her speechless with anger.

Muriel snickered behind her fan. "Oh, lud, Phaedra. How very disappointing. I had expected something a little more spectacular. After all, you are passably pretty. I vow the marquis took more notice of Sophie Grandisant, in spite of her prominent front teeth."

"I have not done with him yet," Phaedra said. How dare he pass her over as if she were nobody? Never had she encountered the likes of such arrogance—not even in those dreadful days of her marriage, when Ewan Grantham had held his untutored bride up to ridicule before all his fashionable friends. She had learned a great deal since the time when one snub would have sent her, teary-eyed, to cower in some corner. She had learned enough to be able to teach Monsieur le Marquis that she was not so easily ignored.

In three quick strides, Phaedra placed herself directly in Varnais's path.

"My lord," she said. "I came here tonight expressly to meet you."

He flicked an imaginary speck of lint from his waistcoat. "How flattering."

Phaedra became aware of more than one head turning in their direction. She longed to draw the marquis off into some secluded nook to conduct this conversation, but Lady Porterfield's ballroom offered no such place. Lowering her voice, she said, "They are now forming sets for the minuet."

"Do I understand you to be asking me to dance, my lady?"

"Yes, I am," she replied doggedly. She must be mad! This was beyond the pale, even for the untamed Phaedra Grantham. She had the satisfaction of at last obtaining a reaction from Armande de LeCroix.

"How very—" She thought she detected a slight quiver in that smooth voice, but he went on, "How very *original* your English customs are, my lady. I had no idea."

Once more Phaedra became aware of the dozens of eyes trained upon her. Dear God, where would she find a hole large enough to crawl into if he refused? She felt herself retreating a step.

One corner of his mouth twitched. "*Ah bien*, how could I maintain my honor as a Frenchman if I refused such a request from a beautiful woman?"

With that he offered her his hand. A bloodred ruby ring set in heavy gold contrasted with the bronzed strength of his fingers. She placed her own within his grasp, bracing herself for the chill. To her astonishment, the hand gripping hers was warm, sending a sudden current rushing through her body at this contact of flesh upon flesh, a current that made the heat of the ballroom seem as nothing. As he led her onto the floor, the buzz of voices threatened to drown out the music; but to Phaedra, all sound, all sight faded into insignificance. She felt as if she were alone with this enigmatic stranger, who made her pulse race with but a touch.

As the opening strains of the minuet sounded through the ballroom, Phaedra gave herself a mental shake. The rest of society, the fops, the silly chits like Muriel Porterfield, might be

content to stand in awe of this man. But Phaedra was determined
to find out exactly who this marquis was, what sort of mischief he
might be brewing with her grandfather. He was a far cry from the
elderly busybody she had expected. So why the devil had he
advised against her return to London?

Gliding toward his lordship, her skirts rustling against his legs,
she tried to penetrate what lay behind the mask. But his eyes were
so hypnotic and piercing that she averted her gaze in confusion.
She regarded his shoe buckles, the firm-muscled calves encased in
white silk stockings, the tight-fitting knee breeches that clung so
well to his lean hips . . .

"Well, what think you, madam?" His soft voice startled her.

"Of what, my lord?"

"Of the buttons on my waistcoat. I told the tailor they would
never do."

"Buttons?" she repeated, wrenching her eyes away from their
admiring perusal of his masculine form. "I—no, my lord, I see
nothing wrong with your . . . your buttons."

"But I affirm that there is. If they so hold a lady's attention that
she never looks up to afford me one glimpse of her beautiful eyes,
then I think my tailor has greatly erred."

Flushing, Phaedra looked up at once. Was he mocking her? She
could tell nothing from the dry tones in which he spoke. "That is
better."

"I am sorry, my lord. I did not mean to seem rude." Her
apology was swept away as they were separated by the movement
of the dance.

Why did he never smile? His lips were set, immovable, but at
least his eyes did not look so cold as she'd first seen them. Or was
it all a trick of the candlelight?

When they came together again, she said defensively, "I was
not staring at you, but merely watching my steps. It has been a
while since I danced the minuet."

Even as she spoke, Phaedra's lips twisted in pained remembrance. The crowded assembly room, Ewan's foot hooking
around her ankle, tripping her into the line of dancers. "Your
pardon," Ewan had called out as he had hauled her up from the
floor. "But I fear my wife tries to gallop through every dance as
if it were an Irish jig." Then the laughter . . . as always, the
cruel, cutting laughter.

Phaedra became aware of a strong hand at her waist, another

clasping her palm. With a start, she came back to the present, realizing that she had almost blundered into the next set, but Armande discreetly guided her back into position.

"There, you see," she said, feeling her cheeks burn. "I did try to warn you. As my husband was wont to say, I—I am not plagued by an overabundance of grace."

"If there was grace found wanting, my lady, 'twould not be any fault of yours, but your partner's."

His lips came startlingly close to her ear until she fancied she felt the warmth of his breath along her neck. How could any voice so deep, so undeniably masculine, be so soft and caressing? She wondered if he could feel the tremor that passed through her and hailed with relief the next pattern of the dance that separated them.

What was she doing? she wondered as she circled the room. She had not informed him as she had planned, that she could do without his interference in her life. She had not asked him even one question. Now Armande had her by the hand again, pulling her close, outwardly maintaining all the formality, the ritual of the dance, while his fingers teased the sensitive hollow of her palm.

"My lord," she said, trying to bring her disordered wits together, "I fear I have a complaint to lodge against you."

He spoke as if he had not heard her, his voice quizzical, pensive. "How sad you appeared a moment ago, my lady, so far away. As if some unhappy memory had suddenly risen to haunt you."

Phaedra felt her face drain of color and nearly snatched her hand away. What sort of man was this, that he could read her innermost thoughts? She began to regret greatly that she had removed her own mask. The marquis had her at a decided disadvantage.

"My grandfather, my lord," she said, firmly steering him toward the one topic she wished to discuss. "You have been at great pains to convince him I should remain in Bath. Why?"

"Now that I have seen you, I almost regret my advice." The look which accompanied these words made her pulse skip, made her nearly forget he had evaded her question.

"Only almost?" she challenged.

"I naturally assumed you would wish to live in seclusion, to be alone with your grief. According to your *grandpère*, it was your own idea to remove to Bath, *n'est-ce pas?*"

Phaedra could not deny this. The trip to Bath had been her own doing. After Ewan's accident, she had desperately needed some time alone, not to grieve, but to reconsider her future prospects away from the presence of her domineering grandfather. But that had always been a temporary measure. She now coldly informed the marquis, "I never intended to be banished to Bath for the rest of my life. I have had more than enough time to recover from my husband's death."

"And yet your widowhood is most recent." The unfathomable blue eyes skimmed over her gown, lingering for the briefest moment upon the creamy swell of breast exposed by her décolletage.

Phaedra stiffened her spine, mustering all her defenses. Did he, too, look to criticize her for abandoning her widow's weeds? What right had he to judge her? He understood no better than anyone else the six years of subtle hell that she had endured. When Ewan died, her tears had been tears of relief rather than sorrow.

"Yes, my widowhood is recent. Too recent to suit me. Ewan should have been in his grave a long time ago." She looked at Armande to gauge the effect of her bitter words.

His eyes widened a moment before resuming their normal hooded expression. "There is no sadness at all in your heart for his death? Not one regret?"

"No!"

"But I understand your husband was a most . . ." He hesitated, as if searching for the correct word, "A most estimable man. Young, handsome, and intelligent."

Phaedra's lip quivered. She was so weary of this eulogizing of Ewan Grantham. So charming, so handsome. Such a tragedy that he should perish so young, in such a gruesome riding accident. Now that he was dead, society would make him a saint, casting herself into the role of black-hearted villainess who had not shed one tear for that "estimable" man. Even this cold, emotionless marquis took Ewan's part. 'Twas so unjust, for Lord Varnais did not know the truth of her life with Ewan. But if he wished to be as ignorant as the others, to perceive her as shallow and heartless, who was she to disappoint him?

As they went down the dance, Phaedra said, "Now that you mention it, I do have one regret. Ewan died in the autumn, and I was obliged to wear black for the Christmas holidays. I do so loathe black. 'Tis not at all my color."

"I would have thought black most becoming to you. Such a foil for that magnificent fiery mane of hair."

Now she was certain that he mocked her. "La, sir, but you Frenchmen are smooth-tongued rascals. Are all those in your family so clever? I have never heard the name de LeCroix before. Where are you from?"

"France, my lady. 'Tis where most Frenchmen are from."

"Have you been in London long?"

"Scarcely long enough."

Phaedra bit her lip in vexation. Damn him! The man was a master of evasion.

" 'Tis a perilous time for you to be enjoying yourself in London, my lord, is it not? With our two countries drawing so close to a declaration of war. 'Tis expected any day that your king will side with the American colonists, championing them in their quest for freedom."

"That is a strange phrase to spring from the lips of a lady. I suspect you have been reading too much of that—what is the name of that *vaurien*—Robin Goodfellow?"

"Yes, I—I have heard of him. A little." Phaedra's eyes swept down and she pretended to concentrate on her steps. "But many others have been discussing the likelihood of war between England and France. What is your opinion?"

Armande shrugged as he took her hand to circle her around him. "The prospect interests me not. I am not a soldier."

A diplomat then? Phaedra wondered. No, the marquis seemed far too uncompromising for such a role. Mayhap he had been drawn to London by business interests. But none that he would disclose.

Each gambit that she flung out met with little success. The marquis fielded her questions with polite boredom until Phaedra seethed with frustration. She flattered herself that she could set any man talking, but never in her life had she encountered anyone as icily reserved as the Marquis de Varnais. His very reticence excited both her curiosity and her suspicions.

If the man possessed no interest in politics or business affairs, then what did he have in common with Sawyer Weylin?

"I was wondering," she demanded at last. "Have you known my grandfather for long? When did you first become acquainted?"

She felt a sudden tension in the fingers touching hers. After a heartbeat of hesitation, he replied tersely, "At a coffeehouse in Fleet Street. And now, my lady, I believe our dance has ended."

To her intense disappointment, Phaedra saw that this was true.

The last notes of the music had died away and she knew little more about Armande de LeCroix than when she had first stood up with him. As she sank into the final curtsy, he bowed over her hand, raising her fingertips to graze them with his lips.

Phaedra was seized by an impulse she could not have explained, not even to herself. Her fingers shot upward, tugging at the strings above the marquis's ear which held his mask in place. The tie came undone, the mask fluttering to the floor.

His lordship straightened, anger flashing briefly in his eyes. The anger passed quickly, leaving a cold stare in its wake. Phaedra's breath caught in her throat at her first full view of Armande's face. He was more handsome than she had supposed, with high cheekbones and an aquiline nose. His brows were dark slashes above those ice-blue eyes. But never had she seen any man's face so dispassionate. He might well have still been wearing a mask.

"I am sorry," she breathed at last. "I fear my curiosity got the better of me."

He said nothing, merely bending to retrieve the mask. As he did so, his coat shifted, revealing a silver hilt that nestled beside the silk-shot folds of his pale blue waistcoat.

Why had she not noticed the slender sheath before? She had thought it but another walking stick. A tiny gasp escaped Phaedra as she stared at the hilt devoid of all ornament, a stark bit of steel wrought for lethal service, not fashion.

"Is something amiss, my lady?" With slow deliberation, Armande refastened the mask about his face.

"I—I was but noticing your sword. So few gentlemen wear them nowadays."

"The streets of your fair city are teeming with danger for the unwary. I wear the sword for protection." He added softly, "It also provides an excellent deterrent for the overly curious."

Was that meant to be a warning to her? Phaedra arched her neck and stared defiantly up at him. "Yes, I daresay curiosity could be a nuisance to a man who had something to hide."

Before she could prevent it, he cupped her chin firmly between his long, powerful fingers. There was nowhere else for her to look except into the hypnotic depths of those blue eyes peering at her through the slits of the mask.

"Your grandfather described you to me as a young woman with an excessively inquisitive nature. It would have been far better if you had taken my advice and remained in Bath. But now that you are here, I suspect you are intelligent enough to understand me when I say how very much I dislike anyone trying to interfere with my affairs."

Phaedra struck his hand aside and stepped back lest he notice how she had begun to tremble. "As much as I dislike anyone interfering with mine! So monsieur, I strongly advise you to keep your opinions about widows to yourself and stay away from my grandfather. Otherwise I might be obliged to—to . . ."

"Yes?" he prompted.

"To find some way to be rid of you," she said with far more bravado than she felt.

For the first time that evening, the shade of a smile touched Armande de LeCroix's face, a smile nowise reflected in the icy, dangerous depths of his eyes.

"How amusing," he drawled, in a voice silken with menace. "I was thinking exactly the same thing about you."

Chapter Three

PHAEDRA STARED NUMBLY AT THE PLAYING CARDS IN HER HAND. HER eyes, bleary from lack of sleep, refused to focus, and the morning breeze drifting through the open window did nothing to clear her groggy senses. The library at Blackheath Hall, her grandfather's house, was a small, narrow room set at the back of the second floor. Sawyer Weylin could not see wasting any of his grander apartments upon a set of rubbishy books. The closely packed volumes that lined every available inch of wall space exuded a strong odor of leather and dust. Even though it was but the first of June and the hour not advanced past ten, the air was humid and stuffy. The summer promised to be a hellish one.

Aye, it would be hellish indeed if she continued to be afflicted with such dreams as had tormented her last night. Every time she had closed her eyes, Phaedra had found herself back in Lady Porterfield's ballroom, circling through the steps of the dance with a silver-masked stranger. Sometimes she would wrench away the mask to see a grinning death's head. But other visions were worse. She would see Armande de LeCroix, his blue eyes glinting with the intensity of a candle flame, his seductive whisper ensnaring her in a silken web. His mouth had sought hers, hot, moist—

It was fortunate, Phaedra thought, that she had been able to force herself awake. No lady would have such wicked dreams—which were all the more disconcerting because the man was her avowed enemy, Varnais. Ewan had always told her that she was possessed of a harlot's nature.

"Are you going to play that jack, my girl?" A good-humored male voice with an Irish lilt broke into her reflections. "You might be better advised to lay down your queen."

With a start, Phaedra realized she was holding her hand too low. Leaning across the mahogany card table, her cousin Gilly unabashedly perused her cards. She raised them and directed a half-embarrassed glance at the young man sprawling in the slender-legged Chippendale chair, which looked too fragile to bear the weight of his lanky frame. How many of her shameful thoughts had her cousin read upon her face?

Patrick Gilhooley Fitzhurst grinned at her, flicking aside one of the strands of hair that drooped in front of his twinkling green eyes. His riotous mass of brown curls defied confinement in the queue he had attempted to form at the nape of his neck.

"'Tis a fine hand you have there, I'm thinking," he said. "Would to God it pleased you to play some of it."

"I intend to, Gilly, if you would only cease interrupting me." Re-sorting her hand, she tried to concentrate on her game. But the vision of steely-blue eyes kept rising between her and the cards. She kept remembering the marquis's final words of warning: he would find a way to be rid of her if she pried into his affairs. Of course, she had made the first threat, but she had been angry and blustering. He had meant it. What sort of deadly game must the man be playing, if the mere hint of a few questions provoked such a response? Phaedra had an unreasoning feeling that she would never know a peaceful night's sleep again if she did not discover the truth about de LeCroix.

"Phaedra!"

She started, almost dropping her cards. "Oh, very well, Gilly." She flung down a jack, scarcely thinking what she did. With a snort of disgust, Gilly trumped her, taking the trick.

Phaedra strewed the rest of her cards across the table. "You've won."

"Won, is it?" Gilly wrinkled his snub nose. "For all the challenge you offer, I might as well have been playing with my old grandmother, and herself half blind. Here, look at this."

Phaedra watched as Gilly tugged one threadbare cuff of his rateen frock coat, shaking it until several aces dislodged from his sleeve, fluttering onto the table. "And you not noticing a blessed thing! I thought I'd taught you better."

"And I thought you would have outgrown such childish tricks." She stood, beginning to gather up the cards, but she paused, regarding him gravely. "Gilly, you—you have not been using these tricks elsewhere. Not when really playing for money."

The jade eyes widened to the full extent of their innocence. "Now, by the grave of my sainted mother . . ."

"Gilly!"

He sighed, then stood up to remove his frock coat, revealing the patched canvas work on the back of his worn silk waistcoat. "There, now do I look as if I were making my living fleecing gentlemen at cards?"

She smiled. "I do beg your pardon, Mr. Fitzhurst."

"And so you should, my girl." He donned his frock coat, adding, "You were such a gloom-faced chit this morning. I only thought to amuse you by reminding you of the old days when we used to play at being cardsharps. Lord, don't you remember how we planned to run off together and live by our wits? We even practiced picking pockets. That, of course, was only supposed to sustain us until we saved enough for pistols and could take to the High Toby."

"Yes, I remember. What dreadful, wicked children we were." She chuckled softly, but her laughter held a hint of wistfulness in it. Aye, she remembered well the old days. Her Irish days, she was wont to think of them. When she had run wild with Gilly, barefoot down the dusty lanes like a pair of urchins, scrumping apples from Squire Traherne's orchard, scaling trees as if they were castle walls, galloping bareback across the meadows on half-wild ponies. It was a wonder they both hadn't broken their necks. Never again in her life had she felt so free.

Gilly, her mother's nephew, was all that she had left of those days. Her English grandfather, angered by his only son's elopement, had always hated her Irish mother. With both her parents dead, Sawyer Weylin had done his best to sever all Phaedra's connections with Ireland, but her affection for Gilly proved too strong a bond even for the old man to break.

Phaedra became aware that Gilly had come round the table to her side. His fingers, roughened from handling the leather of his horses, chucked her lightly under the chin.

"Out with it, Phaedra, my girl. Sure and your mind hasn't been on the cards. What's troubling you?"

She sighed. "It seems I have acquired an enemy."

"The devil you say! And you, with your sweet, gentle disposition."

"I am serious, you rogue," Phaedra said, although she was forced to bite back a smile. "What have you heard of a man who calls himself de LeCroix?"

"Is it the Marquis de Varnais you're meaning? Well, he appears to be far wealthier than I, and I've heard half the ladies in London would willingly cuckold their husbands in his bed."

"Is that all you know of him?"

Gilly regarded one of his worn sleeve cuffs. "The marquis and I do not exactly attend the same supper parties, colleen."

"I would have also thought him to be above my grandfather's touch, but apparently they have become boon companions."

Phaedra's chair snagged on the thick Axminister carpet as she shoved it back, rising to her feet. She paced about the small chamber with quick, nervous steps while she recounted for Gilly the entire tale of her meeting with the Marquis de Varnais, beginning with the nobleman's advice to Sawyer Weylin that she be kept in Bath, and ending with a description of Armande's warning.

"And he as good as threatened to kill me if I asked any more questions about him," she concluded.

To her disappointment, Gilly looked unimpressed. He perched atop one corner of the library's heavy desk, tapping a boot against the claw-foot leg in negligent fashion.

"Astonishing." He exuded his breath in a long low whistle. "Not back in town but one night, and already after picking a quarrel with someone. It must be the Irish in you, my dear."

"It was far more than a quarrel. There is something sinister about the marquis. The man is plotting some mischief, and I have an intuition that it concerns both Grandfather and myself."

"And you intend to make sure that it does."

She glared at her cousin, but he disarmed her with a smile. "Admit it, Fae. You were piqued by this meddling marquis, so you sought out the fellow and provoked him. You've a devilish sharp tongue, enough to rouse a saint to murder."

"It was nothing of the kind. But I cannot expect *you* to comprehend. You were not there. You didn't dance with him."

"Aye, and I don't suppose there's much likelihood of his ever asking me, either," was Gilly's cheerful reply. "I think your marquis is simply too top lofty to give an account of himself to anyone. My advice is to leave the poor man alone. But I see from the mulish look on your face that you're not about to do that."

"No, I'm not. I do not like those who intrude themselves in my family. Nor do I like being threatened." Phaedra stalked over to where Gilly perched upon the desk. "Despite your marked lack of sympathy, I am glad you happened by this morning."

"Happened by, is it? You had me summoned from my bed at the crack of dawn."

Phaedra ignored this grumbling remark. Instead, she leaned past her cousin, indicating the sheets of parchment stacked on the desk behind him. "I have another delivery for you."

Gilly glanced over his shoulder. The next instant he leaped off the desk as though it had caught fire. His air of nonchalance vanished, and he paled beneath his tanned skin.

"Mother of God! Are you daft, woman, to be leaving this about where any dim-witted housemaid might chance upon it!"

Phaedra proceeded to gather up the sheets. "I assure you, no one has been in here this morning but myself. I just wrote it last night." She didn't add that the pages had been scratched out here in the dismal hours before the dawn, when her garret room was too hot and her bedchamber far too confined, far too full of the Marquis de Varnais.

She ran a hasty eye over some of the paragraphs, pleased to see that at least she had been coherent at that hour. But she drew up short at the last page.

"Lud! I almost forgot my signature." She reached for a quill pen, dipping it into the pot of ink. At the bottom of the final sheet, she hastily scrawled the name, *Robin Goodfellow*. The signature looked bold and masculine enough to fool anyone, even her sharp-eyed publisher, Jessym. As she proceeded to sprinkle sand to dry the fresh ink, Gilly peered over her shoulder.

"What the deuce have you been writing about this time?"

"Read it and see."

While Gilly edged himself atop the desk once more and began his perusal, Phaedra picked up a blank sheet of parchment and fanned herself with it. The front of her loose-fitting sacque-style gown already felt uncomfortably damp and clinging. She stalked over to one of the narrow window casements to see if she could force it open further.

Sawyer Weylin's estate lay far north of Piccadilly. The sprawling Palladian-style mansion was nestled in a parklike setting, simulating a country gentleman's estate. But one never quite escaped the reminders that the bustling city of London was not far away. Phaedra crinkled her nose. Even out here, one occasionally caught a whiff of the coal-smoke and that pungent odor peculiar to the River Thames.

"Sweet Jesus!"

Gilly's exclamation drew Phaedra away from the window. She turned around to find her cousin gripping her manuscript, looking far from pleased.

"My essay doesn't meet with your approval?" she asked.

"The parts about the navy's ships being filled with dry rot, and the bit about the king and parliament being negligent are excellent." Gilly raked one hand back through his dark hair, further disordering his unruly curls. "But these passages about the Marquis de Varnais! It sounds as though you are implying he could be anything—from a low-born impostor to a French spy."

"I only hinted at a few reasons why he might be so prickly about his background."

"This borders on libel, Phaedra, and well you know it! Jessym will never print it."

"Jessym prints anything he thinks will sell." But inwardly Phaedra squirmed in the face of Gilly's disapproval. Mayhap she had gone too far in her remarks about Varnais. But she hoped that her writing would make society, and especially her own grandfather, regard the man a little more warily.

Gilly tossed the sheets back down upon the desk. "I'm surprised at you, Fae, that's all. Your pamphlets have been full of masterful writing, about fine, important issues. It's that proud of you, I've been. This is common gossip."

Phaedra gave an affected shrug, although she felt the sting of his criticism keenly. She knew that her earlier writings had been much better. Her secret career as Robin Goodfellow had begun some months before Ewan's death. Then she had written stirring condemnations of the king and his ministers for their shortsighted dealings with both the Americans and the Irish. Her impassioned words had supported the American colonists in their war for independence. She had cried out for justice for the beleaguered

Irish Catholics, whose livelihood was being stolen by greedy English landlords. All her writings had been heartfelt because they mirrored her own despair, her own yearning for freedom from a union that had become a bondage.

Aloud, she responded bitterly to Gilly. "I am sorry you disapprove of my 'common gossip.' But I had not much choice, thanks to Grandfather and his good friend the marquis. It is not easy to write about fine, important matters from exile in Bath. You know I only intended to make a brief holiday when I left town after Christmas, not to find myself banned for the rest of my days."

"But you cannot blame Varnais for that. You are an independent woman now. You can come and go as you please."

"What? With my grandfather controlling the purse strings of the meager pittance Ewan left me? I had barely enough pocket money to get to London on the stage. When Grandfather finds me returned, he may well fling me into the street."

The stern expression which sat so ill on Gilly's good-humored face softened. "Well, we can become highwaymen as we'd always planned. How have you managed to escape the jaws of the old crocodile thus far?"

"He was out when I arrived last night. By now I expect his beloved housekeeper has informed him of my return." Phaedra grimaced. The mere prospect of a confrontation with her grandfather left her feeling deflated. She crossed the room and slowly began to fold the sheets of her essay.

"If you don't wish to deliver this for me, I understand. But the sad truth is, Gilly, that I rather need the money."

"Whist now. Did I ever say I wouldn't take it?" The affection in his eyes nearly brought her to tears. "You could malign the good Saint Patrick himself, and I'd stand by you to the end." Gilly tugged the manuscript from her hand and tucked it inside his waistcoat.

When she deposited a grateful kiss upon his cheek, he groused, "All I say is, heaven deliver you if your grandfather ever suspects that you are the rascally Robin Goodfellow a-tweaking the king's tail." Gilly gave a short hoot of laughter. "Come to think on it, 'tis more likely myself that'll be suspicioned. I think Jessym half does already. Belike one day I'll find your marquis coming after me with his wicked sword."

"I would never let it come to that," Phaedra vowed earnestly.

"If you were ever accused of being Robin Goodfellow, I would—"

She broke off, interrupted by a high-pitched scream.

"What the devil is that?"

"I—I don't know," Phaedra said, looking up fearfully at the ceiling above them. "But I think it is coming from the direction of my garret." Lifting her skirts, she dashed out of the library, with Gilly hard on her heels. Seeking out the backstairs, she took the risers two at a time, not pausing for breath until she reached the small chamber at the very top of the house.

The scream had not been repeated, but when Phaedra stood outside the door to her private sanctum, she could hear the sound of muffled sobbing and above it, a steady thwack, like a poker being pounded against a cushion.

"Sounds like someone is taking the devil of a drubbing," Gilly said. "You'd best let me deal with this."

Phaedra shook her head, her mouth compressing into a hard line. Turning the knob, she flung the door open and burst into the room. The sight that met her eyes occasioned more rage than astonishment, for she had already half-guessed what was amiss.

The chamber, with its low ceiling and plain white plaster walls, was a jumble of furniture discarded from the elegant apartments below. Between a Jacobean daybed and an empty bookshelf, cowered a tall, raw-boned maid, her flat bosom heaving with sobs. The girl held her large-knuckled hands before her face in an effort to ward off the blows. Her assailant, a wisp of a woman garbed in black bombazine, brought her cane crashing onto the girl's back with great energy, her bloodless lips stretched back in a grimace of ecstasy.

Phaedra flew across the room, catching the woman's arm in midswing, and wrenched the weapon away from her. "Mrs. Searle! What is the meaning of this? How dare you strike my maid!"

From beneath the starched lace of her mobcap, Hester Searle's colorless eyes glared at Phaedra with all the malice of an adder contemplating its prey.

"When yer ladyship hears the truth, ye'll want to beat the wicked creetur yerself. I caught Lucy afixin' to burn yer ladyship's finest gowns." The woman pointed an accusing finger toward a pile of black silks strewn before the fireplace.

The girl scrambled over to Phaedra, shrinking behind her skirts. "Oh, milady," she sobbed, "I tried to explain."

Phaedra glanced down at the purple swelling which had begun to disfigure the girl's cheek. Her own countenance flushed with anger, but she managed to place a gentle hand upon the girl's shoulder. "Never mind, Lucy. I will settle this. You run along to Thompson and have him apply some ointment to that eye."

With a hiccup of relief, the girl bolted from the room, nearly blundering into Gilly in the doorway. Phaedra rounded upon Mrs. Searle. Never had she so loathed the sight of that woman's gypsy-brown, sharp-featured face, the coal-black hair puffed back from her brow in a widow's peak. A distant relative of Ewan Grantham's, poor and untutored, Hester had been hired as the housekeeper upon her late husband's recommendation. More often than not, Hester had served as Ewan's spy. Upon her husband's death, Phaedra had hoped that Hester would resign her post, but it seemed she was never to be rid of the sly creature.

"This time, you've carried your impertinence too far, Mrs. Searle. In the first place, I've told you that I consider this my own private room. I don't ever want you coming in here. Secondly, that girl was acting upon my orders. I told her to destroy those gowns. I no longer have a use for them."

Hester Searle pursed her lips. "Begging yer ladyship's pardon. How was I to know? Such a strange command, burning these lovely silks. If you had but told me you wished to be rid of them, I could have . . ."

"You are only the housekeeper. How I dispose of my personal wardrobe is none of your affair."

"Aye, but Fae, I fear for once I must agree with Madame Jester about the gowns." Having all but forgotten Gilly's presence, Phaedra twisted her head to glower at him. He leaned up against the doorjamb. "'Tis more the action of a spoiled, highborn beauty than the cousin I know, to so wantonly destroy such clothes as many a poor woman would be glad to have upon her back. If you don't want them, m'dear, give them away."

Phaedra bit her lip. More than anyone else, Gilly should understand why she despised those black gowns. With irritation she realized that Gilly was right. It was wasteful to burn up the gowns. She had seen enough of poverty herself to know better. Before she could reply, however, she was distracted by the sound of Hester hissing like a cat. Her pale eyes spit fire at Gilly.

"You. You, here in this house! If my dear Lord Ewan were still alive, ye would never have dared."

Gilly gave the woman a mocking grin. "What, Madame Pester? You mean to say you are just now aware of my arrival? Tch. Tch. Your prying little eyes must be wearing dim with age."

"Don't bandy words with her, Gilly." Phaedra stamped her foot. "Mrs. Searle, you will treat my cousin with respect or I swear I shall send you packing."

But Gilly called out, "Now, Fae, Madame Jester has reason to be shocked by my presence. A gentleman in your private room, an Irishman and a Catholic to boot. Fie! For shame."

"Mayhap you are guilty on the last two counts," Phaedra retorted. "But upon my authority as a *spoiled, highborn beauty,* let me tell you, sir, that you are no gentleman. Now be off. I am certain you have a rather pressing errand to attend." She glanced pointedly toward where her manuscript bulged in his waistcoat pocket. "I can pack away these gowns for the almshouse without your interference."

A smile of approval lit Gilly's face even as he swept into an exaggerated bow, encompassing both Phaedra and Mrs. Searle. "Oh, yes, your ladyship. Right away, your ladyship. And Madame Fester, charmed as always to be makin' your acquaintance again." Still bowing and scraping, Gilly backed out of the room.

When his grinning countenance had disappeared from view, Phaedra turned her attention back to Mrs. Searle. The woman had successfully disguised any rage she felt at Gilly behind her normally morose expression. Her hands folded before her, her strangely wrought fingers peeked out of her black lace mittens, crooked only at the first joint like the claws of a vulture.

"I regret havin' disturbed yer ladyship with my error," she said. "If I am excused, I will be about my work."

"Oh, yes. I am sure you are just dying to go see my grandfather and tell him all about my having Gilly here." Phaedra was well aware that Sawyer Weylin despised her Irish cousin nearly as much as her late husband had.

"Nay, I shouldn't dream of disturbin' the master when he's holdin' his levee," Hester said. Although she lowered her lashes, her thin, blue-veined lids did not hood her eyes enough to disguise a glint of malicious contemplation.

"Get along, then. And when Lucy has recovered, send her up here to bundle these gowns. But if I ever catch you striking her or prowling through my room again, I swear I'll wring your scrawny neck with my own two hands. And not even my grandfather will be able to stop me."

Her face emotionless, Hester nudged several of the black gowns aside with her toe, uncovering a cloak. Retrieving it from the pile, she prepared to slip out of the room.

Phaedra sharply drew in her breath. "And where do you think you are going with that?"

Hester shrugged, shooting Phaedra a sly glance. "I only thought as ye be now givin' these things away, I would have it for myself. Being but a poor housekeeper with no wealthy grandfather to ease my—"

"Oh, no, you don't. Give me that." Phaedra wrenched the cloak from the older woman's grasp. "You think I'll let you walk off with this, so I can find it turning up amongst my things again one day? Don't think for a minute I don't know that it is you who keeps slipping this back into my wardrobe."

"Why, ma'am, ye seemed to cherish it so," Hester purred. "I couldn't believe ye meant to discard it."

"Liar!" Phaedra's fingers tightened on the soft folds. "I will tolerate no more of your tricks, do you hear me? Now get out of here. Go make your report to my grandfather. And keep your sneaking face out of my sight."

"Yes, my lady," Hester sneered, her stiff skirts rustling as she glided out of the garret, the door clicking shut behind her.

Phaedra trembled with anger. Meddlesome old witch. She did not doubt for a moment that the housekeeper's true purpose had been to snoop amongst Phaedra's most private belongings.

Anxiously, Phaedra hastened toward a small cabinet lodged in one corner of the room. One of the few pieces of furniture she had brought with her from Ireland, the cabinet was fashioned of blackened bog oak, the sides carved with fanciful figures, spine-chilling animal masks like those found in the Book of Kells. Within its locked drawers resided her notes, first drafts of the pieces she had written under the name of Robin Goodfellow and the copies of the *Gazetteer*, the newspaper that printed her essays.

Reassuring herself that the cabinet had not been tampered with, she resolved to take even greater precautions in future to keep Hester Searle out of her rooms. She'd endure no more of the woman's prying and malicious tricks.

Phaedra's eyes dropped to the garment she yet clutched in her hands. She wanted to fling the cloak from her, but instead she smoothed it out, the cloth exercising the same terrible fascination for her it always had. Fashioned of dove-colored cassimere, it had a folding hood that expanded to frame the wearer's face in layers of ruffles. Phaedra hugged the cloak close to her body, the inches of fabric falling far short upon her. The garment had been constructed for someone far more dainty than herself.

Her eyes misted over when she recalled the first time she had ever seen the cloak. It had been lying draped over that very same indigo-blue velvet wing chair, nestled so close to the fire screen. Of course, then the wing chair had been new, part of the elegant bedroom furnishings downstairs. The velvet was faded now, but not so her memory. Sinking down upon the daybed's stiff brocade covering, Phaedra stroked the soft wool of the cloak, her mind drifting back to her wedding day.

She had returned, exhausted from the celebration of the rites in Hanover Square, to the rooms Sawyer Weylin had had prepared for her and Ewan. Exhausted, yes, but happy—and full of plans for the future. She had not been pleased to begin her married life under her tyrannical grandfather's roof, but was sure it would not be long until Ewan whisked her off to his own estate in Yorkshire. Scrambling into her linen shift, she had sent her maid away, then snuggled beneath the coverlets to await her husband. Her handsome, charming, Ewan—her *husband*. Phaedra's heart had skipped a beat, her youthful body wriggling in anticipation. She was not totally ignorant of what to expect. Although still a maiden, a muscular Irish stableboy, whom she had so adored at age sixteen, had taught Phaedra more things than her parents would have liked. It was at that time the decision had been made to find her a husband. Phaedra had giggled as she remembered how forcefully her mother had put the case to Papa.

"By my faith," Lady Siobhan had snorted, "the girl is overripe, George. Delay much longer, and we shall see her fruit plucked by the wrong hands."

Strangely, Sawyer Weylin had chosen that time to heal the age-old breach between himself and his son. Although Weylin still had refused to receive his Irish daughter-in-law, he had showed an interest in producing a suitable candidate for his granddaughter's hand. At first Phaedra had rebelled, wanting nothing to do with the grandfather who so snubbed her beloved mother. But Lady Siobhan herself had insisted that Phaedra accept Weylin's offer, seeing better prospects for her daughter in England than here in her impoverished Ireland. Phaedra's own objections had lessened when she saw the portrait of the man Sawyer Weylin had selected. Lord Ewan Grantham was decidedly a fine figure of a man.

The betrothal was delayed for another year by the untimely death of her mother. Most willingly would Phaedra have remained with her father, but George Weylin seemed to have no heart left for anything but his grief. He had bundled Phaedra off to England at the earliest opportunity. Banished to a strange country, her mother gone, her Papa far away at Abbey Lough, Phaedra had received a cold welcome from Sawyer Weylin, who from the outset regarded this half-Irish grandchild critically. But Lord Ewan had turned out to be as handsome as his portrait. Most naturally, Phaedra had transferred the full fire of her passionate affections to him, adoring her new husband.

Squirming beneath the sheets on her wedding night, Phaedra had wondered how she could contain herself much longer if Ewan did not hasten to her side. 'Twas then that she had first noticed the dove-colored cloak. With a shriek of feminine joy, she had bounded out of bed, snatching up the garment. Then the door to the bedchamber had crashed open and Ewan had staggered inside. She had turned to him, glowing with pleasure.

"Oh, my love. What a splendid wedding gift. I thank you, oh, a hundred times."

But instead of the urbane smile she had come to expect, Ewan flashed her a look of anger and hatred. He yanked the cloak from her hands, nearly spinning her off-balance.

"Don't you ever touch this again," he had slurred. He reeked of whiskey. Phaedra shrank back, the smile withering upon her lips. "I—I am most dreadfully sorry. I thought 'twas meant for me."

"You?" He gave a vicious bark of laughter. "This little cloak for a great horse like you?" He shoved the fabric almost in her face, and she stepped back, wincing.

"Then whose is it?" she had whispered.

"This, my little Irish bitch, belonged to the woman I loved." Hugging the cloak as if he embraced a lover, Ewan wove his way across the room. He attempted to seat himself in the wing-backed chair, missed, and sank into a heap by the fire.

Phaedra had tried to reach out to him, but he waved her away, shaking one huge fist. "You—stay away from me. Don't want you. Never did." He buried his face in the cloak. "Oh, Anne, my lovely Anne."

Phaedra's hands fell limp to her sides. Her chin quavered. "Is—is she your mistress?"

Ewan had raised his head long enough to roar at her. "No! She would have been my wife! My true wife!" His voice grew thick with weeping and his entire frame shook with sobs. Numbly, Phaedra had retreated to her own bedchamber, but the heavy oak door could not block out the sound of his dreadful sobs, which continued far into the night. It was then that Phaedra had fled to the top of the house and found the abandoned attic chamber that would become her retreat—a place to shed quiet tears of her own for a love lost, for a love that she had never had.

The memory of that night faded as Phaedra realized that she was once again crying, her tears wetting the cloak her husband had wept over so long ago. She had never asked Ewan what had become of his Anne, whether the woman had died or married someone else. The manner in which Ewan had cherished that cloak had told Phaedra all she cared to know. She could see now what a fool she had been, becoming infatuated by a handsome face. How many times had she met Ewan before their wedding day? Mayhap thrice. She had been naught but a pawn, caught between two ruthless men: her ambitious grandfather, who wished to marry a member of his family into the nobility, and Ewan Grantham, in need of Weylin's money to settle his debts. Never, Phaedra vowed, would she permit herself to be so used again.

Wiping her eyes, she resolutely put the garment from her. She had had to endure Ewan's keeping the cloak about, but now that he was dead, she was not going to be haunted by it anymore. Wistfully she regarded the fireplace grate, longing for the courage to stuff the cloak in and watch it burn to ashes. After all these years, the dove-colored wool still seemed to exercise a spell upon her. But, at least, she would have it boxed up, sent someplace where she never had to lay eyes upon it again.

Stuffing Anne's cloak under her arm, she retreated down the stairs to the hall below, directing her steps toward that wing of Sawyer Weylin's mansion that she had shared with her late husband. The carpeted floors seemed unnaturally quiet now without the constant stream of tradesmen, barbers, and other servants who had ceaselessly attended upon Ewan's demands.

Although Sawyer Weylin was generous about paying Grantham's debts, there had been conditions attached. The one that had irked Ewan the most was her grandfather's·insistence that the newlywed couple live under his roof, where Sawyer Weylin could maintain control over her spendthrift husband. Too weak to defy the old man, Ewan had directed his bitterness at Phaedra. He had felt as trapped by their marriage as she. His dying had released them both.

Phaedra's step faltered as she passed the door to Ewan's bedchamber, locked now in accordance with a barbarous mourning custom, which dictated that the deceased's chambers be shut up for a lengthy period of time. Not that Phaedra cared a whit for that. She had no desire ever to set foot again in that room, which held for her only memories of humiliation. On those infrequent occasions when she had had to submit to Ewan in his bed, his lovemaking had been brief, almost savage, as though he sought to punish her for not being Anne.

But her own bedchamber was linked to his by a connecting door, and Phaedra did find disturbing the tomblike silence that now emanated from Ewan's room. It was like living next to a mausoleum.

Clutching Anne's cloak a little tighter, Phaedra prepared to skirt past that still, forbidding doorway. Then she froze, hearing a sound where there should have been none. The light padding of a footfall, a whisper of silk.

Her heart thudded. Not even the housemaids were permitted to enter Ewan's room. Then who would dare? The door had remained locked since the day of Ewan's burial. Stretching out a hand, she tried the knob.

It turned easily. Phaedra scowled. The housekeeper was the only person with a key. Phaedra ground her teeth as she inched the door noiselessly open. If Hester Searle were up to more of her tricks, she would—

Phaedra paused, blinking on the threshold, taken aback by the flood of sunlight. She had expected to find the room shrouded in darkness, but the curtains were flung wide. All the furniture was gleaming with a fresh polish of beeswax from the mahogany dressing table to the four-poster bed where . . .

A gasp caught in Phaedra's throat . . . where a strange man stood with his back to her, shrugging himself into a pair of breeches. Phaedra caught a glimpse of muscular buttocks before the man eased the tanned cloth over his lean hips. Stunned, her eyes roved upwards past a trim waistline to a broad back, as hard-muscled as any strapping farm laborer's. Shagged lengths of sable-colored hair covered the nape of his neck.

"Who are . . . what are you doing in my husband's room?" Phaedra managed to ask at last.

The man started as though aware of her presence for the first time. As he spun around, another gasp escaped Phaedra. Her arms went slack, dropping Anne's cloak in a heap.

"You!" she cried, not trusting the evidence of her own eyes. The elegant satins might be stripped away, along with the mask and white-powdered wig. But there was no mistaking the lean, arrogant curve of the jawline, the thin sensual mouth, the chilling blue eyes. The half-naked man who now stalked toward her was undoubtedly Armande de LeCroix, the most noble Marquis de Varnais.

Chapter Four

VARNAIS HALTED INCHES FROM WHERE PHAEDRA STOOD, IMMOBILE, on the threshold. She had but to raise her hand and she could have touched the dark mat of hair that clung with sweat-sheened dampness to his bare chest. With unshaken aplomb, LeCroix worked to close the last button on his breeches. Phaedra forced herself to wrench her eyes away from the deft movement of those long, tanned fingers.

"*Bon jour*, Lady Grantham." He inclined his head toward her in an ironic bow. "An unexpected pleasure. Is this another of your unusual English customs?"

His light mockery roused Phaedra's stunned senses, flooding her with sudden anger at the shock he'd given her.

"Damn you! What are you doing here?"

"I live here," he said dryly.

"Since when?"

"Since your grandfather most kindly suggested that I give up my lodgings and become his guest—about a fortnight ago."

"A fortnight!" Phaedra sputtered. "Then last night when we met, you knew you already were—would be—" Sleeping but yards away, divided only by one wall from where she had tossed in her bed, tormented with dreams of him threatening her, caressing her. The thought brought heat rushing into her cheeks. "You did not trouble yourself to inform me of the fact!" she accused.

The corner of his mouth twitched, a faint trace of amusement

44

shading the ice-blue eyes. "It was one of the few questions you did not ask me, my lady."

Phaedra muttered an oath under her breath. Taking a hesitant step backward, she scarce knew what to do next. She could not bodily eject Armande from Ewan's room as she would have liked to have done. The most ladylike course of action would be to stalk away in high dudgeon to find her grandfather. The marquis was half naked, and even now she could hear one of the maids about to whisk down the hall.

Impulsively, Phaedra bolted forward and slammed the door closed behind her. The abrupt movement brought her brushing up against Armande. Flinging out her hands as though to ward him off, her palms pressed against the warm, firm flesh of his shoulders. She received the briefest of warnings from the sudden intensity of his gaze and jerked her hands back as though she had been seared. But it was too late. His arms banded about her, imprisoning her against him. Heart thudding, for one moment she forgot herself enough to allow him to draw her close. But at the first heated touch of his lips, his mouth grazing hers with the promise of sweeter fire to come, she began struggling to be free. To her surprise, he readily released her.

"How—how dare you!" she gasped.

He shrugged, and whatever desire she had seen flare to life in his eyes was gone. "*Milles pardons,* my lady. 'Twould seem I misread your intent. In France, there is only one reason for a woman to so rush into a man's bedchamber."

So the kiss had been but another of the marquis's mockeries. Phaedra drew in a tremulous breath, raising one hand to her burning cheek in an attempt to cool it. "This is—was my husband's room. I came to see what you are doing here."

"Dressing myself."

He was baiting her, she thought, and enjoying every minute of it. She replied in as cool and steady a voice as she could muster. "You cannot stay here, especially not now that I've returned from Bath. This room adjoins my bedchamber."

"You can always keep your door bolted, if you wish," he said softly. In his voice was the barest suggestion that she might not wish it.

Phaedra's hand fluttered nervously to the neckline of her gown. "So I shall, for the rest of your *brief* stay here."

He merely smiled and walked leisurely toward the bed, where

his plain white shirt lay spread out on the blue velvet counterpane. He picked up the shirt, easing the linen carefully over the muscular contours of his shoulders. Did not the man have a valet? Phaedra wondered. That was odd for a great nobleman. Either he could not afford a manservant or he wanted no one in such close attendance upon him. The elegant cut of his clothes, and the heavy ruby glinting upon his finger, made a lack of funds seem unlikely.

When he had put on the shirt, he glanced up, looking as though he were surprised to find her still there, but not sorry. "Should I invite you to take a seat, my lady? Forgive me, I am not accustomed to holding levees for ladies."

Phaedra realized she been staring, the blush threatening to rise into her cheeks anew. She blurted out, "You don't look like a marquis."

"And have you examined so many marquises at great length that you can pass such a judgment?"

For once, the half-smile tugging at his mouth was more teasing than mocking. She felt her own mouth curve in reluctant response. "No, you are the first."

She knew she was behaving outrageously, lingering in this room with the same man who had threatened her only last night. And yet he scarcely seemed like the same man. Could the absence of the wig and white powder make that much difference? She studied the way his rich sable-brown hair waved back from his brow. It softened the planes of his face, making him appear less arrogant, and the light in his blue eyes was not quite so chilling. Mayhap Gilly was right. Mayhap it was only her own imagination that made such a sinister figure of the marquis.

"If you continue to stand there watching," Armande said, "I may press you into service, tying my solitaire."

"Would you trust me to knot something about your throat?" she retorted.

His smile faded, his hand going up toward his neck in a half-conscious gesture. The action drew Phaedra's attention to a small scar at the base of Armande's throat, straight and neat, as though the incision had been very precise. Could the marquis have been pierced there with a sword? Phaedra could well imagine him as the sort of man to fight duels, but she rather thought that he would not be the one carried from the field.

"For the sake of your reputation," he said, "I think I'd best tend to the dressing myself. If you will excuse me, my lady, I must see if I can locate my tan waistcoat."

The abrupt change in his manner indicated a dismissal, but as Armande disappeared into the small powdering room that adjoined the bedchamber, Phaedra made no move to leave. Without Armande's presence to distract her, her gaze roved curiously about the chamber that had once been her husband's.

Ewan's personal belongings had all been swept away, giving the room, although completely furnished, a strangely barren appearance. Armande said he had been living here for a fortnight—but, Phaedra thought with a frown, that was not strictly true. The marquis was simply inhabiting this place, the evidence of his presence quite sparse—a pair of immaculate boots perched near a needlepoint-covered stool, his wicked-looking sword resting on the seat of a straight-backed chair.

Phaedra skirted gingerly past the weapon, eyeing the top of the dressing table, cleared except for a shaving mirror, a jar of snuff, and an intriguing box shaped like a treasure chest.

She glanced nervously over her shoulder, but there was no sign of Armande returning. She could still hear him rummaging about in the other room. Maintaining what she hoped was a casual flow of chatter, she began inching her way toward the box.

"I know you are loath to answer questions, but I wonder if you mean to make a long stay. Summer is unbearable in the city. Most of the ton will leave for the country. Only my grandfather adores London so much that he insists upon staying."

Her words trailed off as her fingers closed over the chest and tried the lid. Locked. Her shoulders sagged in disappointment. The next instant she let out a squeak of fright. Armande's hand shot out of nowhere, clamping about her wrist. How had he managed to come up on her so silently?

He turned her slowly about to face him. It had not been the wig, she noted miserably. The silken strands of dark hair now did nothing to soften the expression in his eyes. They pierced her like glinting shards of ice.

"Still so curious, my lady Grantham?" he murmured. "And I had hoped we had reached some sort of an understanding."

Phaedra felt her pulse thrumming beneath the pressure of his fingers. She struggled to be free, but his grip only tightened. Her sense of shame at having been caught trying to pry into the box caused her to glare at him with defiance. "All I understand is that I neither like nor trust you."

"That you mistrust me, I believe. But as for disliking . . ." One of his eyebrows arched skeptically.

Phaedra managed to wrench her hand free at last. She rubbed her bruised wrist, unable to look at Armande de LeCroix. For she feared that his arrogant suggestion might be true. She was conscious of a strange attraction to this man, an attraction she had felt from the first. He called to something primitive in her, that dark side of her own nature Ewan had always warned her about. Not trusting herself to speak, Phaedra whipped up her skirts, heading for the door.

She heard him stalking after her and fought down a panicky impulse to run. He caught hold of her upper arm.

"Let me go!" she cried.

But he said calmly, "You're forgetting your cloak." She glanced down and saw that he had meant to do nothing more than hand her Anne's cloak, which she abandoned upon the floor. He bent down to retrieve it for her.

Her own hands shaking, Phaedra started to snatch the soft gray wool from him, but to her surprise, he refused to release it. A crease deepened between his brows as he shook out the folds of the cloak and stared at it, his expression unreadable.

"This—this is yours?" he asked at last in an oddly husky tone of voice.

"No," she snapped. She scarce knew what bitterness induced her to sneer, "It belonged to one of my husband's paramours."

Phaedra recoiled before the look Armande gave her. The hatred that blazed in his blue eyes was as piercing as a naked length of steel. He flung open the chamber door.

"Get out," he said tersely. When she only stared at him, he took her by the arm, firmly steering her into the hall. He hooded his eyes, the shutters closed on the violent emotion she had just glimpsed upon his face.

When he spoke again, his voice had regained a measure of his icy calm. "You are correct, my lady. It does bid fair to be a most hot summer in the city. I strongly suggest you go back to Bath."

Before she could reply, he had closed the door in her face. Phaedra was left alone to deal with the jumble of her emotions— confusion, anger, fear, fascination. A most disconcerting fascination. She had sworn, after Ewan's true nature had revealed itself, never again to allow any man to rouse such feelings of desire in her. Especially not one as obviously dangerous as Armande de LeCroix. Although she earnestly desired to stay in London, she knew that it would be folly to spend an entire summer under the same roof with this man.

It was high time to speak to her grandfather, Phaedra thought, as she stormed to her own room. It was not until she had reached the safety of her bedchamber that another thought occurred to her. The Marquis de Varnais had kept the dove-colored cloak.

Long after Armande de LeCroix heard Phaedra's footsteps retreat from his door, he stood, head bowed, holding the gray cloak, his fingers clutching at the soft wool. Painful memories flooded back to him of the young girl who had once worn the cape.

Lady Phaedra's bitter words echoed through Armande's mind—*my husband's paramour.*

Was that all that remained of Anne then, that false epitaph and this damned cloak? His hands crushed the fabric as Armande swore softly. He raised his head, his gaze locking upon his own image in the cheval glass. The Marquis de Varnais's chilling mask of indifference had cracked, revealing a visage at once younger and more aged, his cheeks flushed with passion, his eyes storm-ridden with bitterness and anger.

He recoiled in shock from the reflection. Was that how he had looked only moments ago when he had thrust Phaedra Grantham out of his room? He was going to have to be much more cautious, especially now that that most inquisitive lady had returned from Bath. His eyes never wavering from the mirror, Armande struggled to repress all those dangerous feelings that the sight of Anne's cloak had aroused. He slowly forced his features to relax until he had once more assumed the icy calm of the Marquis de Varnais.

"Bien—that's better," he muttered. He strode over to the mahogany dressing table and relinquished the cloak, laying it gently over the back of the chair. He could never again afford to let his guard slip that way—not without jeopardizing his entire reason for being in London, in Sawyer Weylin's house. If the sight of Anne's cape was going to overset him, then he'd best make sure it was out of sight.

A pity he could not do the same with Lady Grantham, Armande thought with a slight frown. If there was anything that could have disturbed him, it was Phaedra's arrival. Some instinct had warned him from the first that Weylin's granddaughter might prove an unwanted complication to his plans. That was why he had done his best to make sure she stayed in Bath.

But even he had been unprepared for exactly how *much* of a complication the lady threatened to be—and he was not thinking of Phaedra's intelligence and determined curiosity. Nay, it was her impact upon his senses that had taken Armande unawares. In the midst of the other artificial beauties at last evening's ball, with their powdered false hair, Phaedra had struck him like the sun blazing forth upon a winter's day . . . her silken hair all gold and aflame, green eyes that sparkled with the fire of finely cut emeralds, the lithe beauty of her slender form in that low-necked gown revealing the gentle swell of her breasts, pearly hued flesh so velvet soft his fingers had ached—

A shudder coursed through Armande as he attempted to choke off his thoughts, to stem the heat of desire coursing through his veins, a desire he could not afford to feel for any woman, let alone Ewan Grantham's widow.

It was not any amorous intent that had brought him to London, but a harsh and deadly purpose. As though to remind himself of this, he bent down and retrieved his sword. The cold hilt, the weight of the finely tempered steel, felt good in his hand. Lightly balancing the weapon, he executed several movements, flashing the blade through the air, parrying imagined blows. The exercise helped to cool some of his turbulent thoughts of Phaedra. Indeed, 'twas an insult to Anne's memory to feel aught but hatred for anyone bearing the name of Grantham.

But Phaedra was innocent, his mind argued. She had not even been in England when Anne had been destroyed. And as for pain—what a wealth of it he had seen in Phaedra's expressive eyes, no matter how defiantly she strove to hide it. The lady's fine-boned features revealed every emotion she felt. No dissembling smiles were part of Phaedra's makeup. Her air of vulnerability stirred feelings other than desire in Armande, feelings he had thought long dead.

His sword arm wavered in midstroke, and Armande slowly lowered the weapon to his side. No, he could not deny it. Phaedra obviously also had suffered at Ewan Grantham's hands. She was an innocent, just as Anne had been—but an innocent very likely to wreak havoc with Armande's own carefully laid designs.

"I did warn the lady not to pry," he said with a heavy sigh. And if she continued not to heed that warning? What then?

His grip tightened upon the sword, his gaze drawn to the sharply honed blade. Then it was the way of the world. In his bitter experience, the innocents were always the first to pay.

Chapter Five

PRUDENCE DICTATED THAT PHAEDRA NOT INTRUDE UPON HER GRAND-
father, but wait for the old tyrant to summon her. He was
undoubtedly even now in the midst of his levee, that morning
ritual where toadeaters and place-seekers gathered to dance
attendance upon a great man while he dressed, to admire his taste,
to discuss business, to beg for favors. Sawyer Weylin would not
be pleased if she burst in upon him while he entertained his
sycophants, especially if she came demanding explanations regarding the Marquis de Varnais.

But prudence had never governed Phaedra's relationship with
Sawyer Weylin. She had been at loggerheads with her grandfather
ever since she had set foot off the packet from Ireland. She sensed
that Varnais's presence in the house would do little to change that.
Very likely the marquis would make matters worse.

Consequently, she resolved to see him. She had Lucy help her
into a pink silk gown, then she seated herself before her dressing
table, while her maid drew part of Phaedra's thick hair into an
old-fashioned topknot.

The surface of Phaedra's dressing table was cluttered with all
the feminine accoutrements any woman could desire. Sawyer
Weylin grudged no expense to make his granddaughter appear
quite the grand lady. But to her, the silver-handled brushes, the
perfumed pastilles, and the gilt-edged mirror were all impersonal
ostentation. Phaedra's own touches were mixed in—a cup of

wilting violets, a copy of *The Rights of Man* open to the last page she had read—and a porcelain statue.

As Lucy applied the crimping iron, coaxing Phaedra's hair into loose-flowing curls, Phaedra picked up the figurine—a diminutive shepherdess with rose-flushed cheeks and wistful blue eyes. She had found the statue long ago, buried behind the ancient bookcase in the garret. Obviously of no value to anyone else, the shepherdess had enchanted Phaedra. Somehow the sculptor had managed to make the brittle porcelain come alive. Phaedra almost expected the dainty bare feet to step forward, the small white hand curving round the shepherd's crook to move, the waist-length cascade of golden hair to stir with the wind.

Lost in contemplation of this small treasure, it took Phaedra several seconds to realize Lucy had finished with her hair. Sighing, Phaedra restored the figurine to its place on the table. Taking one last glance at herself in the mirror, she set off to do battle with her grandfather.

Her petticoats rustling in time to her militant step, Phaedra stalked toward the second-story landing. Twin staircases of polished marble curved down to the floor below. Running her hand along the delicately wrought gilt railing, Phaedra descended into what she termed her grandfather's "chamber of horrors."

The towering walls of the entrance hall were of a deliberate bleakness, rough stone fancifully designed to imitate the interior of an ancient castle. Shields splashed with heraldic devices hung willy-nilly amidst a collection of medieval weaponry. Broadswords, poleaxes, cinquedea daggers, and halberds with wicked sharp-curving hooks now cheerfully jumbled together, bore mute testimony to centuries of mayhem.

If nothing else, however, Phaedra often thought, the gloom-ridden hall provided an excellent setting for Hester Searle. She saw that the housekeeper had cornered the cook's two small children by one of the suits of armor. Phaedra paused at the foot of the stairs, clenching her jaw. Blast the woman. She was at it again, indulging in another of her favorite malicious pastimes, terrorizing poor Tom and Jeannie. The little ones cowered in the shadow of what must have seemed like a great metal giant in their eyes. But surely no more terrifying than Madam Hester herself, who crooked one finger gleefully toward the morning-star mace suspended in the armor figure's iron-gauntleted fist.

"And that was the very weapon, m'dears, that old Lethe used to dash out the brains of Lord Ewan's father."

Jeannie squeaked, clutching her brother and burying her face against his chubby arm. Although Tom tried to pretend he was not afraid, his eyes were as round as those of his small sister.

Phaedra stormed down the length of the hall to put a stop to the gruesome tale, but Hester had already reached her climax. Raising up both arms so that she resembled some black-winged bird of prey, she said, "But they caught that wicked murderer and hung 'im until his face turned ablue with chokin'. So take care, young'uns. They still say old Lethe rises from his grave at midnight to carry off all bad children."

"Hold your tongue, you wretched woman!" Phaedra cried, but her intervention came too late. With a frightened squeal, Tom and Jeannie plunged past her skirts, sobbing as they ran to seek their mamma. They would have nightmares for a week, thought Phaedra as she fought down a strong urge to slap the housekeeper.

"Curse you! I told you before, I will not tolerate your frightening the children with your horrid tales."

Hester folded her hands demurely in front of her. "But milady, the murder is part of the history of this house. The little 'uns find it fascinatin'—as ye would yerself if ye would ever permit me tell you all about it." Hester smiled, lowering her voice to a soft purr. "The foul deed took place nigh the year before ye came here to be Lord Grantham's bride. Arrangin' the details of *your* marriage contract, they was, Mr. Weylin, and Master Ewan's papa, Lord Carleton—"

"I am not interested."

"The servants had been given a holiday. All alone in the house were Mr. Sawyer and Lord Carleton . . . or so they fancied."

"Be quiet!" Phaedra snapped. She could barely restrain a shudder as she glanced at the heavy mace's pointed spikes. She had no need of Hester's embellishments to imagine what such a weapon might do to a man's skull. "Keep your ghoulish tale for those as have a taste for such things. I'd best not ever see you frightening Tom and Jeannie."

"Oh, aye, yer ladyship," Hester smirked, dipping into a stiff-kneed curtsy. "You shan't *catch me* at it again."

Phaedra spun on her heel and walked away before the awful mace could be called upon to do its second murder. When she reached the doors leading to the anteroom, Hester called out, "Go

right in, yer ladyship. I'll wager Master Weylin be powerful eager
to see you."

Phaedra ground her teeth but pretended that she had not heard
the woman's taunting words. Not waiting for one of the footmen
to bow her inside, Phaedra flung open one of the doors and
stepped inside the lofty chamber, all gold and cream, the rococo
plasterwork of scrolls and twisting leaves as elegant as a king's
stateroom. The anteroom was sparsely furnished, with a few
uninviting splat-back chairs. Sawyer Weylin did not like anyone
to be too comfortable while awaiting his pleasure.

Most of the men crowded into the anteroom preferred to stand.
Since her grandfather had managed to obtain a seat in parliament,
his levees seemed more popular than ever. Phaedra pressed
forward a few steps and was obliged to flatten herself against the
wall as two footmen brushed past her, dragging a man from the
room. The haggard-looking individual bore not much chance in
his struggle against her grandfather's burly servants, the young
man's limbs like thin sticks protruding from his shabby second-
hand garb.

"Stop your carryings on," one of the footmen growled. "The
master don't receive slum rats like you here."

"I have to see him," the man sobbed. "I have to have my
wages. My wife and child are ill—" The rest of his protest was
lost as Weylin's servants dragged him out of the room.

"John," Phaedra attempted to call after the footman, to see
what the trouble was, but the minute she spoke, she found herself
surrounded. She could not see past the tops of white-powdered
wigs bending over her.

Masculine voices importuned her on all sides. "Lady Grantham, a moment of your time. I hear your grandfather is seeking
an architect after the style of Adam. I know of just such a
fellow . . ." "Your ladyship, your grandfather promised to get
my son a post in the customs office . . ." "Please, Mr. Weylin's
not receiving anyone this morning. If you could put in a word—"

"Gentlemen, please." Phaedra raised one hand, attempting to
ward them all off, refraining from telling the last poor fool who
spoke that a word from her would surely condemn his cause.

When her grandfather refused to allow anyone into his private
dressing room, Phaedra knew, he was usually in a vile humor.
Otherwise, a privileged few were generally permitted into that
inner sanctum, to wheedle and flatter while the old man donned

his wig. Phaedra elbowed her way out of the circle of anxious place-seekers and tradesmen, squaring her shoulders for the battle to come.

Slipping through the door at the end of the anteroom, she shut it firmly in the faces of the disappointed throng behind. Although designated as a dressing room, this inner chamber was fully as large and ostentatious as the anteroom, with gilt chairs placed as though for a performance. But the chief actor was obviously in too surly a humor to ring up the curtain today.

One gout-ridden foot propped up on a pile of feather-tic pillows, Sawyer Weylin shifted his not inconsiderable bulk upon cushions of Italian velvet, resting his large-knuckled hands along arm rails carved into the shape of snarling lions. The chair resembled a throne that might have been found in the palace of the Venetian Doges; and her grandfather, Phaedra thought, could easily have passed for an Oriental despot, with his impressive jowls, his heavy-lidded eyes, and a powdering jacket drawn about his bull-like neck.

He took no note of Phaedra's entrance, his features florid with a rage directed at the barber trembling before him.

The man timidly held up a gray bagwig. "I assure you, sir, 'tis designed in the latest fashion."

"Bah! I can't abide gray." Weylin slapped his own bald pate. "Think that I shaved off the remnants of my own hair for you to trick me out like some old woman. And charge me thirty guineas into the bargain."

"The price is more than fair, and gray is most becoming to you. Surely my lady agrees."

The barber's remark and his hopeful glance at Phaedra alerted her grandfather to her presence. He twisted round upon his throne as far as his size would allow him, and glared.

Phaedra curtsied. "Good morrow, Grandfather."

"Good morrow is it?" Weylin roared. "Disobedient chit. Get over here and account for yourself at once. What d'ye mean—" He broke off to snarl at the barber. "Don't stand there gawking. Be on your way, rascal."

"B—but your wig, sir . . ."

Weylin snatched it from him. "Be off with you and send me the reckoning. Fifteen guineas, mind you, and not a penny more."

"Sir!" The man's wail turned into a gasp as Sawyer Weylin groped for his gold-tipped cane, poking it at the man. As the barber scrambled for the door, her grandfather managed to deliver a well-placed thrust at the man's plump buttocks. Weylin grunted in satisfaction before turning to rail at Phaedra.

"Stap me, if I ain't beset upon all sides by highwaymen and robbers. There's not an honest tradesmen left in all of London." Weylin jammed the wig upon his head.

"Now, missy, over here!" He tapped a spot near his chair with the cane. "What d'ye mean by sneaking back from Bath, filling my house with Irish papists? Searle told me you received that rascal cousin of yours. I won't have it! Foreign villains creeping about under my roof."

Phaedra gasped with indignation. "You're a fine one to talk about foreign villains. What about your French friend ensconced in Ewan's room? I daresay he is as Catholic as Gilly."

"I'd trust a Frenchman a deal further than I would an Irish or a Scots. At least Armande is not a pauper."

"I'll wager you have no notion whom the marquis might be, any more than anyone else does." Phaedra advanced upon her grandfather. Ignoring the manner in which his chin quivered with anger, she proceeded to straighten his wig, which looked ridiculously askew. The old man thrust her aside.

"And so you've already presented yourself to the marquis, looking like a raggle-taggle gypsy, I suppose." He jerked on one of her own red curls. "Od's lights, girl, why can't you ever powder that carroty hair of yours? 'Tis demned hard upon a man's eyes this hour of the day."

"We have more important matters to discuss than my hair." Phaedra flicked her tresses out of his reach.

"So we have. Why the deuce you couldn't stay put in Bath until I sent for you? You've likely ruined everything."

Phaedra started to snap out her reason for returning to London, but her grandfather's last remark brought her up short. What did he mean, she'd ruined everything? Before she could question him, the old man gasped a flood of curses as the pillows shifted out from under his leg, jarring his gouty foot.

"Demnation. God curse it!"

Phaedra bent down to rearrange the pillows beneath the limb, which was swathed in a linen bandage. "Stop thumping about like that. You are only making it worse." She wondered when the stubborn old man had last been seen by his physician.

When she'd managed to ease the foot into a more comfortable

position, Weylin sagged back in his chair, mopping at his sweating brow with a large handkerchief.

"Ah, that's better." He glanced down at Phaedra with a look approaching fondness. "Foolish, headstrong girl. If only you knew how I have your best interests at heart."

The layers of flesh on his face crinkled, his lips stretching into a bland smile, revealing a row of even white teeth, remarkably unblemished for a man of his years. He was inordinately proud of them.

Her fingers still curled about a pillow, Phaedra stared up at him, her own mouth hardening into a line of suspicion. It suddenly struck her that something was wrong here. She had expected her grandfather to be furious at her unannounced return from Bath. Despite his grousing, she had the feeling he was not altogether displeased to have her back. Smiling down at her, Sawyer Weylin reminded her of a fat, lazy crocodile, sunning itself on the banks of a river. But Phaedra had seen too many fools snapped up in her grandfather's jaws to be taken in.

"What did you mean a moment ago," she demanded, "when you said I'd ruined everything?"

"Only that I'd hoped eventually to present you to Armande in style, once I'd brought him around to the notion."

"Notion? What notion?"

"Of marrying you, you dunderhead. D'you want to be a widow the rest of your days?"

Her grandfather's words struck her like the blunt end of a cudgel. Phaedra scrambled to her feet. "Good Lord! You could not be possibly thinking that I and—and Armande de LeCroix—"

"And why not? He's a marquis, m'girl, with money. That makes him as good as a duke in my books."

"Damn it! You don't even know this man. He's—he's dangerous, secretive, ruthless."

"Hah! So he is." Weylin seemed pleased by her description. "A much more likely specimen than that milksop Grantham."

Phaedra forebore to remind her grandfather that it had been he who had schemed to make Ewan her husband. Sawyer Weylin's fascination with nobility and titles bordered on madness. It had been the chief reason he had delivered her into Ewan's bed, for her grandfather had felt nothing but contempt for her late husband. But this time Sawyer Weylin's obsession for raising his family into the ranks of the aristocracy had taken a far more dangerous turn.

"By God," she said, "I think you would drive me into the arms of the devil himself if he had a patent of nobility."

"So I would," the old man growled.

"I greatly fear this devil has other plans, Grandfather. He could be an impostor for all you know of him. I find certain aspects of his behavior most odd. Only just this morning, he—"

Her grandfather smacked his cane against the floor, his jowls trembling with outrage. "Demnation. D'you take me for an old fool, girl? I've been spotting sharpers since before you were born, aye, before your own father was breeched. I guess I would know whether or not this marquis is the genuine article."

"It scarce matters if he is. Ewan was bad enough. I will not be caught up in your marriage schemes a second time."

"You'll do as I bid you." Weylin expelled his breath in a snort. "You can scarce afford to be picksome, my fine lady. Thanks to your witless father." Her grandfather's face darkened with that bitter scowling expression he always wore when speaking of his only son. He launched into what to Phaedra was an all-too-familiar and hated refrain. "Never knew how I came to sire such a cursed ungrateful dolt. Good for nothing but poking his nose in a parcel of Greek books, dying too young with nothing to show for his life but a pert daughter with red hair and a heathen name. But that's what comes of running off to a godforsaken land like Ireland to wed some slut."

"You will not speak of my mother like that!" Phaedra warned.

"A poor papist slut," Weylin repeated with an ugly sneer. She winced as he dug the tip of his cane into her ribs for emphasis. "The witling couldn't even find one with money."

Phaedra rubbed her side, eyeing him with loathing. At times like this, she hated her grandfather. "My mother was a lady born. Of far better breeding than a coarse old man who smells of gin."

Weylin's features suffused with an alarming purple. He raised up his cane and for one moment Phaedra thought he meant to strike her with it. She glared back, defying him.

He abruptly yanked his gout-ridden foot off the cushions. As his face contorted with pain, he managed to lean upon the cane and struggle to his feet.

"It was gin and small beer that put this fancy roof over your head, missy," he panted when he could get his breath. "And you'd best learn more respect if you wish to remain here."

"I don't," she cried. "I'll take passage on the next boat crossing the Irish Sea."

"And good riddance to you, you baggage." Shoving her aside with one thick hand, he huffed past her. "Go back amongst your savage Irish relations and rot there."

Angry tears stung Phaedra's eyes. "It might interest you to know, Grandfather, that most of those *savage Irish relations* despise me as much as you do, now that my mother is dead. Only they hate me for being English."

"Then hold your tongue, girl, if you don't want me to toss you out." Weylin paused long enough to shake his cane at her. "But cease your nonsense about Armande. You dress like a grand lady and do the pretty by him. If you let him slip between your fingers, I'll send you packing for good this time. Back to Ireland, or to hell, it'll make no odds to me."

The door reverberated upon its hinges as he flung it open. Phaedra caught a brief glimpse of the bewigged men in the next chamber scattering before him like a flock of frightened sheep.

"Where's that demned barber? Does the dolt think I can powder this wig myself . . ." The roar faded as the door slammed behind him, leaving Phaedra alone in the dressing room.

"I hope he powders you until you choke, you old fool." Phaedra wiped savagely at the tears on her cheeks. She might have known it was useless to try talking reasonably with Sawyer Weylin. Both of them were quick-tempered and opinionated; and Phaedra had realized long ago that they took a perverse pleasure in vexing one another. But this latest notion of Weylin's went far beyond mere vexation.

Don't let the marquis slip through your fingers, he had warned.

"That's rich, upon my word," Phaedra muttered, an angry laugh escaping her. What an amusing command regarding a man who was as elusive as a puff of mist.

Her grandfather's ambitions had rendered him blind. It was obvious he gave no credence to her fears regarding Armande, not with such absurd marriage schemes forming in his head. She had to tip her hat to the marquis. In an amazingly short time, he had managed to overcome Weylin's prejudice against foreigners and wangle his way into the shrewd old man's confidence and regard. These were things that she, his own flesh and blood, had not managed in six years.

Phaedra sank down upon Weylin's empty chair, burying her throbbing temple against her arm. What was she going to do now? Simply wait and see what happened? Wait to find out whose instincts regarding the marquis were correct, hers or her grandfather's? She had little patience for waiting, especially if it would involve long, hot nights, knowing she was separated from a most dangerous man by only a locked door.

Phaedra touched one fingertip to her lips, recalling how perilously close she had come to responding to her enemy's kiss. She was beset by a sudden fear that one night it might be she who unlocked that door, a fragile white moth fluttering toward the flame.

No, she would be no man's victim again. Mayhap her wisest course would be to flee back to Bath as Armande had bade her. But she had never fled from any man, neither Ewan and his cruelties nor her grandfather and all his bullying ways. If anyone was driven off, it would not be she. Her only choice was to remain and solve the enigma that was Armande de LeCroix.

She would begin by coaxing Gilly into helping her, setting her cousin to spy upon the marquis, perhaps find out what he kept locked in that small chest. And then there was the matter of Armande's strange reaction to the cloak. If Gilly could but make a few discreet inquiries into his background. They must be very discreet inquiries, for if Armande ever guessed what she was doing . . .

Her mind clouded with the memory of his ice-blue eyes, the well-formed mouth that could be warm, enticing, or cruel when twisted into a menacing smile, warning her not to cross swords with him. She shivered.

It was dangerous, what she meant to ask Gilly to do, but more dangerous still to go on fencing in the dark.

Chapter Six

PHAEDRA PASTED ON A SMILE FOR THE BENEFIT OF THE GUESTS WHO were crowded into the green salon that adjoined the dining room. Nigh a week had passed since she had cajoled Gilly into making inquires about the marquis. Now she had seen the sun set on another day without a word from her cousin.

There seemed little hope he might yet turn up tonight, Phaedra thought with despair as she stole a glance toward the tall windows. Beyond the festoons of the velvet draperies, shadows had long ago lengthened across the lawn. The starless night enveloped the mansion's grounds, the brightly lit salon like a single lamp glowing amidst a world of darkness.

"Damnation, Weylin. Are we to be starved to death?" The growling complaint of one of the guests recalled Phaedra's attention to the approaching ordeal of the supper party. She fixed her gaze with intense dislike upon Sir Norris Byram, one of her late husband's gaming cronies. The stocky baronet thrust an ivory-handled scratcher beneath his wig, chastising the lice so vigorously he nearly knocked the false hair askew.

"We don't keep city hours here at Blackheath House, Byram," her grandfather huffed. All the same, he anxiously dug his hand into the pocket of the orange and pink striped waistcoat straining across his middle, and consulted his watch.

"City hours were good enough for you once," Byram sneered. "I could do well without the sight of this marquis o' yours if it means going without my supper half the night. "

But Byram's grumbles went unheeded. Phaedra noted with cynical amusement that the rest of the guests were all agog to meet Armande. She suspected they would encamp in the green salon until dawn if need be, these honest, hard-working merchants and their wives, who needed their sleep to put in a full day's work on the morrow. Most of those present were acquaintances from the days before Sawyer Weylin had sold his brewery and bought his way into parliament. But mingled amongst the lot were a few impoverished noblemen such as Sir Norris and Lord Arthur Danby, not too proud to cadge a meal at the table of a rich city man.

All except Byram kept peering toward the salon's door as though expecting as grand a show as any performed at Covent Garden. Just when Phaedra had begun to think the marquis meant to disappoint them, the door was flung open. John the footman announced in impressive accents, "Armande de LeCroix, the most noble Marquis de Varnais."

Armande stepped into the salon with his usual effortless grace. Garbed in knee breeches and frock coat of ivory trimmed with gold, his white-powdered hair bound back into a queue, he looked like a crown prince carved from ice and snow.

A hush seemed to fall over the room. Or was it only herself, Phaedra wondered, who had caught her breath at the sight of those cool blue eyes with their distant expression, the handsome, arrogant features hewn into a mask of granite?

Her grandfather's friends made no effort to stop gawking. Phaedra, although she despised herself, could not do so, either. As she followed Armande's every movement, from the stiff bow to her grandfather to the way he unbent enough to be introduced to the company, she thought she now understood the charm Armande exercised upon Sawyer Weylin. The marquis was not condescending. That would have affronted her grandfather. Nay, he remained tantalizingly aloof, so that any mark of his attention conferred a tremor of delight. There was success in attracting the interest of this man, who seemed so far beyond everyone's touch.

The crude Sir Norris was the only one present who seemed unimpressed by the marquis. With a sneer, Byram had extended only his small finger by way of greeting. Armande ignored him, flicking open his snuffbox, allowing just a hint of boredom to settle over his features. Byram flushed beet-red.

Phaedra smothered a laugh, restraining an urge to applaud a

most magnificent performance. But her smile rapidly faded. Aye, why did she have the feeling that was exactly what it was to Armande—a most deadly clever performance?

With an uncanny awareness, almost as though he had heard her thoughts, Armande turned. From across the salon, his gaze locked with hers. The sudden meeting of their eyes gave her a jolt Phaedra felt all the way to her toes. He raised a pinch of snuff to his nose, but she realized with surprise that he only affected to take it. He replaced the snuffbox in his pocket, all the while holding her captive with his stare, his eyes both mocking and challenging. A half-smile tipped his lips, as though he acknowledged the fact that he was not fooling her, yet daring her to destroy the illusion he wove.

She broke the contact first, hastily looking away, ashamed to be caught ogling him like the others. She had scarce seen Armande since the morning she had burst into his bedchamber. He had returned the cloak, but by way of his new valet, Frontenac. The tall thin man had deposited the dove-colored wool into her arms with a haughty sniff and his master's compliments, leaving Phaedra to wonder if she had only imagined Armande's reaction to the garment. Had the marquis deliberately kept out of her way since then? Was he avoiding her questions, or merely heightening the effect of his appearance here this evening?

Phaedra longed to imitate his own expression of lofty indifference, but even with her back to him, she felt his presence in every fiber of her being. His image danced before her eyes, reflected a half-dozen times in the pier glasses set between the salon's rococo panels. Which of those mocking visions, if any, was the real Armande de LeCroix?

"Phaedra?" Jonathan Burnell's low voice at last penetrated her consciousness. Phaedra turned to acknowledge the wine merchant, her grandfather's longtime friend, but she had the uncomfortable feeling that the poor man had been trying to attract her attention for some time now.

His dark eyes regarded her sadly. "I beg your pardon, my dear. Have I done something this evening to offend you?"

"Certainly not." Phaedra bit back a rueful smile at the notion that a man as gentle as Jonathan could ever offend anyone. " 'Tis I who should beg your pardon," she said. "I have been so preoccupied of late."

"With your grandfather's guest, no doubt." Jonathan's smile

did nothing to relieve the gravity of his expression. The glow from the green cut-glass lamps that illuminated the room only served to heighten his sallow complexion, making him appear more melancholy than ever. "I daresay you are as overwhelmed by the marquis's magnificence as the rest of the ladies."

"Indeed. Having him here is more enthralling than attending a frost fair." Phaedra half-hoped Armande might hear her sarcastic remark, but although the marquis stood not more than a few yards away, she much doubted he could hear anything but her grandfather's voice booming in his ear.

"I half-feared something troubled you," Jonathan whispered. "I trust 'tis nothing to do with your writings?"

Phaedra stole a cautious glance about her. No one else was within earshot except the foppish Lord Arthur Danby, and he had sagged down onto one of the armchairs, already in that befuddled condition that her grandfather described as being half-glazed.

"No, the writing is going splendidly," she whispered back. "The next issue of the *Gazetteer* should be circulating amongst the coffeehouses by tomorrow. The contents may disconcert more than a few honorable members of parliament."

To say nothing, Phaedra added to herself, of a certain marquis. She had a notion Armande de LeCroix would not be pleased to find himself the object of Robin Goodfellow's speculations, the light of public attention fixed upon him.

Jonathan captured one of her hands, grasping it between his own. "My dear, if you knew how I worry about you, what you are doing. The things you write border on treason. It could be the ruination of both you and your grandfather. If anyone discovers you, it would be assumed that Weylin provided you with—"

"And how would anyone guess?" she interrupted. "Not even my publisher knows the identity of Robin Goodfellow. My cousin Gilly is the only other person I have trusted with the truth. Unless you mean to betray me."

She meant it as a jest, but she forgot that Jonathan never jested. His eyes darkened with reproach. "My dear, how ever could you think such a thing? I owe my very life to you. Do you think I could ever forget the risk you took for me?"

"Nonsense. What risk? You know my Irish blood is enough to scare off almost everything—including the pox." She averted her face to hide her feelings of embarrassment and guilt. Five years ago she had nursed him through an attack of the smallpox, and

Jonathan had been devotedly grateful to her ever since. But it had been no noble gesture on her part, she reflected bitterly. Disillusioned with her marriage to Ewan, she had scarcely cared whether she lived or died.

She slipped her hand from Jonathan's grasp. As always, his gratitude was making her uncomfortable. "Pray, don't look so solemn," she said with forced gaiety. "This supper party promises to be grim enough entertainment. Grandfather has ordered up so many courses, the poor marquis may be obliged to—"

She broke off suddenly, her attention caught by Lucy's timid face peeking inside the salon door. When Phaedra glanced her way, the young girl beckoned frantically and closed the door.

Phaedra excused herself to Jonathan. She inched her way toward the door as quickly as she could without attracting attention, but the company seemed too absorbed by the marquis to even notice when she slipped from the room.

She found Lucy in the hall, wringing her large hands.

"Lucy," she hissed. "Whatever is the matter?"

"Oh, milady, I thought you'd want to know. Your cousin is here, trying to see you, and Mrs. Searle won't let him in."

"Damn that woman." Phaedra bit her lip in vexation. She could not be gone long, or her absence would be noted, Armande's fascination notwithstanding. But Gilly would not have ridden all the way out here at night unless he had something important to tell her. Something he had learned about Varnais.

Her heart thudding with excitement, she instructed Lucy, "If my grandfather comes looking for me, tell him I have torn the flounce on my petticoat and will return as soon as I've mended it."

She scarcely waited for Lucy's solemn nod of agreement before raising her skirts and running toward the front hall. She brushed past the suits of armor, which stood like a row of silent, eerie sentries. The padding of her slippered feet seemed to raise a fearsome echo off the rafters towering overhead. But Phaedra doubted if the two who struggled near the mansion's open front door would have noticed her approach if she'd been wearing iron-heeled boots.

The pale circle of lantern light spilled across Gilly's cheerful features as he pressed his shoulder up against the door in an effort to keep Mrs. Searle from closing it. "Come now, Madam Fester, there's a sweet colleen. Just whisk to the dining room and be telling my cousin I'm here."

"Out with ye, ye Irish wastrel," Searle screeched as she was inched backward, losing in her struggle to bar the door. "Get out afore I scream for John and Peter to toss ye on yer ear."

"Mrs. Searle!" At the sound of Phaedra's shout, the woman paused to look back.

"Admit my cousin at once." But the command was unnecessary, for Gilly had already managed to disentangle the woman's hands from his cloak and slip past her.

"But yer ladyship, being as ye are now naught but a poor widow, ye ought to have more of a care for yer reputation than to be receivin' the likes of him. What would the elegant company in the salon be thinkin'—"

"I care no more for their opinion than I do for yours," Phaedra said, stalking forward. "Be about your business."

The housekeeper dipped into a sullen curtsy, but she made no effort to conceal her resentful glare before disappearing into the shadows beyond the stairway.

"Whew." Gilly straightened the black solitaire knotted around his neck. "That creature pounced at me like a daft cat. With all his wealth, I should think your grandfather might hire a butler." He rolled his eyes toward the collection of halberds and swords mounted upon the walls, their sharp edges glinting in the candlelight. " 'Tis bad enough stepping into this dungeon, without being greeted by a witch at the door."

"Pay her no heed." Phaedra eagerly embraced him. "Where have you been? I have been expecting you for days. "

But Gilly ignored her question, gazing about him with morbid fascination. "What a place this is at night!" He lowered his voice to a sinister pitch. "Can't you half fancy that old Lethe yet hovers in the shadows, ready to bash his next victim? 'Tis passing kind of your grandfather to have kept the mace, in case the old fellow should decide to rise from his grave."

Phaedra felt the hairs prickle at the back of her neck. "Gilly, will you stop teasing?" Seizing her cousin by the arm, she dragged him into her grandfather's anteroom. The chamber, now devoid of its morning throng of satin-clad beggars, seemed as solemn and silent as the hall beyond. Phaedra hastened to light an oil lamp with a taper from one of the sconces.

"Now tell me," she demanded, "what have you found out? What did you discover about Varnais?"

Gilly swept off his cape. He folded his arms across his chest, a

twinkle of amusement sparkling in his green eyes. "Ah, and to
think I had a notion it was myself you were missing, you were so
glad to see me at your door."

He mournfully shook his head. "Well, if tidings of Varnais is all
you are after, my darlin' cousin, I fear you are doomed to
disappointment."

Phaedra frowned. "You've been gone nigh a week. You must
have learned something. Who is Armande de LeCroix?"

"Exactly who he claims to be. The Marquis de Varnais."

"If such a family and title exists. Did you make inquiries of the
French Ambassador?"

"Ambassador!" Gilly snorted. "My dear, if you truly wish to
know any secrets, you don't go asking an ambassador. You speak
to his footman or his cook."

"And so what did his excellency's footman have to say?"

"That the name of Varnais is well-known in the south of
France. Both title and family are as ancient as Notre Dame. The
present marquis's parents died when he was but a babe. He had
two elder brothers, both of whom are also dead, without issue.
Consequently, the title came to de LeCroix."

"Then he really is the Marquis de Varnais," Phaedra said
slowly. She was uncertain whether she felt relieved or disappointed. "And Armande himself? What did you learn of him?"

"Let me see." Gilly rubbed his chin, staring up at the ceiling.
"Well, he orders his snuff from Trebuchets in Oxford Street. He
prefers French tailors to English, and has ordered no new clothes
while in London . . ."

"Gilly!" Phaedra was startled by the sharpness of her own
voice. Her cousin regarded her with open-mouthed surprise, and,
turning aside, she began to fidget with the pole fire screen, the
panel done up in her own indifferent needlework—a relic of the
manner in which she had filled her days before embarking upon
the far more interesting career of Robin Goodfellow.

"I beg of you to stop tormenting me," she said in a small voice.
"This matter is far too important for jesting. Now did you at least
make inquiries about him at his former lodgings?"

"Aye," Gilly's voice was subdued when he answered her this
time. "From the landlady to the laundry maid, they had not a deal
to say about him other than how generous he is with his vails.

"And the only personal servant he has is that long-nosed valet.
I'm not exactly permitted to run free in this house, Fae. I had to

wait until Monsieur Frontenac came away on an errand. Any decent Irish servant I could have lured into a tavern—but these Frenchies! The man was as secretive as a father confessor."

Phaedra heaved a deep sigh of frustration. This scanty information was not what she had waited nigh a week to hear.

"Admit it, Fae," Gilly said coaxingly, "you've got yourself in a dither over nothing. This marquis of yours is a little more aloof than most men. You've allowed your imagination to run riot, conjuring up all sorts of sinister fantasies."

Phaedra closed her mouth in a tight, stubborn line. Argument would be to no avail. No one, not even Gilly, took seriously her suspicions about the marquis.

"I suppose you did the best you could," she said stiffly. "Doubtless you are right. I am making a fool of myself as usual."

"Fae, don't be angry with me. If you want, I could try to follow the man—"

"I wouldn't dream of wasting any more of your valuable time." She scooped up his cape and folded it across his arm.

He fetched a deep sigh, but made no move to leave. He lingered by the door, regarding her wistfully, his eyes bearing the soulful expression of a great galumphing puppy, begging to be let in out of the rain. It was the same look that had been getting him out of scrapes ever since he was five. Phaedra was not proof against his charm.

"It's an ill-tempered shrew I am," she said, hugging him. "Forgive me, Gilly. But you know well how hard it is for me to admit when I am in the wrong. 'Tis doubly embarrassing when I think what I wrote about Varnais for the *Gazetteer*."

"There's no sense fretting about that, Fae. I daresay Jessym already has that issue at the booksellers by now. All you need do is write something else and stir up a fresh hornet's nest. Whatever you've said about Varnais will be soon forgotten and—bless me! I've nigh forgotten my main purpose in coming out here tonight."

Gilly fished a threadbare and much-mended purse from his waistcoat pocket. "Hold out your hands," he commanded. Bewildered, Phaedra complied. He undid the drawstrings of the purse and poured into her upturned palms a handful of golden guineas.

"Payment, my dear coz," he said gleefully, "wrung out of your clutch-fisted publisher by my persuasive Irish tongue. I told Jessym if he didn't come across with an advance, I'd be like to break his pate."

"Oh, Gilly, you—you darling." Phaedra balanced the coins between her cupped palms. "I'm a woman of substance again," she crowed. "Independently wealthy."

Gilly chuckled. "I don't know as I'd go that far. But I did get the old rogue to promise double for your next piece."

"Double. That's wonderful. I—"

She broke off at a sharp click, signaling the door handle to the anteroom was being turned. One of the heavy oak portals pushed quietly open.

"Lady Grantham?" Armande de LeCroix's cool voice slashed through the sudden silence like a saber's blade.

"Well! Speak of the devil!" Gilly mumbled in Phaedra's ear, but she scarcely heeded her cousin. She stared at the tall, elegant figure, whose broad shoulders blocked the door. The man moved with the stealth of a stalking leopard.

"Your pardon, milady," Armande said. "I had not meant to startle you, but I thought I heard your voice in here."

Heard her voice and how much more? Phaedra wondered, her heart thudding from the shock of his sudden appearance.

"I had some business to attend. *Private* business." She tried to present the picture of haughty composure, but her hands trembled as she hastened to slip the coins back into the purse. Faith, she could not have appeared more guilty than if she were the infamous Guy Fawkes caught stuffing a powder keg under parliament. Gilly, on the other hand, had contrived a smile of the most charming innocence. The rogue probably could have done so even if he stood holding a lighted fuse in his hand, Phaedra thought with some envy.

In her nervous haste, she dropped one of the guineas. It rolled to a halt by Armande's silver-buckled shoe. He bent and retrieved the coin in one graceful, fluid motion.

"I am sorry if I am intruding," he said. Armande crossed to her side and took her hand. He pressed the gold coin into her palm, cupping her trembling fingers about it. His ice-blue eyes delved into hers, seeming to promise that what secrets he had not heard, he would prize from her by force of will. Then his gaze traveled to Gilly. One of the marquis's dark eyebrows arched questioningly.

Phaedra had no choice but to perform the introduction. ". . . And my lord, this is my cousin, Patrick Gilhooley Fitzhurst."

"A pleasure it is, my lord." Unabashed by Armande's cool,

appraising stare, her cousin seized the marquis's hand and wrung it in a hearty shake. Devilish lights danced in Gilly's eyes as he added, "I've heard a great deal about you."

"I'll wager you have, Mr. Fitzhurst," Armande said.

"My—my cousin helps me. With my investments, from time to time," Phaedra said hastily. Then she silently cursed herself. She owed Armande de LeCroix no explanations. "Unfortunately, Gilly was just on the point of leaving."

"You are not staying for supper, Mr. Fitzhurst?"

"Nay, my lord." Gilly swung his cape about his shoulders. "I fear most of Mr. Weylin's guests are the sort to take Mr. Swift's 'Modest Proposal' to heart. Not only do they think all Irish children should be devoured—they wouldn't hesitate to serve me up, tough and stringy as I am."

To Phaedra's surprise, the marquis laughed. It was the first time she had ever heard him do so, the sound rich, deed-timbered, but also restrained, as though the man dared not find genuine amusement in anything. She found the thought disturbing and somehow infinitely sad.

"Farewell, coz. Your lordship." Gilly bowed to Armande and gave Phaedra an audacious wink as he moved toward the door. "No need for you to summon Madam Pester. I can find my own way out."

Gilly was nearly across the threshold and Phaedra had just felt herself begin to relax when Armande spoke up. "One word before you go, about your, er—*investments*, Mr. Fitzhurst."

Her cousin paused on the threshold, his brow furrowed in an expression of polite inquiry. The marquis shook out the lace at his wrists and continued in completely impassive tones, "Half a crown might do for a laundry maid, but it takes far more to induce a valet into gossiping about his master's affairs."

A gasp escaped Phaedra, and she could feel the color begin to drain from her cheeks. *He knew.* Dear God, Varnais knew about the questions Gilly had been asking. For a moment, even her cousin looked shaken, but he quickly recovered himself.

"I shall bear that in mind, your lordship." Although he flashed the marquis an impudent smile, his gaze swept over Armande as though reappraising the Frenchman, his stance growing more wary. He said to Phaedra, "Mayhap I should stay awhile longer—"

"Nay, I wouldn't dream of detaining you," Phaedra said. She

all but thrust him across the threshold, muttering low enough so that only her cousin could hear. "Please, Gilly. You will only make matters worse. I can deal with the marquis."

Although Gilly was not proof against the beseeching look she gave him, he backed out of the room with obvious reluctance, unwilling to leave her alone with Armande. As soon as the door had closed behind her cousin, Phaedra felt her own bravado ebb.

The silence that settled over the anteroom seemed heavier than one of London's fogs. Phaedra avoided looking at Varnais. Nervously she moistened her lips. "We'd—we'd best hasten to the dining parlor. I daresay the others will be wanting their supper."

She took a step forward, but Armande's outstretched arm barred her path, not roughly, but an immovable barrier all the same. His fingers came to rest lightly at her waist.

"My lady, I believe we have need of a talk."

Phaedra backed away from the disturbing touch of his arm. No matter how lightly he grazed her, she could always sense a tension about Armande. He was like a well-honed blade sheathed in its scabbard.

"Well, if you want to talk about prying," Phaedra blustered, then realized with dismay, it was not he who had brought up such a thing, but she. She continued doggedly, "How dare you follow me from the salon!"

"Your grandfather sent me to find you."

"I hadn't realized there was a shortage of footmen." She tried to slip past him, but he planted himself more firmly in her path. Never had he seemed more formidable, his masculine strength thinly veiled beneath the cool exterior of ivory satin.

"What you should realize, my lady," he said, "is that I seldom trouble myself to warn anyone a second time."

Phaedra thrust out her chin, seized by an impulse to deny any knowledge of what he was talking about. But one look at his eyes, glinting like shards of crystal, told her denial would be useless. She faltered. "And just—just how did you know that I—that Gilly—"

A trace of amusement eased the hard lines of his mouth. "My dear Lady Grantham, you and your cousin are not exactly the most subtle people I have ever met. But I will admit that when reports reached my ears of a strange Irishman asking odd, unconnected questions about me, I neither knew his name nor associated him with you until ten minutes ago."

"Oh," she said weakly. She retreated a step, still unable to gauge how annoyed he was. She had a strong fear that if she ever raised Armande's anger, she might not even know it until too late.

"So now you know 'twas I who set Gilly on." She affected a careless shrug. "What will you do about it? Draw your sword and cut off my head?"

He didn't answer her, but his smile unnerved her. With each step she took backward, he stalked closer, until she felt the edge of the fireplace pressing against her spine, leaving her no further room to retreat.

"I suppose you think I owe you an apology," she said. "Maybe I do. You might be pleased to know all of Gilly's questions accomplished nothing, except perhaps to make me feel somewhat foolish for mistrusting you."

Was it her imagination, or did she sense a slight relaxing in Armande's whipcord taut frame, a barely audible breath of relief?

"And does this mean you no longer mistrust me?" he demanded. "You are now satisfied. There will be no more questions?"

"I—I . . ." she stammered. How did he expect her to reply when his lips drew so near to her own?

"I suppose not," she breathed, scarcely aware of what she was saying. He cradled her face between his hands. Although she made a faint protest, she felt strangely unable to resist. Her heart thundering in ears, she half closed her eyes, fully expecting him to kiss her again. His strong fingers were surprisingly gently as he stroked back the hair from her brow.

"No more questions," he murmured. "Ah, Phaedra, I wish I could believe you, but already I fear I know you too well."

He brushed his lips against her forehead, and then abruptly released her. Phaedra trembled with disappointment, and another emotion she refused to recognize. There was something disturbingly final about the way Armande had embraced her, as though he bade her farewell. His blue eyes were warm with regret, his smile tinged with sadness. Somehow the expression frightened her more than any of his threats had ever done.

The footman, John, held back the chair at the foot of the long dining table. Phaedra sank into the hostess's seat, her head already swimming a little, although she had not tasted so much as a drop of wine. For once she could not attribute her reeling senses to the heat of the room. Nay, it all stemmed from her growing confusion, that tangle of emotion generated by the enigmatic man who now seated himself at her right.

What had happened between herself and Armande only bare moments ago? She thought if she closed her eyes she would still be able to feel his hands caressing her face, that gentle kiss which had somehow seared her more than the most heated embrace. For a brief space of time, all her mistrust had been swept away, her defenses lowered. She frowned. Or had it been Armande who had momentarily dropped his guard?

If that were so, he now had it firmly back in place. As she signaled to the footmen to begin serving the first course, she covertly studied Armande. His features were composed into the familiar icy mask. If anything, he appeared even more withdrawn; but Phaedra could not be certain if was she whom he wished to distance himself from, or the rest of the company gathered.

Her gaze traveled past him down the length of the table, the pristine white linen cloth covered with the glitter of crystal, china and silver-plate, and the candelabrum of blue jasper. Only with difficulty had Phaedra kept her grandfather from displaying every piece of expensive tableware that he owned. She caught glimpses of Sawyer Weylin's face framed between the branches of the candlesticks. His thick lips pursed with smug satisfaction as the ladies exclaimed over the table setting. Their husbands expressed more pleasure at the sight of the steaming soup tureen and silver platters laden with meat.

A marquis and Wedgwood china, leek soup and mutton dressed with French sauce. How easily impressed these people were! Immediately Phaedra felt ashamed of herself for being so snobbish. Her grandfather's merchant friends were decent folk, wellmannered, intelligent. It was only that their conversation was more likely to center about the Royal Exchange rather than Sheridan's latest play or the witty speech Lord Chatham had made in the house of lords today.

Not that Sawyer Weylin's so-called noble guests showed any disposition to discuss such interesting topics, either. Sir Norris Byram slurped his soup with such violent enthusiasm that he spattered the cuffs of poor Jonathan, who sat opposite him. Lord Danby had sobered up enough to take his seat at the table. He plucked out his quizzing glass and proceeded to inspect everyone with great astonishment as though he had not seen any of them until just that moment. He paused when his inspections reached Phaedra's end of the table, focusing on Armande. As much, Phaedra thought with scorn, as Arthur Danby ever focused on anyone.

"Stap me, sir," Lord Arthur said, "but we've met before."

Armande dismissed Danby with one bored sweep of his ice-blue eyes. "Aye, in the green salon but a half-hour past."

Danby beamed, looking quite pleased with himself. "So we did. Never forget a face." He squinted at Armande for a few moments longer, then shrugged.

Phaedra picked at the food on her plate. She had little appetite for any of the fancy dishes dressed by her grandfather's new French chef—one more indication of Armande's influence. Although the rest of the guests chatted amicably enough, the first hour of the meal passed for her in a kind of isolated silence. She was scarcely aware of any of them but the tall, proud Frenchman seated so close to her. She had but to reach out for her hand to brush against his. Yet Armande persistently directed his attention toward the woman seated on the other side of him, his broad shoulder and the iron line of his averted profile providing as much a barrier as if he had erected a wall between himself and Phaedra.

The fluttery Mrs. Eulalie Shelton dropped her spoon, looking ready to faint when Armande fixed his gaze upon her.

I should have never seated her next to the marquis, Phaedra fretted. The tiny wool draper's wife was a timid soul, easily overwhelmed.

But to Phaedra's surprise, the lines of Armande's face relaxed. Even his voice grew gentle as he strove to make Mrs. Shelton feel at ease, feigning interest in commonplace topics such as the Wedgwood china.

"I—I prefer Mr. Josiah's fancier sort myself." The elderly woman at last became brave enough to venture. "The kind with the 'Truscan ladies dancing in the center."

"Ah, but madam, the china is most *elegante* when the design is kept simple." Armande indicated the deceptively plain mint-green border that scrolled the rim of his saucer. He displayed an astonishing knowledge as he went on to describe the Dysart glazing process, which gave the china its lighter tints.

Phaedra could only shake her head. She wondered if the day would ever come when she would know Armande de LeCroix so well that he would cease to amaze her. Her gaze strayed to the hilt of his sword, which protruded from the side vent of his coat. She would have wagered that most of his pastimes would be far more dangerous than the collecting of china.

Armande had the nervous Mrs. Shelton quite relaxed by the time the platters of the second course were served. Much to Phaedra's embarrassment, the conversation veered from the cups and saucers to herself.

"Poor dear Lady Grantham," Mrs. Shelton whispered to Armande in a voice meant for his ears alone. "So young to be a widow. Her husband's death was so shockingly sudden. You see, he was out riding on his estates up north when . . ."

Phaedra felt relieved when the woman lowered her tone even further so that Phaedra was not obliged to listen.

". . . the most dreadfully horrid accident I've ever heard tell of," Mrs. Shelton concluded.

"So I had heard," Armande said. He did not seem as eager to discuss Ewan Grantham's death as he had the china.

But Mrs. Shelton, made comfortable by Armande's previous kindness as well as two cups of claret, persisted. "The Grantham family has seen more than its share of tragedy. Did you know that Lord Ewan saw his own father murdered in this very house!"

"Indeed?" Armande asked in a hard, dry voice.

Mrs. Shelton heaved a great sigh. "Poor Lord Carleton."

"From what I heard about 'poor' Carleton," Phaedra started to chime in, then stopped herself. It might sound ill-natured to say that Ewan's father likely had deserved to be murdered. By all reports, Carleton Grantham had been a bad-tempered rakehell, likely to rape a maidservant or to whip a hunting dog to death. As cutting as Ewan's tongue had been at times, Phaedra had oft taken some comfort from the fact that he at least had not been as violent as his father.

Armande in any case showed little interest in the subject. He drained his crystal goblet, his mouth twisting as though the wine was bitter. Then he lapsed into a chilling silence that left poor Mrs. Shelton looking flustered and confused.

Phaedra was far from enjoying the supper party herself. She hailed with relief the arrival of the footman to clear the table for the dessert course. But her relief was short-lived, for now Sir Norris Byram leaned back in his chair and belched loudly. He stole a glance at the rest of the company, his porcine features stretching into the leer of a man contemplating some mischief.

Reaching inside his coat pocket, he produced some folded up pages from a newspaper.

"Look," he said, waving it about. "Another issue of the *Gazetteer*. That rascal Goodfellow is at it again."

Phaedra choked in the act of taking a sip of wine. Armande turned in her direction, his brow furrowed with concern. He reached toward her, but Phaedra shrank back, muffling her face behind a napkin. The last things she wished for right now was to feel Armande's penetrating gaze upon her.

Blast Norris Byram. The man had a talent for making a nuisance of himself.

Sawyer Weylin reddened to such an extent Phaedra almost feared he would have an attack of apoplexy. "How dare you, sir," he bellowed. "How dare you bring a copy of that rag sheet under my roof!"

Unperturbed, Byram unfolded the paper, his gaze shifting toward Armande with an expression of sly malice. "I thought it might be of interest to one of your guests. His lordship's name is mentioned not a few times." Byram shifted in his chair and prepared to hand the paper down the table to Armande.

A flicker of surprise crossed the marquis's face, but otherwise he extended his hand with a look of indifference. Phaedra had to restrain a wild urge to intercept the newspaper. She could not have explained the feeling, but she suddenly knew she did not want Armande to read what she had written about him. There was still much about the marquis that disconcerted her, roused her suspicions, but she now saw that Robin Goodfellow's insinuations about Armande were both mean-spirited and cowardly. For the first time, she felt ashamed of her work.

Armande's fingers closed over the paper and he was about to begin reading the contents. Then suddenly, Sawyer Weylin's chair scraped back. With a speed astonishing for a man of his girth, he stormed the length of the dining hall and snatched the paper from Armande's hands. At the haughty look Armande bestowed upon him, Sawyer Weylin huffed, "Your pardon, my lord. But I am a member of parliament, the loyal servant of good King George. I can't permit the works of that treasonous dog Goodfellow to be passed about under my own roof."

Armande shrugged. "As you wish, sir. I am sure the matter is of no great import to me."

Weylin proceeded to shred the newspaper to bits and cast it into the empty fireplace grate. Phaedra expelled a deep breath of relief as her grandfather resumed his seat.

"Well, I can always tell his lordship what Goodfellow wrote," Byram sneered.

Weylin's fist pounded against the table with a force that made the forks jump. "Hold your tongue! I forbid even the mention of that pernicious rascal's name in my house."

Her grandfather looked so fierce that Byram had the good sense to close his mouth. The uneasy silence that settled over the room was broken only by the arrival of dessert. The rich assortment of creams, sugar puffs, iced cakes, and trifle topped with pudding did much to sweeten everyone's disposition, with the exception of Sawyer Weylin.

Her grandfather now proceeded to break his own rule, launching into an invective against Robin Goodfellow that held the writer responsible for everything from the king's poor health to inciting the American colonists to revolt against the crown.

Phaedra tried to concentrate upon the trifle, driving her fork into the wine-soaked sponge cake and fighting back an urge to break into hysterical laughter.

"Nay, Sawyer," Jonathan's quiet voice broke into her grandfather's tirade at last. Phaedra's friend looked so stricken with fear that she regretted having burdened him with her dread secret. "The *Gazetteer* did not even start publication until after the revolution had begun," Jonathan said earnestly. "I am sure the colonists have never even heard of Robin Goodfellow."

"Aye, they have their own set of rabble-rousers," Norris Byram agreed.

Her grandfather's scowl deepened. "That's what they all are, rabble. Every blasted one of those revolutionaries. A pack of ruffians only fit for the gaol. Destroying property, dumping good tea into the harbor."

Phaedra rolled her eyes to the ceiling. Her grandfather had been harping upon that incident in Boston for the past four years, with as much rancor as though he were a tea merchant and it had been his own cargo destroyed.

But as ridiculous as his sentiments seemed to Phaedra, he received a chorus of approval from most of the men present. Only Armande appeared uninterested, his long fingers crooked languidly about his wineglass, toying with the stem.

"Ungrateful lot, those colonists. No loyalty. After all the years

our army has protected them from savages and the French."
Phaedra listened to the men's comments with growing irritation,
determined to keep her lips sealed. Far wiser to swallow her own
opinions, save them for Robin Goodfellow to expound. But when
one fool piped up, "and we maintained a fair system of trade for
them," the bounds of her self-control burst.

"Fair," she echoed with contempt. "You gentlemen certainly
have a strange notion of what is fair. We sell our goods to the
colonists at outrageous prices, and then we tax their own crafts so
they cannot compete. That is supposed to be fair?"

"No one asked your opinion, missy," Weylin growled.

But Phaedra could not stop herself once she had started. "You
talk about the colonists like they were unruly children who needed
chastising, but they value the same freedoms you do and are not
about to—"

"Be quiet," Weylin thundered. "Od's fish, woman. You don't
have the least idea what you are talking about."

Sir Norris sniggered. "Lord, but the chit has gotten cheeky
since Ewan stuck his spoon in the wall. Poor old fellow must be
turning in his grave."

"'Tis her father's fault," Sawyer Weylin said. "Fool let her
read too many books. Trying to teach her to think, he said. 'Bout
as much use for a thinking woman as there is for a talking dog."

Her grandfather's friends chortled in appreciation of his wit,
even most of Phaedra's own sex joining in or eyeing her with
disapproval. She flushed with mortification.

Suddenly Armande's suave voice cut through the coarse laughter. "Some of the most enjoyable moments I have ever spent," he
said quietly, "were in the company of a certain lady whose beauty
was only matched by her intelligence and her wit."

He looked directly into Phaedra's eyes as he spoke, leaving her
in no doubt of whom he meant, nor of his sincerity. She could not
have been more stunned than if he had leaned forward and kissed
her. Could the man truly be defending her learning? It was
something not even her own father had ever done.

Armande's remark momentarily silenced the others until Byram
smirked. "Strange pleasures you Frenchies have. Next I suppose
you'll be telling us we should be sendin' our daughters up to
Oxford and givin' them the franchise."

His comment produced another spate of laughter, which quickly
changed to gasps when Armande leveled a chilling stare at Byram.

"By all means. If a woman has a good mind, she should use it. Let the ladies vote. The more capable ones might even take a seat in parliament."

He could not have stunned them more if he had advocated home rule for Ireland. Even Phaedra found herself gaping at the marquis. The man was more of a radical than she had ever dreamed of being. She sensed the thunderclap about to erupt from her grandfather's end of the table. His professed friendship for Varnais might have ended abruptly if Arthur Danby had not provided a diversion.

The fop leapt to his feet, spilling his second glass of wine that evening. "Stap me! Oxford. That's it." His finger trembling with excitement, he pointed at Armande. "That is where we met. We were up at Oxford together. Don't you remember? 'Tis me. Danby."

While he thumped his chest, the other guests returned their attention to their plates, looking alternately amused and disgusted with Lord Danby's drunken nonsense.

But Armande's facial muscles went rigid, his lean face appearing almost gaunt. Ever sensitive to his mood changes, Phaedra could not help but note how his fingers tightened about the stem of his wineglass.

"I regret, monsieur, you are mistaken. I took my education in Paris."

But Danby continued as though he had not heard. "I remember you. Your name is—is—"

A tremor passed through Armande's hand, and Phaedra thought that in another moment, he would surely shatter the crystal. She breathlessly awaited Danby's next words.

"Name of—of John or Jason something. You were—" Danby tried to snap his fingers, but couldn't manage it. His concentration broken, he stared cross-eyed at his hand, trying to coordinate the movement of his thumb. Phaedra had an urge to fly at him and shake the fool out of his memory lapse.

Sir Norris reached around Mrs. Byng and caught Danby by the coattails. "Sit down, you fool, and stop making such an arse of yourself." He yanked hard, tumbling the fop back into his chair.

Armande released the wineglass, his hand dropping back to his side. The footman mopped up the claret Danby had spilled, and the incident appeared forgotten. Forgotten, that is, by all but Phaedra and, she was certain, Armande.

For all that Armande had recovered his composure, Phaedra believed that Danby had left him badly shaken. She stared at Arthur Danby with an interest she had never felt in the man before. What had he been about to remember? Of course, he was a simpleton, a drunkard. Even while she studied him, the fool was using the rose water in his finger bowl to rinse out his mouth. No one ever took Danby seriously. If it had not been for Armande's reaction, she would not have done so, either. But she vowed to get Danby alone. She must jar the dolt's memory.

As the footmen began to clear away the dessert dishes and bring in the port, Phaedra realized with reluctance that it was time for her to signal the ladies to rise, and leave the gentlemen alone. Sir Norris Byram was obviously squirming to fetch out the chamber pot kept stored beneath the sideboard.

Phaedra was pushing back her chair to rise when the door behind her crashed open. She had not even time to turn around before a wild-eyed man burst into the room. Several of the women cried out. Arthur Danby exclaimed. "What the deuce!"

Phaedra's own startled gasp was cut off as she stared at the man. It was the same haggard young man who had been ejected from her grandfather's levee last week. The fellow still looked half-starved and ragged, but far more desperate.

Before the footman could move to intercept him, the man staggered the length of the dining room toward her grandfather. "This time, Weylin. This time you'll bloody well hear what I have to say."

From beneath his tattered coat, the man produced a flintlock pistol. Phaedra choked back a scream as he cocked the hammer and leveled the weapon straight at her grandfather's head.

Chapter Seven

PHAEDRA PRESSED HER HAND TO HER MOUTH. THE CLICK OF THE hammer being pulled back made her stomach give a sickened lurch. She caught her breath, anticipating the loud report of the pistol. But endless seconds ticked by and the only sound was the strange man's ragged breathing as he continued to hold her grandfather at gunpoint. Phaedra was dimly aware that Mrs. Shelton had crumpled to the floor in a dead faint; but the other guests sat frozen, their faces presenting a tableau of shock and horror. The only two in the room whose composure appeared unaffected were her grandfather and the marquis.

Sawyer Weylin glowered up at the man who threatened him. "I told you before, Wilkins. I don't receive workmen in my home."

"I only come for what's rightfully owed me." Wilkins jerked the pistol closer to her grandfather's face.

Phaedra could endure no more. She took a half-step forward, not quite clear even in her own mind what she meant to do. Armande seized her arm in an iron grip.

"Be still, you little fool," he said in low, level tones. "Can you not see how that fellow's hands are shaking?"

She halted, noting that Armande was correct. Wilkin's hands trembled as though he were afflicted with palsy. The jerking movement could set off the pistol at any moment.

Yet her grandfather calmly reached for his wineglass. "I don't owe you anything," he said.

"My wages, damn you!" Wilkins cried.

"Your wages, villain, went to pay what was owing at the tavern—as was agreed."

"Not by me. I am not a slave, to be thus bought and sold."

Weylin sloshed his wine about the bottom of his glass. "Any man is a slave who cannot control his drinking habits."

Phaedra gripped the back of one of the chairs. Was her grandfather mad to bandy words so? Could he not see that this man was nigh-crazed? Her heart hammering, she suddenly noticed Armande stealthily inching closer to Wilkins.

The man dashed the back of one torn sleeve across his eyes. "I made a mistake once, but I have not touched a drop since. I am begging you. At least, let me keep half the money. My—my babe died today, and I'm like to lose my wife as well. She's—she's dying of—of hunger . . . God-cursed starving while you—you—"

His wild-eyed gaze flicked to the linen tablecloth littered with cake crumbs and the remnants of the rich desserts.

Her grandfather shrugged his beefy shoulders. He snapped his fingers at the footman. "John, clear away the rest of these scraps. Whatever is left give them to this—this *beggar*."

A sound erupted from Wilkin's throat that sent a chill the length of Phaedra's spine. It sounded like nothing human. She almost thought she could see something snap deep within the man as his face contorted. In that instant, she read her grandfather's death in the man's eyes.

"No!" Her outcry was lost in what happened next. She was never sure how Armande had moved so fast. His sword arced, a silver blur as he struck Wilkin's hand upward. The pistol erupted with a deafening roar, a flash of blue fire.

As the acrid haze of smoke cleared, Phaedra nigh sobbed with relief to see her grandfather still in his chair, unharmed.

John shoved past Phaedra, the burly footman diving for Wilkins and wrestling him to the ground. Amidst the screams of the women and the chaos of chairs overturning, Sir Norris leaped in eagerly to help. Although Wilkins struggled with the strength of a madman, he was quickly overwhelmed.

He collapsed, blood streaming from his nose. Sir Norris drew back his fist to hit the unconscious man again, but Armande seized Byram's wrist.

"Enough," the marquis commanded. Byram's face darkened, and Phaedra thought he meant to turn his fists upon Armande. But he apparently thought better of it, yanking his hand free and getting to his feet. Armande's breath came a little more rapidly than normal, but it was the only sign that he had been in any way affected by the violence. He calmly resheathed his sword.

Now that the danger was past, Phaedra's knees shook, ready to give out beneath her. Somehow she managed to get herself to the opposite side of the dining room.

With a rush of affectionate feeling that surprised her as much as it did Sawyer Weylin, she flung her arms about his neck. "Grandpapa! Are—are you truly unharmed?"

" 'Course I am. Don't be an idiot, girl," Weylin said gruffly. He pushed her away, leaving her feeling foolish. The rejection worked like a slap in the face to Phaedra. Her trembling stopped at once, replaced with anger.

"Me an idiot! When it was you who all but begged that madman to shoot you. How could you taunt him so!"

Weylin struggled to his feet and regarded the powder-blackened hole in the wallpaper just beyond his head. Then he stumped round to gaze down at the inert Wilkins.

"Damme. I doubted the cowardly knave even had the pistol loaded." His voice was a mixture of grudging admiration and contempt. "Well, cart the villain out of here."

John and the other footmen moved to obey, all attempting to make excuses for allowing Wilkins to gain entry. But her grandfather cut short their efforts to blame each other. "Just tie the blackguard up, and see him delivered to Newgate. I will lodge my complaint in the morning."

John hefted Wilkins over his shoulder. The man's limbs hung down limp as a bundle of rags, his white face smeared with blood. The man had just attempted to murder her own grandfather, and yet Phaedra could not restrain a murmur of pity. "Mayhap— mayhap we should summon a doctor."

Her grandfather shot her a look of scorn. "Waste of effort, m'dear, for someone already marked for the hangman's noose."

The other guests nodded approval as John carried Wilkins from the room. He was obliged to edge his way through the crowd of frightened servants who had gathered just beyond the door.

" 'Ere now, you lot. Back to your work," John growled, full of self-importance as he struggled to balance his grim burden. "Nothing happenin' 'ere that's of any concern to you." In the disorder that followed, Phaedra wondered if it was only she who noticed Armande slip out quietly after John. But she had little time to speculate on where he was going.

Mrs. Shelton claimed all of her attention. The woman had recovered enough to be propped up in a chair, but she moaned piteously while Mrs. Byng fanned her. Phaedra moved to fetch Mrs. Shelton a glass of claret, but her grandfather snorted.

"You'll be wanting something stronger than that, m'girl." He rang for a decanter of brandy, all the while giving the gentlemen present a broad wink. "We men don't fret ourselves over such trifles, but the ladies might fancy a small drop."

The laughter that this produced seemed to relieve much of the tension. Few of the guests resumed their seats, instead mingling in small groups discussing the incident. Many of the men were loud in their protestations, describing exactly what they had been about to do with Wilkins before the marquis interfered.

Phaedra's lip curled with scorn. Aye, the fools all had plenty to say, but no one thought to voice the question that most needed asking. Phaedra could keep quiet no longer. She rounded upon her grandfather and demanded, "And who exactly is this Mr. Wilkins, Grandfather? Why did he want to kill you?"

Weylin sloshed down a mouthful of brandy, his nostrils flaring as he sniffed. "A carpenter, hired to do work at the properties I own at the east end. My mistake. The sort of rascal one can expect to deal with when buying carcasses."

There was a chorus of solemn assent from most of the others. Even Arthur Danby seemed to know what her grandfather meant. Only Phaedra felt bewildered.

"Buying carcasses? I don't understand," she said, frowning from one face to another, waiting for an explanation.

"It refers to the practice of hiring labor from taverns, my lady," Armande's silky smooth voice answered her.

Phaedra whipped around. She had not even heard the marquis return to the dining room. He stood just inside the door, neatening the lace at his wrists. "The proprietor of a tavern sells the service of a customer to cover the cost of his drinking debts. All money earned for the work goes straight to the tavern until the reckoning is paid."

Phaedra turned reproachful eyes upon Sawyer Weylin. "But Grandfather! Wilkins said he and his family were starving. What did you expect them to live on?"

" 'Tis not my problem, missy. I never forced the man to go
aswilling himself that deep into debt."

"Oui, the poorer classes are such weak-willed wretches,"
Armande said. "They only have to *enter* the taverns to collect
their wages—nobody is forcing them to drink. The tapsters are
ready to ply them with a glass—the credit is so easy to obtain, and
they have not the strength to resist."

Armande's ironic tone was entirely lost upon her grandfather.
Weylin nodded his head in vigorous agreement. "Weak-willed
indeed. Why, I once both distilled gin and ran a brewery. Yet I
never had any problem remaining temperate."

Arthur Danby hiccuped. "I'm a four bottle man, m'self."

On this absurd note, the discussion of the unfortunate Wilkins
ended. Though the others seemed able to forget the man, Phaedra
could not. She feared her sleep tonight would be haunted by the
memory of Wilkins's wild-eyed despair. There was no doubt in
her mind of what fate awaited him. Her grandfather would see to
it that Wilkins suffered the full penalty of the law for this night's
work. There was little enough she could do to save him, but she
might be able to do something for Wilkins's poor wife if she could
find the woman. Phaedra thought wistfully of parting with her
small hoard of golden guineas, then shrugged. So Robin Goodfellow might be obliged to waste a bit more ink before Phaedra
Grantham could declare her independence from tyranny. It had
taken the Americans years to do so. Surely she could endure a bit
longer. In any case, she had no choice. Her grandfather would
never think of helping the woman.

There was another action that Phaedra felt obliged to perform—
because Sawyer Weylin never would. Stiffening up her courage,
she sought out Armande de LeCroix, managing to draw him a
little aside from the others.

"My lord," she said. "I fear my grandfather has forgotten to
thank you. You saved his life tonight."

Armande's brows drew together, his expression far from
encouraging. She placed one hand timidly upon his sleeve.

"Well, *I* want to thank you. I will always be grateful for—"

"I don't want your gratitude." His voice rang out harshly, then
he amended in milder tones. "It was the most trifling service, my
lady. I beg you will say no more about it."

He grasped her hand and raised it to his lips, the kiss he pressed there both brusque and fervent. Then he turned abruptly away as though unwilling to meet her eyes.

Armande could be one of those men, she supposed doubtfully, that found it embarrassing to have someone in their debt, who hated being thanked. Yet she had difficulty imagining the self-possessed marquis ever being embarrassed by anything.

Nay, t'was more like, like . . . A troubled frown creased her brow. Perhaps, having saved her grandfather's life, the marquis now bitterly regretted having done so.

Phaedra hoped that the Wilkins incident would bring about an early end to the supper party, but she was disappointed. With the exception of the Sheltons, who called for their carriage at once, the other guests refused to allow their evening to be spoiled by such trivial incidents as attempted murder or a man being beaten unconscious and dispatched to prison.

If she could not be rid of these people, Phaedra determined to pour out coffee in the green salon rather than the music room. She dreaded being pressed into playing the spinet. An indifferent musician at best, she was in no humor to plod through *Rule Britannia*, the only composition her grandfather appreciated.

She felt relieved when the card tables were brought out, thus easing any further demands upon her to play hostess. Disinclined to play herself, she paced before the salon's long windows. The moon had come out at last to war with the clouds, making a feeble effort to spill pools of light into what was a sea of inky blackness. Not that the salon's windows presented a breathtaking vista in any case, for they only looked out on a broad expanse of lawn. Her grandfather's gardener Bullock had tried to imitate Capability Brown; but alas, although he absorbed some of the great land-scaper's precepts, he had not acquired his taste. Bullock had leveled every tree and flower about the mansion, leaving Black-heath standing in the midst of an uninspired green prairie of neatly trimmed grass.

Phaedra sighed and drummed her fingers restlessly against one of the panes of glass. Sir Norris Byram glanced up from his cards to glare at her, and she stopped, hugging her hands beneath her arms. The evening's events had put a greater strain upon her nerves than she had at first realized. How she longed for the solitude of her garret, where she could curl up on the daybed, her chin upon her knees, and be alone with her thoughts . . .

thoughts that she was obliged to admit centered upon one man. Ever since she had stood up with Armande de LeCroix, dueling wits with him to the strains of a minuet, the marquis seemed to have taken possession of her every waking moment.

She permitted her gaze to stray back to the salon. Most of the guests were grouped in foursomes, but Armande sat with one of the younger men, engaged in a hand of piquet. The candle's glow cast a soft illumination over Armande's face, somehow easing the lines of those haughty, patrician features; his blue eyes looked hazy and preoccupied. Phaedra could only wonder what dark, mysterious roads his mind traveled, what haunting secrets lay sealed beneath the curve of those sensual lips.

Her longing to discover those secrets burned as strongly as ever, but the desire had taken a subtle turn she scarcely comprehended herself. Somehow she no longer wished to expose the man as much as she wanted to understand him. Armande had done something this night that filled her with wonderment whenever she recalled it, something even more wondrous then the saving of her grandfather's life.

Armande had defended her. Not her honor. That would have occasioned no gratitude in her. She supposed there were gallant fools enough who would have done that. Nay, Armande had defended her mind, her right to have opinions on matters other than the cut of a gown or the latest dance step. He had made her feel for once that it was not so unfeminine for a woman to think, that the intelligence she cloaked beneath the guise of Robin Goodfellow was not so shameful, after all. Any man who held such views would have attracted her interest, but that it was the enigmatic Armande who had done so intrigued her almost beyond bearing.

She could nearly hear Gilly's voice cautioning her. *If you spied a will-o'-the-wisp, Fae, I vow you'd follow it until you were hopelessly lost.*

"Mayhap, I already am, Gil," she murmured. Without making it obvious what she did, she glided closer to Armande. Fanning herself, she affected a casual interest in his game.

There was no change in his negligent posture. His broad shoulders remained relaxed, one leg crooked back, the other lazily extended, displaying the outline of his muscular calf sheathed in silken hose. All the same, Phaedra felt that he was very much aware of her presence. Still waters, both of them, with not a ripple in one that the other couldn't sense.

With a shake of her head, Phaedra immediately dismissed the peculiar notion. She tried to concentrate on the game, noting uneasily the large amount of money strewn on the table between the two men. Frowning, she studied Armande's partner, striving to recollect his name from the introductions. Mrs. Byng's eldest son; Charles, she believed he was. Deeply flattered by the marquis's attention, the young man was obviously playing too deep in an effort to impress him.

Phaedra did not know why, but it pained her to think that Armande might be taking advantage of the man's inexperience. Once more than willing to believe the worst about Armande, she now regarded with fierce shame the notion that the marquis might be nothing more than a common cardsharp.

Much to her relief, the marquis was a most indifferent card player, taking no time over his discards. Charles Byng easily took the next hand. He emitted a crow of triumph as he scooped in his winnings. "Your luck is certainly out tonight, my lord."

Armande displayed no more concern over his heavy losses than if he had been tossing pennies to urchins. "One cannot expect always to be attended by good fortune," Armande drawled. "A bitter fact you may have to learn one day, my young friend."

"Pooh! If you mean to start preaching like one of my maiden aunts, I'll have done with you." Charles proceeded to reshuffle the deck and gave Phaedra an audacious wink. "Your game might improve if you paid more attention to the cards and spent less time stealing glances at Lady Phaedra."

Had Armande been looking at her? Phaedra wondered with a start. In any case, he did so now, the glint in his blue eyes bringing the heat to her cheeks. "Indeed," he murmured. "I begin to despair of ever winning the game. Her ladyship does present a danger of breaking my concentration."

Although his words were light, Phaedra sensed an edge of steel in his voice, another meaning hidden like a dagger beneath a cloaking of velvet. Did he truly perceive her as dangerous?

Although she managed to dip into a mocking curtsy, she sounded rather tremulous as she tried to laugh it off. "My apologies, sir."

As she glided away from him, he offered her that smile of his which was all too fleeting. She suddenly realized she did not want him to think of her as a threat. She wanted him to . . . Aye, she thought, feeling stunned, *she wanted him to trust her*.

Lost in her study of Armande's downswept eyes, his hooded expression, it took her several moments to realize someone was tugging at her sleeve. She glanced around to find John, his broad forehead knotted with concern.

"My lady," the footman whispered, "about that Danby fellow. He wants . . ."

"More wine?" Phaedra interrupted, grimacing at the bottle of Madeira John balanced upon a silver tray. It seemed the last thing Danby needed, but she shrugged. "I suppose you'd best give it to him. He's over . . ." She started to indicate the French gilt sofa where she had last seen Danby sprawled. The cushion still bore the imprint of his head, but the sofa was empty.

"That's just it, my lady," John said. "His lordship's gone upstairs. I think he's fancyin' he's in his own house and is trying to find his bedchamber."

"Well and have you informed my grandfather?"

"Aye, but all master said was to let him pass out wherever he liked."

Phaedra rolled her eyes. Always the perfect host, her grandfather! With her luck, it would likely be her own bedchamber that Danby selected. She sighed. "Thank you, John. I shall take care of the matter."

John looked relieved. "If you would be requiring my help, my lady—"

"No, you are needed here." She rustled away from him to the bellpull, intending to summon another of the servants. It would serve Hester Searle right if Phaedra sent her to deal with Danby. She smiled at the thought, remembering all of Danby's drunken buffoonery at the dinner table, climaxing in his absurd declaration that he knew Armande from Oxford.

Yet exactly how absurd was that statement? Her fingers hesitated when she reached for the silken cord, temptation beckoning to her. She had no desire to confront Danby herself in his idiotic state, yet might she not be losing a perfect opportunity? If she could find him alone, perhaps somehow she could sober him up enough to find out if he really did remember something about Armande.

A guilty flush spread across her cheeks. She had just been thinking that she wanted Armande to trust her. This scarcely seemed the way to begin, by continuing to question and pry. She glanced toward Armande, half-fearful of his uncanny knack for reading her thoughts from across the room. But Charles appeared to be keeping him fully occupied.

How much harm could she do Armande just by having a few words with Danby? Obviously the marquis himself was not much concerned about Lord Arthur, for he had made no move to seek out the man. Certainly if Danby posed any real threat, Armande would . . . Phaedra shivered. Having seen the ruthless grace with which he wielded that sword, Phaedra harbored no doubt as to what Armande would do. With her customary impulsiveness, she snatched up a candle and darted out of the salon.

The marquis continued to sprawl in his chair, his cards held languidly before him. It would have taken someone far more observant than Charles Byng to notice the tension coiled within Armande—although the young man *had* discerned the manner in which Armande kept stealing glances at Phaedra.

I must have been all too ridiculously obvious, Armande thought, but he was finding it increasingly difficult not to be, harder and harder not to devour Phaedra with his hungry gaze. Never had he been so achingly aware of any woman, the fresh, feminine scent of her warm skin, the animated lilt of her voice, those candid green eyes that were such mirrors to her thoughts.

Only moments ago he had caught her studying him, but in a gentle fashion, far different from her former suspicious gaze. Upon her delicate face, he had read traces of his own loneliness, a longing so poignant, it had nigh stilled his breathing, flooded him with regret . . . regret that he could not suppress the memory of what had happened to Anne, and postpone his dire purpose in coming to London for at least one sweet night with Phaedra in his arms.

It had been most fortunate for his composure that the footman had come up and spoken to Phaedra just then. More fortunate still when the lady abruptly left the room.

For the first time that evening, Armande felt some of his tension ease. Without Phaedra to distract him, he could focus his attention upon his fellow guests. There were others in this room that bore watching far more than Lady Grantham. Without seeming to do so, Armande permitted his gaze to flick toward the gold brocade sofa. He froze in the act of drawing a card.

When last he'd checked, Danby had been sagged against the cushions. But now the fop was gone. Had his carriage been summoned, or was the fool still lurking about somewhere?

Forcing himself to behave naturally as though he had no thought but for his cards, Armande inwardly swore at his own carelessness in losing sight of Danby's movements. He needed to know that the drunk was safely on his way home and no longer sharing any more reminiscences about Oxford. That was exactly the sort of thing to excite Phaedra's suspicions all over again.

Armande's mind was suddenly filled with a fleeting vision of Phaedra as she had quit the room. Had she left a shade too abruptly? Was her manner, mayhap a trifle furtive?

All unconsciously, he drew in his breath with a sharp hiss.

"Is anything amiss, my lord?" Charles inquired innocently.

"*Non.* Nothing, except that it waxes too warm in here." To himself, he murmured Phaedra's name, cursing the reckless stubbornness that made her ignore his warnings, yet at the same time admiring her courage. His heart wrenched with anger, bitter sorrow, but most of all regret for what might have been.

Then, with a most deadly calm, Armande folded his cards upon the table and rose to his feet.

Phaedra hastened up the sweeping stair to the second floor. Once on the upper landing, she was forced to pause, considering which way to turn next. Blackheath was a veritable maze of spare bedchambers, a fact which made it all the more perverse of her grandfather to lodge Armande in Ewan's room.

She saw no sign of Danby stumbling about the halls. Directing her footsteps toward the wing of the mansion that housed Weylin's prized picture gallery, she caught a glimpse of Mrs. Searle conducting her nightly inspection, making sure all the windows were locked. Phaedra ducked into the shadows until the housekeeper passed. She was not about to stop that sly old witch to inquire after his lordship's whereabouts.

When she was certain Hester had gone, Phaedra resumed her search. She had reached the last bedchamber before she met with any success. The door to the Gold Room stood ajar. Phaedra was certain the vulture-eyed Searle would never have left it so.

Tiptoeing forward, she eased the door open. Barely inching her slipper over the threshold, she called softly, "Lord Danby?"

She was greeted by a silence in which she could have heard the dust settling. The white bedhangings shifted slightly from the draft of the open door, the gossamer fabric stirring ghostlike against the lumbering shadow of the bed frame.

Phaedra shivered, retreating. But just as she began to close the door, she spotted what looked like a dark bundle of cloth dumped on the carpet before the window.

"Lord Danby?" Phaedra repeated uncertainly. Despising herself for a faint heart, she forced herself to step farther into the room. She lowered her arm, guiding the candle's unsteady light toward the floor.

The figure slumped by the window was indeed Arthur Danby. His arms sprawled out, his head lolling at an awkward angle, he looked so still, the man might well have been . . .

Dead? The thought struck Phaedra with a sickening jolt. She tipped the candle, splashing hot wax upon her hand. As she steadied the candlestick, she tried to steady her nerves, as well. Rubbing the rapidly congealing wax from her hand, she gently massaged her sore skin.

She crept nearer to Danby. His mouth lolled upon, his eyes closed, his face as waxen as her candle. Trembling, she leaned over him, stretching out one tentative finger.

He was dead all right . . . dead drunk. She might have guessed as much. Phaedra drew back, disgusted by the sour smell reeking from Danby, equally disgusted with herself. As Gilly was wont to say, she had permitted her imagination to get the bit between its teeth and gallop away with her.

Bracing herself against the window sash, Phaedra pulled up to her feet. She glowered down at Danby. Useless creature! Unless she could find some way of reviving him.

Her gaze roved about the darkened room until she caught the gleam of the ewer and basin upon the washstand. She cocked her head to one side, considering. Aye, it might be worth the effort.

She set the candle down on a dressing stand and hurried over to the washstand. The possibility of some of the guests lingering overnight must have occurred to Sawyer Weylin, for the room had obviously been readied. The pitcher was filled with water, some thick towels draped nearby.

Phaedra glanced at Danby, her fingers crooking about the pitcher's white porcelain handle. But she hesitated, recalling with sudden clarity Armande's voice asking her if she would continue to mistrust him, to pry into his past. But—she had not exactly promised him she would not.

Why, now, did she feel as though she were about to betray him? Simply because he had defended her from ridicule when she had dared to voice her opinions, something no one had ever done? Or because he had saved her grandfather's life?

She thought of the gentle kiss he had pressed against her forehead, the look of sadness shading his eyes. Mayhap she was playing the role of Pandora; mayhap her curiosity would let loose all manner of evil. Yet if Armande did harbor a dreadful secret, surely she had the right. She felt little short of desperate to discover it.

Slowly, she carried the pitcher across the room and stood gazing down at Danby. She thought briefly of wetting one of the towels, then gently dabbing the cool water over his face. Then she shrugged and poured the entire jugful over his head.

Danby spluttered, and floundered about like a fish dragged up into the air. After much blinking, he raised himself up onto one elbow. "Stap me," he groaned. Then he rolled over and muttered, "Bargeman, bargeman. Thish boat has a leak."

His head thunked down as though he were fading back into another stupor.

"No, you shan't," Phaedra cried. She seized him by the collar and after much struggle, managed to flop him on his back. Shaking him, she called, "Wake up, my lord."

His lids fluttered open and he regarded her with muzzy eyes. "Ish time to go to Dushess's rid—riditto?"

"No. 'Tis time to sober up so we may have a little talk."

"Never good time be shober." He squinted toward the window. "Very dark. Time for bed."

To Phaedra's horror, Danby began to fumble with the buttons of his breeches. He apparently had acquired much skill in the art of undressing himself while roaring drunk, for he managed to undo several of them.

"Stop that!" She grabbed his hands to halt the movement.

He peered up at her, a sickly leer crossing his foolish countenance. "Charmelle, that you, m'pet? C'mere."

Danby tugged Phaedra down, his mouth trailing a line of sloppy kisses along her neck, his hands fumbling with her hair. With an oath of disgust, Phaedra wrenched herself free. But at the same moment, Danby's fingers hooked around the neckline of her gown, tearing it down one shoulder.

"Damn!" Phaedra hissed. She plunked Danby away with such force, it bounced his head upon the floor. She doubted in his state, he even felt the jolt. He smiled at her beatifically and passed out again.

Phaedra struggled to her feet, making a futile attempt to pull the silk fabric up over her bare shoulder. She glared at Danby in frustration, resisting the urge to administer him a sharp kick. Whatever, if anything, the idiot knew about Armande, the secret was safe this night. She would have to sink Arthur Danby in the Thames before rousing him to his senses—if the man had any, which she had begun to doubt.

But there was little use railing at an unconscious man. She would have to wait until tomorrow. Retrieving her candle, she prepared to seek out her own bedchamber and have Lucy repair the damage to her gown.

When she crossed to the other side of the bed, she was surprised to find the door closed. Odd. She had no memory of having shut it. Reaching for the handle, she turned it. But nothing happened.

Phaedra tried again. It seemed to be stuck. She set down the candle and rattled the knob with both hands. She tried twisting and pulling with both feet braced at the same time.

Not stuck . . . locked. Phaedra bit her lip in vexation. Somehow she had managed to lock herself in with Arthur Danby. She had little choice but to hammer on the door and shout until one of the servants heard her.

But she had just drawn back her fist to strike the first blow when the full force of her predicament struck her. Aye, she would have some pretty explanations to offer when the door was unlocked. Herself with her hair all disheveled, her gown falling off her shoulder, Danby lying there with his breeches half undone. No one would be quite certain as to who had been attacking whom. There was only one certainty. Her grandfather would be sure to believe whatever put her in the worst possible light.

Phaedra lowered her arm. Then what the devil was she going to do? She started to curse herself for being so careless when she froze, startled by a sudden recollection. Nay, she had seen no key in the lock. She could not possibly have trapped herself. That could only mean that someone else . . . A trickle of foreboding iced its way along Phaedra's spine.

The entire time she had bent over Arthur Danby, she must have been watched by a pair of eyes peering out of the darkness, an unseen presence observing her every movement, before quietly closing the door and locking it.

So then someone must be playing a malicious jest or . . . Phaedra tensed, then placed her ear to the door, catching the unmistakable sound of voices coming from the hallway beyond. She held her breath, scarcely daring to hope. With luck it would be Lucy or one of the servants she felt she could trust.

Her heart sank when she clearly distinguished her grandfather's booming voice. "I've got one of the best picture collections in London, gentlemen. Most are in the gallery, but a few of the better ones are scattered throughout the house."

Someone else growled a reply. Sir Norris Byram, she guessed. But it required no guessing on her part to identify the next speaker.

"*Très bien*. I am most interested in seeing the Titian you said lodges in the *Chambre d'Or*."

Phaedra froze in horror, at the same time, everything clicking into place for her with bitter clarity. Armande. But of course, it was he. She had not given the man enough credit for ingenuity. Somehow he must have extricated himself from Charles Byng in order to follow her. It would have been such an easy matter for him to lock her in with Danby.

It was not at all a malicious jest, but a well-conceived plan to ruin her. Armande's quick mind had taken advantage of her own recklessness. And she did not attempt to fool herself; it would be ruin if she were found thus. Her prudish grandfather would fling her into the streets this very night.

As she heard the men drawing closer, Phaedra looked about frantically for a place to hide. No, that would not serve. If Armande guided her grandfather here on purpose, the marquis would not rest until she was found. Dragged out from behind the wardrobe or from beneath the bed, it made no odds which. She would appear all the more guilty.

Only one recourse was left to her. Her mind working quickly, Phaedra raced over to the window. Blowing out her candle, she struggled to fling open the casement before her eyes had even time to adjust to the dark. The moon, drifting behind the clouds provided her just enough light to see what a deadly drop it was to the ground below. The rough stone wall might have been as smooth as glass for all the toeholds it looked capable of providing.

Even the ivy seemed to cling precariously, its green tendrils but slender threads unable to support her weight.

Phaedra's courage failed her for a moment. Then she heard someone just outside the door. She sucked in her breath. Better to risk breaking her neck than be caught in such humiliating circumstances. Giving herself not another moment to think, she plucked off her slippers and flung them out the window.

Scooping in her skirts as best she could, she quickly followed. Thrusting her legs out first, she eased her stomach across the sill until she dangled by her hands. It was still a perilous long way to the ground.

Yet she could not hang forever. Her palms already felt slick with sweat and she could hear the bedchamber door opening. Uttering a silent prayer, she let go, risking a grab for the vines, trying to find even the hint of a holding for her feet. Her legs tangled in her skirts, her silk stockings more slippery than her shoes of velvet might have been. The vines tore free beneath her clawing fingers, scratching her arms, scraping her shoulder on the way down. She broke her fall partly by clutching at the wooden casement of one of the lower windows, then she dropped hard, landing upon her side.

Momentarily stunned, Phaedra lay still. Then she rolled over, drawing in a painful breath. But she scarcely had time to ascertain she was still alive, her bones miraculously intact, before a light appeared at the window above her.

Stifling a low groan, Phaedra crouched in the grass. There was not so much as a shrub to hide behind. All she could do was to creep backward, drawing herself into the long dark shadows thrown by the massive walls of the house itself.

Long, painful moments passed before Phaedra saw the tall graceful silhouette of a man at the window. Candle shine haloed Armande's white-powdered hair, his features lost in shadow so that he appeared almost as some pale phantom staring into the night. Searching for something? Phaedra wagered bitterly that he was and hoped that he was feeling most keenly disappointed.

She remained flattened upon the damp grass until Armande vanished. The light went out, returning that portion of the house to its customary darkness.

Phaedra sat up slowly, not so much conscious of the scrapes and scratches stinging her flesh as she was of the nettles that seemed to have been driven deep into her heart. Well, at least now she understood more about Armande de LeCroix, about that tender kiss, that look of regret she had surprised upon his hard features earlier. Even then, he had been but biding his time. Had he not sworn from the beginning that he would find a way to be rid of her if she didn't stop questioning?

Yet he had nearly lulled her into doing just that, with all his feigned admiration, his sinister charm, his deceitful way of appearing gentle when she least expected it. It was almost as if he knew how starved she felt for someone to show her even a small modicum of—

She drew her lips together so tightly it almost hurt. He had been more quick than a serpent to take advantage of the opportunity to ruin her reputation, to see her driven out from the only home she had. But she felt more astonished at her own reaction than by what he had done. Why should she feel pierced with this sense of stark betrayal?

She had suspected all along how ruthless Armande could be. A most clever man, the marquis. Clever, subtle, and cruel. Dear God! At one point, she had almost felt guilty for prying, actually indebted to the man. Well, no more! Now that he had taken the tip off his foil, she would no longer fight with a blunted weapon, either. She also knew how to bide her time, finding the moment to strike back. Phaedra gritted her teeth. She could be every bit as hard and cold as Armande de LeCroix.

But as she crawled about in the dark, hunting for her discarded slipper, she felt something hot splash down her face. She touched her hand to her cheek, astonished to find she was crying.

Chapter Eight

MORNING SUNLIGHT FLOODED PAST THE BROCADE CURTAINS, ALMOST merciless in its cheerfulness, the frolicksome song of a lark invading the heavy silence of Phaedra's bedchamber. The only sound from within the room was the whisper of a brush as Lucy quietly feathered the tangles from Phaedra's red curls.

Phaedra scarcely noticed the bright promise of the day or her maid's efforts. She stared deep into the mirror that folded out from the top of her dressing table. Despite the elegance of her yellow figured silk gown, she looked exactly like what Gilly often called her, "Fey." Her green eyes glittered, huge in the pale oval of her face, and the fiery tendrils of her hair wisped about her temples.

How old would she have to be, she wondered bitterly, before she lost that look of vulnerability, that wounded little-girl expression? Phaedra slammed the mirror down with a sudden violence that nearly toppled her porcelain shepherdess off the dressing table's edge. Moving the figurine to a more secure position, Phaedra said curtly to her maid, "Send down to the stables and tell them I will be wanting the carriage today."

"Yes, my lady." Lucy ducked into a quick curtsy. Phaedra was aware that the girl studied the scratches and angry red scrapes that crisscrossed Phaedra's hands and arms. But the girl said nothing, merely handing Phaedra her bonnet and a swansdown muff before hastening to carry out Phaedra's command.

When the door had closed behind Lucy, Phaedra slowly raised herself from the cushioned stool, wincing as she did so, her body painfully stiff from the bruises battering her hip and side. She felt the old familiar fog of depression about to creep over her, and fought it with the only weapon she had, her anger. Her eyes turned balefully toward the connecting door that led to Armande's bedchamber. She burned with a desire to confront him outright with the villainy he had practiced upon her last night.

He must be desperate indeed to stoop to such ignoble tricks. To think she had almost begun to believe she might have been wrong about the marquis! She had nearly been gulled into believing him different, not only from the villain of her imagination, but also different from Ewan, and from all the petty, narrow-minded men she had ever met. Different he certainly was, his cruelty far more subtle, couching his betrayal in words of velvet tenderness and feigned admiration. She had almost begun to believe in Armande de LeCroix, and the warm, beckoning light she had glimpsed in his eyes. She had almost believed that maybe, just this once, she was not about to pursue the will-o'-the-wisp.

Phaedra tried to push aside the hollow sense of disappointment that washed through her. In another moment, she would be weeping like a fool again, snuffling into her pillow as she had last night. Pleading illness, she had never returned to the salon; she had thus at least avoided Armande, for she had been unwilling to let him see her reddened eyes, to know how much his treachery had affected her.

It was unwise to reveal one's weakness to the enemy. And that was what he was—a most dangerous foe. All the more reason she should not burst into his bedchamber and confront him. Nay, when next they met, she must be in control of herself, as icy and subtle as he, if she ever hoped to beset him.

She wondered how Armande had been affected by the failure of of his vicious scheme. She hoped he had spent a night of hell, wondering how she had escaped his trap, worrying that she had learned something from Arthur Danby. Yet she doubted it. She could picture him but hunching those elegant shoulders in a careless shrug, laying his plans for a more clever scheme to rid himself of her the next time. Phaedra's fingernails dug into the downy surface of the muff. She didn't intend to offer him any further opportunity.

A rap sounded at her bedchamber door. Most likely it was Jane come to fetch the breakfast tray away, Phaedra thought, shouting out a command for the housemaid to enter.

It was not Jane's apple-pink cheeks framed in the open doorway, but the sly, dark features of Hester Searle. The housekeeper hovered on the threshold like a specter.

"What do you want?" Phaedra demanded, charging forward before the woman could set foot in her room.

"Some lad brought a message for yer ladyship. I knew if 'twas important, ye'd be wishful of readin' it at once."

"How excessively thoughtful of you," Phaedra said in dry tones as she reached for the note grasped in Hester's hand. The woman's fingertips crooked through the ends of her black lace mittens, curling about the vellum like talons. She seemed deliberately to be prolonging the moment, taking her time about handing the note over. Phaedra yanked it from her clutches.

Searle's beadlike eyes glistened. "Why, whatever's happened to yer ladyship's arms? Ye look as though ye been scrapping with the cat."

Phaedra didn't answer, simply slamming the door in her gloating face. What a pity for Hester that she hadn't broken her neck last night, Phaedra thought. It would have given the woman something grisly to talk about besides old Lethe.

She quickly forgot the housekeeper as she examined the folded piece of vellum. Her name was inked across it in a rushed series of blots which could only be Gilly's handwriting. Phaedra flipped the note over to break the seal, but the red wax came away easily. Phaedra would have wagered her last groat that Hester Searle had read the letter.

"Damn that woman," she muttered, unfolding the note. Her fingers trembled as she scanned the contents, fearful of what might have been set down there for Hester to see. Fortunately, this message made no mention of Robin Goodfellow. She would have to caution Gilly to take care what he committed to paper. Future missives might not be so harmless as this one, which dealt, in Gilly's jaunty, haphazard style, with Armande.

My dear Fae,
    By the time you read this, I should be well on my way to France, my darlin' coz. Having met your marquis, I'm thinking perhaps there is something more to your fears than mere imagination. I'm after making a few more inquiries to see if I can induce the Varnais family into passing the time of day with a charming Irish lad. Not to fret yourself over my

lack of funds. I won a grinning contest at the Boar's Tooth, myself pitted against a dour Scot, name of Dermot MaCready with a handsome set of teeth. I outgrinned him by a full five minutes. Hope to return in a fortnight. My tender regards to Madame Pester.

Much love, Gilly

Despite the letter's lighthearted tone, Phaedra felt no inclination to smile. Gilly might have been her twin as far as impulsiveness was concerned. Why could he not have consulted her first before undertaking this rash voyage to France?

Mayhap it would prove a good notion, but right now she felt abandoned, deserted by her one true friend. A fortnight . . . much could happen to her in a fortnight. If Armande attempted to serve her another such turn as he had last night . . .

Fear and loneliness tugged at her, threatening to swirl her down into dark eddies of depression. No, she thought, resisting the pull. She could manage without Gilly. Let Armande scheme as he would. The next move would be hers.

Phaedra shoved the note in a drawer. Donning her bonnet, she scooped up her muff and hardened her jaw with resolution. Never had she been so nervous about descending the stairs of her own home. Her fingers trembled inside the muff; she was not at all certain she could maintain her composure when she came face to face with Armande.

When she came downstairs, she discovered that she needn't have worried. John informed her that both her grandfather and the marquis had gone out.

"Thank you, John," she said, some of the stiff, militant set to her shoulders easing. She could almost regret Armande's absence, having composed in her head several greetings, all of them alike in their acid sweetness.

She forgot every single one of them as her gaze focused on the man meandering aimlessly about the front hall, in flashy clothes that looked much the worse for having been slept in. Armande might be gone, but Lord Arthur Danby was not.

His lordship strutted toward the front door as though coming from the king's levee. He paused by one of the suits of armor, stopping long enough to level his quizzing glass at the pointed spikes of the infamous mace.

He appeared on the point of making his departure when Phaedra rushed after him. "Lord Danby?" she called.

The quizzing glass swiveled in her direction. Phaedra skidded to a halt in front of him. "Good morrow, Lord Danby. I—I trust you slept well."

"'Deed I did. Most kind of you to ask." He brushed back the straggling ends of his disheveled gray wig and offered her a vacuous smile. Except for a certain puffiness about the eyes, he appeared not much the worse for last evening's revels. Even sober, he still bore the expression of a besotted sheep. Phaedra sought for a way to introduce the subject of Armande de LeCroix without seeming too abrupt, when Dandy disconcerted her by saying, "Forgive me, my beauty. But I have not the honor of knowing your name."

"Why—why, I'm Lady Phaedra Grantham."

He dipped into an awkward bow. "Charmed to be making your acquaintance. Simply charmed."

"You made my acquaintance last night," Phaedra said, biting her tongue lest she add, "You silly clunch."

"Alas, I'm a poor hand at names. I never forget faces, though."

"So you said last night. How much I enjoyed it when you entertained us with your anecdotes about *Oxford.*" She laid special stress on the word, trying to jar his memory.

"Did I? Well, I daresay I was quite witty." Danby turned back to his inspection of the suit of armor.

Phaedra stuffed both hands inside her muff and laced her fingers tightly together. Patience, she counseled herself, patience if you expect to learn anything from this fool.

"You mentioned that you knew Armande de LeCroix."

"Who?"

"The Marquis de Varnais." Phaedra gritted her teeth. "You said that you attended Oxford together. Except that you thought his name was . . ." She paused, waiting expectantly.

Danby lifted the visor of the armor cautiously as though he feared to find a face peering back at him.

"No Frenchies at Oxford that I recall. 'Course, there could have been for all I know. I never went there."

"Never went there!"

"Cambridge man, myself." He let the visor slam shut with a loud clang. "Well, good day to you, Lady Grantley. Thanks ever so for your hospitality. Must all meet again sometime."

Somehow he gained possession of one of her hands and planted a moist kiss above her knuckles. He didn't even appear to notice that her fingers were clenched into a fist.

Phaedra stood there fuming. The one weapon she had most counted on in her battle against the marquis now sauntered away from her. The footman let Danby out before she swore. Of all the incredible dolts. The man was a worse fool sober than drunk. She stalked from the hall, resigning all hope of ever learning anything from Arthur Danby.

Soon Lucy brought her news that only increased her frustration. Her grandfather's elderly coachman, Ridley, had refused to hitch up the carriage until he knew where she meant to go.

"Anywhere." Phaedra's gaze traveled up the hall's gray stonework. She had no intention of spending her day imprisoned here, awaiting Armande's return with a mixture of dread and longing, anticipating his next attempt to drag her to the devil.

"Anywhere," she repeated, "away from this accursed house." Yet she realized such an answer would not suffice for Ridley. The elderly coachman was obliged to render a strict accounting to Sawyer Weylin. Anyone might have thought her grandfather took her for a prospective horse thief.

Where was she going? There was only one reasonable answer she could think of to give. "Tell the old martinet I wish to go to Oxford Street."

Her grandfather would never succeed in making a cit of her, Phaedra thought, as the carriage lumbered along the cobbled pavement. Only one part of London had ever succeeded in capturing her heart and imagination . . . Oxford Street, choked with its hackney cabs, sedan chairs, dirt and noise, a seemingly endless row of bowfront shop windows displaying tempting wares behind latticed panes.

All the raucous music, the riotous poetry that was London sang out here in the rumble of iron coach wheels, the bells tinkling from the collector for the penny post. Milkwomen yodeled, and the ballad singers bellowed, all striving to be heard above the litany of the street hawkers . . . "New-laid eggs, five a groat." "Hot mutton pies, hot!" "Oysters, buy my oysters."

Phaedra let down her coach window, thriving upon the din and confusion. Gilly had once teasingly remarked to her, "They say

Nero fiddled while Rome burned. In the midst of the mayhem, you, my girl, would have gone shopping."

Phaedra was obliged to admit there was some truth to the charge. In the grimmest times of her troubled marriage to Ewan Grantham, she had fled to Oxford Street. Not to shop, but to lose herself in the crowds, to banish her depression in all the bustle and color, to draw from the vitality and life teeming about her some reason for clinging to her own miserable existence.

It had always worked. Somehow jostling elbows in such a sea of humanity had reduced Ewan and all his petty cruelties to a level of insignificance. Phaedra hoped the street could work its magic again, hoped the din and uproar would diminish Armande de LeCroix and the pain and confusion he had brought into her life, so that she could but snap her fingers and he would be gone.

The younger footman, Peter, let down the coach steps and helped swing Phaedra up onto the raised footpath. Behind her, she could hear Ridley, up on his box, give a loud humph of disapproval. Most ladies of quality, ever mindful of the dangers of mud and rascally pickpockets ready to snatch one's very handkerchief, did not wander the street, but preferred to be deposited directly at the steps of the shop they wished to visit.

Phaedra merely offered Ridley a sweet smile and instructed him to wait for her at the next corner. Stuffing her hands deep within her muff, she set off down the street, followed by her maid. "What would my lady be looking for?" Lucy inquired timidly.

A diversion. A way to keep from being driven mad by the deceptive charms of a certain ruthless Frenchman. But Phaedra kept to herself such thoughts as her maid would scarce have understood. Lucy had always been mystified by these street ramblings of hers. Phaedra usually found some practical reason for the outing, simply to erase the perplexed lines from the girl's brow.

She said airily, "Oh, I am hoping to find a gift for a dear friend of mine who is to be married soon." Inwardly Phaedra grimaced, reflecting how astonished Muriel would be to receive such a token of Phaedra's tender regard.

No matter. The explanation satisfied Lucy, leaving Phaedra to wander where she would, her thoughts free to roam likewise. She strolled past a succession of shop fronts, the glass glinting like mirrors set into treasures boxes, reflecting back gold buckles and quill pens, parchment maps and perfumed soaps, bagwigs and Dr.

James Restorative Powders. The tradesmen liked to boast that what one could not find in London shops, one simply didn't need.

Except what Phaedra desired could not be found there or anywhere. What Phaedra wanted was a mirror that would help her see into the dark corners of Armande de LeCroix's cold heart.

She found herself standing in front of a jeweler's shop, where a pair of twin sapphires were displayed in the window. In one light they flashed blue fire, in another glinted as cold as shards of ice—exactly like Armande's eyes. Phaedra shook herself. Now she must become as hard and calculating as he; but she despaired of ever being able to do so.·

"Does my lady wish to go into this shop?" Lucy asked hopefully.

"No." Phaedra moved farther along the street. She paused in front of a peruke-maker's establishment, frowning at the white bagwig displayed there, with its elaborate sausage-roll curls. Armande was far more attractive when he abandoned his wig and powder. She could not help remembering the sweep of sable hair waving back from his brow, the bronzed, hard-muscled flesh he kept concealed beneath his satins and lace. A man of frustrating contradictions, he seemed a different person when he set aside all the accoutrements of the elegant aristocrat.

Every puzzling thing she had ever noted about Armande now crowded into Phaedra's brain. His inexplicable position as a guest of her grandfather, the painful flash of memory in his eyes occasioned by the gray wool cloak, the way he had tensed at Danby's seeming foolishness, his refusal to be thanked for saving Sawyer Weylin's life, the violent aversion to questions about his past that had led him to try to ruin her. Thinking about Armande was like holding in her hands shattered fragments of crystal that could not be pieced back together.

She rubbed her temples. It was no good. She had come to Oxford Street to escape, for a time, Armande's all-pervasive presence. Yet everything seemed to remind her of him. Only a few yards away, a group of ballad singers burst into a chorus of bawdy songs, so loud she could scarcely hear herself think. She glanced about her, suddenly wondering why she had come here. Why had she never noticed before how dirty Oxford Street was? The shop displays were garish, and the people thronging past her were loud-mouthed and vulgar. And the noise—the noise she had oft thought so delightful was enough to split one's head!

Feeling the tension begin to build within her anew, Phaedra started at a touch upon her sleeve. She had all but forgotten Lucy's presence. Her maid said, "Mayhap madam could find something in that shop to please your friend." Phaedra turned toward the shop front that Lucy so shyly indicated. Her gaze flicked over some indifferent pieces of china and a silver tea service.

"No, I think not—" Phaedra began, preparing to continue on her way, when she was arrested by the sight of something almost lost in the shadow of the tea urn. She peered closer, pressing near the glass. It was naught but a pair of candlesticks—and yet there was something in the delicate artistry of the china that reminded her strikingly of the shepherdess she had found in the attic. Of course, there was nothing remarkable in the fact that the same artisan should have fashioned other pieces than her own figurine. But Phaedra's curiosity was aroused enough to slip inside the shop, with Lucy following doggedly at her heels.

The interior was quiet, appearing not to enjoy much trade. She was the only customer—perhaps the only one in some time, Phaedra thought, eyeing the layering of dust on the shelves. They were stuffed with an odd assortment of jewelry, buckles, snuff-boxes, ladies' fans, and trinkets.

The shopkeeper who bustled forward to serve her struck Phaedra as being something of a trinket himself. He barely came up to her shoulder. Both his smile and his black hair looked painted on, as much as if he had been a wooden toy soldier.

"Good afternoon, milady," he trilled. "My stars, such a fine day. So perfect for your outing."

Phaedra suspected he would have greeted her in the same fashion even if it had been pouring rain.

"And how may I have the honor of serving your ladyship?"

"Well, I did wish to inquire about—" But before she could finish, the little man rushed on.

"An enameled sand box for dusting dry the ink upon your letters? Wonderful charming."

"No, I believe not. I would like to examine—"

"Or some Egyptian pebble teeth for your grandmamma, perchance? Mayhap a new fan. I have an excellent assortment—"

"No!" Phaedra said. "I merely wanted a closer look at the candlesticks in the window."

The shopkeeper raised himself up on his tiptoes and preened. "Ah, the candlesticks! Your ladyship has most excellent taste."

He scurried toward the window display and in another moment he was blowing the dust off the candlesticks and setting them upon the counter with a flourish.

"Treasures. Wonderful charming." He beamed.

Phaedra carefully lifted one of the candlesticks. A maiden, molded of blue and white jasper and garbed in flowing Grecian robes, held aloft a petal stem on which the taper was to be mounted.

Although Phaedra did not possess Armande's expert knowledge of china, she had a fine eye for detail. The similiarities in style to her own shepherdess were remarkable.

"I know this sounds foolish," she said hesitantly. "But I believe I already possess a figurine made by the same artisan."

"Indeed, milady?" The merchant smirked. "Such a coincidence. Lethington china is extremely rare."

Lethington. The mere sound of the name stirred some chord of memory in Phaedra, but she could not place it.

"The piece I have is a shepherdess," she said, and went on to describe it for the shopkeeper. He permitted a rather doubting frown to disturb the surface of his too smooth politeness.

"W-e-ell, 'tis a popular subject for china manufacturers, but I suppose you might have acquired one of a famous set. A shepherd and shepherdess were commissioned for the Emperor Franz Joseph of Austria and his sister, the French Queen Marie Antoinette; but unfortunately the figurines were never delivered."

Phaedra tore her eyes away from the entrancing candlestick long enough to inquire. "Oh? Why not?"

"Alack, the Lethington manufactory was forced to close its doors. I procured many of the pieces when the property was sold to pay off debts. But the shepherd and shepherdess were missing." The merchant added almost too casually, "If your ladyship would like to bring me the figurine, I would be only too pleased to examine it to see if it is genuine Lethington."

"Is it worth a great deal of money, then? I have heard of Wedgwood china," she murmured, "but never Lethington."

"The Lethington family were well-acquainted with Josiah Wedgwood, I assure you. All of them from Staffordshire, all of them skilled craftsmen. Of course, the Lethington shop was a family concern. The mother and her two sons, James and Jason, as I recall. Also a sister, Julianna. Fan me ye winds, but Mrs. Lethington must have had a penchant for the letter J."

When the shopkeeper finished chortling at his own jest, he added, "Most of the actual designing was done by Miss Julianna."

That information caused Phaedra to examine the candlesticks with renewed interest, admiring Julianna Lethington's skill. How it would astonish her grandfather, who thought women could do naught but embroider handkerchiefs. She remarked almost to herself, "With such artistry, I am astonished that the Lethingtons should ever have been obliged to close their business."

" 'Twas owing to a tragedy in the family—a scandal far too sordid for your ladyship's delicate ears." For all his protestations, Phaedra could tell the man was perishing to impart it to her. "The elder brother James was hanged for murder, and some say his sister committed suicide, flinging herself into the Thames. As for the younger brother and the mother, they simply packed their bags and fled to Scotland, so I've heard."

Although she made a murmur of sympathy, Phaedra's interest in the tale had already begun to wane. Mulling everything over in her own mind, she decided that it was highly unlikely that her porcelain shepherdess could be the famous piece designed by Julianna Lethington for an emperor. After all, Phaedra had found the statuette discarded in the attic—and she knew her grandfather's shrewdness too well to think he would miss a prize. Although Sawyer Weylin had no appreciation of the arts, he had a canny instinct for anything of value.

Having reached this conclusion, Phaedra returned the candlesticks to the counter and thanked the shopkeeper for all of his time. The little man's chin dropped when he realized she intended to quit the shop without purchasing anything.

He followed her to the door, filling her ears with his importunings. "Nay, milady, if the candlesticks do not please, let me show you some of my other pieces. I have many other things—wonderful charming . . ."

But Phaedra put an end to this by frankly admitting she had no extra money for china at the moment. Gathering up her maid, she escaped from the dark shop into the brilliant flood of sunlight. Considering that Phaedra's avowed intent had been to purchase a wedding gift, Lucy was looking rather puzzled.

To distract the girl as much as anything else, Phaedra entered a milliner's and made a trifling purchase of some sash ribbons, then sent Lucy to take the parcel back to the carriage, thus giving herself a moment alone. She had espied a bookseller's stall across the street and intended to secure herself a copy of the *Gazetteer*, to secret away with the other copies of her writing she kept in the locked desk in her garret.

As soon as she made certain Lucy was a safe distance up the street, Phaedra hiked up her skirts and darted through the traffic, barely escaping having her toes crunched by the wheel of a farm cart. In the next instant she was nearly knocked down by a running footman. The fellow did not even pause, but continued his sprint, waving his white baton in an effort to clear a path for the Duchess of Avalon's carriage. Phaedra leaped past the posts separating the street from the footpath just in time to save herself from being trampled by her grace's leaders.

She collided against a hard male chest with a force that nearly sent her sprawling backwards into the mud. A strong pair of arms closed about her, steadying her.

Phaedra took but a moment to catch her breath before mumbling. "Thank you, I beg your pardon." She struggled to pull free, aware that her rescuer appeared to be taking undue advantage of the situation, holding her longer than was necessary. As she focused on lean, chiseled features and ice-blue eyes, her heart gave a mighty thump instead. She could feel her face turn ashen. It was as well that the strong arms of Armande de LeCroix yet held her, or she might have fallen.

"Lady Grantham," Armande said, his lips tipped into that reluctant smile which was so peculiarly his own. The waves of his sable-colored hair captured the sunlight, whose reflected warmth shone in the depths of his eyes, as well. How dare he pronounce her name like that, in those low, intimate tones! He almost made it sound like some sort of an endearment. She shoved away from him, the color flooding back into her cheeks.

All the composure with which she had planned to face him—where was it now? She could have cursed him for retaining his. It was not fair, his taking her by surprise this way, but then she already knew that the marquis played by his own rules.

"Lord Varnais. Only fancy encountering you here," she managed at last. She had meant to be all chilling sweetness, but she could not seem to avoid a flinty, accusing tone. "We do have a habit of meeting at the most unexpected times. One would almost think you had been following me." She nearly added, "*Again.*"

" 'Tis equally astonishing for me, but not unpleasant." He

smiled. "I am glad to see you have recovered from your illness of last eve. Are you out here all alone?"

Armande's silken voice could make the most innocent questions sound sinister. She retreated a step, her eye drawn to the window of the shop from which she realized Varnais must have just emerged. A single black-edged placard proclaimed, FUNERALS FURNISHED HERE.

"No!" she blurted out, her fingers tightening upon her muff. "My maid, the coachman, and footman are just at the next corner."

"I am glad to hear it. 'Tis not safe for you to wander the streets unescorted."

"I'll wager I am as safe here as I would be in some of the rooms of my grandfather's own house." She stiffened with annoyance when she saw that her pointed remark produced not so much as a twitch of an eyebrow on Armande's handsome impassive face. What a cool villain he was. Determined to force some guilty reaction from him, she continued, "Oxford Street is no longer what it was like when my grandfather was a boy. He told me this part of the city was but a pit of mud, a likely spot to be set upon by cutthroats. But I imagine such villains are a little more subtle these days—perhaps more after the style of the French."

"We have villains in France with no more claim to cleverness than your English ones, madame."

"But I daresay you have *some* that are masters of the art of calculation."

"You could encounter such rogues anywhere." To her outrage, a flicker of amusement shaded his eyes. " 'Tis all the more reason you should be careful, *ma chère*. Mayhap you would permit me to walk you back to your carriage?"

He reached for her hand, but a sudden frown creased his brow. Phaedra tried to draw away, but he would not let her. Maintaining a firm but gentle clasp on her wrist, he examined first the back of her hand and then the palm.

"Mon dieu. What have you done to yourself?"

The light tracing of his finger made her skin tingle. His feigned concern caused her more pain than the knowledge that he was responsible for her injuries.

"A trifling accident." She had difficulty speaking past the sudden lump that formed in her throat. "I assure you that no such mishap will ever befall me again."

She jerked away from him and stuffed both hands in her muff. Damn him! She could endure no more of his performance. She would dash her fist into his face, if he continued to regard her with that mock-tender light in his eyes. As though he worried over a few minor scratches, when she knew well he'd just as lief she had broken her neck.

"You will excuse me if I decline your offer of an escort," she said through gritted teeth. "I am not returning to my carriage. I was on my way to the bookseller."

"Then I will stroll with you. I had a purchase I wished to make myself." He slipped his arm through hers, the movement full of graceful gallantry, yet inexorable. There was no way to be rid of him unless she wished to make a scene in the streets.

She acquiesced in silence, walking stiffly beside him, the whole time very much aware of the pantherlike movement of his muscular limbs, the latent masculine strength he so well concealed beneath the fancy cut of his French frock coat.

As they drew nigh the bookseller's stall, Phaedra attempted to shake Armande off by feigning a deep interest in purchasing a book. The variety that this particular seller offered was small, a mixture of old and new. Goldsmith and Johnson were tumbled haphazardly amongst volumes of Fielding and Smollett. Not far off Phaedra could see a copy of the *Gazetteer,* but with Armande hovering so close to her side, she dared not reach for it. She snatched up a book without noticing the title.

"You and your cousin seem to have an admiration for Swift." Armande's comment made no sense until Phaedra realized with a start she was holding the first volume of *Gulliver's Travels*.

"Yes," she said slowly, stabbed by a painful remembrance. " 'Tis one of the few books my mother ever bought for me, though I scarce ever appreciated the satire. I read it more for . . ."

"For the fantasy. For the pleasure of traveling to such faraway exotic places as the kingdoms of Lilliput and Brobdingnag."

Phaedra could only stare up at him, for a moment forgetting her anger, as she wondered how he could know such things about her childhood. He almost sounded as though he had shared her dreams, had been her fellow traveler when she had voyaged with Lemuel Gulliver. How utterly absurd! To imagine such a thing about a man of such cold, cruel logic as Armande.

He pointed to the book in her hands. "Well, you can scarce wish to purchase what you already have."

"But I don't have it." Her fingers tightened almost unconsciously. "My husband burned it . . . all my books." Why was she telling Armande all this? He could not possibly care. No one but she had ever mourned the loss of the books from her childhood. She had mourned them like old friends, the one legacy from her parents lost to her forever.

She could still recall that day she had come in from riding, preparing to take tea with Jonathan. She could experience again that sick feeling, when she had found the garret bookcase empty, and had seen Ewan's cruel smile when he had indicated the heap of ashes in the fireplace grate. It was yet another punishment for her being "too clever." He had nearly broken her that time, Ewan had. It was as though he had thrust every dream she'd ever cherished into those flames, reducing a part of her very soul to ashes. That day she had finally begun to hate Ewan Grantham . . .

"Phaedra?" As though from a great distance, she heard Armande's voice. She blinked, coming back to the present to find Armande studying her with grave concern, the bookseller eyeing with suspicion the volume she hugged to her chest as though she meant to steal it.

"Will my lady be wanting that wrapped?" the man asked.

Much to the bookseller's evident disgust, she shook her head. Armande appeared about to protest, so she said quickly, "I doubt I could afford it. My grandfather has no more liking for Irish authors than Ewan had. I could not bear to see another book cast into . . ." She laughed weakly. "Coal is so much cheaper to burn."

She replaced the book, then said in a low voice, "I believe I have done enough browsing for one day."

"*Bien*. I will make my purchase, then we'll go. I fear 'tis I who must risk offending your *grandpère*. My curiosity has been aroused by the crude Sir Norris."

Phaedra watched as Armande proceeded to buy the copy of the *Gazetteer* she had noticed earlier. But the urge she had felt last night to prevent his reading it was gone. With a kind of cold fascination, she watched him flick through the pages. She knew when he had read down to the section that concerned himself. His fingers tightened upon the newsprint, a wintry expression replacing the warmth with which he had regarded her earlier.

"You do not seem to have found Mr. Goodfellow's essay all
that diverting," she ventured.

"No, I didn't. I would have thought the man could have found
more important matters to write about, but it seems he shares your
interest regarding my background."

Phaedra flinched before the sudden hard look of suspicion
Armande directed her way. Nay, he could not possibly have
guessed. She fidgeted with her muff, saying as indifferently as she
could manage, "I—I daresay Mr. Goodfellow's curiosity could
make things far more uncomfortable for you than I ever did."

"He could if I continue to let him write this tripe."

"How ever would you stop him?" Phaedra asked, much
misliking the knifelike glint in Armande's narrowed eyes. "Even
the members of parliament, who have been used much worse by
the man than you, have been tolerant. Especially after the John
Wilkes affair."

When Armande shot her a questioning look, she explained, "He
was another writer who dared criticize the king. When he was
imprisoned, riots broke out on his behalf."

"There are more effective ways to stop a man's pen than
prison," Armande said coldly.

Phaedra plucked at the ribbon adorning her muff until it came
off in her hand. "Alas," she stammered. "No—no one has the
least notion who Robin Goodfellow might be."

"I will find out." The steely resolution in Armande's voice left
her in no doubt that he would. It would not be difficult for
Armande to track down her publisher. Gilly had told her that
Jessym was tough, a close-mouthed individual, but Armande,
Phaedra feared, would know how to be most persuasive. Even if
Jessym knew naught of her, he would be bound to mention Gilly.
Armande knew that her cousin had been investigating him. The
marquis might assume that Gilly was Robin Goodfellow. And
then . . . No, she couldn't let it come to that.

Phaedra shuddered, feeling beads of cold sweat breaking out
upon her forehead. She tried to behave naturally, permitting
Armande to take her by the arm to lead her back to her carriage.
But beneath her outwardly calm exterior, her heart pounded. All
unknowingly, Armande suddenly posed a greater threat to her than
he had when he had locked her in with Danby.

If she ever meant to fight back, find a way to be rid of him, she had to do it quickly. But her mind was all but numb from panic. What could she do? What on earth could she do?

She could not have said how the idea first popped into her head. If she had been thinking more clearly, she would have dismissed the thought at once as insanity. The mere notion of attempting such a thing left her in a cold sweat. No, she couldn't. What if it backfired? What if Armande caught her?

Yet even though she was nearly choked by her fears, she was already clearing the way to set the plan into motion. When her maid reappeared at last, she found an excuse to send the girl away again immediately. "Nay, you may wait in the carriage, Lucy. You can see I have the marquis with me now. I am sure I can depend upon him to escort me upon one more errand. Just tell Ridley to bring the carriage around by the goldsmith's shop."

She hoped her voice sounded flirtatious, like Muriel Porterfield's, instead of shrill with panic. But it scarce mattered. Armande seemed to have withdrawn into himself, too preoccupied with his own grim thoughts to notice her nervousness. He made no protest about escorting her to the goldsmith's, holding the door open for her with a kind of stiff gallantry. How could she possibly be scheming to do such a thing to him? No, she adjured herself, steeling her shoulders. After what he had done to her last night, the threat he posed to herself and Gilly, he deserved it. That is, if it worked . . .

Phaedra started when the low-voiced proprietor approached her. A solemn, businesslike man with a balding forehead, he appeared accustomed to the vagaries of female clientele. He made no demur when Phaedra had him drag out almost every item in the shop for her inspection, every necklet, ring, chain, watch. She pretended to examine them all, while furtively drying her moist palms on her skirts, flexing her fingers. It had been many years since she had played at sleight of hand games with Gilly. She had no way of knowing if she still possessed the skill—at least not until she tried.

Swallowing hard, she dropped her muff. While the goldsmith bent to retrieve it, Phaedra palmed one of the gold seal rings. That of course was the easy part. Her knees trembling, she skirted over to where Armande stared moodily at a delicate lady's watch and chain. Phaedra brushed up against him. In one swift movement, she slipped the seal ring into his waistcoat pocket.

He glanced down at her, his eyes widening in momentary

surprise. Phaedra's stomach lurched with fear. Had he felt her planting the ring?

"Oh—oh dear," she faltered. "I—I think I've lost my . . ." She nearly said muff, realizing in time she was still clutching it. "My—my handkerchief. It was one my mother embroidered for me. I must have dropped it back at the bookseller's. I don't know how I could have been so careless. I cannot bear the thought of having lost it."

The story was absurd. She was certain Armande would see through it at once. But the genuine anguish in her voice must have made it sound quite convincing. She actually felt tears start to her eyes.

Armande's grim expression softened. He lightly touched her cheek. "There is no need to so distress yourself, *ma chère*. I will go back at once and look for it."

Phaedra lowered her eyes, no longer able to bear to look at him. "Would you?" she quavered. "I'd be most grateful."

As Armande left the shop. Phaedra fought down an urge to call him back. Even now she could put a halt to this.

And do what? Sit back and wait until Armande found another way to destroy her? Taking no time to reconsider, Phaedra forced her trembling legs to propel her toward the goldsmith.

"Oh, sir. That—that man in your shop just now—"

"My lady's husband?" the goldsmith asked.

"Heaven forfend. I—I never saw him before in my life. I think he was following me."

The goldsmith's balding forehead furrowed with indignation. "The rogue. There are plenty of that sort about to accost innocent women. In future, might I suggest your maid . . ."

"You don't understand, sir." Phaedra wrung her hands. This must not take too long. She had to be out of here before Armande returned. "His advances to me were all a ploy. He but used that for an opportunity to steal. I—I saw him slip a ring into his pocket. I was so frightened, I could not speak to warn you."

The goldsmith frowned. "Are you certain, milady? The gentleman was most well-dressed for a thief."

At Phaedra's insistence, the man examined his merchandise. She went through agonies of fear while he did so. It seemed to take him forever to notice the large seal ring was missing.

The goldsmith shook his head. "Aren't these rascals getting bolder all the time? Such elegant raiment, too. Only fancy!"

"While you are fancying, the man is making good his escape."
Realizing her voice sounded too sharp, Phaedra quickly resumed
her fluttery tone. "I mean, you must get the constable after him.
He's only gone a small way up the street."

"Well, if milady would be so good as to bear witness—"

"No, I could not bear to set eyes upon the villain again."
Phaedra struck her hand to her brow. "You will have all the
evidence you need, I assure you, in his right front pocket. I must
get to my carriage before I faint."

That was not far from true, Phaedra thought as she stumbled
from the shop. Her knees felt so weak she was relieved to find
Peter waiting to hand her into the coach. She all but collapsed
inside, wrenching the door closed herself. She wanted to order
Ridley to drive back to the Heath at once, but she had to have
some idea if her plot had succeeded.

She instructed Peter in breathless accents. "Tell Ridley to drive
around the next square and then come back up Oxford Street."

Peter looked astonished but said, "Very good, my lady."

Ridley would think she had taken complete leave of her senses,
but Phaedra did not care. She leaned back against the squabs and
closed her eyes, tensed and waiting. She had some notion of how
pale she must have looked, for her maid tried to administer the
vinaigrette.

Phaedra waved her aside. "No, I need nothing except—except
a little air."

She slunk to the coach window and peered out as the carriage
at last wound its way slowly back up Oxford Street. The vehicle's
progress was even slower than before, thanks to the crowd that
had gathered outside the bookseller's stall. Armande stood in its
midst, his tall figure appearing haughty and detached by comparison to the accusing mob. Phaedra caught a glimpse of the
goldsmith's bald head, saw his arms wave in angry gesticulations.
In a supremely scornful gesture, Armande flung back the flaps of
his frock coat, feeling into the pocket of his waistcoat. Phaedra
watched his hauteur dissolve into astonishment as he himself
produced the missing ring.

The crowd fell upon him then, seizing his arms before he could
move. Phaedra clenched her hands, terrified of what would
happen next. But Armande appeared too stunned to offer any
resistance as he was hustled off to be taken into custody. Phaedra
drew back as he was dragged past her coach. She was uncertain

what caused Armande to glance up just then. Perhaps he recognized the markings of her grandfather's carriage. Perhaps it was that uncanny instinct he seemed to possess. For one brief moment Phaedra found herself staring into Armande's upturned face. Like quick strokes of lightning she saw realization flash across his countenance followed by a look of betrayal Phaedra thought would haunt her forever. Then his face seemed to turn to stone. If Armande de LeCroix had not despised her before, his glacial stare told her that he had now become her deadliest enemy.

Chapter Nine

THE LONG, JOLTING RIDE OUT OF THE CITY AFFORDED PHAEDRA FAR too much time to think about what she had just done. She closed her eyes, but all she could see was Armande's face tensing into gaunt lines of shock, his eyes shadowed with the pain of betrayal. She had caught the same tormented expression in her own mirror once too often not to recognize it in Armande.

Yet what right had he to feel betrayed? she thought bitterly. Had he not brought it all upon himself? He had come to her grandfather's house, cloaking himself in secrecy, threatening both her and Gilly. He could not expect to endanger her and those she loved, then imagine that she would behave like some witless doll, letting him do as he pleased.

Nay, there was no reason in the world that she should feel guilty. All the same, she kept envisioning Armande being dragged away by the malicious, triumphant throng. For some reason, it also conjured up memories of the carpenter Wilkins, his bloodied form being slung over John's shoulder, being removed from her grandfather's elegant dining parlor like a sack of refuse.

But it made little sense that she should thus connect the two men. Aside from the fact that both Wilkins and Armande would lodge in Newgate this night, there was no similarity. No one had carted Armande off. Even surrounded by a threatening mob, he had carried himself with a kind of scornful hauteur. Theft was not nearly so dreadful a charge as attempted murder. And the most important difference of all—Armande's wealth and title—would

settle over him like a protective mantle. Likely his trial would be
but a token affair. The scandal was what Phaedra was counting
upon to drive the marquis from her life. After being proclaimed a
thief, Armande would not dare show his face at the Heath again.
Her grandfather bore more tolerance for a would-be assassin than
he would for one charged with stealing.

But for the first time, some of the flaws in her impulsive plot
began to occur to Phaedra. What if Armande revealed to her
grandfather the trick she had played upon him? She would deny it,
of course. But who would her grandfather believe?

And then, what if Armande simply returned to the Heath with
no idea but one—to exact his own vengeance upon her in full
measure? If he did so, Phaedra was only sure of one thing, his
revenge would be cruel, subtle, and well-planned, not conceived
in the heat of a panic as her own had been.

The only thought bolstering her courage was that it would take
Armande time to extricate himself. Justice moved slowly, even for
a nobleman. By the time he was free, perhaps Gilly would have
returned. Or she might have thought of another way to deal with
Armande.

What she needed to do now was compose herself for the
moment when she faced her grandfather across the dinner table
and he wondered what the deuce had become of Armande. She
would have to be able to turn upon him a pair of most innocent
eyes . . .

The carriage was well on its way out of London, turning upon
that stretch of road that led out to the Heath, when Phaedra's
thoughts reverted to the Wilkins affair. Her preoccupation with
Armande had nigh driven all thought of the unfortunate carpenter
and his wife from her head.

Remembering it now scarcely did her any good. She had
counted upon being able to send Gilly to find out where Mrs.
Wilkins lived, but Gilly was gone. Mayhap it might be possible to
get one of the younger male servants to undertake the errand for
her, despite the possibility of incurring her grandfather's displeasure. The footman, Peter, was a most amenable young lad.

For once, luck was with Phaedra. When she mentioned the
matter to Lucy, her maid imparted the startling information that
very likely Peter would go. He knew the Wilkins family quite
well.

Phaedra banged on the roof of the coach, shouting for Ridley to stop. She almost thought the old man meant to ignore her, but after a time, she felt the carriage slow, the wheels themselves seeming to grind to a grudging halt.

Peter came to the coach door at once. The carriage had pulled past the environs of the city, and there was naught in sight but a rolling green meadow with several cows peacefully grazing.

"Peter," Phaedra said. "Lucy tells me you knew the Wilkins man."

Peter shot a reproachful glance at Lucy, then began to bluster. "I only talked to him a time or two when he did some carpentry work down at the stables. It wasn't me who let him in that night, Lady Grantham. I swear—"

"Nay, Peter," she said soothingly. "I wasn't accusing you. I only wanted to know if you knew where the man's wife lives."

"Eliza Wilkins? Well, aye I do, but—"

"Good. Then direct Ridley to turn the coach about and drive there at once."

Peter's jaw dropped. "Surely not, my lady. You'd never be wanting to go to *that* part of London."

"I assure you that I do. Tell Ridley at once, Peter." Her tone brooked no refusal. Peter reluctantly withdrew from the coach doorway, but she could hear him muttering, "I can always tell Ridley, my lady. But I doubt he'll do it."

Peter was soon proved correct. Ridley balked at the notion and prepared to whip up his horses, continuing on for the Heath. But Phaedra leaped down from the carriage and engaged in a heated argument with the stubborn old coachman. She only won in the end by threatening to set out on foot if need be.

Ridley surrendered with a bad grace, snarling that her grandfather would hear of this, that if they were all murdered down there in Canty Row, Sawyer Weylin would receive full report. Phaedra bit back a smile as she reentered the coach. Having achieved her object, she enjoyed a small feeling of victory, almost unspoiled by the knowledge that she would later have to deal with her grandfather's wrath.

Ridley set the horses off at a slow pace, as though determined to thwart Phaedra in whatever small way he could. But a full hour later, when the carriage rumbled down Canty Row, Phaedra began to appreciate Ridley's reluctance.

The carriage wheels jounced and ground their way through ruts compounded of mud and offal, the sickly pungent odor pervading the air as though the decay of centuries festered in the narrow lane. Coal smoke hung thick above the street, casting a pall over buildings that looked as though they should long ago have crumbled to dust. The tenements leaned against each other, like drunkards groping for support. Everywhere windows were boarded up to avoid the window tax, yet it made no odds—for the sun itself seemed to have forgotten this part of London.

What ragged inhabitants Phaedra saw were mostly children. They stared at her coach, their eyes aglitter with the hunger and savagery of half-starved rats. Phaedra plucked nervously at her muff, half-expecting them to fall upon the carriage at any moment and gnaw at the wooden wheels.

Lucy shrieked when one scrawny youth chunked a rock. It hit the side of the coach with a startling thunk. But Ridley brandished his whip, setting the urchins scattering back into the dark shelter of the doorways.

Ridley adamantly refused to let Phaedra dismount from the carriage. She did not argue with him, letting Peter go in search of Mrs. Wilkins. He disappeared into one of the more respectable-looking buildings. Phaedra waited several minutes, the first daunting impression of Canty Row beginning to fade, losing its ability to intimidate her. She should never have let Peter go alone. Mrs. Wilkins was supposed to be ill. Most likely the woman would not be able to come out to her.

She had almost made up her mind to follow Peter when the footman emerged. He leaned in the door of the coach. " 'Tis all right, my lady. I believe 'twould be safe for you to come in." Ridley started to howl a protest, but Phaedra had already leaped from the coach. She turned a deaf ear to both Lucy's frightened pleas and Ridley's more vociferous ones.

She followed Peter beneath the shadow of one of the tenements, up a flight of rickety wooden stairs. The sour smells of urine and sickness assaulted her in a great wave. She pressed a scented handkerchief to her nose, beginning to doubt both Peter's wisdom and her own. From a corner of the hallway, she caught a glimpse of the child who had thrown the rock, staring at her with sullen eyes and swilling from a bottle of gin.

But she had scarce time to register any feeling of shock when

Peter ushered her into a large room. He closed the door, respectfully maintaining a watchful post by the threshold. Phaedra adjusted her eyes to the room's dim atmosphere, then glanced about her with astonishment. It was not in the least what she would have expected.

The room bore signs of the building's general state of decay, but it was obvious someone had been at great pains to keep the chamber clean. An oil cloth was spread across the wooden floor, its worn surface well swept. The sparse furnishings—a mattress, a table, one chair—bore no hint of the grime of Canty Row. Upon the windowsill stood a clay pot, in which some bright red poppies managed to bloom, catching what little light filtered past the window boards. The flowers provided a splash of color in what was otherwise a most drab world.

Eliza Wilkins came slowly forward to greet Phaedra. Her much-mended gown hung upon her thin frame, her features almost ethereally pale. Her blond hair fell past her shoulders, the strands of a lackluster hue. Yet naught could erase the delicate structure of the bones beneath the transparent skin, nor the beauty of a pair of soft brown eyes, the strength latent in the proud set of her emaciated shoulders. At one time, Phaedra thought, Eliza Wilkins must have been a very lovely young woman.

Phaedra half-retreated a step. It suddenly occurred to her that as Weylin's granddaughter, she would likely not be welcome.

"Mrs. Wilkins?" she stammered. "I—I've come. That is, I am . . ."

"I know who you are, Lady Grantham," Eliza Wilkins said. There was no rancor in her voice, only infinite weariness. She did not look at Phaedra as she invited her to sit down.

Phaedra glanced at the room's single roughhewn chair. "No, thank you." Eliza Wilkins looked as though she were the one who ought to be sitting. Indeed, Phaedra wondered what was holding the woman on her feet. But she stood patiently waiting, Phaedra was sure, for Phaedra to declare her business and get out.

"I was so sorr—" Phaedra broke off again. What was she going to say? That she was sorry for the woman's misfortunes. Dear God, Wilkins had said that their babe had died recently. Added to Eliza's grief must be the knowledge that her husband was certain to hang. All phrases of condolence seemed woefully inadequate, almost patronizing.

What could she say then—that she had come to help? Phaedra fingered the small purse of coins knotted beneath her jacket. That too seemed inadequate in the face of all this. Her gaze once more roved over the barrenness of the room's furnishings, the sorrow set deep in Eliza Wilkins's dark eyes.

She became miserably conscious of how she must look, trailing in here with her livery-garbed footman, her silk gown, the lace dusting of her petticoats peeking out. She felt suddenly ashamed that she had ever dared fancy she knew anything of poverty, ashamed of being Sawyer Weylin's granddaughter.

She drew in a deep breath and tried again. "I have heard something of your misfortunes, and I regret that my grandfather should have been the cause of some of them. I cannot do much, but I would like to help you—if you will let me."

Perhaps the humbleness of her tone inspired Eliza Wilkins to look up at Phaedra for the first time. "Thank you," she said. "But the other gentleman has already been more than kind."

"Other gentleman?" Phaedra repeated uncomprehending.

"Aye, he was a guest at your dinner party last night when my husband tried to—" Eliza's voice faltered. She concluded, "The French gentleman called upon me only this morning."

The French gentleman. The phrase struck Phaedra with all the force of a lightning bolt.

"You cannot mean Armande de LeCroix," she cried incredulously.

"How odd." Eliza's eyes became almost luminous with wonder. "I never realized until just now he never told me his name."

"Then describe him." Eliza Wilkins regarded her for a moment, no doubt surprised by the anxiousness of Phaedra's command. But obediently, the woman sketched for Phaedra an exact picture of Armande de LeCroix as Phaedra had seen him last, exact except for the description of the marquis's expression.

"He had the most gentle blue eyes of any man I'd ever met," Eliza mused aloud. "Yet so sad. I hope he finds whatever he is looking for."

Phaedra stared at the woman. "What makes you think he is looking for something?"

"I don't know." Eliza slowly shook her head. "He simply gave me the impression of a man who has lost something very precious, who is not at peace with himself." The woman gave a brittle laugh. "And God knows, I have met enough men like that. My Tom . . ." She let the thought trail off.

Phaedra continued to gape at her. She tried to imagine the cold, haughty Armande, coming to such a place, seeking out Mrs. Wilkins. It was not so difficult. She was aided by the memory of how gentle his fingers had been only that morning when examining her injured hand. Phaedra recalled how Armande had slipped from the dining room last night, after Wilkins had been taken away. Had it been to find out where the man lived?

But it made no sense. What reason would the icy Armande have to help these people? Suddenly eager, Phaedra turned to Eliza Wilkins. She wanted to know everything he had done and said. Fortunately Eliza Wilkins was not at all loath to talk about the marquis.

"Why did he come here?" Eliza repeated Phaedra's question, a furrow creasing her pale brow. "I wondered that myself. All that he said was that he too knew what it was like to be at the mercy of the powerful and ruthless."

Armande? Phaedra's jaw dropped open. She could not picture the indomitable marquis ever being at anyone's mercy. But she did not interrupt Eliza as the woman continued, "He was very generous with—with his money and oh, so much more. He even promised me . . ." A shadow passed over Eliza's pale features. "He promised me that he would see my babe had a proper burial and was not thrust into the poor hole. And for my husband—" Eliza brightened, her eyes wistful with hope. "He swears that he will see Tom is not hanged, but only transported."

"Only transported!" Phaedra could not refrain from blurting out. "But you would still likely never see—I mean . . ." She stumbled over her words, trying to amend the error of her clumsy tongue. But it seemed wrong to give Eliza Wilkins any false hope of ever being reunited with her husband.

"I would follow him, wherever he was sent," Eliza said.

Phaedra glanced dubiously at the frail woman, considering it unlikely the woman had the strength to follow Tom Wilkins to the other side of London let alone Georgia.

"I love him, you see," Eliza said simply, as though that accounted for everything. Mayhap for her it did, Phaedra thought, staring with a kind of envy at the woman's rapt expression. She suddenly felt as though it were Eliza Wilkins who was garbed in silk, and she herself the one deprived, lacking.

She drew toward the door, preparing to depart. "I am relieved to hear you are being so well taken care of," she said stiffly. "I will not intrude upon you any longer."

Eliza Wilkins seized hold of her hand. She gave Phaedra's fingers a gentle squeeze, her brown eyes unwavering as she stared up at Phaedra. "And don't you go away from here distressing yourself. You are not to blame for anything."

Phaedra started. It was almost as though the woman's gaze shone softly into her heart—but not quite. In truth, she could not blame herself for anything her grandfather had done. The guilt Eliza was obviously reading upon Phaedra's countenance stemmed from a far different cause.

The woman trembled with hope, believing that Armande was wielding his influence to save Tom Wilkins from the jaws of Newgate. Only Phaedra knew that at that moment, thanks to her, those prison gates were slamming tight upon Armande himself.

"Where the deuce is de LeCroix?" her grandfather asked for the third time. His bulk weaving along the green salon, he consulted his watch, occasionally stopping to wince. His gout was acting up again, no matter how he might pretend to the contrary. He grumbled, "Frenchies. Got no notion of being on time for dinner."

With only Phaedra and Jonathan Burnell for an audience, Weylin appeared to have forgotten all his quips about not keeping city hours. Phaedra was grateful that only Jonathan had been invited to dinner. There was no way she could have managed even one gracious commonplace to entertain a guest this evening.

She sat poised on the Queen Anne's chair by the hearth and started to thrust the poker into the grate when she remembered there was no fire to stir. There was something depressing about a fireplace in the summertime, she thought. With the grate swept clean, the andirons slicked with grease and stored away, the soot-blackened opening yawned before her, ugly and dismally empty, like a condemned man's cell the day after—

Phaedra nearly dropped the poker, then silently cursed herself for allowing her mind to keep running on such things. Yet why on earth had word of Armande's arrest not reached Blackheath? Surely the gossip must be circulating through London by now, and her grandfather and Jonathan had spent the entire afternoon haunting their regular coffeehouse.

"My dear Phaedra." Jonathan's voice bit through her like the crack of a whip. She hoped her grandfather did not notice how she jumped, how tense she was.

"Are you well?" Jonathan asked anxiously. "You look so pale."

Phaedra forced a smile to her lips and shook her head. Jonathan was one of the kindest men living, but must he forever be plaguing her with questions about her health? She started wearily to reassure him, when her grandfather answered for her.

"Of course the wench looks pale. That is all the more good it did, sending her off to Bath to drink the cursed waters." He leveled upon her the irritation he was evidently feeling toward the absent marquis. "Why can't you paint yourself up a bit like the other fashionable gels I see, and powder that cursed carrot-top hair? Small wonder the marquis is not here. That Friday face look of yours is enough to drive any man from our door."

Phaedra had heard this refrain too often even to bother defending herself. Jonathan's face rarely ever registered anger, but now he glared at Sawyer Weylin. "If—if the marquis can find any flaw in Phaedra, why, why the man must be blind."

The intended compliment came out twisted, an awkward attempt at gallantry from a plain man not accustomed to making such gestures. Phaedra could not even offer him a smile of gratitude. She felt miserable enough without being made more so by the undeserved admiration of an old friend.

Weylin continued ranting at Phaedra as though Jonathan was not even in the room. "More than likely you've caught something, likely spotted fever or a pox, sneaking off to Canty Row with my best horses, paying social calls at the house of my assassin."

Jonathan paled. "Canty Row! My dearest Phaedra!"

But his distress was ignored as her grandfather shook his thick finger under Phaedra's nose. "Did you think Ridley would not report the whole of your doings to me, missy?"

"It wasn't a house, only a room," she said, thinking of the Wilkinses' bleak abode. "And as to assassins, you still seem very much alive to me, Grandpapa."

"No thanks to that villain Wilkins."

Jonathan's gaze darted between Phaedra and her grandfather. "But Phaedra! What ever induced you to go there?"

"I only thought to help Mrs. Wilkins."

"Meddlin'!" Sawyer Weylin's jowls puffed with indignation. "You silly chit. I expect you were taken in by Wilkins's whining tale. Set out to right the wrongs of your wicked old grandfather, did you? I'm an ogre because I expect able-bodied men and women to do an honest day's work, and keep their debts paid without looking for handouts. I never in my life asked for charity, and I don't intend to have my granddaughter running round behind my back dispensing it, either."

"I would scarce describe Mrs. Wilkins as able-bodied, Grandfather. Wilkins's tale was perfectly true. She has been very ill since the death of their child."

" 'Twas most kindhearted of you to help the woman, my dear," Jonathan said. "I only wish you had come to me first. I could have used my patronage to have the poor woman taken into a hospital."

"If you aren't another pretty fool." Her grandfather poked the tip of his cane at Jonathan. "Taking the money you've worked so hard for all your life and flinging it into patronage. Hospitals, bah! More like shelters for a pack of sluggards feigning sickness."

Weylin flung up his arms in a frustrated gesture as though he washed his hands of the folly of the entire world. "Stap me, you might as well lock me up in Bedlam. I suppose I must be mad, since I seem to be the only one not inclined to empty my pockets for a lot of undeserving rascals." A scowl wrinkled his broad forehead. "Mind you, if I had known about the child . . ." he muttered. Then he shrugged his beefy shoulders, stumping impatiently to the door, looking at his watch again.

What would her grandfather say, Phaedra wondered, if he knew it really had been Armande who had helped the woman? It would vastly change his impression of the marquis, even as it had done her own. It was no coldhearted villain who had called upon Mrs. Wilkins today. Phaedra still marveled at what Armande had done. It went beyond a gesture of *noblesse oblige*, beyond flinging a handful of coins to the peasants. Nay, he had obviously put himself to no little trouble, seeking out Eliza Wilkins, arranging for the funeral of her child. A small thing, yet it showed a great depth of feeling she would have never thought Armande possessed.

And what of his reason for behaving in a manner that seemed so out of character? Eliza Wilkins's explanation echoed through Phaedra's mind. *He said he knew what it was like to be at the mercy of the powerful and ruthless*. Men like her grandfather, men like Armande de LeCroix himself. So Phaedra had once thought. Now she was not so sure. Armande's sympathy for Wilkins, that haunted expression she had on occasion glimpsed in his cold blue eyes. What was there in his past that inspired such things, the past that he was at such pains to conceal?

If only instead of threatening her, Armande had chosen to confide. But mayhap she had seemed to him like naught but another Muriel Porterfield, a selfish lady of the *haut ton*. Perhaps he thought she would never have understood. There was little use in speculating. It was too late now, far too late.

Phaedra stared back into the fireplace grate, the stones so cold. Despite the warm summer's eve, she could almost fancy the chill from it creeping into her bones. What was it like to spend a night in Newgate Prison? She shuddered.

As if her nerves were not stretched taut enough, some imp of perversity had taken possession of her grandfather this evening. Perchance her own guilty reflections made it seem so, but her grandfather appeared able to talk of naught but the very subjects Phaedra most wished to avoid.

"I declare," he huffed. "London is naught but a shore of rogues these days. I was coming up High Street and what did I see, but a footpad as bold as you please, leaping atop a sedan chair. The rogue cut a hole in the roof and snatched a wig from a man's head. In full light of day! A twenty-farthing wig! The villain will swing for that if he is ever caught."

Phaedra, who had been trying to blot out the sound of her grandfather's haranguing, stiffened at his last words. "Hang for twenty farthings?" she faltered. "Most surely not."

"Most surely could." Her grandfather rocked back on his heels, his lips pursed in evident satisfaction at the thought. "A man may hang for any theft over five shillings, and so he should. Lazy rogues fleecing honest, hard-working men!"

Five shillings. Phaedra's hand crept to the lacy shawl knotted round her shoulders and she tugged uncomfortably at the fringe. The ring she had planted upon Armande was well above five shillings in value. But they don't hang noblemen, she reminded herself. All the same, she hadn't known men could die for so little cause. What if she was wrong about the immunity of noblemen, as well? Of a sudden, she remembered Muriel's gossip about Tony

Aackerly being flung into Newgate. *Only fancy! That some shabby shopkeeper could have a gentleman treated thus!* Of course, Tony was not a lord. But so many of the English had a strong antipathy toward foreigners, especially the French. What if Armande's rank as Marquis de Varnais counted for naught? Phaedra had difficulty swallowing. A lump of apprehension had closed up her throat.

Jonathan's heavy sigh echoed her own feelings. "I have always thought the law a trifle harsh," he said. "The gallows at Tyburn are put to far too great a use."

Weylin eyed him contemptuously. "Fortunately we are all saved a great deal of trouble by gaol fever. It carries off most of the rascals."

"Gaol fever?" Phaedra asked weakly.

"Aye, girl. What d'you think Newgate is? Some charming country manor house? The fever runs rampant through that pest hole so that few who ever take it recover." A grin crinkled Weylin's florid countenance. "I heard old magistrate Harbottle goes in such fear of the fever, he came to court with a nosegay pressed to his face the other day. He kept the prisoners at such a distance from him, he could scarce hear their confessions."

Her grandfather might find that amusing, but Phaedra was wracked with a vision of Armande tossing upon a filthy cot, caught in the grip of a raging fever. In the midst of his agony, would he curse her? Dear God, she had never meant to kill the man. She had only wanted to . . . Phaedra dropped her head into her hands, wishing her grandfather would be quiet.

But his voice droned on without mercy, talking about executions now, recounting every one he had ever witnessed with great relish. "Now I've seen it take a good hour for some of 'em to die. They struggle so hard, fair dancin' at the end o' the rope. And then others snap!" Her grandfather gestured as though breaking a twig. "Just like chicken bones popping."

Phaedra's fingers flew involuntarily to her own throat. *No! They would never hang him. They never would.*

". . . and they hung this one rogue, see, for pilfering a snuffbox, chunked his body into a coffin. Well, the guards given the task of his burial stopped off for a pint of bitter." Weylin shook with chuckles. Phaedra pressed her hand to her mouth lest she shriek at her grandfather to hold his tongue.

Oblivious to her distress, the old man chortled. "The guards had been followed by a pair o' rascally resurrection men, with an eye to swiping the body, to sell it to a surgeon for his ghoulish studies. While those fools were a swilling at the inn, the resurrection men snatched the coffin and—"

"Truly, Sawyer." Jonathan made a mild attempt to intervene, casting a pained glance at Phaedra. "I think you are about to make Phaedra ill with all this—"

"Here's the best part o' it." By this time, Weylin wheezed with suppressed laughter, scarcely able to speak. "The lid o' the coffin was not properly nailed down. They'd not got far, when the lid burst open and the—the corpse sat up."

Weylin doubled over, slapping his knees. "The man wasn't dead. They said those resurrection men t—took off running, all the way to Y—Yorkshire. Hah! And by the time the guards caught up to the cart, they were so fearful of losing their posts because of their bungling, they quick found a tree and h—hanged the poor wretch all over again."

Weylin clouted Jonathan on the back and roared with laughter. Jonathan summoned a thin smile in response. Phaedra bolted to her feet, her hands trembling. She could not endure a moment more of this.

"Grandfather, about the marquis . . ." she began.

Weylin wiped his moist eyes with the back of his hand. "Aye, what about him, girl?"

She glanced down at the carpet, her voice rife with guilt and misery. "I—I don't imagine that Armande will be here."

"Do you not, milady?" The low voice issuing from the salon doorway chilled Phaedra to the marrow of her bones.

She spun around with a tiny cry. Armande de LeCroix stood framed just inside the door. Dressed for dinner, his garb appeared as elegant as though he had but returned from an assembly. But he had not taken the time to powder his hair, and the dark strands were pulled back into a severe queue.

"Armande." Phaedra could have fallen upon him with a sob of relief. She was only halted by his expression. His eyes blazed at her like a fire ready to rage out of control and consume her. She had oft wondered how the icy marquis might look when angered. Now she knew. Her heart slammed against her ribs.

"Astonishing," he rasped. "One might almost fancy you were glad to see me, milady."

He stalked into the room, but Phaedra's courage deserted her. She did not wait to see what he meant to say or do next. Regardless of her grandfather's startled expostulation and Jonathan's look of surprise, she gathered up her skirts and bolted from the salon.

She ran blindly, overcome by an unreasoning feeling of panic, seeking by instinct the one place she felt safe. Her feet just touched the stairs leading to her garret when her heart leaped into her throat. Dear God, he was coming after her.

She shot forward and almost hurled herself through the door to her garret room, but she was not fast enough. She tried to slam the door closed behind her, but Armande's hand thrust through the opening, blocking her attempt. She let go, retreating further into the room. Armande stepped inside, slamming the door behind him.

The last rays of the dying sun cast shadows over his haughty profile, accenting the high arch of his cheekbones, his lean face hollowed by anger. His eyes glinted like points of steel.

Panting, Phaedra glanced wildly behind her, but there was nowhere to retreat. Where were her grandfather and Jonathan?

As Armande crossed the room with slow, deliberate steps, she held up one trembling hand in a weak effort to ward him off. "You—you make one move to touch me, and I'll scream."

He halted but a sword's breadth from where she shrank against the wall. He didn't have to touch her. She could feel the fury crashing from him like invisible waves, sensed the enormous control he exercised to keep from reaching at once for her throat. It was like being near something savage, wild, held back by the thin thread of a very taut leash.

"Whatever is amiss, Phaedra? You look so pale. Has my return astonished you that much?" He abandoned the mocking tone, a quiver of suppressed rage rippling along his jaw. "You damned little fool. Did you really think they would hold me once they knew who I was, once I had paid the cost of that cursed ring?"

Phaedra only pressed herself back further against the wall, unable to meet his angry, accusing gaze.

"Answer me, Phaedra! What did you think they were going to do to Armande de LeCroix, the most noble Marquis de Varnais?" There was self-mockery in the way he pronounced his name, the bark of laughter that accompanied it striking cold to her heart.

She found her voice at last. "I don't know. I only thought to—to—"

"To have me hanged?" He loomed so close, if she but breathed she would brush up against him. His harsh voice grated against her ear. "They don't hang aristocrats, *ma chère,* nor even fling them into rat-infested cells. With a few bribes I could be lodged in an apartment fit for a king, no matter what I'd done. Even if I were to snap your deceitful little neck."

"Why don't you do it, then?" she choked. "You threatened to destroy me once, didn't you? Go on and finish what you tried to do last night."

She was mad to goad him thus, sensing he teetered on a dangerous brink the self-contained marquis seldom reached. Yet wracked by guilt and fear, Phaedra hovered too near her own snapping point to care.

The fury still burned in Armande's eyes, but she detected a flicker of uncertainty, as well. "Last night?" he repeated.

She looked up at him, incredulous that he could keep up his pose of innocence even now. "Stop it." Her breath caught in a ragged sob. "I am not a fool. I know it was you who locked me in with Danby. So you can just stop pretending."

Long moments passed as he stared at her. She saw the light of anger slowly die, to be replaced by the inscrutable expression she so hated. It was as though his abandoned fury coursed into her, the overwrought emotions of many endless hours breaking forth in a flood of tears.

"Damn you! I said stop pretending." His image blurred before her eyes as she slammed her fist against his chest, again and again. As immutable as a wall of stone, he made no effort to stop her, merely waiting until her arm dropped weakly to her side. "Damn you to hell," she repeated in a whisper. He caught her as she swayed and collapsed weeping against him, then lowered her onto the Jacobean daybed. Phaedra struggled out of his arms, muffling her sobs into a silk pillow, giving full rein to the storm that had been brewing inside her for many days.

Given over to her misery, she lost all sense of time and place. It seemed an eternity before she could halt the flow of her tears and regain a semblance of composure. At last, she sat up, drawing in deep, hiccuping breaths. She almost believed Armande had gone.

He hadn't. He sat poised near her on the edge of the daybed. He extended his lace handkerchief to her, all traces of his anger vanished, like a tempest that had never been.

After a moment's hesitation, she accepted the handkerchief and applied the linen to her eyes.

"And now, milady," Armande said, his voice so level, he might have been addressing pleasantries to her across the tea table. "If you will not again attempt to thrash me for asking, what about last night? Let us imagine that I know nothing, and explain to me your remark about Arthur Danby."

"You locked me in the Gold Room with him." She glared at Armande through swollen eyes, hating him for so easily having regained his composure when she was sure she must look like the very devil. Her voice sounded tinny, almost childish with accusation as she continued. "Then you fetched my grandfather by pretending you wanted to see the paintings upstairs, hoping he'd catch me with Danby. You knew full well what'd he do if he thought I was—" She sniffed. "What a perfect scheme to be rid of me and my troublesome curiosity."

"The Gold Room. But when I entered there, Danby was passed out cold and there was no sign of you—" Armande broke off, his gaze flying to her scratched hands. "The open window! *Mon dieu!* You little idiot. You could have broken your neck." He flushed with anger again, but of a far different kind than she had seen upon his face before. She did not feel threatened, although Armande looked ready to shake her.

"I thought that was the idea," she said, although she was no longer so certain herself. Could the most brilliant actor in the world possibly appear as shaken and surprised as Armande did at this moment? She continued stubbornly, "I suppose that if you couldn't manage to ruin me, my death would serve as well."

"Then that was why you placed that ring in my pocket today? For revenge?"

"For protection! Did you think I was going to wait to see what malicious plot you next had in store for me?"

To her astonishment, he smiled, the expression half-rueful, half-incredulous. He covered her hand where it rested on the bed with his own. "Phaedra," he murmured, shaking his head.

She stiffened, looking away from him. "Don't—don't touch me. And don't you dare use my name that way."

But he made no effort to draw his hand back. "Phaedra," he repeated. "Look at me." When she refused, he caught her chin, gently but firmly forcing her to gaze up at him.

"Considering what our past relationship has been, the suspicion and the mistrust, I know this will be difficult for you to believe. It was not I who locked you in with Arthur Danby."

She tried to force her mouth into an obstinate line, but her lips quivered. "Then I suppose it was mere coincidence you just happened along with my grandfather."

"Yes. It was his idea to see the paintings, not mine."

Phaedra squirmed, feeling more uncertain of her position by the minute. But she continued to argue. "You were the one I heard suggesting that you examine the Titian in the Gold Room."

"I like Titian," Armande said softly. "We share the same failing—a weakness for tempestuous red-haired women."

He leaned back, resting his head upon one of the silk pillows. He exhaled his breath in a long sigh. "You are an impulsive woman, Phaedra Grantham, with a distressing habit of leaping to conclusions. You sent me to hell and back today."

Phaedra studied him, still not certain if she believed his denial about Danby. But he was not lying now about what she had put him through. She could see it in the lines of fatigue etching his eyes. "You—you couldn't have possibly been frightened when you were arrested." She hung her head, adding in a small voice, "You said yourself you never were in any danger."

"No danger except for that of encountering old ghosts that I thought to have . . ." His voice trailed off, a haunted expression clouding his eyes. He swallowed, then said thickly, "I knew a man once, a—a friend who was imprisoned."

It was the first time Armande had ever volunteered any information about his past. Phaedra felt as though she had coaxed some creature, wild and untamed, to her side at last.

"And this friend of yours. He died?" she asked quietly.

"Aye." Armande passed his hand across his eyes.

"At Newgate?" she prodded gently.

The blue eyes flew open to stare at her. Phaedra could almost see the walls going up.

"*Non*. In France, in—in the Bastille."

He rolled onto one side, propping himself onto his elbow, resting his head against his hand. He gave her a disarming smile, and Phaedra knew he was about to turn the subject.

"And I suppose there is no point in my asking what you were doing in the Gold Room with Arthur Danby."

"I was not making love to him, if that's what you mean." She flushed, then wondered why she had said that. She became uncomfortably aware of the languid sensuality in Armande's pose, just how intimate it was to be sitting with him upon this bed.

"I didn't suppose you had followed Danby out of any amorous intent," he said. As he sat up, she could not help noting the way his muscles rippled beneath his frock coat. "The man is a dolt. I hope you will be wise enough to place no credence in anything he might say."

Armande moved closer, his fingers tracing the curve of her jaw. "I wish the mistrust between us could end."

"If only you would not be so secretive," she murmured, knowing she ought to draw back and resist. How easy it would be for her to forget all that had passed between them, to become ensnared in the web of that silken voice.

He pressed butterflylike kisses against both her eyelids. "If only you would not be so inquisitive. If you could trust me enough to believe that I have no desire to harm *you*."

He laid such peculiar stress on the last word. Then who did he want to harm? The question was swept from her mind as his lips found hers, the contact spreading warmth through her veins. A voice deep inside her cautioned that this could be but another ploy of Armande's. When all else fails, try seduction. Yet despite the gentleness of the kiss, she could sense the longing of his own desires. For whatever reason, by design or misunderstanding, both of them had journeyed to hell and back today. 'Twas as though he kissed her now to offer her comfort, as well as to seek it for himself.

Only half-realizing what she did, Phaedra ran her hands along the nape of his neck, her fingers caressing the silken ends of his dark hair. When she melted against him, he needed little urging to deepen the kiss, his tongue exploring her mouth with a kind of lightning-hot sweetness. What had been warmth became fire. He tumbled her back onto the bed, never breaking the contact of their lips.

"Lady Phaedra."

The sound of Lucy's voice rang out so near, it struck Phaedra's passion-drugged senses with the force of cold water. She felt Armande freeze. In another moment Lucy would charge through the garret door and find them thus. As Armande wrenched himself away from her, she scrambled up from the daybed, flying over to the door. She held her weight against it as the doorknob turned.

"Milady?"

"Aye, Lucy?" Phaedra asked, trying not to sound as breathless as she felt. "What do you want?"

"Your grandfather is demanding to know what has become of you. He sounds most dreadful angry."

"Tell him I will be down at once."

She waited until she heard the girl's footsteps receding, then leaned against the door for a moment to compose herself. She turned to discover Armande now standing and straightening his frock coat. He bore the same look of disorientation—like a dreamer too violently awakened.

She stared from him to the rumpled daybed, scarcely able to believe what had nearly happened. It had all been so sudden, the flaring of their passion—like a spark set to dried tinder. But the flame appeared to have died as quickly, leaving her embarrassed and shaken in the cool aftermath.

It helped some to see that Armande was not looking his urbane self, and the smile he gave Phaedra was uncertain. "I am not sure whether we should curse that girl or thank her. 'Twould seem I was nearly the undoing of your reputation, after all."

He strode briskly toward the door where she yet leaned. Was he planning to leave her like this, with no more to say than that? He might attempt to dismiss what had happened so casually, but she could not. She caught his arm. "Armande, I—"

He placed his fingertips gently upon her lips. "I fear we both have been behaving with less than wisdom, *ma chère*. Nothing has truly changed. We still cannot trust one another. We will only make matters more—" he hesitated, "—more complicated by embarking on a relationship sparked by mutual loneliness."

Mutual loneliness. Was that all it was, this tug of attraction she felt between herself and Armande, that at times seemed both to draw them together and pulse them apart?

"I wish I could simply forget." His sudden vehemence startled her, but it vanished as quickly as his passion had done. "But I can't," he concluded dully.

Forget what? she wanted to demand, watching in despair that shuttered look settling over his eyes. He said, "'Tis best we continue as we began, keeping each other at sword's length."

"I have every intention of doing so," she said primly, striving to mask the hurt his words gave her. He briefly saluted her hand with his lips. They might have parted thus if his eyes had not chanced to meet hers. For once the pretense between them could not be maintained. She read freely in his gaze the single truth she felt burning deep in her own soul. He might make what declarations he pleased. But it could not change what they both knew was going to happen, what had been inevitable from the night they first met.

Chapter Ten

THE MUSIC GALLERY'S CURTAINS OF GOLD VELVET WERE DRAWN, closing out the night, but not the distant rumble of thunder. Phaedra's hands faltered as she ran them along the spinet's keyboard. She wished the storm would break and be done with. The heavy stillness in the skies beyond the shielding of velvet seemed to magnify the tension gathering within her own bosom.

Her fingers jabbed at the black and white keys, plunking out a tune from Gay's *Beggar's Opera*. A song she'd oft played, it required little concentration—which was as well, for she had little to give. Her gaze traveled repeatedly from the instrument to the man who stood half-turned away from her, appearing lost in the study of an elaborately framed work of Salvator Rosa's, mounted upon the red damask walls. The lace tumbled over Armande's wrists and gathered at his throat seemed so at odds with the lean, dangerous slant of his profile. As though he felt her staring at him, he turned to face her. The silver candelabra mounted upon the torchère cast a bright glow, but the tiny flames burned no more brilliantly than what smoldered in the depths of Armande's eyes.

Phaedra's pulse skipped a beat as she felt the embers of a similar fire stirring deep within her. Her fingers stumbled, missing a few notes. Armande had insisted that nothing had changed between them. He was wrong.

All during the course of the long, tedious dinner, a meal they had both left nigh untouched, their eyes had often met, furtive stolen glances as though in acknowledgment of the secret they shared—that sweet, brief moment of passion. It was that secret, Phaedra believed, that prevented Armande from retreating behind his mask of impassive hauteur as he had done before, and shutting her out so completely.

He might deny the mutual desire they had known, declare that he had no intention of ever caressing her again. It mattered naught, Phaedra thought, raising her gaze from the keyboard to find him staring at her. His eyes were speaking for him.

Her cheeks flushed, her fingers somehow located the right keys to end the song. The last note she struck seemed to reverberate forever in the gallery's deathlike quiet, a phantom echo resounding off the high, scrolling ceiling.

She had cut the song short, but no one—certainly not Armande—appeared to have noticed. Half-asleep on the bow-fronted chaise, her grandfather's snort startled her. She had nigh forgotten that he and Jonathan were still in the room.

Jonathan broke into a smattering of polite applause while Sawyer Weylin blinked and smacked his lips. "Eh—what? Oh, yes. Delightful, my dear, simply delightful."

Phaedra dragged her eyes from Armande long enough to stare at the old man. Her grandfather was strangely mellow this evening, all his earlier perversity gone. He had not even rebuked her for her inexplicable behavior in bolting from the Green Salon. Throughout dinner, he had beamed at her. She could not imagine what she had done to deserve his approbation.

"Play something else for us," Jonathan requested humbly.

Her grandfather bolted upright. "What! Nay, 'twas not that delight—" He harumphed, then struggled to his feet with a wide yawn. "Demnation, how groggy I feel. 'Tis the fault of that port you brought me, Jonathan. Demned heavy stuff."

"It was far superior to the other lot Scroggins tried to pass off on me," Jonathan said. "The knave! I only dealt with him at all upon Lord Danby's recommendation."

"Danby!" Her grandfather hooted. "You should have known better than to listen to him. That fool'd drink anything."

Phaedra could not help covertly studying Armande to see if the mention of Danby's name produced any reaction. He appeared absorbed in stacking her sheets of music into a neat pile.

"Even Danby would have balked at this wine," Jonathan continued. "Scroggins had sought to make the wine seem more full-bodied by treating it with oil of vitriol. Vitriol."

Weylin shook with amusement. "Hah! That might have made a temperate man of Danby. One glass of that, and I trow he'd have no *stomach* for another."

Jonathan waxed bitter over the foul tricks he had oft detected amongst his fellow merchants, sulphuric acid substituted for vinegar, alum used to whiten bread. The exposing of such deceits held a keen interest for him, one of the few subjects that inspired the quiet man to passion. But he was cut short by her grandfather, bellowing for John to unfold the card table.

Phaedra heard the command with dismay. She had barely managed to get through dinner and her music. How could she possibly spend long hours of card-playing seated across from Armande, half-dreading, half-inviting his glance?

She felt Armande circle behind her. Even the simple gallant gesture of his pulling out her chair so that she could rise from the spinet made her achingly aware of the lean, honed grace of his tall frame.

Jonathan prepared to seat himself at the card table when Weylin prevented him. "Leave the cards to the young people." He rested his thick hand upon Jonathan's shoulder, giving him a wink. "What say we old men enjoy some of my fine Canary wine whilst I show you the sketches my architect has done to refurbish this room." He made a sweeping gesture of disparagement which encompassed the music gallery's heavy elegance. " 'Twould seem this Roman palazzo stuff is now *demaday*."

And the heavens forbid, Phaedra thought wryly, that anything in Sawyer Weylin's manor be classified *démodé*—whether he understood the term or not. She fancied that Jonathan looked a trifle annoyed to hear himself described as an "old man." He cast a wistful look in Phaedra's direction when Sawyer Weylin dragged him to the gallery's opposite end.

The music gallery was a long chamber that could double as a ballroom, allowing a dozen couples to perform the gavotte when the massive armchairs, sofas and torchères were shoved aside. With her grandfather and Jonathan taking a silver candelabrum and ensconcing themselves at the end near the marble chimney piece, she and Armande might well have been left alone.

She seated herself at the card table, avoiding looking at Armande. She sensed that he was doing the same. Her voice sounded unnaturally high as she asked. "What will you, my lord? Piquet? *Vingt-et-un*?"

"The choice is yours, milady," he replied silkily, settling into the chair opposite her.

Was it, indeed? Phaedra wondered, recalling how he had tried to avoid her touch. "Piquet, then," she said aloud.

Beyond the curtains, the wind whistled and rattled the panes. Her hands trembled as she donned a pair of mufftees to protect the delicate embroidery of her sleeve hems. Armande's lips quirked into a smile.

" 'Twould seem that I have been left to the mercy of a hardened gamester."

She shuffled the deck with rapid jerking movements, trying to make her voice sound light. "Aye, you shall find me a far fiercer opponent than Charles Byng."

She dealt the cards, then quickly arranged hers, scarcely noticing what she held. Armande fanned his out between his fingers. Moments ticked by without his making another move.

The thunder rumbled again, closer this time. Phaedra shifted restlessly in her chair and cleared her throat. Armande's gaze at last drifted over the rim of his cards. His blue eyes appeared almost hazy in this soft light. She didn't think he was focusing on her cards so much as dreamily contemplating the curls falling past her shoulders.

Self-consciously, she fingered one tendril and brushed it back. "I have dealt the hand, my lord. It is for you to open."

"Is the game to begin with no wagers?" he asked.

"I fear I am not accustomed to playing as deep as you."

"I know you are not. That is what makes any gaming betwixt us seem like I would be taking a most unfair advantage."

When their gaze met across the table, Phaedra was no longer sure they were talking about cards. "I have but little coin for you to take advantage of," she said uncertainly.

"Money is of no value to me. The only wagers worth making concern matters more precious. Mayhap . . ." He hesitated. "Mayhap a bid for what you desire most in the world."

"What I desire most?" She gave a shaky laugh. "I have never been quite sure what that might be."

"Perhaps that I should leave your grandfather's house and never return."

Once Phaedra had imagined so herself, but now . . . However, she made no attempt to contradict him.

"And you," she demanded. "If you propose that to be my prize, what do you ask for yourself if you should win?"

He took a long time about answering her. Then he looked up, making no attempt to mask the raw hunger blazing in his eyes.

"One night with you," he said.

The cards fluttered from her nerveless fingers, his unexpected words striking her like a jolt of lightning, leaving a searing heat in its wake.

Armande's face darkened as though he regretted his reply. He folded his cards, placing them in the center of the table. " 'Twould seem the stakes I set are too high for both of us."

Her hand flashed out, pinioning his atop the cards he sought to abandon. "Done!" she cried. "I—I accept your wager."

She scarcely drew breath as she waited for his reaction. She expected him to pull his hand free and withdraw at once. He regarded her impassively, his features so still they might well have been sculpted of marble. But for the muscle that worked along his jaw, she would have had no clue at all as to the struggle that raged within him.

Then he slowly moved her hand from his and gathered up his cards. Her heart hammering, Phaedra did likewise with her own, splaying the small rectangles before her face in an effort to conceal the blood she felt rushing to her cheeks.

Dear God, what was she doing? The passions seething inside her must at last be driving her mad, just as Ewan had always assured her they would. She tried to concentrate on the cards she held, but they faded before her eyes in a blur of black and red.

The rain broke at last, pattering against the windows. Phaedra dimly noted Jonathan taking his leave and bid him a preoccupied good night. The merciless flick of cards being laid down seemed to cut through all other noise, the rain, the muted sounds of thunder, her grandfather snoring upon one of the settees.

Although her hands shook, Armande seemed to have recovered his composure. He played with a grim intensity, yet continued to lose points. It was some time before the truth occurred to Phaedra. He was throwing the game by design.

But it had been he who had first proposed the wager, and the desire firing his gaze was so heated, she did not doubt it was real. Was his present behavior prompted by gallantry or some other, darker apprehension she could not begin to understand? She bit down upon her lip to still its trembling. If he lost, did he truly mean to honor the bet and leave, never to return?

Phaedra reached for the pack and drew out an ace. Now she was almost sure to win both the next trick and the game. She risked a glance at Armande, who appeared too absorbed to notice anything she might do. With all the deftness Gilly had taught her, she slipped the card into her mufftee.

She drew again, and almost cursed aloud at the perversity of fate. What must the odds be against turning up another ace so soon? With a quick, trembly movement, she sent the card to lodge with its fellow up her sleeve.

She finally succeeded in pulling the right cards to sabotage her hand. When Armande revealed his, she laid out her losing sweep with a kind of defiant triumph. His impassive expression did not change, but when she scooped up the cards to deal again, his hand shot out, gripping her wrist. She had no time to protest before his fingers delved into her mufftee, producing the missing aces.

Phaedra hung her head. She felt as though every forbidden desire she'd kept locked away in her heart all these years lay exposed before Armande's merciless gaze. Was there ever any lady who would have thus bartered her virtue? She might as well have begged for Armande to take her, like any street harlot. Her cheeks burned with shame, and she could not meet his eyes.

"You cheated, milady," he said softly. "I declare this game forfeit to me."

But she heard no censure, no triumph in his almost gentle tones. If anything, he sounded infinitely sad.

By the time Phaedra reached her bedchamber, the storm had ceased its ominous threatening and erupted in all its fury. The rain became a sheen of dark water glazing her windowpanes. The night raged, a tympany of thunder and violent clashes of lightning, as Lucy helped Phaedra shrug into her night shift. The linen clung to her skin as she slipped beneath the sheets. She was so tense that she scarce permitted her head to rest against the pillow.

As soon as Lucy had gone, Phaedra flung aside the bedclothes. Stumbling through the darkness, she fumbled with the tinder box and managed to light the stump of a candle. It would likely not burn for long, but enough to guide her steps until she . . . Her gaze traveled to the door connecting to Armande's bedchamber.

Her heart fluttered like the wings of a bird about to fly of its own volition into the hunter's snare.

And Armande? She wondered what he was feeling, waiting for her on the other side of that door. He had walked away from the card table, trying to summon a mocking smile as though the entire game had been but flirtatious nonsense.

But his laughter had been hollow, the longing in his eyes keen enough to break her heart. He would not hold her to the wager; she knew that. She had but to return to her bed, pull the covers up tight about her neck and try to lose herself in the oblivion of sleep.

Her gaze shifted to the dressing-table mirror. Her image appeared almost unearthly in the dim light, a pale spirit garbed in flowing white. She arranged the ripples of red-gold hair over her shoulders in a modest effort to conceal the rose-tipped crests of her breasts, visible beneath the nigh transparent gown. She began gliding toward the connecting door like a sleepwalker, no more able to control the course of her wandering than she could put a halt to the thunder rending the skies.

She reminded herself that Armande de LeCroix was still a man enshrouded in mystery, his hidden past a threat to her. He could be the Prince of Darkness himself, for all she knew. She tried to recall the passion that had betrayed her once before, delivering her into seven years of hellish captivity as Ewan's bride. But memory grew dim until all she could remember was the heated fury of Armande's kiss.

Her numb fingers slid back the bolt, the door whispering open beneath her trembling hand. She held the guttering candle before her like a talisman as she stepped across the threshold into Armande's chamber, a quiver shooting through her as though she had passed some point of no return.

"Ar—Armande?" she called softly.

"I am here." His voice sounded at once distant and startlingly close. She jumped as the room was illumined by a jagged flash of lightning, revealing the outline of Armande's muscular form but a few feet from her, as though he had been lingering by the door, tense and waiting. He was garbed in his close-fitting breeches, and his white shirt, unbuttoned to the waist, exposed the vee of his bronzed chest. He slowly stretched out one arm to her, extending his hand.

Her faltering steps guided her closer, the dim light of the candle giving the pitch-dark room a misty quality. It reminded her

strangely of the dream she had had of Armande so many nights
before, when she had returned from Lady Porterfield's ball. That
tormenting dream of so many endings, as she had stripped away
Armande's mask, one time to find death, another desire. What
awaited her now in those angular features lost in shadow, the
watching eyes but a glint in the darkness?

She had an urge to snuff out the candle and not look upon an
expression that might turn the dream into a nightmare. But
Armande took it from her before she could do so. In the brief
moment he held the taper, his face was fully revealed to her. His
sable-dark hair swept back from his brow in damp waves, beads
of moisture clinging to the high planes of his cheeks almost as
though he had been out walking in the storm. The force of the
tempest appeared caught in his eyes, stripping away all illusion of
the cold, haughty marquis, leaving but a man, vulnerable, his
emotions as raw and untamed as her own.

Phaedra never had imagined anything like the tender way he
pulled her into his arms. She could feel the pulse in his throat
drumming against her temple.

"I should send you away, but I need you," he said hoarsely.
"My God, Phaedra, you have no idea how long I've needed you."

His voice sounded so strange. She did not understand what
anguish deepened those lines about his mouth. For tonight, she
did not want to know. No man had ever needed her before, and her
heart responded to that appeal.

She longed to ease the pain wracking his brow. Stretching up on
tiptoe, she whispered kisses against his mouth, his jaw, the
curious tiny scar at the base of his neck. He groaned and buried his
face in her hair. The candle sputtered and went out, leaving them
in darkness, clutching each other as though they stood not in the
security of the bedchamber but lost somewhere in the rage of the
storm itself.

He swept her up in his arms, carrying her to the bed. She wound
her arms about his neck, clinging to him even after he had laid her
down, stretching out beside her.

"Phaedra," he murmured. There was again that strange huski-
ness, a kind of wonder in the way he spoke her name. "You seem
more spirit than flesh. I can scarce believe you are real."

"I am real," she assured him. Indeed she had never felt so alive
as she did this night. She upturned her face to receive his kiss,
allowing her lips to part in invitation. His tongue mated with hers,

filling her with sweet fire, the kiss becoming increasingly more urgent, more demanding.

His hands deftly undid the ribbons of her nightgown, his breath coming quickly. When he stripped away the linen, Phaedra shivered as the cool air struck her skin. Even in the darkness of the room, she felt conscious of her nakedness. Ewan had never bothered to undress her.

She knew Armande couldn't see her face, but somehow he read her feelings all the same. He pulled back the counterpane and nestled her beneath its downy depths, then stood to remove his own clothing. As he peeled off his breeches and shirt, the lightning burst outside the window behind him in a series of quick flashes, outlining the sinewy strength of his limbs, his broad chest and stalwart shoulders. He hovered before her like some bronzed god from the pagan tales of old, borne in by the winds of the storm, come to fulfill every fantasy she'd ever dared to dream in her lonely bed.

He slipped beneath the coverlet, drawing her back into his arms, resuming their kiss. The first contact of his bare flesh with her breasts sent shock waves tingling along her skin.

"Phaedra . . . my sweet Phaedra." He breathed her name in a fierce whisper, making her love the sound of it upon his lips. Yet once again she found something vaguely disturbing and different in the seductive tones of his voice, like notes of a familiar melody played out of key.

But she forgot all else as he kissed her again. His hands moved over her, paying homage to every curve of her body. She fought to keep her own hands still. In those brief times he had taken her, Ewan had never liked her to touch him. He had said her fingers were coarse and clumsy.

Yet as Armande brushed against her, her hands seemed to move of their own accord, reveling in the texture of his hair-roughened chest, the feel of hard muscle corded beneath the pulsing heat of his flesh. Fearful of his reaction, she hesitated, but when he made no move to stay her, her palm skimmed lower, seeking out the most mysterious region of his masculinity, the velvet sheath of his manhood.

She heard the hiss of Armande's indrawn breath as her fingers closed about him. She was wicked, shameless. In another moment, he would thrust her away in disgust. But he emitted a low groan and pressed kisses behind her ear, a shudder shaking his frame. His caresses became more urgent.

Gently he forced her to her back, suspending himself above her. "My love . . . can wait no longer." His voice was a plea, nigh an apology. But she already was opening to him, bracing herself for the first violent thrust.

To her surprise, he eased himself so carefully inside her, it was she who felt the need to pull him closer. His slow, rhythmic stroking evoked waves of pleasure, and yet a part of her tensed, resisting the culmination of their passion, the fulfillment which had been forbidden her for so long.

Armande bent down and kissed her, deep and hard. "Don't deny . . . yourself, Phaedra," he breathed. "Surrender."

Mercilessly, he increased the tempo of their mating, each movement calculated to drive her to the fever pitch of desire. She closed her eyes, dimly aware of Armande's hoarse cry, the shudders wracking his frame, moments before a fury of wondrous sensation seemed to burst inside of her. The exquisite pleasure was far too intense to last for long, but when it was gone she was filled with a sense of sweet release.

Most sweet and miraculous still, Armande's strong arms yet banded her close to him even as he sank exhausted beside her, drawing in deep breaths, pressing his lips against her hair. Ewan always had . . .

As her own pulses slowed to a more normal rhythm, Phaedra cradled her head against Armande's shoulder, not suppressing the thought of Ewan so much as simply losing it. Suddenly, it did not matter what her husband had done or said. Somewhere in the dark, in the gentle fury of Armande's lovemaking, it was as though the shadow of Ewan Grantham had been banished from her life. She felt so warm and secure lying in Armande's arms, aye, and content—a rare emotion indeed for her restless heart. A deep sigh escaped her.

Armande planted a kiss upon her forehead, and she could feel the smile curving his lips as he asked, "Was that a sigh of pleasure or regret, milady? Mayhap you now are sorry you strove so hard to lose the game."

Phaedra vehemently shook her head. Sorry? How could he even ask such a thing? She had no words to describe what Armande had done for her. He had given back so much of what Ewan had stolen from her—her belief in herself as a woman, a desirable woman, capable of giving love and receiving it.

"No, I shall never regret this night. No matter what happens."

"Hush, Phaedra. You tempt fate with such reckless vows." He tipped back her head, covering her mouth with his own as though in some superstitious dread of what her words might invoke, their kiss the charm that would hold evil at bay.

Phaedra melted willingly into his embrace. She wanted only for him to hold her, any doubts vanquished by the darkness and the warmth of their bodies entwined. Once more she was lost to everything but Armande and his tender caress.

It was some time later when she first realized the storm had ceased, leaving only the rain. She nestled against Armande, both of them lulled by the pattering against the window. Aye, there was no need to think or say anything more tonight, to remember anything but Armande's lovemaking, how gentle, how fierce he had been.

Her eyes fluttered closed, drifting into a state of half-dreaming, half-waking. She splayed her hand upon Armande's sweat-dampened chest, her fingers rising with the deep, regular rhythm of his breathing. He felt so warm. Even as he slept, she could yet sense the pulse, the passion of his lifeblood rushing through his veins. And to think, the first night she had met him, she had thought him so cold, a man carved of ice and snow.

Her lips tilted into a drowsy smile. Ah, but he was French. Did not Frenchmen like to boast they were the most skilled of lovers? From the beginning, she had been seduced as much by the silken tones of his voice calling her *ma chère*—

His voice . . . Once again something niggled at the back of her mind, a vague uneasiness. But Phaedra could no longer resist the pull of her own exhaustion. The disturbing thought drifted further and further out of reach. Cocooned in the security of Armande's arms, she fell asleep.

Dawn crept past the windowsill, shading the bedchamber in hues of pearly gray and soft rose. The morning star came up on a world new-washed by the storm, tinting the sky with promise of a bright summer's day. But for Phaedra, the piercing strength of those first rays striking her eyelids were an annoyance, an intruder come to steal away her dreams.

Such sweet dreams they were—of a dark-haired lover with chilling gaze and burning touch, a man of ice and fire.

She flung one hand over her eyes, trying to shut out the insistent sunlight, cling to the image of the bronzed hero the storms had cast into her bed. But as she stirred, she became aware of something pinning her to the bed.

Her eyes opened and focused with some confusion upon the naked length of her own body, the paleness of her skin in marked contrast to the tanned, sinewy arm banding across her waist. Her gaze traveled up the length of the arm, to a powerful shoulder, a broad expanse of bare back, her eyes finally coming to rest upon the countenance of the man who slept beside her, flat on his stomach, his face half-buried in the pillow.

It hadn't been a dream. Phaedra experienced a fluttering of panic as she came fully awake, a blush firing her cheeks as the events of last night flooded back to her. She had truly taken Armande de LeCroix as her lover. But what had seemed so right, so natural in the warm mantle of night now seemed a little frightening, even shameful, in the cold light of day.

She tried to ease herself out from beneath the weight of Armande's arm, groping for the counterpane. But the movement woke him at once. He flung himself over and jerked to a sitting position, his hand flying to the scar on his throat in a gesture that seemed almost reflexive. In that unguarded moment, Phaedra thought she saw an expression akin to terror in Armande's eyes.

Timidly, she touched the smooth bare skin of his shoulder. "Ar-Armande?"

The ice-blue eyes slowly focused on her. "Phaedra." Her name on his lips was almost a breath of relief. He gave her a misty smile, then stretched out beside her, pulling her in his arms, seeking her lips. Although not prepared for the sudden fierceness of his embrace, she did not resist, wanting as desperately as he to recapture the magic she had shared with him last night. How right he had made it all seem between them! She had felt she belonged nowhere else but in his arms. It would have all been perfect except—except for that uneasy feeling that now crept over her, the same disturbing sensation that had tugged at her just before she fell asleep. What had triggered it again? Was it something in the way he had said her name?

Phaedra strove to forget her uneasiness as Armande kissed her. His mouth was warm and enticing, the look he gave her so tender that it was as though the sun had risen in his eyes. His fingers tangled in her hair as he murmured, "Good morrow, my love."

Phaedra froze. That was it. *His voice.*

She thrust herself away from him, sitting bolt upright. "Wh—what did you say?" She hoped, nay, prayed that he would answer her in the familiar silky French accent. Looking puzzled by her reaction, he said, "I wished you a good morrow, love. It is one, is it not?"

"I—I suppose," she stammered. What she wanted to cry out was, *no!* It was far from being a good morrow when she had just realized her French lover was speaking to her in accents that might have been bred in the hills of Staffordshire. He might call himself Armande de LeCroix, but the man who had made love to her last night was an Englishman.

How long she had waited for Armande to make some mistake, to reveal his true nature. But why did it have to happen now, after what they had shared? She crossed her arms protectively over her breasts, suddenly feeling miserably aware of being naked in bed with a man who was little more than a complete stranger.

"Are you cold, sweetheart?" he asked. He still did not realize how he betrayed himself with every word. The intimacy between them had caused him to lower his guard. He tried to pull her back into his arms, but she squirmed to be free of him.

"N—no!" She said breathlessly. "I—I mean . . . I never intended to—to wake you. I—I am sorry."

"Don't be. I have never been awakened so pleasantly in my entire life."

"But—but I really should be—"

"Kissing me," he said, giving one of her curls a playful tweak.

She gave a hard shove, breaking his hold on her. Scrambling to the very edge of the bed, she tugged on the coverlet, holding it into place just above her breasts. "The servants will be up soon. I dare not be caught in here. It would be so difficult to explain."

Aye, she could not even explain to herself the madness that had overtaken her, leaving her to set aside all her doubts and mistrust of Armande, to render herself as vulnerable as a woman could ever to be a man.

Armande raised himself to a sitting position, the warm glow on his countenance fading. He said slowly, "Yes, I suppose it is . . . difficult."

Her blush deepened, and she could not meet his earnest gaze. "I cannot seem to find my nightgown."

He reached over the side of the bed and retrieved the linen

garment from the floor. She all but snatched it from him. Considering all that had passed between them, would he laugh at her if she begged him to turn his head while she fled the room?

The request seemed to stick in her throat. Before she could say anything, he rose from the bed himself. She averted her gaze as he shrugged himself into his breeches and shirt.

Then he came round the bed and silently held out to her his own dressing gown of wine-colored satin. She hesitated for a moment before taking it, then awkwardly scrambled into the garment. Tailored to accommodate Armande's broad shoulders, it hung loosely upon her smaller frame. His musky male scent clung to the garment; donning it seemed almost as intimate a gesture as having made love to him.

"Th-thank you," she said.

"Not exactly the latest mode in lady's fashions, but the effect is quite charming." He smoothed the fabric over her shoulders, unable to refrain from making the simple gesture a caress.

Phaedra felt a shiver of response run along her spine, but her mind condemned her mercilessly. *How can you! You don't even know who he really is.*

She shrank away from Armande, knocking a candlestick off the night table. Nervously, she drew the ends of the dressing gown more tightly about her, then fingered the tendrils of her disheveled hair.

"I suppose I do . . . I must look totally absurd."

His mouth tightened. "You look like a guilty little girl who has been caught doing something naughty."

His remark scarcely provided the reassurance she was seeking. "I—I never have taken a lover before." She heard her own words with dismay, not knowing why she said that, but somehow finding it important that he should know. She added, laying pointed emphasis on the foreign words, "I fear, *monsieur le marquis,* that I lack your *savoir faire* in these matters."

The thrust found its mark. She saw Armande pale with realization. But when he replied, he coolly slipped back into his accent with what Phaedra feared was the ease of long practice.

"I never supposed that you had, *ma petite*." He approached her again, and she could see from the longing on his face how badly he wanted to gather her into his arms. Stiffening, she merely shook her head.

His outstretched arms dropped slowly back to his sides. "And

so now come the regrets, despite all your vows and protestations."
His voice held a bitter, accusing edge. "I feared such would be the
case. Only I never expected it to happen quite so soon."

"Then what did you expect of me?" she cried. "I fear I am far
too unsophisticated not to feel awkward, waking up in the bed of
a man who—who I doubt has even told me his true name."

"We are harking back to that again, are we? *Mon dieu*, it didn't
take you long." He closed the distance between them. Forcing her
head up, he traced the sensitive skin beneath her eye. "You look
as though you have lain awake all night. Were you hoping that I'd
talk in my sleep. I've had women bed me for many different
reasons, but I must admit that this is a new—"

He got no further for her hand lashed out, cracking across his
cheek in response to his hurtful words. She lowered her stinging
palm, momentarily stunned by what she had done—but not more
stunned than Armande, who rubbed the red imprint left by her
hand.

She spun away from him, running toward that threshold
between their rooms. She felt she had crossed it a lifetime ago.
With several quick strides, he caught her, whipping her around to
face him.

"Let me go!" She struggled uselessly against the iron strength
corded in his hands, feeling the sob rise in her throat.

"No, Phaedra. Please." His manner was gentle but urgent as he
sought to restrain her. "I deserved that—deserved your anger. But
I cannot let you go this way. Please stay."

Tears spilled down her cheeks. Armande forced her head
against his chest. He rocked her in his arms, saying huskily.
"Hush, *ma chère*. Don't cry. I never wanted to hurt you."

Phaedra resisted a moment longer, then sagged against him.

"Forgive me, Phaedra." He pressed his lips against the crown
of her head. "I had no right to be resentful of your doubts. You
should have doubts about me. God knows, I have done naught to
allay your suspicions."

"If you would just tell me who you *really* are." She sniffed.
"What you want here at the Heath."

He cradled her head between his hands, using his thumbs to
wipe the tears from her cheeks. She thought she had never seen
such a depth of sadness in anyone's eyes as she saw in Armande's
at this moment. He looked like a man who had lived with pain for
so long that he had despaired of ever knowing happiness again. He

put her gently from him, turning to fetch a square of white linen from the dressing table. He handed her the handkerchief, then almost hesitantly reached for something else.

Brushing aside the tears blurring her vision, she watched as Armande lifted the same small chest she had once tried, without success, to peer into. It was as though within the confines of that box reposed all the hidden thoughts that tormented him. Phaedra caught her breath as she sensed the struggle raging within him, the urge to unlock those secrets, set them free.

He spoke at last, his voice taut with anguish. "I—I cannot. I cannot even ask you to trust me."

She knew the struggle was lost as he carefully returned the box to its place on the night table. The familiar mask settled over his features. He walked over to stand by the window.

She could sense his retreat in every rigid line of his body, the sunlight streaming through the window merciless in its illumination of the harsh lines carved deep beside his eyes, making him look jaded with weariness.

"The wager is settled," he said. "You have given me my night. I will leave your grandfather's house today."

His words struck her with dismay. "Y—you will leave? But why? It was not you who lost the wager."

"We both lost, *ma chère*. Before we had even begun."

"Are you doing this as some sort of gallant gesture to protect me?" she demanded. "I have looked out for myself any number of years now. 'Tis not as though I were a green girl."

He laughed softly, the saddest sound Phaedra had ever heard. "You will always be a green girl. 'Tis one of your charms. I think you must be the most vulnerable woman I have ever known, save one."

She started indignantly to refute his words, then broke off, recalling that her behavior this morning was scarce calculated to contradict him. She blew her nose into the handkerchief with a defiant sniff. He had not intended to leave the Heath upon awakening this morning. She was sure of that, remembering the glow in his eyes as he had first reached for her, the warmth of his kiss. This change in him was her fault. She had overreacted, perhaps, to discovering that all her worst suspicions were true, that he was indeed an impostor. Mayhap if she had not slunk about as though she were ashamed, frightened, blubbering all over him, if she had behaved differently . . .

But it was of no avail to consider that now, she thought, studying the immutable set of Armande's jaw. What could she do? Fling all pride and common sense to the winds and beg him to stay? Nay, Armande was right. It was far better that they not continue to reside under the same roof. She had known that herself from the very beginning.

She could only salvage what was left of her pride and exit with dignity. "When will you go?" she asked.

"As soon as possible, I think. After breakfast."

So soon! A part of her wanted to protest. Instead, she nodded briskly, replacing his crumpled handkerchief upon the dressing stand. He crossed the room to her side. If only he would hold out his arms to her as he had done before . . .

But he did not. Instead he sketched her a formal bow. Raising her hand, he just barely grazed it with his lips. "Farewell, my lady."

Phaedra stifled an hysterical laugh at the absurdity of it. He, clad only in breeches and shirt, his hair yet tousled from their lovemaking, she with his dressing gown half-falling off her naked shoulder—and they were behaving like mere acquaintances, parting after tea. Yet she had no choice but to see the farce through to its end.

"Farewell, my lord."

He didn't release her hand. His eyes traveled over her with a poignant intensity as though he were trying to memorize every detail of her.

"You only meant you are leaving the Heath, is that not so?" she asked anxiously. "You are not leaving London, as well."

A deep sigh escaped him. "No, I cannot leave London as yet. There is something I came to do. But until that task is accomplished, I think it best that we do not meet."

She could make little sense of this cryptic words, only understanding one grim fact. He meant this to be a final farewell. Without realizing what she did, Phaedra's fingers tightened convulsively over his. It was as though a huge chasm yawned between them, but only Armande could see what lurked at the bottom. It wasn't fair.

"And when this task of yours is done—" She could not keep the plea from her voice. "What then?"

For a moment her own fears and despair were mirrored in his

face. Then he abruptly shook off her hand, distancing himself from her with the hardness in his eyes.

"When my task is done," he said with a conviction that chilled her to the marrow of her bones, "you will never want to see me again."

Chapter Eleven

HOURS LATER, PHAEDRA STILL COULD NOT GET ARMANDE'S WORDS out of her mind. Shut away in the inner sanctum of her garret, she sat at her desk, failing to notice the ink dripping from her quill pen onto the page until it was too late. She made a halfhearted attempt to blot the stain, Armande's grim prophecy yet seeming to echo in her ears. *You won't ever want to see me again.*

What could he intend to do that was so dreadful? The man talked as though he meant to commit a monstrous crime, some fraud or theft, or as though he were thinking of *murdering* someone. Despite the warmth of the late-morning sun streaming through the garret window, Phaedra shivered. She tried to tell herself she was being absurd. Yet although she might wish to deny it, she feared Armande would be capable of anything. For all his tenderness, she had seen the chilling light in his eyes too often. When she had left him, he had already taken refuge behind the icy facade she had learned to hate.

Phaedra's hand tightened upon the pen, nigh snapping the delicate quill in half as she fought against the tides of despair and fear that beset her. Flinging the pen down upon the desk, she tried to whip up her anger as a defense.

To the devil with Armande de LeCroix and all his cursed secrets! Her throat burned raw with unshed tears. And to the devil with herself, as well. She shoved back from the desk, getting to her feet. The violence of the movement caused her chair to tip over backwards and clatter to the floor.

She left it where it had fallen, stalking over to the window. Both segments of glass, like two small latticed doors, were tightly closed. No wonder it was so stuffy in here. Phaedra struggled with the casement, trying to force one side open. The wood resisted her efforts until her face flushed damp with perspiration.

Cursing, she shoved with all her might, venting her temper upon the frame as though her very life depended upon opening the glass. When the window finally did give, swinging wide with a mighty slam, she lost her balance, her head and shoulders thrusting out into nothingness.

For a moment Phaedra had a dizzying view of the Heath's stone gates and the cobbled drive below. Quickly drawing herself back in, she mopped at her brow with the heel of her hand.

Her heart pounded with fright, but she adjured herself not to be a fool. After all, it was not as though she had actually been in any danger of falling the three stories to the ground below. She would have to squeeze herself through the window to be in peril of that.

Phaedra lingered by the window, resentful of the pale blue sky, so indifferent to her misery, and the sun, glinting with appalling cheerfulness off the cobblestones wet from last night's rain. She wished there was some way she could spring from the window ledge and fly like some silver-winged bird, far from the Heath, fleeing these gray stone walls that had never harbored aught for her but pain.

But what made the longing to escape so keen this particular morning, she scarcely could have said. Mayhap it was the memory of a night that would never come again, of blue eyes whose longing and despair tore at her heart, then froze her with the menace of secrets she was not permitted to understand. Mayhap it was merely to avoid the pain of watching Armande ride away . . .

"I'm glad he's going. Glad!" she whispered fiercely.

But her heart condemned her for a liar. She blinked hard, staring out at the summer-blue sky dotted with fleecy clouds. No, she would not weep again. For the truth was, that no matter how genuine Armande's desire for her, his need for her, it made no difference. Nothing could change the fact he was a man caught up in the web of some dangerous intrigue. She would not make the mistake of being ensnared in those silken bindings, of once more becoming enamored of a man whose life held no place for her.

She had a life of her own to live, and it was time to get on with it. Her resolve taken, Phaedra squared her shoulders, determined to think no more of Armande, at least not this day. Stalking away from the window, she uprighted the chair and resumed her place at the desk. Reaching for her quill pen, she dipped the tip in the ink, forcing herself to concentrate on finishing her composition.

> . . . and how can a nation which declares itself to be enlightened continue to cower behind the ancient cry of "No Popery," like children howling in terror of bugbears in the night? Too long have Catholics been denied their rights to vote and hold office simply because of the bigoted fears of king and parliament.

She continued in the same strain for a few more terse paragraphs before signing the name of Robin Goodfellow with a large flourish. There. Although the writing was done in haste, her message was clear. Freedom! Freedom from English rule and emancipation for the Catholics who made up the suppressed majority in Ireland. Honest folk martyred for the sake of their religion, like her own cousin. At this thought, a reluctant smile curved Phaedra's lips. Truthfully, she could not picture a less likely candidate for sainthood than Gilly. But for all his nonchalance, she knew there was a serious side to his nature, one that had oft been angered by the persecution of his countrymen. Mayhap this essay of hers would merit more of Gilly's approval than her ill-conceived piece about Armande had done.

Aye, and mayhap Gilly would be more inclined to forgive her for the fact that he had gone on a fool's errand. She suffered a pang of conscience when she thought of her cousin wasting time and money in France to discover what she already knew, that Armande was not the Marquis de Varnais. It scarcely mattered, anyway. After today she would never see Armande again.

Phaedra briskly sanded the parchment to dry the ink, trying to keep her mind busy upon matters other than Armande's departure. She thought of the considerable sum of money Jessym had promised for her next essay. The difficulty would be, with Gilly away, in finding a way to get the writing to her publisher. She trusted no one else, with the exception of Jonathan, to act as courier for her. But she could not bring herself to take advantage of her old friend's devotion, knowing full well how such an errand would distress the nervous man. She might well be forced to await Gilly's return—but who knew when that might be?

Her reflections were interrupted by the sound of the ormolu clock chiming the hour of eleven. Her gaze traveled to where the timepiece sat. It was the only ornament on the shelves that had remained empty since the day Ewan had destroyed her books. She supposed Armande would be packed, preparing to leave.

Phaedra folded the essay and locked it inside the desk drawer. She suddenly knew she could not endure being in the house when Armande left. Her grandfather was sure to rage at her for not exerting enough charm to make Armande wish to stay. Her lips twisted into a bitter expression when she thought of exactly how much charm she had exerted. But it had not been enough.

No, she could not face Sawyer Weylin's wrath just now, could not endure waving farewell to Armande as though he were but the merest acquaintance just passing through her life. Her only hope of maintaining sanity lay in losing herself on the grounds until she was certain Armande had gone.

Fearful of encountering him, she did not even risk returning to her room to fetch her bonnet. She crept down the backstairs, drawing a sharp-eyed glance from Hester Searle as she skirted through the kitchens. Ignoring the woman, Phaedra let herself out the kitchen door, making her way through the rose garden at the back of the house, and headed for the gravel walks beyond.

But she had not gotten as far as the dense shubbery when a voice, barely audible, pronounced her name. "Phaedra?"

She bit down upon her lip, despising herself for the hope that flared in her heart, but she could not suppress it all the same. She held her breath as she turned around. Her heart sank.

It was not Armande rising from the stone bench, the morning breeze riffling the dark strands of his hair. Phaedra watched as Jonathan Burnell crossed the garden to her side, wondering what on earth he was doing at the Heath so early. She had no desire for the comfort of Jonathan's solemn smiles this morning, and regretted she hadn't walked on, pretending not to have heard him. But she felt immediately ashamed of her impulse to avoid her old friend, who had always been so kind to her. Concealing her impatience, she managed to greet him in cheerful tones. "Why, Jonathan. What a surprise. What brings you out to the Heath at such an hour?"

He blinked at her, his smile fading in confusion. "Don't—don't you remember? I spent the night at the Heath because of the storm. I *told* you I meant to do so."

"Oh." A guilty flush mounted into Phaedra's cheeks. She bore but vague recollection of parting from Jonathan. She had thought he'd summoned his carriage to return to the city—but then she had been rather absorbed in her card game with Armande.

Quickly she attempted to recover her error lest she hurt Jonathan's feelings. "Aye, of course. What I meant was, it is such a surprise to see you sitting alone in the garden. Why are you not breakfasting with Grandfather?"

"I never eat much in the mornings." He regarded her eagerly. "Were you going out walking, my dear? I should be only too pleased to accompany you."

Phaedra heard his suggestion with dismay. She needed solitude now, needed it like a drowning man needs air. But how could she spurn his offer without wounding him? Only one reason occurred to her.

"To own the truth, 'tis already so warm and sticky I was not planning on a walk." She fingered the high neckline of her saffron morning gown in what she hoped was a convincing manner. "I should rather pay a visit to the pond instead."

"The pond! You are not thinking of going swimming again." Jonathan looked horrified, as though one had proposed leaping from London Bridge into the treacherous depths of the Thames.

"I have been swimming since I was a wee girl," she said. "My cousin taught me. I could likely swim the channel if I chose."

"I—I know that well, but . . ." Jonathon faltered, his pock-marked cheeks flushing beet-red with embarrassment. Phaedra guessed he must be recalling the day he had come upon her enjoying the waters of the pond in quite her natural state. The incident had occasioned poor priggish Jonathan far more distress than it had herself. Although he could not meet her eye, he continued, "But I always worry so about currents . . . intruders."

"Pooh, what could happen to me on my grandfather's own land? And as for a current, that would be an astonishing thing to find in any pond, let alone a man-made one." Her unhappiness caused her to add with a shrug. "So if I did drown, 'twould be entirely my own fault. Not that my death would be of any great loss—"

"Don't ever say that!" The unexpected violence in Jonathan's voice startled her. He seized her hands, a feverish light glinting in his eyes as he declared, "You cannot imagine what it would mean to me if I lost you. I would as soon be dead myself."

"I only spoke in jest, a poor one, I admit. I am sorry." Recovering from her surprise at his outburst, Phaedra tried to withdraw her hands, but his grip was astonishingly strong. "Please Jonathan, you—you are hurting me."

He did not seem at first to hear her murmured protest, but then he blinked several times and slowly released her. The peculiar light in his eyes that had so unnerved her vanished, and Jonathan seemed once more himself. "I—I am sorry, Phaedra. I did not mean to hurt you. You know that is the last thing in the world I would ever wish to do. You simply do not realize how I worry about you. All I have ever wanted is to see you protected."

Phaedra managed a weak smile and nodded, rubbing her bruised hand. Jonathan had frequently made such avowals to her, and Phaedra had always been touched by his devoted friendship. Why now did his words leave her feeling strangely disquieted? She shook her head, attributing her unease to all the other highly charged emotions she had been feeling that morning.

She ended the conversation by saying with forced lightness, "My! How—how maudlin we have become. And on such a beautiful day, too. If I mean to have my swim, I'd best be going. Pray excuse me, Jonathan."

Feeling somewhat guilty for thus abandoning him, Phaedra slipped past the hedge, affording him no opportunity to speak again. She was aware of how despairingly his eyes followed her. He reminded her of a faithful hound being forbidden to accompany his mistress.

"Forgive me, dear friend," she murmured. Since he was still watching her, she had no choice but to continue on toward the pond as she had stated. In truth, as the sun rose higher, becoming a fierce blaze in the sky, swimming began to seem not a bad notion. It had been a long time since she had done so.

Next to the garret, the pond was the only other refuge she had ever found at the Heath, a place of delicious solitude. Her grandfather and his friends preferred the comfort and order of the gardens by the kitchen to the wilderness which had been created for him at great expense. The pond was situated well past the manicured lawns and the intriguing gravel walkways considered *de rigueur* for any gentleman's estate these days. Sawyer Weylin's landscaper, Bullock, had leveled all the towering oaks and diverted the course of the brook that had once flowed naturally over the Heath's lands. In their stead, he had thrust a woodland cluster of flowering trees and shrubbery, an artist's conceit, attempting to improve upon nature.

Phaedra pressed through the thicket of carefully arranged bushes toward the pond. The symmetrical shape of the clear silvery water would have fooled no one into thinking this bucolic scene had been crafted by the hand of God. The red deer imported to lend it credence had fled long ago, seeming to vanish into thin air. Although Phaedra had never informed her grandfather, she thought she had once detected the aroma of roast venison wafting from one of the crofter's huts down the lane.

As she swept off her sash, she regarded Bullock's creation with affectionate contempt. She supposed it was no more tasteless than the fake Greek temple or hermitages that adorned other estates. At least her grandfather had never gone so far as to hire a hermit to stalk about his lands. And the pond did serve a most useful function—at least for her.

Phaedra struggled to undo the lacings of her gown and stripped it off over her head. Her petticoats and stockings followed. Here she felt none of the shyness that had made her so awkward in Armande's bedchamber. This was her element, reminding her of her childhood in Ireland, when she and Gilly had paraded in the buff, learning to swim in a God-created pond with all its familiar discomforts of reeds and rocks. In those days she had basked in complete innocence of the nudity of her own body, an attitude most of the Irish shared. It had taken years as an Englishwoman to teach her to be a prude.

Phaedra paced to the edge of the pond. Despite the warmth of the sunlight, she regarded the glassy surface of the pond with momentary trepidation. The waters were never aught but chilly. But she had been taught long ago there was only one way to approach it. Drawing in a deep breath, she plunged into the pond feet first, allowing the water to close over her head. The shock of the cold water enveloping her was at first terrible, then delightful, as though every pore in her body had been jarred awake. Striking the surface of the water, she swam about with vigorous strokes until her blood felt warmed by the exercise.

Pausing to catch her breath, she tread water, before stretching out, trailing her arms in a floating posture. She basked in the feeling of her own numbing exhaustion, the soothing way the cool waters buoyed her up and lapped against her.

But it was not long before the sheer quiet of the place began to oppress her. Even the larks and the chattering squirrels seemed to shun the little copse, as though they detected the artificiality of it. Yet she continued floating, determined to keep her mind from straying back to thoughts of Armande.

She had no use in her life for any man. Had she not just escaped her bondage to Ewan? What was Armande de LeCroix but a distraction? He diverted her from her real goal—to somehow earn enough money to become independent of her grandfather and all his schemes. She set her mind to the task of finding a way to deliver her material to Jessym. She could not afford to wait for Gilly's return, even if this meant she had to run the risk of going to the printer herself. Londoners were notoriously fickle. Robin Goodfellow could easily become last week's sensation, if she did not stir up some new controversy with her pen.

A breeze scudded across the surface of the pond, rippling the waters, and raising gooseflesh upon her bare skin. Phaedra shivered, then kicked her feet beneath her and dog-paddled for the bank.

Hauling herself out, Phaedra flopped into the cool grass, waiting for some of the moisture sheening her skin to dry before dressing again. She plucked a blade of grass and stroked it across her cheek, peering at her reflection in the water. With her hair sprayed across her bare shoulders in fiery rivelets, her wide green eyes haunting her pale face, she looked like some lonely sprite trapped beneath the surface of the water.

She stirred the blade through the reflection, dispelling her image into a myriad of shimmering ripples. Very well, then. Mayhap she would admit it. She was lonely. Why else would she have responded so eagerly to Armande's caresses, gone so willingly to his bed? At times she felt starved for affection—and there was so much about Armande that was perfect.

Too perfect, she thought bitterly. Beyond his skill as a lover, and the enticement of his lean, dangerous profile, he knew how to be kind and gentle. Her longing for that was nigh as keen as her longing to be loved. Armande seemed to understand so much of what she felt. Add to that the fact that he didn't want her to be a simpering fool, that he respected the power of her mind and admired her for it . . . as long as she didn't ask too many questions. Phaedra was glad she remembered that. It saved her from something like regret.

"Damn you, Armande de LeCroix," she muttered, but this time her cursing of him lacked conviction. She rolled over on her side, peering upward to where the sun peeked through the leaves. It must be past noon, she thought dully. By now he must be gone.

She suddenly hated the whispery shadows of the leaves, cast over her like grasping fingers out to steal the very sunshine from her soul. Sitting up, she hugged her bare knees, feeling hollowed by despair.

For the first time, she wondered if it were really so important to her what Armande called himself. What mattered his real name, or what secrets he kept? Quite unreasonably, she was struck by an unexpected memory of Eliza Wilkins, the woman's willingness to risk her life, her security, all to follow her husband Tom wherever he went. "Because I love him," Eliza had said in her quiet way. Phaedra had not understood then, but maybe now, she thought she did, just a little.

If ever she did see Armande again—

The thought broke off as Phaedra was startled by the snap of a twig. She tensed, glancing about her, but the copse was silent, the only movement the rustle of a leaf. All the same, she had the uncomfortable sensation of being spied upon.

Without making obvious her nervousness, Phaedra reached for her clothes. She scrambled into her petticoats and was lacing the corset across her bosom when she heard another snap, followed by the crunch of boots. Someone *was* there.

Phaedra whirled around, clasping her gown in front of her breasts, preparing to scream for help if necessary. She tensed at the sight of the tall man stalking past the bushes. Her lips rounded into a weak oh.

She gaped at Armande, attired for riding in a plain brown frock coat and tan breeches protected by spatterdashes, his silky dark hair drawn back in a neat queue. Her heart set up such a hammering, she could do little more than stare at him. "I—I thought you'd gone."

He dug the toe of one boot into the ground, avoiding her eyes. Never had he looked less the picture of a polished marquis. Fingering the brim of his cocked hat, he said in a low voice, "How could I—after we parted so abruptly? We never truly said farewell."

She thought they had said nigh everything there was to say. An angry blush heated her cheeks. He swore he didn't want to hurt her, yet he seemed determined to prolong this parting, make it as painful as possible.

He moved to the edge of the pond, staring moodily down at his own image, the reflection as mysterious and elusive as Armande himself. Phaedra turned her back on him. With unsteady jerks, she strove to finish lacing the front of her bodice.

"How long have you been watching me?" she blurted out.

"Too long for my peace of mind," came his strained reply.

"Damnation!" Somehow she had tangled one of the lacings, snarling it into a hopeless knot. She yanked on the ribbon, tearing the delicate silk. Whipping around, she hissed through gathering tears, "Curse you. Why did you have to come looking for me? Why didn't you just go!"

He glanced up at her, his eyes rife with misery. "I can't," he said hoarsely. "I think I am falling in love with you."

He spoke with such quiet simplicity she could not doubt he meant it. The words had been wrung from the depths of his heart.

Inexplicably something he had said the first night they had met echoed through her mind. She heard herself replying with a shaky, nigh hysterical laugh, "H—how amusing. I was thinking the exact same about you."

Phaedra never knew how her trembling legs carried her across the clearing, but suddenly she was flinging herself into Armande's arms with a force that nearly tumbled them both into the pond.

"Phaedra," he groaned, burying his face against her neck. "What a selfish bastard I am. I tried to tear myself away . . . tried. But I swear, somehow I will manage—make sure you never have cause to hate me."

"Nay, hush, love." Her fingers tangled in his hair. "Everything will be all right."

It was a rash and reckless pledge to make when she had no idea what *everything* was. But nothing mattered to her now, nothing except that he not vanish from her life. At this moment, she could imagine no greater pain than that.

His mouth burned against hers as they sank down as of one accord and tumbled into the grass. There was no hint of the accomplished lover in the trembling way Armande fumbled with her clothes. He nigh tore her petticoats in his haste to disrobe her, she nearly doing the same to his cravat and coat. Their bodies bared, they came together, flesh to flesh, in a kind of fierce desperation. It was as though they were both aware of how close they would always be to losing each other, forever hovering on the brink of some dark calamity. They had to seize what precious moments the begrudging fates would allow.

Their passion rose and swelled in a heated rush, leaving them spent with exhaustion. Even then, Phaedra held Armande inside her for as long as she could, as if drawing back would allow all the shadows of secrecy to creep between them.

"Phaedra. Phaedra," he murmured. "How have I ever managed to live without you? I feel like a man who has been lost in an endless winter. And you are the blazing sun."

He rolled onto his side, still crushing her against him. She gazed up at him through the tears sparkling at the edge of her lashes. "I have never been anyone's blazing sun before." She emitted a watery chuckle. "Although Grandfather complains most fiercely about the color of my hair."

"He's a fool!" She was startled, almost frightened by the savage bitterness that twisted his mouth when speaking of Sawyer Weylin. She felt relieved when he forced his features to relax. "Your hair is glorious, *ma belle*. You would have driven Titian nigh mad with the longing to paint—"

She laid her fingers across the sensual curve of his lips, stopping him. The love they dared speak of was yet new. But Phaedra knew with dread certainty, two things which would always put the tenuous bond between them at risk.

"I want to exchange a promise with you," she said solemnly. With a future as uncertain as theirs, there was only one pledge they could offer each other. Despite the tender light in Armande's eyes, one brow shot up in an expression that was as wary as it was questioning. Nonetheless, she continued, "I promise to ask no more questions that you cannot answer if you will pledge—"

She felt Armande tense.

"You pledge that there will be no more *ma belle* or *ma chère*, no more playing the French marquis. Not when we are alone together—like this."

For one moment, she feared he would refuse her even that much honesty. Then, he relaxed. "Very well. *My beautiful* Phaedra."

He laughed and pulled her close for another long and satisfying kiss that set the seal to their promises . . . promises that could never be kept.

* * *

Phaedra slipped back to the house much later in a far different mood than when she had fled from it earlier. She sought out the backstairs, humming snatches of outrageous Irish ditties she had learned from Gilly—songs no lady ever ought to know. But then, she smiled, she had never looked less like a lady than she did now. Anyone who saw her would guess what she had been doing in the sweet grass by the pond.

Armande's passion might well have been stamped upon her face for all to see. She could feel her skin glowing, how tender her mouth was from the force of his kisses, her hair tumbled about her like some wild-eyed gypsy's. It was as well she encountered none of the servants, for she could not have concealed the strange and fluttery feelings she had inside.

Armande said he loved her. His unexpected declaration filled her with wonder. She had never thought to hear those words from any man, certainly not the icy Marquis de Varnais. Ah, but he was not the marquis, and whoever he might be, she assured herself, that was not her concern. It was enough to know him as the man who loved her, whom she loved in return. She would make it enough.

Even living on the edge of this precipice was preferable to the lonely existence she had known before Armande came. Now she reveled in the riotous thrum of her pulses, the excitement tingling through her veins. The crash might come, bringing in its wake a despair darker than she ever had known. But it wasn't coming today.

Armande loved her, *her*, Phaedra. Not "Lord Ewan's relict." Herself. She twirled about, then skipped toward her room so gaily that for a moment she might well still have been that barefoot little girl from Donegal. She barely noted that the door to her bedchamber stood ajar until she bounded across the threshold. She nearly collided with the grim figure of Hester Searle.

A gasp, half of fright, half of annoyance, escaped Phaedra. She drew back in a gesture as reflexive as shrinking from a repulsive toad. "What are you doing in here?"

Even though she towered over the housekeeper by a full head, it was she who felt at a disadvantage as Hester's beadlike eyes took in Phaedra's mud-stained skirts, studying her flushed face. A soured expression twisted Hester's pinched white visage.

"I've been checking on the housemaids to make sure as yer rooms be cleaned proper. It scarce happens by magic, ye know."

"Or by witchcraft." Phaedra offered her a too-sweet smile. Not even Madame Pester should be allowed to spoil her happiness this day. She arched her neck in a prose of haughty disdain and stalked past the woman toward her wardrobe.

"How sorry I am to be intruding," Hester sneered. "I had no idea yer ladyship would be wishful of changing clothes at this hour of the day."

Phaedra yanked open the wardrobe door, searching through the silks for a fresh gown. "One usually does after slipping on the wet grass and taking a tumble." She immediately despised herself for offering any explanation of her disheveled state. She was not obliged to render an accounting to the likes of Hester Searle.

Hester stooped to pick up some blades of grass that had dropped from Phaedra's petticoats. Crushing them between her crooked fingers, she said, "I've also just put the maids up to doin' the bed in the marquess's room. Do ye reckon he will be needing to change his garb, as well?"

There was no mistaking the contemptuous insinuation in Hester's voice. Phaedra felt the blood drain from her face except for one spot of heat that glowed high in each cheek.

"Why don't you ask him yourself?" she snapped. She snatched a sacque back gown of peach-colored silk from the wardrobe and stormed into the powdering room to change, slamming the door behind her.

That Searle creature was going to push someone too far one of these days, Phaedra thought. She only hoped she was there to see it. The woman could not have made the connection between herself and Armande if her prying eyes had not been at work again. Mayhap the woman had been listening at the keyhole when she and Armande . . . Phaedra suppressed the thought, the mere suspicion of such a thing enough to make her feel quite ill.

She tugged off the soiled gown without summoning Lucy to aid her. Searle's suspicions had been bad enough without her maid wondering why her mistress returned from a morning's walk with her corset strings all tangled in knots.

As Phaedra struggled into the peach silk, she thought of Hester's spiteful expression with increasing dissatisfaction. It occurred to her that the woman's penchant for spying could present a real danger to Armande. Hester might search through Phaedra's bedchamber as much as she liked, for all Phaedra's secrets were carefully locked away in the garret. But could

Armande say the same for his? She thought of the wooden casket he kept in plain view upon his dressing table. One of Hester's hairpins might be enough to pry it open. She ought to warn him.

Phaedra's lips curled into a wry smile. Faith, after trying so hard to expose him herself, it was rather ironic she should now seek to protect him. Being enamored of a man made a great many changes in one's perception. If love was not precisely blind, it did render one far more willing to look at things a different way.

Still smiling, thinking of Armande, Phaedra rustled back into the bedchamber. To her displeasure, Searle was still there. The woman stood smoothing the lengths of Phaedra's ivory counter-pane, although the bed had already been made up by one of the maids. Hester's rough fingertips snagged on the satin brocade, a strange brooding expression darkening her features.

How out of place, in her stiff, black bombazine, the wizened creature looked amid the eyelet lace and frills of Phaedra's bedchamber. Phaedra frowned, the image of Hester caressing her bedclothes somehow disconcerting, like the shadow of death passing through a bride's bower.

"You can go now, Mrs. Searle," she said in her frostiest accents. Not waiting to see the command obeyed, Phaedra swept over to her dressing table. Settling herself into the gilt carved chair, she pulled up the mirror and began brushing the tangles from the silky threads of her fiery hair.

Phaedra had never been given cause to feel vain before, but as she regarded her reflection in the mirror, she could nigh begin to believe Armande's words of endearment when he had called her *"ma belle."* What fairy spell had he worked upon her in the pond's hidden glade? Never had her eyes shone so bright and luminous, her skin been tinted with such a soft pink glow. The rosebud shape of her mouth quivered as though harboring the sweetest of secrets only a woman could know. How she—

Phaedra dropped her hairbrush, a frightened cry escaping her. Another face flashed beside hers, like some hobgoblin appearing by witchery within the depths of the mirror, the leathery features contorted into an ugly mask of hatred. It took Phaedra a moment to realize it was only Hester Searle hovering behind her. She placed her hand across her bosom in an effort to steady her jumping heart.

She retrieved the fallen hairbrush, unwilling to let Hester see how much she had startled her. She glared at the woman. Was there something else you wanted, Mrs. Searle?"

The woman's eyes burned like two live coals, and in their depths Phaedra glimpsed a jealousy that could burn like acid to the core of a soul. Without knowing why, Phaedra shivered. Never before had she been afraid of Hester Searle, but in that brief moment, she felt terrified.

The woman's blue-veined lids slowly lowered, the dark eyes slanting into their customary sly expression. Once more she was naught but the prying housekeeper, a source more of irritation than terror. Phaedra let out her breath.

"No, milady. There was naught else." Still, Hester did not go. She lingered by the dressing table, daring to finger Phaedra's fan, her dainty kid gloves. Although no longer afraid, the woman was making Phaedra decidedly uneasy.

When Hester picked up the porcelain shepherdess Phaedra had found in the garret, Phaedra commanded, "Put that down."

Mrs. Searle's clawlike fingers tightened around the delicate figurine until Phaedra feared she meant to crush it. "Where'd ye come by this?"

"That is none of your concern." She moved to take the shepherdess from the woman, but to Phaedra's complete outrage, Hester whisked it out of her reach.

"Miss Lethington meant this geegaw for Master Ewan, so she did. How did *you* come to have it all this time?"

Lethington. Phaedra started. That was the name the shopkeeper had mentioned just yesterday. But how strange to hear it fall from Hester's lips. Although she had a strong urge to box Hester's ears and send her packing, Phaedra's curiosity got the better of her. "Miss Lethington? You don't mean Miss Julianna Lethington?"

"Certainly I do. This here statue was meant for the Emperor of Austria, but Miss Julianna, she vowed to give it to my Master Ewan instead. Only he never got it. He always believed as how someone stole it."

Despite her growing anger with Hester, Phaedra felt a tingle of excitement. Was it possible after all that her shepherdess was part of the famous Lethington set? Or was this only more of Hester's odious tale-spinning?

As she managed to snatch the shepherdess back from Hester, Phaedra said loftily, "I found this in the attic, so I consider it mine now. And if it is the treasure you claim, why on earth would Julianna Lethington have wanted to give it to my husband?"

Greatly to Phaedra's astonishment, Hester broke out laughing. She could never remember having heard the housekeeper give way to mirth before. It was a screechy, unpleasant sound, like the strident cry of a raven, and Phaedra felt it slash right through her.

"I don't see what is so amusing about my question."

"Don't you?" Hester rubbed the back of one black lace mitten against her watering eyes. Phaedra marveled that such a mirth-filled gaze could at the same time harbor so much malice.

"I only be surprised, that's all, what with you not being able to bear having the woman's cloak about, that ye should so cherish her china."

Cloak? China? What the devil was the woman talking about? Phaedra stared at Hester, certain the petty impulses stirring in the housekeeper's crabbed little soul had finally driven the creature mad.

"Lord bless us, ye really don't know, do ye?" Hester craned her neck eagerly, looking for all the world like an adder about to deliver a choice bit of venom.

Phaedra did not know, but as she glanced uneasily from the housekeeper's malicious face to the figurine, she wasn't sure she wanted to.

"The gray cloak, my dear Lady Grantham," Hester purred. "Ye recall it. The one that belonged to—"

"I know full well whom the cloak belonged to. What of it?" Phaedra no longer felt disturbed by the memory of Ewan's precious lost love, Anne, but she loathed discussing her former humiliation with Hester all the same.

"We-e-ell," Hester drew the word out, obviously determined to savor every moment of the revelation to come. "The lady who owned that cloak is the same who fashioned the china." She crooked one bent finger toward the statuette Phaedra cradled so protectively in her hands. "Miss Julianna Lethington was Master Ewan's lost love."

Julianna Lethington had been Ewan's Anne? Dear Lord, no wonder Hester nearly wept from laughing. It was indeed an irony that the figurine that Phaedra so loved should turn out to be but another memento of her husband's lover.

Phaedra turned the golden-haired shepherdess carefully in her hands, almost able to picture the graceful fingers that had wrought the statue's beauty. For years, fear, hurt, and jealousy had stifled her curiosity about the mysterious Anne. But she felt far differently now. That likely had much to do with Armande's whispered words of love. She no longer need feel any envy of a phantom woman whose memory her husband had cherished in her stead.

"So Anne was the daughter of china makers," she mused. "No wonder Ewan never wed her." The greedy and proud Grantham family would never have suffered one of their members to marry a girl of such low birth. Indeed they had scarcely accepted Phaedra, despite the lure of her grandfather's fortune and the fact that her mother, Siobhan, had been a lady.

"Such a great tragedy it all was." Hester fetched a deep sigh, her soulless black eyes never leaving Phaedra's face. "Master Ewan, he loved Julianna Lethington so."

Did Hester think to wound her still with that sort of spiteful reminder? Phaedra favored her with a scornful glance. "And what would you know about it? You were not even employed here at the time."

"Lord Ewan didn't treat me with the contempt as *some* in this house do. Oft his lordship would confide in me—"

"I doubt that. I knew my husband well. He was never the sort to pass his time of day with the housekeeper." Phaedra placed the shepherdess back on the table, starting to stroke the brush through her hair again. She broke off with a gasp as Hester's hand hooked over her shoulder, the woman's nails biting through the gossamer fabric of Phaedra's gown.

"Ye never knew him, nor me, neither," Searle hissed. "I was more than just the housekeeper when Master Ewan lived. The same blood flows in my veins as any Grantham. Aye, the Searles be just as good, though we fell upon harder times."

Phaedra struck the woman's hand from her shoulder. Her flashing green eyes met Hester's malevolent black ones in the depths of the mirror. "You'd best go now," Phaedra said through clenched teeth.

"He loved *her*, he did, not you." Hester stabbed the words at Phaedra as though she wielded a knife. "Loved his beautiful Julianna. As fair and delicate as that there china. He never stopped loving her—no, not even after what her murderin' brother did to my poor Master Ewan's papa, Lord Carleton."

Phaedra twisted around in her chair, preparing to thrust Hester from her room if she had to. But she froze, blinking as though she had been dazzled by the light of a hundred chandeliers. A light that suddenly made all crystal-clear.

"Lethington . . . old Lethe," she said wonderingly. "The old Lethe who killed Carleton Grantham was—was Anne's brother."

Hester regarded her with the contemptuous patience usually reserved for the village idiot. "That's aright. James Lethington. He be the one. The same tale as I've tried to tell you many a day, but ye've always been too high-minded to hear it—or perhaps too afraid."

"I've just never had any interest in a past that does not concern me."

She turned her back on Hester once more and tried to resume brushing her hair, annoyed to see that her hand trembled a little. Mayhap Hester's sneering suggestion was correct. Mayhap she was a little afraid, as suggestible as any of the little children Hester loved to terrify. Perchance Phaedra was oft haunted enough by the specters from her own past. She didn't want to add anyone else's to the collection.

But Hester's voice dropped to its low, sinister pitch, and Phaedra could not seem to stop her. The crone peered over her shoulder again, her haggard image hovering, nigh mesmerizing Phaedra with her witch-black eyes. 'Twas as though she had conjured up some evil spirit within the depths of the mirror and could not put it down again.

"'Twas in a springtime of long ago, it was," Hester droned. "That my handsome Master Ewan declared his love for Miss Julianna. Fair she was, a maiden all gold and roses, so dainty she scarce reached the master's shoulder. He could neither eat nor sleep for thinking of her, and he vowed to make her his bride despite the difference in their stations.

"That pleased neither the Granthams nor the Lethingtons. Oh, yes, they were proud as Lucifer, too, her mama and them brothers of hers who were no more than street rabble. James and Jason. But it would have taken more than the likes of them to have stopped Master Ewan getting what he wanted. It was his father Lord Carleton as done that. And all for the sake of *you*."

Hester fairly spat the word at Phaedra. Phaedra lowered the hairbrush, the bristles digging into her palms as she held it clenched tight in her lap.

"By then your grandfather was dangling prospects of fortunes afore Lord Carleton's greedy eyes, offering to pay off family debts—the Granthams, they were always in debt. And then, of course, you were the daughter of an *Irish lady*."

The term might well have been an insult the way Hester pronounced it. "The match was clapped up without scarce consultin' Master Ewan. He'd never been strong about opposing his father—Carleton Grantham was the very devil of a man. But for the sake of his sweet Anne, Master'd have defied them all. Lord Carleton, he figured he'd find a way to buy Julianna Lethington off—or mebbe fright her away. And the devil, he succeeded. 'E got 'is way, all right. There came a night—the girl had a tryst planned with Master Ewan. She was asupposed to be acoming, and to bring him that little statue as a pledge of her love. But she vanished from the face of the earth."

Phaedra's eyes traveled to the fragile porcelain figurine, which would be so easily crushed—just as its delicate maker must have been.

"Master Ewan was brokenhearted," Hester continued. "But that brother of hers, that James, fetched after Lord Carleton in a perfect fury."

"I well imagine that he might," Phaedra said warmly. "And if Ewan so loved the girl, he should have done the same."

Hester's mouth pinched, but she otherwise ignored the slur upon her beloved Master Ewan. "Mr. Weylin and Lord Carleton were below in the study going over the details of the marriage contract, not knowing James Lethington had followed Lord Carleton here. All the servants were gone that eve. They'd been given a holiday. So 'twas easy matter for old Lethe to creep into the hall unseen and take his choice o' weapons."

Hester's lips snaked back into a ghoulish smile that sickened Phaedra. "He took the mace down from where it had hung on the wall and waited—"

"Aye, so he did," Phaedra interrupted sharply. "Then he killed Lord Carleton and was hanged for it. But what of the rest of his family? Did they ever find Julianna?"

"Naught but her dove-gray cloak, left alaying upon the river bank not far from the spot where they say she chose to end her life."

Phaedra frowned. She sensed there was more than one detail missing from this tale that Hester spun for her with such wicked delight. It seemed far too convenient that Julianna would have obliged Lord Carleton by committing suicide—unless Ewan's father had terrified her into doing so. But if Julianna had perished in the river, how did the missing shepherdess come to be abandoned in her grandfather's attic?

"And what became of Julianna's mother and the other brother?"

Hester shrugged. Apparently, having committed no gruesome murders, Jason Lethington held little interest for her. The housekeeper resumed her grisly detailing of the murder.

"A most wicked heavy weapon that mace was. Capable of crushing a man's skull with but a light blow—"

"That will be all, *Searle*," Phaedra said sharply.

Hester's eyes snapped to hers in a hate-filled glare. "Oh, aye, aren't you the one for dismissin' me after ye've heard all ye care to hear. The great lady with yer fine peach silks and cream satin bed."

Phaedra jerked to her feet and stalked over, pointedly opening the bedchamber door. She must have been mad to have listened to Hester even this long.

"For all yer airs," Hester said. "Yer naught but a poor relation, same as me. Only I grub and truckle fer a livin' on the poor salary yer grandfather flings me. Ah, but he's too kind, letting me have the used tea leaves to sell fer a little extra. Since I be lackin' other attributes to peddle, such as ye bear."

Phaedra flushed a deep red. "Get out of here!"

"First flingin' yerself at that drunkard Danby and now at the marquess with my poor Master Ewan not buried a year. Well, ye'll never be no marchioness. That Lord Varnais don't love ye no more than Master Ewan ever did. He'll but use ye—"

"I said get out!" She advanced upon Hester, not quite sure what she might have done had the housekeeper not at last shown the good sense to cringe away from her. She bobbed an insolent curtsy.

"Aye, just as ye wish, yer ladyship."

As the woman slunk out the door, Phaedra sank down upon the gilt chair, her knees trembling. She dropped her head against her hands, cursing herself. She had allowed Searle to get the better of her again, drive her to anger just when she had fancied herself immune to the woman's vicious barbs.

The creature must indeed be a witch, searching out Phaedra's soul with her hag's gaze. When one tender area had healed, she knew just where to direct a new thrust. *That Lord Varnais don't love ye . . . he'll but use ye.*

No! Phaedra slammed the palm of her hand upon the dressing table. She would let no more of Hester's poison enter her heart. The housekeeper was naught but an embittered, jealous old crone. Phaedra would not allow one particle of her happiness to be snatched away by her grasping fingers.

Tossing her head, she tried to resume brushing her hair. But she found herself staring at the golden-haired shepherdess perched before her. It was as though Hester's touch had somehow tainted even her enjoyment of that, the figurine's eyes appearing hauntingly sad, the delicate hue of the lips as crimson as a slash of blood.

Her eyes glittering with angry tears, Phaedra seized the statue and buried it deep in the dressing table drawer.

Chapter Twelve

THE MEMORY OF HER QUARREL WITH HESTER CLUNG IN PHAEDRA'S mind like finely spun cobwebs, refusing to be brushed aside. Even days later, as she jounced through London in the faded splendor of a hackney coach, she found herself thinking about Mrs. Searle.

Mayhap it was the evening fog that swirled about the carriage, rendering the familiar streets of London into a nightmare world of illusion, of lurking mists that kept reminding Phaedra of Hester. Or mayhap it was the knowledge of the risk she took in being out alone, on a mission of just the sort of secrecy the spying housekeeper would most have liked to discover.

Nervously, Phaedra patted the packet that contained the writing she soon hoped to deliver into Jessym's hands. She was supposed to be taking tea with Jonathan Burnell and the elderly cousin who kept house for him. Her plan was to drop off the packet and continue on to Jonathan's house in Cheapside before her absence could be noticed. She knew her friend would willingly lie to cover her activities, but Phaedra had no desire to place Jonathan in such an awkward position.

In any case, she did not intend for her business with Jessym to take long. Phaedra adjusted the heavy veil over her face, trusting that the fine black silk would obscure her features when she thrust the manuscript out the coach window. She would not alight from the carriage, thus keeping Jessym from studying her at any great length.

Leaning forward, Phaedra risked a peek out the hackney's

grimy window to see if she could determine how close they might be to Fleet Street. But the fog blanketed everything, drawing down the curtain of night far sooner than she had anticipated. The few other carriages that dared risk travel on such an evening clattered past her and disappeared like shadow riders into the thick mists; even the clatter of the horses' hooves was muted into a dreamlike unreality.

Many of the town houses had already lit their oil lamps, which the law required them to burn above the pavement in an effort to discourage the rogues who roved London's streets by night. This eve, the lamps flickered but dimly in the graying haze. The illumination did not even reach the center of the street where the hackney coach ambled, leaving Phaedra feeling cut adrift in a sea of darkness far from the welcoming beacon of any shore.

She shivered and huddled back against the seat, wondering why she had not asked Armande to accompany her, why even now she did not trust him enough to tell him the truth of Robin Goodfellow's identity. She was certain he was no longer angry about the article she had written maligning his pose as the Marquis de Varnais. She had never even heard him mention Robin Goodfellow again since that day they had met by the bookseller's in Oxford Street. Then why not confide in him as she had Gilly and Jonathan?

Perhaps it was because, deep down in her heart, she feared Hester was right. Armande did not love her, was indeed planning to use her for some sinister purpose of his own.

No! She nearly cried aloud in her vehemence to deny it. How could she yet doubt the soft glow she had seen in Armande's eyes when he looked at her, the sweet fury of his kiss? She would think no more about what Hester had said. The woman's malicious whispers about Armande were but more of the poison festering inside Hester's own wretched heart.

Phaedra was thrown slightly off-balance as the coach lurched to a stop. Through the haze she glimpsed a plain, straight building of ugly red brick, grim and uninviting. The hackney driver swung down from his perch, yanking the door open.

"This be it, milady. The address where you asked to be set down."

"N—no, I didn't," Phaedra protested, the mist itself threatening to seep into the hackney's interior, leaving her damp and chilled.

"I mean, could you please knock at the door and request a Mr. Jessym to come out to me."

The driver scowled, and it took a great deal of effort to persuade him—almost as though he feared Phaedra meant to make off with his cab and horse the minute his back was turned. By adding a considerable tip to the fare, an expense she could ill afford, she convinced the coachman to fetch Jessym.

When he had gone, she fussed with her veil, making sure not so much as one strand of red hair was showing. Her fingers felt slick with perspiration within her tan kid gloves. What if Jessym, accustomed to dealing with Gilly, refused to have aught to do with her?

The moments now seemed to drag by even more slowly. Phaedra was beginning to fear she had come to the wrong address when the driver returned, followed closely by a short man wrapped in a navy greatcoat and wearing a gray powdered bagwig.

Momentarily, Phaedra forgot all caution as she let down the coach window, straining for her first glimpse of Farley Jessym. The middle-aged man who thrust his face close to the coach window was quite ordinary in appearance, with a hard set to his mouth and a look of jaded weariness in his eyes. When he spoke, his voice was sharp, startling Phaedra into backing away from the window.

"Eh, what nonsense is this? What do you want that you summon me out into the streets from my home?"

Her hands shaking, she thrust the packet containing her writing out the window. "From Robin Goodfellow," she rasped in a deep voice.

Jessym's brow arched, his cynical face registering a flash of surprise. He yanked the packet from her grasp. Much to Phaedra's dismay, he jerked the hackney's door open, as well. She shrank back as Jessym leaned inside, his eyes narrowed as though he would penetrate both the gloom-filled interior and the layerings of her veil, as well.

"So now I'm to deal with a wench, am I?" he growled. "What happened to the Irishman?"

Phaedra shrugged, trying to avoid speaking any more than was necessary.

Jessym muttered an oath. "Well, you can tell Mr. Goodfellow

for me, I'm a bit weary of all this secrecy. I like to know who my writers are."

Phaedra merely extended her hand, wishing that it did not tremble so. "The—the advance as promised, please."

"Not so fast, my fine lady, until I see what I have here. This could be naught but a parcel of your love letters for all I know."

Phaedra stiffened indignantly while Jessym undid the packet, hauling forth the first few pages of the manuscript. He squinted at it in the meager light offered by the coach's lanterns.

"Emancipation for Catholics, eh?" Jessym grunted. "This is bound to stir up a pretty rumpus. Not altogether sure I should print it."

Phaedra's heart sank, but she ventured bravely, "My—I mean, the money, if you please."

Jessym stared at her for a long moment, before taking a worn purse from beneath his frock coat. He counted off a handful of coins, but when Phaedra reached for them, he held the money just out of her grasp.

"Trouble's abrewing. Goodfellow ought to be aware of that. The king's ministers are growing tired of the license of the press, and they are looking to make an example of him."

"Nonsense!" Phaedra forgot herself, speaking in her normal voice. "I . . . we've heard those threats before. Ever since the John Wilkes affair, the king has been afraid to persecute writers lest he create another popular hero and martyr."

"Don't you be so sure about that," Jessym scoffed. "All I'm saying is, if the day comes and I'm arrested for spreading sedition, I don't mean to stand in the docks alone. You just make sure Goodfellow knows that."

Jessym tumbled the coins into her hand and stepped back. He closed the door, signaling the hackney driver to move along. The coach lurched into movement before Phaedra had time to react to Jessym's parting words.

As the hackney lumbered off down the street, she fumed inwardly, angry at herself for not having exercised more control over the interview which had just taken place. She had not even counted the money to make sure it was the sum Jessym had promised.

But she merely fingered the coins in her lap, not attempting to do so even now. What did Jessym mean by making such a spiteful threat, that he would not stand trial alone? He knew no one else to accuse except . . . Phaedra froze. Except mayhap Gilly.

Sickened with fear, Phaedra reprimanded herself for thinking like such a dolt, allowing herself to be so easily terrified. Jessym had not yet been arrested for printing the *Gazetteer*, and she had already lampooned King George and his ministers many times with impunity. The harsh-faced publisher was raising alarms over nothing.

But what if Jessym was right, and her luck was indeed running out? What if the king's forbearance were drawing to an end . . . ? She glanced out the window, the gray mists somehow assuming before her eyes the grim guise of Newgate Prison and its horrors, as detailed by her grandfather. No, she could no longer afford to take the risk. Not when she was playing with Gilly's life and her grandfather's reputation, as well as her own safety.

Robin Goodfellow would simply have to make his fortune in some far less dangerous fashion. Phaedra sighed, her fingers tightening over the coins. A most wise decision. She only hoped that she had not reached it too late.

Chapter Thirteen

PHAEDRA COULD NOT BRING HERSELF TO BURN THE COPIES OF THE essays she had written. Instead she tied the articles neatly together with a black mourning ribbon and made sure they were locked safely away in the garret desk. Beyond that, she gave small consideration to the demise of Robin Goodfellow or what the future might hold for her. Relieved when no tidings ever came concerning Jessym's imminent arrest, she was content to live in the present, making the most of every precious moment with Armande, giving no heed to what the morrow might bring.

August descended upon London in a blaze of heat, each day more searing than the last. Those who could afford to do so had long ago fled the city for seaside resorts. Those that had to remain sweltered in the shade and suffered. One afternoon as she and Armande rode out into the meadowland beyond the Heath's neatly trimmed lawns, they saw nary another living creature save for a flock of newly shorn sheep.

Phaedra galloped across the pasture's brittle grasses, scarcely attempting to shield her face beneath the brim of her riding hat. Her roan gelding strove in vain to match stride with Armande's great white stallion, Nemesis.

With but the merest touch from Armande upon the reins, his horse shot forward, scattering the flock of frightened sheep in all directions. Phaedra drew rein upon Furlong before she exhausted the poor beast entirely. The gelding's sides streamed with sweat as he wheezed his way across the meadow.

Armande appeared at last to have noticed that he had lost her. Halting at the edge of the pasture under the spreading shade of an oak tree, he waited. With sweat glistening on his tanned face, he unbuttoned his linen shirt enough to reveal his neck and the dark dusting of hair upon his chest.

A teasing light glinted in Armande's eyes as Phaedra drew alongside. He bent forward, addressing his stallion in a conspiratorial whisper. "In good faith, Nemesis, if I had but known, I could have fetched a knacker for that poor beast to put it out of its misery."

"You never told me you meant to ride as though a band of savage cutthroats were after us," Phaedra said. "Nemesis. What sort of name for a horse is that, anyway?"

"It seemed an apt enough choice when I christened him. But I'm not so sure, anymore." A faraway look crept into Armande's eyes. Then he seemed to snap himself back to the present and slid from his horse.

"If we are to cherish any hope of returning to the Heath," he teased, "it is obvious we must give your spirited mount a rest."

She raised no objections when he lifted her from the saddle. Not far beyond the oak tree, Armande found a rill; rather sluggish with the heat, it yet managed to carve a bed for itself at the edge of the pasture. They allowed the horses to drink, then moved to a spot farther down the bank before kneeling themselves. Phaedra hitched up the voluminous skirts of her sky-blue riding habit and petticoats, dabbing the cool water on her cheeks, then cupping her hands for a drink. She stole glances at Armande, watching him splash the cooling liquid over the strong cords of his neck. Phaedra's gaze was once more drawn to the scar on his throat. Armande had once told her vaguely that the wound was a result of something a friend had once done to him. Was it the same friend he had once mentioned as having been imprisoned, whose memory had haunted him the day she had had Armande arrested? No. Phaedra drew firm rein on the forbidden direction of her thoughts. No more questions.

She sank back on her heels, running her finger inside the collar of her jacket. "I may well be obliged to walk home." She sighed. "I should not have pushed Furlong so hard in this heat."

Armande stood up and tethered both horses firmly to a branch of a small apple tree, whose shade afforded the animals some cool, sweet grass unscorched by the sun. As he stroked Furlong's neck, he said, "You are a skilled horsewoman. 'Tis a shame to see you mounted on such an old slug."

"I have a great deal of affection for my old slug!" But she could not help adding wistfully, "I sometimes wish for a mare with a little more pepper in her step, but my grandfather is not much of a judge of horseflesh. He and Ewan used to have terrible rows over the expensive hunters Ewan wanted him to buy. But he did manage to wring a few fine ones out of Grandfather."

She tugged off her riding hat and stretched out dreamily, flat on her back in the meager shade. "The last hunter Grandfather bought was magnificent. He had the most showy chestnut mane and extremely powerful hind quarters. It was a great pity Ewan had to have been riding Brute the day he—"

She broke off, flushing at the waywardness of her own tongue. She hardly ever mentioned her late husband to Armande, let alone referring to the manner of his death. She glanced up to find Armande eyeing her gravely.

"I—I suppose you feel I am a most terrible, heartless woman," she said. "That I could so mourn the loss of a good horse and not spare one tear for my husband's broken neck."

"Nay, I don't think you are terrible at all."

Despite his soft reply, Phaedra felt driven by a need to defend herself. "The accident was Ewan's own fault. He was always careless with his horses, tearing about like a madman, even over unfamiliar ground. He was out riding alone that morning and decided to cut across some poor farmer's fields. He never checked his pace when jumping that stone fence, never bothered worrying what might be on the other side, that some field hand might have been careless enough to leave his plow—"

Her eyes shut tight as though a vision of the accident might rise up before her. "M-mercifully, Ewan must have died at once. They say he never suffered, but Brute took the worst of the blow, breaking his leg, gashing his side on the plow and . . . it was some time before anyone found . . . It was all so strange."

"Strange? How?"

Armande's question startled her. He had been quiet for so long, she had almost begun to wonder if he were even listening. She opened her eyes to find his gaze intent.

"Well, I scarce know," she said slowly, sitting up. "Mayhap ironic is what I really meant, ironic that Ewan should have been riding alone. Ewan hated solitude. Why, sometimes he even sought out *my* company rather than be left alone."

"Your life with him was very unhappy, wasn't it?"

"Pure hell," she said with a shaky laugh.

"Then I'm doubly glad he broke his neck."

Phaedra shivered. She had come close often to thinking that herself; but the deathlike quiet with which Armande gave voice to her guilty thought left her feeling strangely cold.

She now regretted ever having mentioned her late husband. The mere sound of Ewan's name seemed to have cast a pall over the bright summer's day she and Armande were sharing together. And she had no idea how many more such days she might be granted.

"Well, the worst of those days are all behind me." She sighed, hugging her legs in close. "I am a free woman now."

"But you will marry again." Armande's voice sounded strained. "I have noticed that one friend of your grandfather's seems most devoted to you. I would imagine Mr. Burnell could offer a woman a most secure future."

Was this Armande's way of telling her that he had no future to offer her himself? She had sensed that long ago, and one glance at the sadness darkening his eyes was enough to confirm it. She looked away again, not wanting to face that just now.

"Nay, I shall never allow myself to be shackled by the bonds of marriage again. I intend to be an independent woman one day."

"I am sorry you feel that way," Armande said. "Marriage was never meant to be like the misery you shared with Grantham. If things were different, I would try to make you change—"

He broke off abruptly, standing and walking away from where she sat to stare out across the meadow.

"But what would you know of it?" she asked. "You have never been married . . . have you?"

His throat muscles constricted. "No, I have never been that fortunate. But I have the example of my mother and father to draw upon. There were never two people who came closer to achieving perfect happiness in this very imperfect world."

"Your parents were supposed to have died when you were only a babe," she said gently.

For a moment he looked startled, then he flung up one hand in the manner of a fencer acknowledging a hit. "Piqued again! *Merci beaucoup, madame,* for the reminder."

"I wasn't trying to be clever." She frowned up at him. "I only hope you are not as careless in the presence of others as you are with me."

"It was at your insistence, my dear, that I abandoned my pose as the marquis."

"Only with me. I never meant for you to risk exposure with anyone else. God knows what my grandfather would do if he discovered you were an impostor. And there are many who would take malicious delight in telling him. Hester, for one—"

"So you have warned me many times before. I know full well how to protect myself, Phaedra." The hard planes of his face softened with longing. " 'Tis only with you that I have ever been in any danger. I sometimes think I would sell my soul to be able to tell you everything, hear you call me by my real name."

"The price would be far too dear," she said. She no longer wanted any confessions from him, fearful that she now stood to lose as much from the revelation of his secrets as he. She stood up briskly, shaking blades of grass from her skirts.

She forced a more cheerful inflection into her voice. "Well, sir," she said, "since it was you who were so ungallant as to make me race, if Furlong doesn't recover, I think it only fair that you lend me your mount."

"If you think you could ride Nemesis, milady."

"Pooh! My mother gave birth to me on the back of a horse. I learned to ride before I could walk," she boasted. "We Irish are famous for our horse sense."

"For your horse thieving, too—so I've heard."

When Armande made comments like that, Phaedra harbored no doubts as to the man's origin. The smug expression settling upon his handsome features resembled nothing so much as what she termed, "the Englishman's superior smirk."

She scooped up a handful of water and flicked it at him. Unruffled, he wiped the spray from his cheek with the back of his hand, his desire for reprisal only betrayed by the devilish light that flared in his eyes.

"And of course," he drawled, "there is the Irish lady's fondness for taking a swim . . ."

But Phaedra, guessing his purpose, tore off running across the meadow. She could hear Armande coming after her, and she had no more chance of outdistancing him than Furlong would have Nemesis.

Armande caught her roughly about the waist and tumbled with

her to the grass. They rolled over until they both became entangled
in her skirts, gasping with laughter. Armande pinned her beneath
his weight and swooped down to capture her lips, the sweet, rough
texture of his tongue mating with hers.

Breathless moments later, he drew back. He entwined a lock of
her hair until it formed a fiery ring about his finger.

"Sorceress," he murmured. "Your name should be Circe,
luring a man into forgetting all he ever knew of his past before
being ensnared by your charms."

Phaedra's own smile was tremulous. She only wished she did
possess witchlike powers, to free Armande from whatever dark
motives had first swept him into her life—from those anguished
memories she feared would one day tear him from her. In the
innermost corner of her heart, she knew this idyll they shared
could not last. Phaedra flung her arms about his neck with a
fierceness akin to desperation, pulling his mouth down to meet
hers, heedless of the hot August sun blazing down upon them.
This was her season, hers and Armande's, a season of fire. But the
frosts of autumn and the chilling winds of winter could never be
far behind.

The sun was much lower in the sky by the time Phaedra and
Armande rode back to the Heath; they shared a quiet mood born
of contentment, languorous with the afterglow of making love. As
the gates leading to the stable yard came into view, Phaedra made
one last effort to smooth back the wildly curling ends of her hair.
She feared she had even sunburned her face. She wrinkled her
nose, wincing.

Her disheveled appearance alone would not have been so bad,
but somehow Armande contrived to appear as neat as when they
had set out, his white shirt once more buttoned decorously to the
top, his hair bound trimly in place. Phaedra found this neatness
disturbing; it galled her that the passion they had shared this
afternoon in the meadow had left no visible mark upon Armande.

He glanced across at her and smiled. "It is as well we are
returning. It would seem you have a visitor."

He reined in, drawing Nemesis to a halt. Phaedra did likewise
with her gelding, staring in the direction that Armande indicated.
Another rider was just cantering into the stable yard ahead of
them, taking his sorrel mare at an easy loping pace.

Phaedra covered her eyes with one hand, squinting in the new arrival's direction. But she did not need to be that close to recognize the lazy grace with which the man rode his horse, or the familiar tumble of black curls.

" 'Tis—'tis Gilly," she said, her words coming out in a joyful breath of excitement. "My—my cousin. You remember—"

"Aye, I remember him," Armande said dryly. "Though it has been some time since I have had the pleasure of his company."

"He's been in France," Phaedra began, then stopped abruptly. The minute the words were out of her mouth, she realized her mistake. Armande looked as though she had just kicked him in the stomach. He quickly recovered, his features setting into the mask of ice she had hoped to never see again.

"To France?" he repeated. "I see."

"Nay, you don't see at all. Armande, please, 'tis not what you are thinking. Gilly left long before we ever—"

But Armande had already kicked Nemesis in the sides. The stallion eagerly responded, charging off toward the stables, leaving Phaedra in a choking cloud of dust.

Gritting her teeth, she whisked Furlong's reins, following him. Even as she did so, bands of misery seemed to tighten about her heart, leaving her chilled with premonition. Their summer idyll was about to come to an end.

Chapter Fourteen

BY THE TIME PHAEDRA REACHED THE STABLE YARD, ARMANDE HAD dismounted and flung Nemesis's reins into the hands of a waiting groom. She caught a glimpse of her lover's tight-lipped expression before he turned on his heel and strode away.

"Armande, wait," she called desperately. "I can explain." She slipped out of the saddle before Furlong came to a complete halt. Her toe caught on the train of her riding habit, sending her crashing to her knees, hands outflung to save herself. But she scarcely noticed the stinging flesh of her palms. Scrambling to her feet, she started to run after Armande as he disappeared beneath the archway which led back to the house.

But a wiry male arm caught her about the waist, halting her roughly in midstride. "Here now, Fae." Gilly's lilting voice sounded close to her ear. "Where would you be off to in such a hurry you've no time to greet your own cousin?"

Phaedra struggled to pull free. "Please, Gilly. I am glad you have returned, but let me go. I will come back directly."

"Directly, she says, and me gone on her own errand for nigh a month. Nay, I'm thinking we'd best have a chat right now, coz."

Phaedra detected a hard edge in Gilly's voice she'd never heard before. When he whipped her about to face him, all thoughts of chasing after Armande were momentarily forgotten. She stifled a gasp at the sight of the ugly bruises purpling one side of her cousin's face. His lower lip was puffed and split, one green eye fairly swollen shut. The other glared at her with no trace of Gilly's customary roguish twinkle.

Phaedra's gaze shifted downward to where his hands gripped her arms. His knuckles were raw.

"What on earth?" she breathed. He released her and she gently touched his bruised jaw. He flinched.

"Curse it, Gilly. You've been fighting again. Who the devil was it this time?"

"That scarce matters. The more important question is—what the devil have you been writing while I was gone?"

Phaedra offered him a blank stare. "Writing? I don't understand."

Gilly started to speak, but glanced at the stableboy who had come to take charge of Furlong, as though fearing the lad showed far too much interest in their conversation. Seizing Phaedra by the wrist, he hauled her into the stable itself, past the horse stalls to the small tack room at the back. It was completely deserted now, and Gilly rounded upon her with an angry whisper.

"I had just disembarked, and I barely managed to keep those rascally customs agents from having the very shirt off my back. The next I know, three dockhands approach me. 'Ye've the sound of an Irishman,' they said, none too friendly-like. 'That's right, me fine buckos,' I replied."

Phaedra grimaced, well able to imagine the defiant manner in which Gilly must have thickened his brogue.

Gilly continued, "Then the tallest one—a lout with squinty eyes like my grandmother's meanest sow—he up and says, 'Then ye must be one o' those Irish Papists that there Robin Goodfellow wants set free to vote all God-fearing English Protestants out o' the government, aye and bring in a Catholic king to murder our good King George and have us all up before the Inquisition.'"

"Why, I never wrote any such thing," Phaedra cried indignantly. "All I did was call for an end to English rule in Ireland, and say that Irish Catholics should have their rights to vote and sit in parliament returned."

"All!" Gilly groaned, slapping his palm against the side of the last stall, startling the coach horse within into emitting a frightened nicker. "You must be completely daft, woman!"

"I've written about Ireland many times before, and you've never thought so!"

"All you have done before is complain about absentee English landlords exploiting the Irish. That's another matter entirely, so it is." Gilly paced before her, raking his hands through his disorderly curls. "But when you start stirring up this Catholic business, you're like to get us all lynched. There's too many Londoners as still remember the Scottish attempt to sweep out these dull Hanoverians and bring back the Pretender. Or have you forgotten the bonny, and most Catholic, Prince Charlie?"

"But Gilly, the Jacobite rebellion was years ago."

"The English have damnable long memories. I know some as are still jawing about Bloody Mary feeding the Protestants into the fires at Smithfield. You don't understand your fellow countrymen as well as I thought, Fae. They are more afraid of Catholics than they are of the devil."

"I'm not exactly sure anymore who my fellow countrymen are," Phaedra said bitterly.

Gilly stopped his pacing long enough to give a sigh laden with exasperation. "I know you were meaning for the best when you did that bit of writing, but it hasn't worked out that way. I saw them burning copies of the *Gazetteer* down on the docks today, and I think they'd like to do the same to Robin Goodfellow and any Irishman they can get their hands on."

Phaedra sank slowly down upon a bale of hay. Burning copies of her work? They might as well set fire to herself. Never had she heard aught but popular acclaim for her daring essays. She felt strangely betrayed. She had always imagined those that bought her paper as honest, simple men whose common sense taught them to loathe injustice as much as she did. Now she saw them as naught but thick-skulled fools, understanding nothing, only looking for another excuse to riot and break heads. How cruel, how unfair it was that the winds of opinion could sway thus easily against her. Even more unfair was it that Gilly should bear the brunt of her careless pen strokes. Stricken with guilt, she glanced up at him, her eyes brimming with tears. "Then 'twas all my fault that you've been beaten. And God knows how many other innocent people will suffer. I—I never thought . . ."

Gilly scuffed the toe of his boot against the stray bits of straw littering the stable floor. "Whist now," he said gruffly. "You know caterwauling never remedied anything."

"B—but what can I do?" she asked, her voice thickened by unshed tears. "I have to try to make it right."

"I don't see as how you could be doing that."

She raised her head, swiping at her moist eyes with the back of her hand. "Well, I—I could write another article and say—"

"And say what? That you didn't really mean it—that 'tis a proper thing that a man's religion should bar him from the freedoms granted other men? Nay!" Gilly stared at a point past her, yet his gaze almost seemed to turn inward. He said softly, "Mayhap 'tis wrong of me to be scolding you. You wrote from the heart, only saying what is right."

"But you might have been killed! And a poor consolation it would be to me then, simply knowing I was right."

Gilly's swollen lip curved into a lopsided smile. He looked a trifle sheepish as he confessed, "We-ell, the affair at the docks today was not entirely one-sided. I did make a remark to the pig-eyed one concerning his mother, but I think what clinched the matter was when I made the sign of the cross over him."

"Oh, Gilly!" Phaedra choked, half-weeping, half-laughing at his recklessness. He plunked down upon the hay bale beside her, draping his arm about her shoulders.

"Ah, 'twas not much of a set-to at that. There was only the three of them, and one was but a scrawny fellow. I've been in far grander fights."

Phaedra mournfully shook her head, resisting his efforts to cheer her. "I just wish there was something I could do."

"Well, there isn't, except wait for the furor to die down. I think you'd best not write anything at all 'til then."

"I had already resolved to put an end to Robin Goodfellow, especially after meeting Jessym. Why did you never tell me he was such a horrid little man?"

"He's a businessman, hard-headed and practical, exactly what you needed." Gilly frowned. "But I wish you hadn't gone near him. He didn't know who you were, did he?"

"Of course not. I'm not that stupid. I went disguised. I only wish he didn't know you."

"I'm not worried about that. If you do mean to stop writing altogether, it seems a pity. But the name of Goodfellow will be forgotten by summer's end. Right now, tempers are running a trifle short." Gilly rubbed the back of his neck. " 'Tis this blasted heat. It does peculiar things to a man's brain." He shot her a sidelong glance out of his good eye. "You don't seem to be bearing up so well under it yourself."

Phaedra squirmed under the unexpected intensity of Gilly's

scrutiny. She wiped away the last of her tears and tugged nervously at the front of her riding jacket, almost afraid to look down in case she found one of the buttons undone.

"I—I have been fine," she stammered. "Just fine."

"Have you now? I wonder. I thought by this time you would be all over me with questions about what I learned in France."

She stood up, smoothing her skirts with a fluttery motion. "Naturally I am most curious. Why don't you come up to the house? I should like to try to do something more for that eye of yours, and I'll wager you would be glad of a cold glass of ale."

She tried to lead the way out of the stable, but Gilly caught her by the elbow, hauling her back. "What were you doing just now when I came up, tearing after that de LeCroix as though your life depended upon catching him? He looked as though he'd caught someone robbing his mother's grave."

"Was that how he looked?" Phaedra asked, unable to keep the misery out of her voice. "He was angry. He believes I sent you to France spying, hunting for proof to expose him."

"And so you did."

"No!" she fairly shouted, then remembered to lower her voice. "I mean, that was before—before—"

"Before what?"

Phaedra found she could neither answer her cousin nor continue to look him in the eye. She felt glad of her sunburned cheeks, hoping it concealed some of the blush she knew must be spreading there.

"Your intuition about the man was right, Fae," Gilly said as she remained silent. "He is an impostor, but I have no way of proving it yet. The real Armande de LeCroix thumbed his nose at his highborn relatives years ago and set off adventuring to Canada. But this fellow who claims to be Varnais bears no resemblance to the rest of that family."

"That doesn't mean anything," she said, a shade too quickly. "No one else in our family has ever had red hair, and yet that wouldn't prove me an impostor."

"Besides, de LeCroix is a man in his early forties."

"Mayhap Armande is simply one of those men who bears his age well." She became uncomfortably aware that Gilly was staring at her with growing consternation.

"So it is '*Armande*' we're calling him now, is it?"

Phaedra fidgeted with the sleeves of her jacket as though she had nothing more important on her mind than straightening the cuffs. "Well, very likely you are right about him," she said in what she hoped was a voice of airy unconcern. "But what does it truly matter? Most likely Armande . . . this man is carrying out this pose for a wager. I'm sure it's all some sort of a lark. When you get to know him—"

"A lark!" Gilly seized her chin, forcing her face upward. She tried to look indifferent, but he had known her far too long to be fooled. "Sweet Mother of God. You've gone and fallen in love with the man."

Phaedra shoved his hand away. "And what if I have?"

"What if you—" Gilly nearly choked. "Now you just listen to me, my girl. No one takes the kind of risks that man is taking for a *lark*. You, if anyone, should have the sense not to trust your heart to a man you scarce know. You allowed yourself to be charmed by one bastard, and lived to regret it."

"Armande is different," she cried, resenting the comparison. "He's nothing like Ewan—nothing at all. Armande is—is warm, sensitive, and caring."

"And a bloody damn liar!" Gilly flung up his hands, almost as though he could scarcely credit what he was hearing. "I can see that I've returned none too soon. You've taken complete leave of your senses."

"This is no longer any of your concern," she said stiffly. "I am grateful you went to France for me, but—"

"Grateful be damned." He glared at her, looking as though he would have liked to lock her up somewhere. Splaying his hands against the flat plane of his hips, he tapped his fingers. "I can see that it is high time I took charge of this matter and found exactly who the deuce this fellow is."

She thrust out her chin belligerently. "I know as much about him as I need to know. In my judgment—"

"Your judgment!" Gilly snorted. " 'Tis clear you have no judgment left at all. The man's put you under some God-cursed spell."

"I don't wish to discuss this any further."

But her haughty words might as well have gone unspoken for all the heed Gilly paid her. "What I need is free access to that damned house so that I can search his room."

"Don't you dare." Phaedra gasped. "I won't let you."

"Why not? If this fellow is as wonderful as you say, what are you so afraid I'm going to find out?"

"Nothing . . . I mean, I don't know." She could feel talons of dread sinking deep in her stomach at the mere thought of Gilly's suggestion. How could she possibly make Gilly understand why she no longer wanted to know Armande's secrets? How could she communicate her fear that a little more knowledge might be enough to separate them forever? She had been so happy—and if it took willful blindness to cling to that happiness for even a little bit longer, why then, so be it.

"Fae," Gilly pronounced the childhood nickname, his voice gone tender with concern. "You have to listen to reason . . ." He tried to put his arm about her again, but she jerked away.

"No, leave me alone. I wish you hadn't come back. I wish you would just go away again."

Hurt welled in his eyes, but his jaw stiffened into an expression every bit as stubborn as her own. "I'm not about to do that. I love you too damn much to see you setting yourself up for years of grief all over again."

"If you truly love me, you will please just—"

Her anguished words were cut off by a gruff voice booming down the length of the stables, "Eh, what's all this?"

Phaedra did not have to turn around to realize that her grandfather was bearing down upon them. She heard the floor-boards creaking beneath Sawyer Weylin's bulk. Gilly muttered, "Now there'll be the devil to pay and no mistake."

Despite her desire for Gilly to leave, Phaedra whipped around to face her grandfather. She stepped in front of her cousin like a protective mother tigress, ready to defend him against Sawyer Weylin's certain demand for Gilly's eviction.

Weylin hobbled forward, puffing with the exertion, leaning heavily upon his cane. "Why, bless me, girl," he growled. "What's come of your manners when you think to entertain honored guests down in the stables?"

Phaedra gaped at him, sure she could not have heard him correctly. She glanced at Gilly, who was looking around, as though trying to find the guest to whom her grandfather referred.

"This is your cousin, if I am not mistaken," Weylin continued in tones that sounded almost cordial. "The Honorable Mr. Patrick Fitzhurst." Although her grandfather did not go so far as to offer

Gilly his hand, Weylin leaned on his cane, his wide mouth spreading into a bland smile.

"Aye, the—the selfsame, sir," Gilly said faintly, sounding as though he were not quite sure himself.

"I do have a right to see my own cousin whenever I choose." Phaedra squared her shoulders, preparing for the familiar battle.

"So you do, my dear." Weylin reached out thick fingers and roughly tweaked her cheek. "But why keep the poor man down in the stables? Why not bring him up to the house?"

"But I—I . . . you've always said . . ." Phaedra floundered. She knew her grandfather had been quite mellow of late, but never had he regarded her with such an expression. He looked almost affectionate. He wagged his finger at her as though she were a naughty child.

"I declare," he said, turning to Gilly. "I don't know what I shall ever do with this wild granddaughter of mine. I quite despair of ever teaching her our civilized English ways. Only look at this hair."

Chuckling, Weylin yanked one of Phaedra's tangled red strands. "And I'll be hanged if she doesn't have the marquis running about now, unpowdered like a savage, as well."

Phaedra felt entirely too dumbfounded by this smiling good humor even to muster a retort. Her grandfather cocked his head, studying Gilly's face.

"Stap me, Mr. Fitzhurst, but what have you done to your head, lad? Were you in some sort of accident?"

"No, sir," Gilly drawled. "I've been having a bit of trouble with my eyesight. I seem to keep walking into some of your civilized English fists."

Weylin guffawed and slapped his thigh, shaking all over as though Gilly had made the greatest of jests. Her cousin rolled his eyes at her, indicating that he thought her grandfather had run completely mad. Phaedra was beginning to wonder about the old man's sanity herself when Weylin said, "Well, Fitzhurst, I daresay your cousin has been too modest to tell you. She's made quite a conquest this summer."

Weylin's teeth parted in a crocodilelike smile. "She will likely soon astonish you by becoming the Marchioness of Varnais."

"That would astonish me," Gilly said. He added in a low mutter that only Phaedra could hear, "I'll bet it would surprise the marquis, too, wherever he is."

Phaedra furtively trod on her cousin's foot, flashing him an angry warning look, as a quiver of uneasiness shot through her. The reason for her grandfather's abrupt change of manner was abundantly clear. She had been a fool to think the shrewd old man would not notice some of what had passed between herself and Armande this summer. Now he obviously assumed that his fondest wish was about to come true—her marriage to the Marquis de Varnais. What would his reaction be when this delusion ended, as it inevitably had to do?

But she had more immediate problems to deal with, such as Gilly's vow to search Armande's room. With a stab of dismay, she heard her grandfather inviting Gilly to come sup with them at the house that evening.

She and Gilly spoke with almost the same breath.

"I should be only to pleased to do so, sir."

"No, Gilly has another engagement!"

They glared at each other, both squaring off with grim determination.

"Well, well. Another time perhaps," Sawyer Weylin said, much to Phaedra's relief. But then he put in, "Why don't you come out tomorrow, Fitzhurst? We will be having the sort of simple entertainment out here that you Irish might enjoy. I call it my working lads' fete."

Phaedra winced. The fete. Was that to be so soon? She had nigh forgotten all about it. Once a year, in the summertime, her grandfather sponsored a holiday for many of the young apprentice boys of London. It was the only charitable sort of activity she had ever known him to indulge in.

"We'll have a luncheon under the trees," her grandfather explained, "then games of wrestling, tug-of-war, wringing the neck of a greased goose, all sort of jollifications."

Phaedra did not like the gleam of interest that sparked in Gilly's eyes. "What a grand idea, sir, to get all your household out of doors, frisking in the fields."

"Aye, they like it, sir. I realize 'tis infernally hot this year." Weylin drew forth a linen handkerchief and swabbed at his coarse, sweating countenance. "But 'twill still be a splendid opportunity for a bit of amusement."

"Splendid, indeed." Gilly's gaze narrowed so that his good eye was nearly as closed as his black one. Phaedra had no difficulty in guessing what he was planning.

She began, "Unfortunately, Gilly cannot be—"

But this time her cousin stepped in front of her, interrupting, "I accept your invitation with the greatest of pleasure, sir." His lips parted in a wolfish smile, and Phaedra was certain only she heard the double-edged meaning in his next words. " 'Tis an opportunity I would not miss for worlds."

Gilly left before Phaedra could deter him from the course she feared he meant to pursue. Her grandfather lingered in the stable until Gilly mounted his horse, thus rendering her unable to argue her cousin out of his intention to search Armande's room. When Gilly had gone, she had excused herself from her grandfather's presence as quickly as possible, unable to endure any more of his benign humor. There had been a time when she would have been more than grateful for one modicum of Sawyer Weylin's approval. But to bask in his favor now, knowing the cause of it, made her feel ill with apprehension.

Leaving the stable yard, she hastened toward the house, determined to find Armande. She had to make him understand about Gilly's journey to France, how the whole thing had been conceived long before she had fallen in love with him. But she could scarcely warn him what her cousin now planned to do. She would have to find some way of stopping Gilly herself. Aye, stop him before Armande did. Phaedra shuddered, uncertain where that chilling thought had come from, but she was quick to banish it to those same dark regions.

Much to her chagrin, she could not find Armande anywhere, neither in the house, nor upon the grounds. She even sprinted out to the man-made pond, but it was as though the man had vanished. Sweat trickling down her cheeks, she trudged back to the stairs leading to the Palladian mansion's front door when she heard the clatter of hooves on the gravel drive behind her.

She whirled about in time to see Nemesis flash past in a blur of white, heading for the Heath's main gates. Phaedra raced back down the steps, starting to shout Armande's name, but she stopped in midstep, never letting the cry escape her lips. It was hopeless. If she had admired the stallion's speed before, she was now stunned by the breakneck pace Nemesis set going down the drive. It was as though Armande rode to outrace the devil. An impossible task, Phaedra thought sadly—for she greatly feared he carried his demons within his own breast.

She dragged herself inside the front hall only to be confronted by Hester's gloating smile. "The marquess will not be dining in this evening. I daresay he's found other interests to keep him occupied."

Phaedra said nothing, determined not to accord her the satisfaction of a reply. She swept up her skirts and stalked on past. Only when she was within the confines of her own bedchamber did Phaedra permit her shoulders to droop with disappointment. So Armande did not mean to return for supper. How could she possibly bear it—to know what bitter aching thoughts he must be nourishing, and to be unable to make all right again?

Damn him, she thought, clenching her jaw. He had to come back sometime. He had taken nothing with him, so his clothes must still be here. He was simply behaving with a man's childish stubbornness. She stomped her foot, her eyes filling with angry tears. Her heart ached to think that he could believe she had spent days, nights in his arms, whispering of her love for him, all the while plotting to betray him. Well, she could be stubborn, too. She would sit up all night if she had to until he returned. She would force him to listen.

But her resolve provided cold comfort as the hours of evening dragged by. Never had she spent a more dreary evening at the Heath, dining alone with her grandfather, making halfhearted replies to his jovial teasing about Armande, watching the clock hands move as though weighted by lead.

When she discovered he had invited Jonathan, Sir Norris Byram, and a few other gentleman over for a quiet evening of cards and a late supper, Phaedra was quick to excuse herself. Rising from the table, she said, "Your pardon, Grandfather, but I fear I've had a touch too much of the sun today. My head is aching fit to burst, so I pray you will excuse me."

"O' course. 'Tis not the sort of evening's entertainment I expected to appeal to you, especially with your Armande absent." Weylin gave her a broad wink, then tossed down the rest of his glass of port and awkwardly heaved himself to his feet.

But when Phaedra curtsied and moved to go, she was surprised to feel his arm upon her elbow, detaining her.

"You needn't rush off that fast, girl. There's a matter I need to speak to you about."

"I am very tired, Grandfather. Could it not wait until the morrow?" But her protestations were ignored. Weylin insisted she accompany him as he stumped from the dining room, leading her to that one area of the house where he rarely permitted anyone, his private study.

All dark oak and leather, the chamber was the only room at the Heath that did not reflect Sawyer Weylin's love of ostentation. The room was reminiscent of his days as a simple tradesman, with its scarred desk more designed for work than show, and straight-backed, austere chairs.

Phaedra hesitated on the threshold of this forbidden sanctum, but her grandfather impatiently motioned her onward, setting down a multibranched candlestick atop the desk. Phaedra followed, searching her mind for some reason for the unexplained invitation. Could he be meaning to scold her about Gilly's visit, after all? Or mayhap, she thought, drawing her breath with a sharp intake of apprehension, he had gleaned some hint of the Robin Goodfellow business, after all.

No, if that were the case, her grandfather would hardly seem so—so— She could scarcely determine what he seemed. If it had been any man other than the blustery Sawyer Weylin, she would have described his manner as almost shy, uncertain.

He slid open the desk's center drawer, groping for something. "What is amiss, Grandfather?" she asked, unable to endure the suspense any longer. "Have the bills from the mantua-maker been too high? 'Twas you who insisted I have that last gown—"

"Certainly I insisted. Couldn't hope to have you net a marquis dressed in rags. Nay, 'tis naught to do with bills." He found what he had been searching for, but secreted it so quickly behind his back, she caught nary a glimpse. He faced her, his round countenance flushing a dull red. "I wanted to make you a small present, that's all."

All? Phaedra's mouth hung open. Her grandfather had always paid the reckonings for any expenses incurred, both hers and her late husband's. But always the gowns, the jewels, the fripperies were things she had been required to purchase for herself. Never had her grandfather troubled himself to visit the shops, select something, and present it as a gift.

"A—a present?" she faltered, still unable to credit her hearing. "But why?"

Her question restored some of his bluster. "Why? You silly chit! Because I chose to—that's why. Here, take it."

He held out a velvet-covered jewel case. When she continued to stare, he thrust it at her, growling, "Take it! Take it, I said!"

Her fingers closed hesitantly over the rectangular box. Knowing her grandfather's tastes, she half-imagined some gaudy jewel, flashy and too expensive. But when she opened the box, it revealed a strand of pearls, each bead a perfect circle of milky-white translucence.

"They—they're beautiful," she stammered, feeling quite at a loss as to what to say or think.

"Your grandmother's," he said.

She gaped at him again, overcome with astonishment.

"You did have a grandmother, you know." His bushy brows drew together in a fierce glower. "I didn't produce your father all on my own."

" 'Tis only that you've never mentioned her," Phaedra said wonderingly, caressing her fingertip over the smooth, hard surface of the pearls. "I don't believe I even know her name."

"Corinda. She died young—too young."

"Father never told me anything about her, either."

"Didn't know anything to tell. He was but a lad of three at the time." Weylin lapsed into a frowning silence, and Phaedra thought that was all he meant to offer on the subject. The candlelight played harsh tricks with his face, making the fleshy pockets about his eyes and jowls appear to droop, adding years to his already age-lined face, his shrewd eyes dulled by an expression of remembered pain.

Phaedra longed to know more about the young wife he had lost, but doubted that he would tell her. He rarely spoke about his past, except to boast of his financial achievements. She was surprised when he continued to speak.

"Your grandmother and I—we didn't live in a house like this one—nothing even approaching it." He glanced about him as though half-expecting the Heath's magnificence to disappear at any moment. "Two rooms is what Corie and I shared, but we made do. I was but a journeyman brewer then. My wages didn't stretch to even an adequate supply of coal to heat the place."

Weylin crossed his beefy arms, rubbing them as he stared into the candle flame. "Those dratted rooms were never warm enough for Corie. I always had to keep telling the foolish wench not to huddle so close to the fire. 'Mind your petticoats, Corie, afore you scorch em.' Chit of her age should have had more sense."

Phaedra had the uncomfortable feeling her grandfather had left her, journeying down the road of a far-distant past, a place where he did not care to dwell. He emitted a heavy sigh.

" 'Twas powerful cold that winter. Corie had been suffering from a chill, and she was always bundling up the boy in her own cloak. She—she was alone that day, no one else with her but the lad. I supposed she just couldn't get warm enough, and I wasn't there . . . wasn't there to warn her." He swallowed thickly.

"They reckoned afterwards that the hem of her dress must've caught fire, and she pure panicked—just ran and ran. They found her facedown in the snow—" Weylin broke off, blinking hard. "Demned foolish child." Abruptly he turned his back on Phaedra.

Her hands clenched tightly about the jewel box, and as she stared down at the pearls, it was almost as though she could see a reflection caught in each tiny lustrous bead, that of a sweet-faced young girl, with her father's gentle eyes and delicate features and her hair . . . Phaedra scarcely knew why, but without ever having set eyes upon Corinda Weylin, she felt certain her grandmother had had flowing masses of red hair.

Phaedra longed to go to her grandfather and wrap her arms about him in a comforting gesture. But she had been thrust aside too many times to risk it. Weylin stood, with his hands clasped behind his back. He said gruffly, "I always told Corie one day I'd be able to give her whatever she wanted, furs, fine carriages, jewels. But there was only one bit of finery she ever hankered after, and that was a rope of pearls. I was never able to—so now I'm giving them to you."

"Thank you, Grandpapa," Phaedra said. She at last dared to plant a quick kiss upon his rough cheek. He did not push her away, but he squirmed with obvious discomfort.

"No need to make a fuss. You've turned out a good, obedient wench, so you have—far more sensible than your father. I could have made a grand gentleman of him if he had had the wit to let me. But you're going to surpass any hope I ever had of him."

A smile played about Weylin's lips. "The Marchioness de Varnais. Not bad for a brewer's granddaughter."

Phaedra abruptly set the pearls back on the desk, the poignant pleasure she had taken in the gift fading. "The marquis has not favored me with a proposal yet, Grandfather."

"He will." Weylin nodded confidently. "I've seen the look in his eye when he gazes upon you."

Not lately you haven't, she thought. Her heart ached with the wish that it all could be exactly as her grandfather fancied—that Armande could be who he claimed to be, and so much in love with her that he would sweep her off to his chateau, there to live happily ever after. Impossible. They were bound up in such a fog of lies and deceit that there appeared no hope of lasting love or happiness.

She was startled from her melancholy reflection when Sawyer Weylin clapped his hands together. He rubbed them almost as though the brisk gesture could cleanse him of the tender emotion he had not liked to reveal.

"You'd best hie yourself off to an early bed. We shall have a busy day on the morrow, with all the young lads frisking about."

"Aye, the apprentices' fete," she said without much enthusiasm.

But Weylin's eyes sparkled with boyish eagerness. "I vow the boys will be in high spirits, glad of a holiday. I would have myself all those years I slaved beneath old Master Hutchin's lash."

Phaedra could only stare at her grandfather. He was a man of so many odd contrasts. She wondered if she would ever understand him. "'Twas a most hard road, was it not, Grandfather?" she asked thoughtfully. "The road that led you to all of this."

"'Deed it was, girl."

"Then I don't understand why you bear so little sympathy for other unfortunate men—men such as that Tom Wilkins."

Weylin gave a disdainful sniff. "I've no pity for any paupers, save mayhap the children. If I could make my way alone, so can other men. I daresay you think me a ruthless old man, but I always worked hard, never begged, never did aught I'd regret."

He scowled suddenly, a shade of uneasiness beclouding his eyes. "Except once—" He broke off and shuffled away from her, snatching up the branch of candles.

"We can't be talking here all night. My guests will be arriving. Come along, girl, and don't forget your pearls."

Phaedra would as soon have left the pearls, grieved as she was by the feeling that she accepted them under false pretenses. She knew quite well she would never be the Marchioness de Varnais. But at Weylin's insistence, she guiltily tucked the box under her arm. At the foot of the stairs stretching above them, her grandfather bid her a curt good night.

Too hard to feel sympathy for others, Sawyer Weylin might

have been astonished to realize how much pity Phaedra felt for him, as he watched her retreat up the steps. Despite his satin-clad bulk, he appeared quite small, nigh swallowed up in the vastness of his great hall, a lonely old man clutching his silver candlestick. Mayhap if she did manage to pursue her own dreams of finding her fortune, one day she might also be like . . .

No. Phaedra thrust aside the thought and fled the rest of the way to her chamber, where Lucy helped her undress for bed. When the girl had gone, Phaedra sprawled out on her mattress, leaving the silken bed-curtains flung wide. For what seemed like hours, she tensed, listening for any sound that Armande had returned to the room next to hers.

Exhausted by the events of the day, she felt more tired than she would admit, her eyes stinging beneath her stubborn determination to keep them open. The chamber felt overly warm, despite the fact her windows were flung wide. She kicked away the clingy satin sheet and tossed fretfully upon her pillow. In an effort to stay awake, she tried staring out the window at the moon, a golden disk set amidst a diamond scattering of stars. 'Twas a beautiful summer night. "Far too beautiful to waste in such a foolish misunderstanding, Armande de LeCroix," she spoke aloud, wanting to be angry. But her words, as they echoed in the empty bedchamber, sounded unbearably sad. A melancholy thought washed over her; this was all her relationship with Armande had ever been, one long, wretched misunderstanding.

She drifted away, not into a peaceful deep slumber, but a twilight land of tormenting dreams, haunting night visions. She was skating, wearing a gown that shimmered about her like spun silver, gliding upon endless reaches of a lake layered with crystalline ice set beneath a steel-gray sky. She was dancing, soaring in the arms of a stranger garbed for a masquerade.

Again and again, she tried to draw away from him, the ice beneath her feet so thin, she could see her own reflection a dozen times over trapped beneath the surface. But like the pull of a strong tide, she could not resist the warm strength of the hand closing over hers.

Then she heard a voice, oh so far away, intoning her name, "Phaedra." She could see Gilly paused on the edge of the lake shore, struggling to reach her. No! No, go back, she wanted to cry. The ice would never bear his weight. But try as she would to shout, when her lips parted, no sound would come. Gilly loomed closer and closer to where she linked hands with the stranger. He swirled between them, breaking their hands apart, trying to rip the stranger's mask away.

Everything was moving so slowly. Why couldn't she stop Gilly? The mask tore, coming away in his hands, and she found she was gazing at . . . Armande, his eyes clouded with despair, his arms stretching out to her. She tried to run to him, but the ice was breaking, dissolving beneath her feet. As she plunged downward into the dark, chilling waters, she saw shards of the ice driving into the depths of Armande's eyes, leaving a crimson trickle of blood.

"No!" Phaedra whimpered, flailing her arms, forcing herself awake. The dream yet clung to her while she stared into the darkness of her bedchamber, still feeling herself lost beneath the icy waters of the lake. She lay panting for a few moments, her body covered with a fine sheen of cold sweat. With a low groan, she sat up, rubbing her temples as though to chase away the last fragments of the nightmare. The clock upon her mantel chimed twice. Was it really two o'clock? She didn't think she could have slept that long, had not wanted to. She had been waiting . . . waiting for Armande.

Feeling yet groggy, she staggered toward the connecting door and placed her ear to the panel. All was silent within Armande's room. She turned the handle and pushed, but the door did not yield. She tried again, but as she came more fully alert, she realized Armande had bolted it from his side.

"Damn you, Armande," she whispered. Regardless of who heard her, she was driven by an unreasoning urge to pound on the door, force him to come and let her in.

Just as she raised her fist, she was startled by the sound of a high-pitched laugh that raised the hairs along the back of her neck. Her heart racing, she glanced fearfully over her shoulder, half-dreading to find some mocking specter risen up behind her.

That laugh, though, had been far too real, far too like one she had heard before in the broad light of day. The sound of violin strings being grated by a clumsy hand at the bow . . . Hester Searle's laughter.

Phaedra froze, waiting for the sound to be repeated, but she heard naught but the distant hum of voices drifting through her bedchamber window. She skittered over to the open casement, keeping well back into the shelter of the sheer white curtains.

Peering toward the ground below, she saw no one in the moonlit stretch of lawn or the graveled walk that led to the rose gardens behind the kitchen. The gardens themselves were a shadowy outline of rustling shrubs, but above the whispers of the leaves, Hester's voice cut through the night again.

Her words carried up to Phaedra in indistinguishable snippets. ". . . handsomely, sir . . . wouldn't want to . . ."

Someone answered her, the second voice, low and deep, surely a man's. Abandoning caution, Phaedra leaned out the window, straining to hear, but she could not decipher a word being said.

Hester spoke again. ". . . not wait longer. Tomorrow."

Her mysterious companion rumbled a reply, but was cut off by Hester's shriek. "Tomorrow!"

Phaedra could hear the crunch of a boot, then the rustling of the garden hedges. She craned her neck, but minutes ticked by and no one emerged from the opening between the shrubs. The night resumed its silence, and Phaedra could only assume that Hester and her companion had gone out by the other side.

Frustrated, she drew back from the window. What witchery was that woman up to now, conversing so late with a man in the gardens? Phaedra stifled a yawn, turning what few words she had caught over in her mind, but could make little sense of them. She could not even be sure from the tone of Hester's voice—never genteel—whether the woman had been threatening someone or simply passing along information. Only one word had stood out with undisputed clarity—tomorrow.

Wearily, Phaedra dragged herself to her bed. Her mind was far too unfocused for her to sort the matter out tonight. As she stretched out upon the sheets, her gaze traveled wistfully toward the connecting door.

'Twas obvious she would have to wait until the morning's light before she found the solution to the worries besetting her. Tomorrow, she would take care of everything, Armande, Gilly, Hester . . . tomorrow.

Phaedra closed her eyes, but as tired as she was, sleep eluded her. An absurd thought kept nagging at her.

Tomorrow might be too late.

Chapter Fifteen

"VOICES IN THE GARDEN LAST NIGHT?" HESTER SEARLE'S MOUTH SET in a prim line, but the morning light streaming through the kitchen window fully betrayed the sly mirth playing about the corners of her eyes. "Why, I'm sure I don't know what yer ladyship would be meaning."

"And I am perfectly sure that you do." Phaedra whisked past the spit boy turning a haunch of beef over the kitchen's massive hearth. She followed Hester round the broad oak table heaped with biscuits, cakes, and enough hunks of gingerbread to feed an army of hungry boys.

Hester reached for a straw basket, affecting to count the currant cakes.

"I heard you talking to someone. A man," Phaedra persisted, her temper fraying. She'd had too little sleep, and now was oppressed by the heat rolling over her in waves from the cook's fires. "It must have been past two o'clock in the morning."

"I am not the sort of woman to be found entertainin' gentlemen in the gardens after midnight." Hester sniffed. "It must've been one of the parlor maids or—"

"I know your voice quite well," Phaedra said. "It was you, although I could not tell who the man was."

"Couldn't you?" Hester's smile was smug. She shrugged her blade-thin shoulders. "Yer ladyship must have been dreaming, 'tis all that I can say."

"Damnation! I was not dreaming!" Phaedra slammed the palm

of her hand upon the table with a force that nearly toppled a stack of cakes. Hester merely bustled past, issuing commands to the kitchen girls to look sharp and see that all the pastries were packed into the baskets.

"I've got to make sure the master gets his breakfast afore all those young devils of his descend upon us." Reaching for the silver coffee tray, Hester shot a sly glance at Phaedra as she addressed one of the footmen. "John, there'll be no need fer ye to set a place for his lordship the marquess. I'll doubt he'll be bearing much appetite for his breakfast. Proper done in, he looked when he returned."

Phaedra, who felt on the verge of seizing Hester and shaking the truth from her, paused, thrown off-balance by the reference to Armande.

"H—his lordship has returned?" she asked, trying to hide her eagerness.

"Late last night. If ye had truly been awake, *as* yer ladyship claims, I don't doubt but what ye would have heard him, yer rooms being so close and all." Balancing the coffee tray, Hester disappeared through the kitchen door, a smirk upon her face.

Phaedra let her go. Hester's moonlit tryst in the garden dwindled to insignificance when set beside the news of Armande's return. She had tried his door first thing this morning, even risking a light knock. But the room had responded with the same grim silence as it had known in the days after Ewan Grantham's death. Phaedra had despaired, fearing that Armande would never return. Mayhap he thought she and Gilly had been about to expose him.

She was therefore filled with great relief at Hester's seemingly casual information. But she was not about to humble herself further to Hester by asking after Armande's whereabouts. Leaving the kitchen, she obtained the information she wanted from Peter.

Aye, the footman informed her, his lordship was indeed up and about. In the music gallery, so Peter believed. Phaedra ran toward the back of the house and quietly opened the door to the salon. The long gallery was as still and empty as the nave of some great church on a working day. The discordant notes being sounded upon the spinet were all the more jarring, almost a mockery of the chamber's solemn aura of stateliness.

Half-turned away from her, Armande stood over the instrument, his features beclouded despite the sunshine pouring in through the tall French windows, his fingers plucking listlessly at the keys. One look at him was enough to send Phaedra's heart sinking to her toes. He was garbed in a blue embroidered frock coat and cream-colored breeches, all traces of his dark hair hidden by his powdered wig. Gone was the bronzed sun god whose loving had warmed her but yesterday in the meadow's sweet grass. Resurrected in his place was the lord of winter, come to chill her heart.

Phaedra sighed, pulling the door shut behind her. Armande's head snapped up at the sound. She braced herself for his most frozen stare, but the expression on his face was one she'd never seen there before. His eyes were frighteningly empty.

"I have been looking everywhere for you," she said, wanting to rush into his arms. Instead, she managed a nervous, half-coaxing smile. "I knew you were fond of music, but I didn't know you played."

"I don't," he said, moving away from the instrument. He swept her a mechanical bow. Her ears, fine-tuned to every nuance of his voice, caught the edge of sarcasm as he said. *"Bon jour, madame. I trust you—"*

"Don't!" she said sharply. She had to suppress a strong urge to fly to him, wrench the wig from his head, kiss away the jaded weariness that marred his features. "You know I hate that pretense."

"I thought it was only in bed that the performance didn't amuse you." His attempt at a languid drawl did not quite disguise the bitterness behind his sneering words.

He tried to hold her at a distance, but Phaedra refused to let him. She flung her arms about him, pressing her face against his waistcoat. The satin felt too cool, too slick beneath her cheek, his chest as unyielding as iron. He made no move to thrust her away, but his arms did not close about her, either.

"Please, Armande. I know you are feeling hurt, betrayed. But you will not give me a chance to explain. You were gone nearly all night. I feared that you were never coming back."

"I almost didn't. Then I remembered why I had come to London. I've taken too many risks to be undone by you now. I simply never realized how much *his* granddaughter you are."

Her head snapped back to regard him with frowning puzzlement. "What is that supposed to mean?"

He didn't answer her, merely waiting with studied patience for her to release him. But she clung to him more tightly, fearing that if she let him go now, it might be the last time she ever touched him.

"So what did your Irish spy find out in France?" he asked as though the answer really held little interest for him. "Obviously not enough for you to go running to your grandfather and have me whipped at cart tail's end for the low impostor that I am."

"Gilly found out nothing that I didn't already know," she said. "He went to France the same day I tried to have you arrested for theft—before I ever came to your bed, before I even dared whisper to myself that I loved you."

She searched his face, praying for but one sign that he believed her words. But his eyes were like blue steel. She continued desperately, "I spent yesterday afternoon trying to persuade Gilly you really are the Marquis de Varnais, deliberately attempting to deceive him. Gilly, my dearest friend, who has always been like my own brother."

Armande raised an eyebrow. "And did he believe you?"

"No." Her mouth quivered into a lopsided smile. "I'm such a terrible liar."

"One improves with practice." Armande's hard words seemed to mock himself as well as her.

"The important question is whether you believe me," she said. "You cannot think that I seduced you in order to—"

" 'Tis scarcely important whether I believe you or not."

"Not important?" He had not moved a muscle, but he might as well have struck her. "How can you say that when 'tis wrenching us apart?"

"You cannot wrench apart what never has truly been together." His words, laced with disillusionment, filled her with despair. "We have been living in a fool's paradise, my dear. But even fools must eventually grow wise."

Her arms slowly slipped from around his neck, dropping back to her sides. It was as though his coldness had finally seeped into her own soul, leaving her numb.

"Was it so foolish," she whispered, "your loving me?"

"The most stupid thing I've ever done." His harsh answer caused her to flinch. "Love cannot survive where there is no trust. I realized that at the outset and should have spared us both this misery. There is no way you can ever have any faith in me, no way you will ever be able to trust me."

She drew herself upright, stung by his words. All these weeks she had demanded no explanations, never even pleaded to know his real name. What more proof of her love and trust did the man require?

Yet her anger was tinged with guilty realization. Aye, she had willingly closed her eyes and turned her head the other way. But mayhap self-deceit was not the same as trusting, putting complete faith in the man one loved. She had held back as much from Armande as he from her.

Seized by a sudden determination, her hands clenched into fists. "You give up on our love far too easily, Armande de LeCroix," she said. "If it is trust you want, damn it, I shall bring it to you. The kind you can hold between your hands."

She scarcely took time to note his bewildered frown as she ran from the room. With her customary impulsiveness, she rushed to her garret, unlocked the desk drawer and yanked it open. Grabbing up a handful of the ribbon-bound papers, she raced back down to the music gallery.

Armande hovered uncertainly upon the threshold as though he had been on the verge of coming after her. Phaedra shoved him back into the room, closing the door.

"Here," she said. "This will show you how much I trust you." She tugged the ribbons off the paper, then slapped the unfolded parchment upon a table before Armande, almost as though she were flinging down a gauntlet.

Armande regarded her uneasily. "Phaedra, I don't understand—"

"Just read," she commanded.

He picked up the sheets with reluctance and skimmed the black ink, his brow furrowing into an even deeper frown. "I still don't understand. These seem to be some sort of political tracts—pages of text copied from—from what is that blasted paper? The *Gazetteer*."

"Not copies," she said. "The original drafts. What you see before you is the hand of Robin Goodfellow."

She waited breathlessly for his reaction, but he still looked confused.

"My hand," she added softly.

The truth broke over him at last, his eyes flashing to meet hers in a startled expression. "You—you are Robin Goodfellow!"

"That's right. So never again tell me that I cannot trust you.

You are holding enough there to ruin me—aye, and my grandfather, as well."

All color drained from his face as Armande clutched the sheets. The first feelings of doubt began to niggle at Phaedra. She had not known quite what to expect from Armande at this moment. Amazement certainly, but where was his realization of how much she did love him? She had expected even a little praise perhaps, some pride in those achievements of her mind that he had always claimed to admire. What she had not expected was this silence.

"Don't you understand what I have given you?" she cried. " 'Tis my life bound up in those pages—"

" 'Tis you who do not understand!"

Phaedra recoiled before the sudden fury that flared in Armande's eyes, striking her like a jagged edge of lightning. It was a fury not unmixed with fear, the despair of a man who finds himself irrevocably trapped.

"Damn you! I was trying to make it as plain as possible that you dare not trust me." He flung the papers back at her and they fluttered to her feet, like leaves tossed by the wind. "If you have any more cursed secrets, keep them to yourself!"

He turned on his heel and stormed from the room, slamming the door behind him. Phaedra stared after him, scarcely daring to draw breath. She had begun to tremble so that her legs felt likely to give beneath her, but even so she could not tear her eyes from the doorway through which Armande had disappeared.

At last, like one coming slowly awake, she bent and began gathering up the scattered papers. Too numbed by shock to even cry, she felt rather like a gambler who had taken an enormous risk and lost. Most disturbing of all, she wasn't even certain how high the stakes had been.

Phaedra snapped open her parasol to shield her face from the afternoon sun beating down upon the lawn, hoping that it shielded her unhappy expression as well. She picked her way past her grandfather's servants struggling to clear away the remains of the fete luncheon.

The table looked like a field of battle at the end of a fray, with linen cloths hanging askew, some of the crockery broken, and forks strewn through a trail of cake crumbs like discarded weapons. But the combatants had not retired. Tearing past Phaedra's skirts whooped some fifty boys, their voices ranging from the childish treble to those cracking on the brink of manhood. Most of them were from hard-working families known to Sawyer Weylin, lads he and Jonathan Burnell had seen placed beneath the tutelage of good, honest masters to learn a trade.

Some of the boys still crammed their cheeks full of gingerbread, while others wrestled, traded cuffs, or played at tag, as frolicsome and clumsy as puppies in a kennel. Phaedra started back as a horseshoe whizzed past her nose.

Several stout lads who were supposed to be playing at quoits were growing more unruly by the minute. The game that had resulted in the misfired shoe broke into a bout of fisticuffs. Grinning like a boy himself, Sawyer Weylin guffawed, encouraging the rough-and-ready behavior. It was left to a harassed-looking Jonathan and one of the footmen to separate the small pugilists before any came away with a bloodied nose.

"Tell Mrs. Searle to fetch more cakes for the lads," Sawyer Weylin bellowed. "Blast it all, where is that woman?"

"More cake is the last thing they need," Jonathan snapped. The heat appeared to be affecting even his solemn composure, bringing an unaccustomed tinge of color to his sallow cheeks. He tried desperately to catch Phaedra's eye.

"Phaedra, I must talk to you," he whispered as she glided past, but she ducked deeper into the shade of her parasol.

Her mind was yet too full of the scene with Armande so that she scarcely heeded Jonathan or the boys' antics, not even when one bold rascal let loose a frog near her petticoats.

"You must have been mad." She rebuked herself for perhaps the dozenth time. "Whatever possessed you to do that? Confess to Armande that you were Robin Goodfellow?"

And yet, she thought, why should she continue to fret so over the incident? 'Twas not as if Armande were the enemy she had once imagined him to be. Nay, this was the man who had cradled her in his arms so many hot summer nights, vowing his love for her. And she had believed him.

If only his reaction to her secret had not been so strange. She had never seen such anger in his eyes, an anger that she sensed had been directed against himself as well as her.

Her gaze strayed to where Armande stood at the far edge of the lawn. No trace of his wrath remained now as he tried to help a chubby, freckle-faced lad string a bow that was much too large for him. The boy thrust his tongue between his teeth, puffing and turning red as he tried to bend the supple wood back far enough to slip the string into the notch.

"I doubt biting your tongue off will help, *monsieur*," she heard Armande say. The teasing light springing into his blue eyes played havoc with her heart. How oft had she glimpsed that same expression in the hours when they exchanged banter—banter that so frequently concealed a growing desire.

"A little more muscle is what is wanted." Armande's strong, slender fingers closed over the small pudgy ones, helping the child accomplish the task. He handed the boy the arrow, and then tousled his hair. "Now don't shoot any of your comrades, *hein?*" He smiled as the boy gave his promise and ran off.

Hope fluttered inside Phaedra. At this moment Armande looked very like the man who had so tenderly lifted her out of the saddle but yesterday afternoon. She rustled toward him, but his smile faded the instant their eyes met. It was the Marquis de Varnais who raised his head and attempted to stride past her.

His rejection of her pierced her more keenly than any wound Ewan, with all of his studied cruelties, had ever been able to inflict.

"You needn't take to your heels the instant I approach, *monsieur*," she said with a brittle laugh. "I assure you, I don't intend to burden you with any more of my secrets."

"I pray you don't have any more such to reveal," he muttered. He had started to move away, when he turned and came back as though drawn to her side much against his will. "I am sorry if I lost my temper with you earlier." His apology was as stiff as his manner. "You—you took me by surprise when—"

Armande's eyes darkened as he bent forward, his voice hard and bitter. "Why in blazes did you choose to confide in me now? What were you hoping for—some trade? Your secrets for mine?"

"And you presume to lecture me on the subject of trust!" Phaedra arched her brow, trying to look scornful—but it was difficult with tears burning behind her eyes. "No, *monsieur*, I was not seeking a trade. I merely had some foolish notion 'twould help if I offered you proof of my love. I fear I always have been too stupid to know when matters are past mending."

This time it was she who tried to walk away from him, placing her parasol between them like a shield.

"Phaedra." He breathed her name, but whatever Armande had

been about to say was blotted out by the sound of another voice, whose lilting notes carried above even the shouts of the boys.

"Top o' the afternoon to you, Master Weylin. Master Burnell. 'Tis that sorry I am to be late. I can see I've been missing a feast fine enough to take the shine out of Paddy Duggan's wake."

Phaedra whipped about in time to see her cousin, resplendent in a scarlet frock coat, sweeping off his three-cornered hat and favoring Sawyer Weylin with a jaunty bow. Gilly! The bruises marring his eye and jaw had faded to an unbecoming shade of yellow, but they did naught to tone down his impudence.

She had nigh forgotten he was coming, as well as his reasons for doing so. Never had she thought the time would come when she would view the sight of those sparkling green eyes with such dismay.

She glanced at Armande and saw him go rigid at Gilly's approach, the wary expression upon his face far from welcoming. Her stomach knotted tighter.

After greeting her grandfather and Jonathan, Gilly vaulted toward her in three quick strides. "Phaedra, my sweetest coz. Sure and you're looking as fair as the shamrocks in the springtime." Despite his jovial expression and the damnable thick brogue he was putting on for her grandfather's benefit, she saw the hard glint of determination in Gilly's eyes. His resolution to search Armande's room had not abated a jot in the past twenty-four hours. That was all she needed. Armande was already grim with his suspicions of her.

Her cousin nigh bruised her ribs with his rough embrace. She hissed in his ear, "Gilly, I swear if you go near the house today, I will break your head."

He merely laughed, giving her chin a hard pinch. "Ah, sweet, indeed, and a tongue to match."

He turned to Armande, sweeping into a mocking bow. "By all the saints, if it isn't his lardship, the Marquis de Varnais. A good day to your worship. You're looking elegant enough to coax the snakes back into Ireland."

"Mr. Fitzhurst." Armande's smile was cold. "You seem to become more Irish each time I meet you."

"Ah, well, 'tis a damn sight cleverer than becoming more *English*."

Phaedra's breath snagged in her throat, but Armande's only acknowledgment of her cousin's biting comment was a slight twitch at the corner of his mouth. He bowed stiffly and tried to move on his way, but Gilly barred his path, her cousin's chin tilted to a most pugnacious angle.

"I have recently returned from France. A charmin' country. But sure and I don't have to be telling your lardship that."

Armande's lips compressed into a taut line as he nodded in polite agreement. Once again he tried to sidestep her cousin, but Gilly laid a restraining hand upon his arm.

"I even had the good fortune to travel by your lardship's own estates, and what do you fancy I—"

"Gilly!" Phaedra cried. She sensed the belligerence coursing beneath her cousin's lazy smile, the tension masked behind Armande's expression of indifference.

Armande removed Gilly's hand from his sleeve in an elaborately courteous manner. "I am glad you had such a rewarding journey," he said. He took out his snuffbox, flicking open the lid, the gesture laden with weariness almost as though he himself had conceived a distaste for the role he had to play. "You have not been spending your money unwisely again, I hope?"

"After all your grand advice when last we met? Certainly not." Gilly sneered. "I expect far greater results from my investments this time."

Armande closed the snuffbox with a click. Phaedra wondered if he realized he had forgotten to pretend to take a pinch.

"Indeed, Mr. Fitzhurst?" he said. He looked directly into Gilly's eyes, but there was no rancor in Armande's gaze or his words as he added, "Well, I wish you a long life in which to enjoy it."

Gilly blinked, astonished; and in that moment Armande managed to walk past him with an air of quiet dignity. Her cousin let out his breath in a long, low whistle.

"What a cool devil! I think I have been rather silkily threatened, but stap me, if for an instant I didn't fancy his good wishes were sincere."

Phaedra glared at him, realizing how her hands had been trembling during the exchange. It had been like watching two duelists facing each other and wondering who would be goaded into striking first. "I shouldn't wonder if he had threatened you when you were doing your damnedest to provoke him."

"I was only seeking to know the man better, my dear." His innocent expression was belied by the acid in his tones. "Bring forth his warm, caring side you've been telling me so much about. Perchance I'll become better acquainted with himself before the afternoon is out."

Phaedra placed her hands upon her hips. "*Perchance* you'd best stay away from Armande—and the house."

"Oh, I promise to stay away from *him*."

"I warn you, Gilly," she said, "I will be watching you."

He shot her an aggravating smile and sauntered away, twirling his hat. She had little choice but to dog his footsteps, fearful that at any moment he intended to slip off to the Heath.

While Gilly joined a group of the older lads in playing at ninepins, she hovered in the background, taking care to keep her cousin constantly in sight, all the while affecting a deep interest in the game.

When someone tugged at her sleeve, she pulled away without glancing around.

"Phaedra," Jonathan's voice pleaded. "You must give me but a moment of your time."

"Not now," she started to protest, then swallowed the words as she recalled rather guiltily that she tended to avoid Jonathan too often of late. The poor man appeared nigh ill with worry over something. She sighed, offering her hand in a gesture of acquiescence, permitting Jonathan to lead her to a bench where she could still keep Gilly within her line of vision.

Knowing Jonathan, she was certain whatever had caused this state of anxiety would prove nothing more than a tempest in a teapot. She did not even feel startled when Burnell announced gravely, "Phaedra, I am afraid you may be in danger."

Phaedra forced a smile to her lips, her eyes drawn to where Gilly hurled the ball, scattering the heavy wooden pins. "Jonathan, I assure you, despite the heat, I am not planning to go swimming or do anything else which might distress—"

"I am worried about this Robin Goodfellow affair," he interrupted with a sharp edge to his voice. She glanced up at him in surprise.

"Phaedra, 'tis that last piece you wrote. You have caused riots in the city."

"I know all about that. Gilly told me."

"Did he also tell you Jessym's house was attacked by a mob last night, the windows broken while they howled for the real name of Robin Goodfellow?"

"N-no." She faltered. "I am sorry to hear that. I trust Jessym was unharmed?"

"Aye, but I hear he would sell his soul to reveal the identity of Goodfellow and deflect the anger from his own door."

"He can sell away," Phaedra said. "As long as the only two people who . . ." Her words trailed off as she was about to offer Jonathan the familiar assurance only he and Gilly knew her secret. But there was now a third. Armande. But, she assured herself, no matter how angry he was with her now, he would never betray her. Never! Even if he had ceased to love her, what possible reason could he have for doing so?

"Everything will be all right," she told Jonathan, although the words sounded weak even to her. "This will all pass. And I have decided never to write as Goodfellow again."

"Have you, my dear?" Jonathan brightened. She had never seen his careworn features suffused with such relief. At least, she thought wryly, her decision to fling aside her only chance for independence had made someone happy.

He clasped her hand between his own. "Such a wise choice. I am so glad of it." He immediately sobered. "Of course, I realize what the writing meant to you. Your husband has left you in such dire straits, and Sawyer sometimes can be so difficult."

Such a mild description of her grandfather's irascible temper almost made Phaedra laugh aloud, but she suddenly became uncomfortably aware of the way Jonathan was stroking her hand. It was the lightest of touches, and yet somehow it raised gooseflesh along her arm.

"A woman as young as yourself," he said timidly, "must marry again one day."

Phaedra gently but firmly disengaged her hand. "You are beginning to sound like Grandfather. He has been doing his best to thrust me into the marquis's path all summer."

"Varnais?" Jonathan paled. "Surely not! Such a strange, cold man."

Phaedra stiffened, not liking Jonathan's assessment of the man she loved any more than she had Gilly's.

All the worry lines returned to crease Jonathan's brow. "Blast Sawyer and his cursed ambition. How could he even think of forcing you to marry that—that—"

"Do stop fretting, Jonathan. No one is forcing me to marry anyone."

"But I know too well what Sawyer is like when he gets one of these notions in his head. Nothing ever stops him."

"Jonathan, I assure you," Phaedra said wearily. "I will never be the Marchioness de Varnais."

She regretted she had ever mentioned the matter, only seeking to divert Jonathan's thoughts from the Robin Goodfellow affair. Now she had given him something else to worry about. At times his concern for her could be almost oppressive.

"I am sorry, Phaedra," he said. "I do not meant to annoy you. 'Tis just that I would do anything in the world to protect you."

"Anything," he added with passionate emphasis.

"I know that, Jonathan." She sighed, making one last effort to dispel his anxiety and coax a smile from the solemn man. "Long before Grandfather bullies me into marrying anyone, I will have run off to become a highwayman, just as my cousin and I have always planned." She nodded to where Gilly played at ninepins.

Where Gilly *should have been* playing. Phaedra froze, her heart giving an apprehensive lurch. Her cousin's place had been taken by a chubby boy with a jam-smeared face.

Phaedra jerked to her feet, glancing wildly about her. But her desperate gaze encountered naught but a sea of boys, the florid face of her grandfather urging them on in a tug of war, the servants bringing forth more cakes and ices. Gilly was nowhere in sight. Nor could she see Armande.

"Damn him!" she said through clenched teeth, although she was not certain which man she cursed. Mayhap both of them. Not taking the time to offer a word of explanation to the startled Jonathan, Phaedra tore off running toward the house. She heard him desperately calling her name, but she dared not stop.

She was out of breath when she reached the set of long doors that brought her in at the back of the Green Salon. Clutching her aching side, she hastened into the front hall.

The house was hauntingly silent except for the sound of her own ragged breathing. She might have fancied herself in some abandoned castle with all the grim accoutrements of war gathering dust upon the walls above her. So quiet, so still was the vast stone chamber, as still as that long ago night when James Lethington must have hidden behind the armor, the mace clutched in sweating palms—

Phaedra darted up the stairs almost as though the armored suit itself could come to life and pursue her. She buried her fear beneath angry muttering. " 'Tis I who shall be doing the murdering this time. I will kill Gilly when I find him."

That is, if Armande had not already done so. She suppressed the horrid thought, hating herself for even imagining her love capable of such a thing.

The deathlike silence pervaded the landing as well. Had not one servant remained behind to guard the place? Any other time, Phaedra thought bitterly, that wretched Hester Searle would be lurking about to intercept her cousin. Where was the blasted woman the one time she needed her?

Phaedra crept toward Armande's bedchamber and pressed her ear to the door. She did not know whether to feel relieved or more alarmed when she detected not a single sound. She tried the door and found it unlocked. Inching it open a crack, she risked a peek inside.

"Gilly?" she whispered, but received no answer. The room appeared undisturbed, Armande's scant belongings untouched, even down to the small locked chest upon the dressing table. Still, Phaedra did not quite trust her wily cousin not to be hiding somewhere, merely waiting for her to leave.

She tiptoed into the room, peering into the dressing chamber, behind the draperies and the wardrobe, beginning to feel rather foolish. Mayhap she had once more allowed her mind to leap to conclusions. Mayhap Gilly was not in the house at all, but still somewhere upon the grounds, waiting for his opportunity. She had better hasten out of here, before Armande caught her prowling.

Scrambling to her feet, she left the room, softly closing the door behind her. Should she linger here to see if Gilly did attempt to make good his threat?

Uneasily, she glanced down the hallway, which seemed to yawn before her. She hated being alone here. 'Twas as if the Heath itself brooded, watching her with unseen eyes. Adjuring herself to stop being ridiculous, she made her way toward the backstairs. Knowing her cousin yet, she thought it likely that he might be trying to slip in through the servants' passageway.

At the bend of the servants' stairway she paused, trying to decide whether to go up or down. If Gilly's object was to search Armande's room, it was hardly likely he would have gone to the Heath's uppermost floor. But when she glanced up the stairs, she was startled to see the door to her garret flung wide.

She supposed Gilly might have hidden up there if he thought he heard someone coming, but somehow she ·doubted it. As she mounted the steps slowly, her heart thudded in a discomforting rhythm.

She craned her neck, trying to peer inside without actually entering. She could not even bring herself to breathe Gilly's name this time. Why had she never noticed before how gloom-ridden her precious garret was, even in the daytime?

At last she took a cautious step inside, telling herself she was being even sillier than she had been in Armande's room. Her garret appeared much as it had this morning when she had bolted inside to gather up the papers to show Armande. Of course, she had been in a tearing hurry then.

Her gaze flew to the desk, the carved gargoyle heads on the legs grimacing back at her, seeming as ever to guard her secrets. Then why was she beset by this eerie feeling of something being not quite right about the garret, something different or out of place?

She studied each feature of the room in turn, trying to determine what it was that bothered her. Her glance skimmed past the window, the desk, the daybed, the jumbled assortment of three-legged stools, the little table that held her supply of candles, the bookshelf tucked away in its dark corner . . . The bookshelf which should have been empty.

Phaedra's lips parted, but no sound came. She stared, uncertain whether what she saw was reality or some startling phantom image. The shelves, which had stood as vacant as a dead man's house, now were crowded with books.

Stumbling across the room, she stretched trembling fingers toward the leather-bound volumes of every size and thickness, half-afraid they would crumble and disappear at her touch. Smollett, Johnson, Goldsmith, Fielding, even her Shakespeare and Aristotle, they were all there, like old friends miraculously restored to life, resurrected from the ashes of Ewan's fire. Only the bindings were newer, as yet unworn by her loving hands. Nearly every book Ewan had robbed her of had been returned, along with a few new ones. For a moment all she could do was caress the fine-tooled leather, too stunned to do aught else. Then slowly she reached for one-rose-bound book on the top shelf which stood a little out from the others, as though beckoning her.

Gulliver's Travels.

Phaedra carried it over to the light streaming through the garret window in order to see it more clearly. Her hands shaking, she opened the book to its flyleaf, half-expecting she might see the inscription her mother had written so long ago, somehow knowing what she would really find.

The words were not in Lady Siobhan's delicate, spidery hand, but a bold, elegant scrawl. *To Phaedra,* the inscription read, *From your fellow voyager on the sea of dreams.*

He hadn't written his name, but she needed no signature to identify the writer. She thought back to the time she and Armande had spent together these past weeks, those precious stolen moments of making love and those other, equally precious moments when he had encouraged her to talk. She realized now he had been drawing her out, carefully gleaning the title of every treasured volume she had lost, committing the names to memory. What hours he must have spent combing the bookseller's stalls until he found them all.

She snapped the book closed. And this was the man she regretted having trusted with her secret, the man she feared might do some harm to her beloved cousin. Nay, Armande had been right to accuse her of a lack of trust. How quick she always was to doubt him, to lose her faith in his love.

Even as bitter and betrayed as he was feeling, he had done this for her, gifted her with the return of all her childhood fantasies, that and so much more. Yet she knew he would turn away, not even permitting her to thank him.

Her lips quivered with a determined smile. Well, she would find him and force him to accept her gratitude, aye, and her love as well. She leaned out the garret window, allowing a soft breeze to caress her face. Suddenly the world that had seemed so dark this morning was bright with promise, as shining as the sun over her head. She started to pull herself back in when she glimpsed something below that brought her to an abrupt halt.

Frowning, she stretched out as far as she dared, peering downward at the cobbled pavement. How strange! It looked as though someone had dropped a bundle of black rags. She strained for a closer look and saw that the rags appeared to be sopping up a pool of something . . . something red. Blood.

A strangled sound escaped Phaedra, and she lost her grip on the book. Frozen with horror, she watched the book fall as though time itself had slowed. The volume spun end over end until it landed with a dull thud, only yards from where Hester Searle's lifeless form lay crushed upon the cobblestones.

Chapter Sixteen

WITH LUSTERLESS EYES, PHAEDRA WATCHED THE FOOTMAN DRAWING the heavy curtains across the Green Salon's windows as Sawyer Weylin had commanded. It was as though her grandfather thought by shutting out the darkness of night, he could shut out the specter of death as well, although the broken form of Hester Searle had been laid out in the housekeeper's room only hours ago.

Phaedra huddled deeper against the sofa cushions and shivered. It seemed all she would ever remember about this day—the crumpled black silk, Hester lying twisted like a marionette whose strings had been cut, the blood yet staining the cobblestones. The rest would be a montage of faces—the hysterical housemaids, the ghoulish curiosity of the apprentice boys, Jonathan turning away to be sick, Gilly's grim shock, her grandfather's angry disbelief. And Armande—the only one who had not answered her cries, the only one not there.

Her gaze traveled across the room to where Armande now stood, pouring a small quantity of brandy into a crystal goblet. Except for the fact that he had discarded his frock coat and was garbed in naught but his breeches, ruffled shirt, and waistcoat, he appeared the image of the elegant nobleman. But the lines of his face were grave, etched with a weariness no gentleman of leisure had ever known. Phaedra studied him, trying to recall exactly when Armande had slipped up to join the rest of them. Had it been when Jonathan had left, bearing the last of the apprentice boys away in his carriage? Or later than that, just before she, Gilly, and her grandfather had retired to the Green Salon?

Phaedra rubbed her forehead, massaging the dull throb behind her temples. She didn't know. She supposed she should simply be grateful he was here now.

Armande crossed the room to her side, the glass of brandy cupped in his hand. He carefully avoided Gilly, who paced before the empty hearth like a caged beast scenting danger, sidestepping the sprawled legs of her grandfather. Weylin had ensconced himself in a wing-back chair opposite Phaedra, where he sat drinking brandy, a soured expression twisting his lips.

Armande bent over her, holding out the glass he had just filled. "Here. Drink this," he commanded gently.

She shook her head, having already refused Lucy's offers of sal volatile, burnt feathers, and whatever other restorative the girl could think of. But Armande was more insistent than her maid had been. He raised Phaedra's hand, curling her fingers about the goblet's stem.

"You need it, love," he said softly. " 'Tis stifling in here, and you look half-frozen to death."

He was right. Her grandfather mopped at the sweat on his brow, yet she felt cold, so very cold. She barely sipped the golden liquid, which seemed to spread fire through her, but no real warmth. Phaedra glanced anxiously up at Armande, but she could read nothing in his winter-blue eyes except concern for her. Her gaze traveled involuntarily to the small table beside the sofa. Atop its glossy surface reposed the dirt-smudged copy of *Gulliver's Travels*. Someone, she had no idea who, had retrieved the book from where it had fallen beside Hester.

Another shudder coursed through her and her hands shook, nearly spilling the brandy. She felt Armande's fingers close over hers, their strength helping her support the glass and raise it again to her lips. She forced herself to drink.

He settled beside her on the sofa and she had a strong urge to fling herself into his arms, an equally inexplicable urge to shrink away from him. A silence settled over the salon, as oppressive as the heat within the closed-up chamber.

Her grandfather was the first to break it, setting his own glass down with such a sharp sound that Phaedra jumped. Weylin glared at no one in particular. " 'Tis one hell of an end to my fete-day. That wretched woman's accident could not have been more ill-timed. Now I suppose I must look out for another house-keeper."

Gilly stopped his furious pacing long enough to stare at her grandfather, his green eyes sparking with contempt. "Accident! Holy Mary, Mother of God!"

"You watch your nasty papist tongue, m'lad." Weylin wagged a warning finger at Gilly, his thick finger slightly unsteady owing to the unaccustomed amount of brandy he had consumed. " 'Twas an accident, and I'll have no one saying any different. Or next I know the rector will be refusing to bury the woman in the churchyard, and there'll be all manner of scandal. Demn the creature, anyway. If she wanted to kill herself, couldn't she go fling herself into the Thames like everyone else does?"

"Suicide? Now there's an interesting theory," Gilly said. He cocked one eyebrow, his gaze no longer leveled at her grandfather, but at Armande. "I wonder what his lardship would be thinking. Tell us, *me lard*, do you believe Madam Pester to be the sort of woman who would take her own life?"

Phaedra could not begin to guess where Armande's thoughts had been—from the hazed look in his eyes, he had been miles away. But Gilly's question wrenched him back. He regarded her cousin with frowning surprise. "I scarce knew the woman well enough to say what she was likely to do."

"Didn't you? I would have wagered that Madam Pester num-bered amongst your most intimate acquaintances."

Phaedra saw Armande tense as though he had been flicked with a lash. His eyes blazed at Gilly, the line of his mouth turning white and pinched. Phaedra uttered a faint sound of protest, though what she sought to deny, she scarcely dared to think. She set down her brandy glass before she dropped it, feeling ill.

The only one who did not seem to comprehend Gilly's insin-uation was her grandfather. He glowered at Gilly. "Demnation, boy! What would the marquis be intimate with the housekeeper for? Not even Arthur Danby ever took notice of Searle. And Lord knows when he is drunk enough, that fool would take after anything in petticoats."

"I was not referring to the carnal sort of intimacy," Gilly said. Weylin growled, "Then what the devil are you talking about?"

Armande jerked to his feet. "I am not pleased to understand Mr. Fitzhurst, either."

Phaedra wanted to beg Gilly to stop, but she was strangely

helpless. It was all a nightmare, spinning out in her mind. She could neither direct its course nor waken from it.

Gilly leaned one arm up against the mantel, the hard set of his jaw belying the casualness of his pose. "I could not help remarking how shaken your lardship appeared to discover Madam Pester's untimely end. Of course, it took you the deuce of a long time to arrive. You must have been the last of us all to come gawking."

"I don't share your penchant for grim spectacle," Armande said.

The two men squared off, Gilly's eyes hard as emeralds, glittering with accusation, Armande's like frozen flame. She thought she saw Armande's hand inch toward the hilt of his sword. Phaedra struggled to her feet to fling herself in front of Gilly, but she wobbled, her legs feeling too weak to hold her.

Her movement had the effect of deflecting Armande's gaze from Gilly, drawing the full force of it upon herself. As Armande reached out to steady her, she felt Gilly's arm close about her shoulders, drawing her protectively back against him.

She stared at Armande, trying hard to see the face of the man she loved. But it was impossible to focus on the present as the fragments of memory whirled through her brain. She heard the echoes of her own voice warning Armande against the house-keeper, and Hester threatening the unseen man in the garden; saw the garret door ajar, finding the books put there by Armande, and the open window, through which she well knew no one could have fallen, not without help . . .

Phaedra had no idea what her face revealed until she saw her own tormented thoughts reflected in Armande's eyes. She might just as well have taken a knife and plunged it through his heart.

He turned abruptly away, as though he could no longer bear the sight of her.

"If you will excuse me, Mr. Weylin," he rasped. "I will leave this inquest to Fitzhurst and your granddaughter. They appear quite capable of reaching a verdict without any help from me."

With a stiff bow, Armande stalked from the room. Phaedra took a hesitant step, wanting to go after him, but Gilly's arm only tightened about her.

Sawyer Weylin huffed out of his chair, his heavy jowls quivering. "What the deuce is going on here, Fitzhurst? I'll not have you insulting guests under my roof. I only permitted Phaedra to have you about in the first place as a reward, a small treat."

Although still pale, Gilly had recovered some of his insouciance. "Mayhap you should have been after giving her one of those little lapdogs instead. Far tamer than an Irish hound."

"You insolent whelp! I'll have you thrown out on your ear. These manners might do for Ireland, sir. But in an English drawing—" Weylin broke off with a sharp gasp, doubling over, his hand clutching at the region of his heart. A spasm of pain distorted his features, his flesh turning as gray as his wig.

"Grandfather!" Phaedra reached out to him, Gilly seeking to support the old man from the opposite side. Drawing in several ragged breaths, Weylin straightened, pulling away from them both.

"No—no need to shriek in my ear, girl. I am all right. Just cannot deal with any more tonight—" He stumbled toward the door. "Been too long a day, far too long. Need my bed."

When Phaedra tried to accompany him, he waved her aside. "Just—just remember when you retire yourself, make sure you put out your *hound*."

He hobbled through the doorway, his gout-ridden foot, as ever, giving him pain; but his shoulders were squared, and he appeared to have recovered from his momentary spasm. Phaedra watched anxiously from the doorway until she saw Peter coming to help him up to bed.

Closing the door, she leaned up against it. Quiet descended over the room once more, the silence itself seeming to threaten her. The air felt heavy with all the things she knew Gilly wanted to say, things she didn't want to hear. She gazed back at him, pleading with her eyes.

Her cousin's grim expression softened. He closed the distance between them, gathering her into his arms. She buried her face against the worn fabric of his coat while he stroked her hair, murmuring gently to her, as though she were crying. But she felt far beyond tears as she clung to Gilly for comfort—much the way she had when they were children, and one of their reckless escapades had led to a scrape.

He drew her back to the couch, forcing her to sit down, her head resting upon his shoulder. "The old gaffer was right," he murmured. "Sure and it's been the very devil of a day."

"I shall never forget it as long as I live," Phaedra whispered.

"When I looked down the window and saw her lying there—the blood . . ."

"Don't think about it anymore, Fae." Gilly gently kneaded the back of her neck. " 'Tis over. They'll take her off to be buried in a few days' time."

But Gilly knew as well as she that it was not over. There were too many questions, too many painful suspicions, that would not be buried in that grave alongside Hester.

"I suppose she could have killed herself," she said. "Such a strange, bitter woman!"

She felt Gilly's shoulder blade tense beneath her cheek. "Nay, darlin'. I cannot allow that. You full well know to be thinking such a thing would be but self-delusion."

"Why would it be?" she asked, pulling away from him. "Why is it so impossible that Hester could have leaped from that window by her own free choice?"

The brief moment of comfort and kinship between them had faded. Gilly's lips tightened as he answered, "Setting aside the question of Hester's *sensitive, delicate* nature, there's another damned good reason why suicide cannot be considered. If someone else besides me had troubled to take a good look at her body, I wouldn't be the only one raising up doubts."

"What about Hester's body?"

"She landed face down, but there was blood smeared in her hair. She had taken the devil of a crack on the back of her head. No, Madam Hester never went through that window of her own accord."

Phaedra stood up and took a nervous turn about the room. "Well, she—she could have hit the side of the house on the way down. There was no sign of any sort of struggle in my garret."

"Then why didn't anyone hear her scream? A woman taking a plunge like that would have been bound to cry out. Considering Madam Hester's genteel set of lungs, she should have been heard all the way to Westminister."

"Not if she had willed herself to be silent."

"Damn it, Fae!" Gilly shot to his feet. He caught her shoulders in a bruising grip. "You can't keep walking about with the wool pulled over your eyes. You know cursed well that woman was murdered, and only one person could likely—"

"You have no reason to suspect Armande," she started to cry, then stopped, betrayed by her own words. It was not Gilly who had brought up Armande's name, but she.

She continued desperately, "It could have been some vagrant who crept inside the Heath, a footpad come to steal."

"And it might have been the ghost of old Lethe. Phaedra, you've got to face the truth this time."

She squeezed her eyes, battling the tears, but several droplets escaped past her lashes, making two hot trails down her cheeks. "You are asking me to believe the man I love could be a murderer. Don't you understand that is as painful as asking me to believe that you killed Hester?"

Although Gilly continued to frown, his grip upon her slackened, becoming more gentle.

"Do you know what Armande did for me?" she said, her voice thick with misery. "He replaced all the books for me that Ewan destroyed, put them back on my shelves in the garret. Do you think a man capable of such consideration could—could—"

"Spare a few minutes from the shelving to stuff Madam Hester out the window? Aye, I do."

"Don't!" She wrenched away from him. "'Tis vile of you to make such jests."

"I'm not jesting!" Gilly's voice became as hoarse as her own. "For the love of God, Phaedra. You know what manner of a prying woman Hester was. I won't even pretend to grieve for her. 'Tis a wonder someone didn't fling her off the eaves a long time ago. My only concern is to make sure you're not next."

"Damn you! 'Tis bad enough for you to imply that Armande killed Hester, but to say that he would ever hurt me—"

"He's a man with too many secrets. We both know that. I think he'd destroy anyone who seemed a threat to him." Gilly heaved an exasperated sigh, looking as though the argument had at last begun to wear him down. "Though the Lord alone knows how Madam Hester ever managed to find out anything about de LeCroix. He might be as innocent as my grandfather for all there is to be found in his room."

"Then you were there," Phaedra accused bitterly. "You did search, even after I begged you not to."

Gilly ground his fingers wearily against his eyelids. "Aye, for all the good it did. Even that blasted locked box of his which looked so promising yielded nothing."

"You pried into Armande's wooden chest?"

"You needn't look at me as if I stole something of value from the man. All I found in the box was this." Gilly began to fumble for something tucked in his inner pocket.

Phaedra blanched with horror. "Gilly, you shouldn't have taken anything from his room! Whatever it is, you must put it back before Armande finds it missing."

"Not until you've seen it. 'Tis nothing to make such a great fuss about, unless you can see more significance in a pretty bit of porcelain than I do."

"Porcelain?" Phaedra repeated. Her brow furrowed in puzzlement until she focused on the delicate object Gilly balanced in his hand. It was a shepherd boy with curling dark hair and blue eyes. There might have been a dozen such ornaments to be found upon the shelves in London's great houses, but the style of this particular one had a flair all its own. Phaedra knew immediately whose hand had wrought that delicate statue.

She stared at it until the entire room blurred. As from a great distance, she heard Gilly's voice calling to her. "Fae? Devil a bit! Phaedra! 'Tis only china, not a blasted ghost."

Her lips parted, and she had to fight down the desire to break into hysterical laughter. For Gilly was utterly wrong. That was exactly what he clutched between his fingers, a ghost from seven years past. Its phantom twin was buried upstairs in her dressing-table drawer.

The light from the small candle in Gilly's hand provided but feeble illumination, hardly enough to hold at bay the engulfing darkness of her bedchamber. Yet it was sufficient for her task. The taper's soft glow flickered across the two sculptures Phaedra set side by side atop her dressing table—the winsome shepherd lass with her melancholy smile reunited at last with her mate, the sad-eyed shepherd boy playing upon his pipes in a pose so lifelike Phaedra half-expected the haunting melody to fill her room. Works of art, both of them, fitting gifts to have delighted the monarch Franz Joseph and his sister, the lovely Marie Antoinette.

Instead the figurines served as a memorial to another brother and sister, James and Julianna Lethington. In halting whispers, Phaedra told Gilly all she knew of the Lethington tragedy, from Julianna's hopeless love for Ewan which had led to her destruction, to James's own death upon the gallows.

When she had finished, Gilly touched the head of the porcelain shepherdess almost as though he caressed a living thing, his green eyes bright with compassion. "And now," he said, "now you know what became of the younger brother."

Phaedra's gaze flew to the shadowy outline of the door leading to Armande's chamber. She still wanted to deny that Armande was Jason Lethington, but there was too much evidence now against him.

Besides his cherishing the shepherd figurine, there was his extraordinary knowledge of the processes that went into making china, and the flash of pain in his eyes that long-ago day when he had recognized the dove-gray cloak belonging to Julianna. Phaedra now realized with anguished clarity what torment she had put Armande through when she had had him arrested and carted off to Newgate. The prison's grim interior had reminded him, he had said, of the death of a friend. Not a friend, Phaedra thought miserably, but his own brother, James.

"Forgive me, my love," she murmured. She had been privileged this summer for an all-too-brief time, to glimpse the young man that Jason Lethington must have been, the blue eyes formed for laughter, the sensitive mouth for tenderness. Now that she understood the bitter sorrow that had made it possible for him to transform himself into the icy marquis, she grieved for him. Aye, and feared for him at the same time.

"Hester likely found the shepherd," Gilly mused aloud. "After seeing the piece you had, she must have guessed the significance of Armande's, threatened him with exposure, and he—" Her cousin broke off, his hand clamping down over hers, giving it a fierce squeeze. Gilly's face bore no trace of his former belligerence, only a sadness that matched her own.

"I understand what you're feeling for the man, Fae. The poor devil. He's endured more than enough grief to drive any man to madness. And Madam Pester only got what she's long deserved."

Gilly stroked the back of his fingers along the curve of her cheek. "But no matter what pity I might feel, I can't take the chance that he might hurt you. If he realizes that you also know his secret—"

"He would never harm me," she said. "Just because of what his brother did, you talk as if murder runs in his blood. After some of the things I have done to him, Armande had cause and more to—I mean Jason had . . ." She halted in confusion, raking her fingers through her hair, scarcely knowing what to call the man. She took refuge in the one fact she was sure of, saying fiercely, "He loves me, Gilly."

"Mayhap he does. But even if he does not seek to silence you, he could harm you in other ways."

She shook her head, wanting to convince her cousin he was wrong. But she couldn't. Too oft had she received similar warnings from Armande himself. How hard had he struggled to put distance between them because of his own fear of hurting her.

"You've not thought this through, Fae," Gilly persisted gently. "What do you imagine Jason Lethington is doing here in your grandfather's house, pretending to be some French marquis?"

"I don't know," she said in a small voice.

"He could only have one motive—revenge against those that destroyed his family. With Ewan dead, that leaves only one man Lethington might yet hold accountable, the old gaffer."

Gilly's suggestion chilled her. "My—my grandfather? Don't be ridiculous. He was not involved in the feud between the Granthams and Lethingtons. All he did was arrange my marriage to Ewan."

"For a man bent on vengeance, that might be enough."

"But he saved my grandfather's life." Phaedra's argument seemed suddenly faint however, as she remembered Armande's strange behavior that night. He had refused to be thanked for his deed, and even then she had marked in him a shade of regret that amounted almost to self-disgust. She recalled his cryptic words—that he had come to London with but one purpose in mind, and he feared that she would hate him when he had done.

"It doesn't make sense," she said. "If Armande has come to the Heath to harm my grandfather, why hasn't he done so? He's had plenty of opportunities."

"There still may be much we don't understand. Hester's ramblings about the Lethingtons and this—" Gilly picked up the shepherd, "scarce offer proof of Jason's identity. We have to attempt to turn back time, by about seven years."

"How are we supposed to do that?" Phaedra demanded.

"By going back to where the Lethingtons lived, I suppose. Jason would have to have left some traces of himself behind, something to link him more definitely to the man we know as Armande de LeCroix."

"And when we have the proof that he is Jason, what then?" Gilly didn't answer her, but he didn't have to. Phaedra's eyes locked with his and saw her own misery reflected there. She wanted to frame one last plea, beg Gilly to give up the pursuit. But she no longer could do so. For Armande's sake as well, the truth had to be revealed.

She couldn't believe that her Armande, nigh insane with grief, had cut down Hester Searle. But if her lover kept on down the dark road he now traveled, she feared it could lead to madness, the loss of his very soul.

Phaedra bowed her head, silently giving assent to Gilly's proposal, all the while struggling with her own despair and fear. Seven years ago, Ewan's vile father Lord Carleton had begun the destruction of the Lethington family. She prayed with all her heart she would not be the one who finished it.

Chapter Seventeen

THE COTTAGE STOOD ALONE, FAR REMOVED FROM THE OTHER buildings that nestled together in the small village of Hampstead. A thick blanket of ivy crept up the walls, all but obscuring the whitewashed stone, giving the isolated structure the appearance of some outcast seeking to hide misery and shame beneath a heavy veil.

The house appeared deserted in the gathering dusk, the mullioned windows glinting like dark, unwelcoming eyes. Drawing deeper into the folds of her cloak, Phaedra shivered and shrank closer to Gilly. The soles of her feet felt worn to the bone after so long a day. They had slipped from the Heath at dawn's first light, and now it was evening. She had taken great care to avoid Armande, knowing but one glimpse of her eyes would reveal to him the truth, that she was once more working against him.

She had carried away with her a burden of guilt, weighting her very soul with the despairing reluctance of a woman being dragged to the dock to bear witness against her own lover. Trudging along in Gilly's wake, she had listened while he made inquiries about Jason Lethington, starting at the trinket shop in Oxford Street where Phaedra had spied the candlesticks fashioned by Julianna and had first heard the Lethingtons' tragic story. The little shopkeeper had been as eager as ever to sell Phaedra something "wonderful charming." Although disappointed to discover that information was all she and Gilly wanted, the merchant had willingly obliged. He had furnished them with the address at which the Lethington manufactory had once stood.

Traveling to that part of London, she and Gilly had discovered the Lethington shop now taken over by a confectioner; the chambers where Julianna had once done her designing were now occupied by the confectioner's burgeoning family. None of these good folk had ever heard of Lethingtons nor showed the slightest interest in their fate. Phaedra had been more than willing to abandon the search at that point, but Gilly had insisted on making enquiries amongst the neighboring shops. They had at last discovered a milliner who was able to help them.

Aye, indeed, she did remember the Lethingtons, the elderly woman had said with a sigh. Such a tragedy. No, she had no idea what had become of Mrs. Lethington or Jason after James's execution, but she recommended that Phaedra and Gilly visit Hampstead. An old doctor lived there who had been a close friend of the family, having none of his own. If anyone knew where Jason Lethington might be found, it would surely be Dr. Glencoe.

Thus their weary search had brought them at last to the outskirts of Hampstead by this lonely dwelling place. But as Phaedra studied the cottage's heavy oak door and gloom-enshrouded walls, she shook her head.

"Gilly, this cannot be the right place." She glanced anxiously up at her cousin. Gilly's usually smiling lips were pulled down at the corners with weariness.

"Nay, it has to be, Fae. The vicar was most specific in his directions."

Aye, she thought, when the impatient young man had been able to spare them a few moments from his Bible and quill pen. Upon entering Hampstead, they had stopped at the vicarage as the most likely place to gain directions to Dr. Glencoe's dwelling. Although the clergyman had made quite clear his opinion of being disturbed by visitors in the midst of his sermon-writing, he had, in the end, grudgingly pointed out to them the way.

But despite the irritated vicar's information, Phaedra continued to look askance at the cottage. As Gilly took her by the elbow, steering her forward, she attempted to hang back.

"I cannot believe anyone lives here," she said. "Not even an elderly doctor. The cottage looks utterly abandoned."

But as if to belie her words, a shadowy figure moved behind one of the curtains and set a candle in the window. Phaedra had to swallow her objections and continue on. The light provided no welcoming beacon but only added to the house's aura of melancholy. The tiny glow was not enough to hold back the darkness.

With each step she took, the more of an interloper she felt. When Gilly raised his fist to knock, she made one last effort to stay his hand.

"Gilly, I am so tired. Mayhap we could come back tomorrow. The doctor is likely to be at his supper and as displeased as the vicar was to find strangers come acalling."

Gilly's arm encircled her shoulders, and he gave her a bracing squeeze. "I am weary as you, Fae. But this is the first good information we've had all day. If Dr. Glencoe was such an intimate friend of the Lethington family, he will be the one most likely to have the proof we seek to link Armande with Jason Lethington."

Aye, Phaedra thought dully, the proof she was seeking, yet hoping not to find. No more questions, she had promised Armande, that magic sunlit day by the pond, wanting him both to love and trust her. But it was a promise she had already betrayed past all hope of forgiveness.

She made no further demur, allowing Gilly to hammer upon the oak portal, raising up a thundering summons. "What—what are we going to say to this doctor?" she asked, fidgeting nervously with the hood of her cloak.

"You just leave that to me," Gilly said.

The door inched open, allowing a streak of light to escape. She caught a glimpse of gray curls tumbled from beneath a lacy cap, but no more gray than the eyes that peered out at them.

"What do you want?" a brusque feminine voice inquired.

Gilly flashed his most ingratiating smile, but Phaedra doubted the woman could see much of it in the growing darkness. "We wish to see the doctor, my good woman."

The oak barrier shifted enough to permit an arm to emerge holding an oil lamp. The woman directed the glow toward them. Phaedra flung back her hood and shifted her cloak so that the woman might better remark the quality of her garments and be assured she and Gilly were not some wandering vagrants.

The woman asked, "The young lady is ill, then?"

Aye, Phaedra nearly assented, but her sickness was of the heart, well past any doctor's curing. She kept silent, leaving it to Gilly to reply.

"No, neither of us require medical services. 'Tis a matter of some personal interest we wish to consult the doctor upon."

"I'm sorry. Dr. Glencoe don't receive callers—not at this hour. He retires early because his sleep is far too oft disturbed. Good evening to you."

With that the woman prepared to shut the door, but Gilly's arm shot forward, blocking the movement. "Wait. Please. I am sure he will see us. Just show him these."

Before Phaedra could protest, Gilly had shoved the parcel containing the precious figurines through the narrow opening. There was a pause, then the crackling of paper told her that the woman had seized the package.

The door slammed shut.

"Gilly . . ." Phaedra began, uneasily.

"She'll be back."

But Phaedra was not sure she shared her cousin's confidence. Long moments passed, leaving her to shift wearily from foot to foot. She was about to instruct Gilly to knock again, when the door swung open wide.

The gray-haired individual bobbed her lace cap. The wariness in her eyes had been replaced by curiosity. But all she said was, "Come this way."

Gilly was forced to duck his head as they passed through the doorway. The woman led them through a chamber which was obviously where the doctor operated on his patients. Wincing, Phaedra averted her eyes from the collection of sharp surgical implements laid out in orderly fashion upon an oak table.

The woman flung open the door to a tiny parlor, indicating with a jerk of her head that they should step inside.

"Doctor will be with you directly." With an abruptness that seemed quite natural for her, she left them alone.

Huddling close to Gilly, Phaedra glanced about her. The parlor once might have been bright and cozy, but now everything about the room spoke of faded memory, like flowers, brittle with age, pressed between the leaves of a book. The velvet settee shone bare in some spots, and the matte of the carpet was worn. The veneer on the mahogany sideboard and cabinet was no longer glossy, but dull and scarred.

Shut behind the cabinet's glass doors, Phaedra glimpsed rows and rows of tattered leather volumes. She stepped closer to scan the titles. Intermingled with heavy tomes of medicine and science, the more slender books of novels and poems appeared almost dwarfed. When she saw *Gulliver's Travels* amongst them, her breath caught in her throat. Her heart aching, she wondered if it was here then, in the house of this old friend, that Armande had first begun his own "voyage on the sea of dreams." She lowered her eyes, feeling like an intruder trampling into regions of Armande's heart where she had not been invited to enter.

She felt Gilly tap her shoulder, silently directing her attention to the lower shelf of the cabinet. Somehow it did not astonish her to see the shelf crammed with china. Whimsical medieval chessmen of black basalt jostled for space with vases sporting frolicking cherubs and lambs. So different from the shepherd and shepherdess, yet Phaedra could still detect the delicate artistry of Julianna Lethington. All but hidden behind the chess pieces were other oval disks of china with profiles painted upon them.

She froze, realizing what they were in the same moment that Gilly muttered, "Miniature portraits. That might be exactly what we're looking for."

"No. Don't," she said as he hunkered down, preparing to reach inside the cabinet. She feared at any moment he would draw forth a likeness of Armande, the undeniable proof of his identity as Jason Lethington.

But before he could do so, the parlor door opened behind them. Gilly straightened abruptly, both of them whirling at the same time to face the old man shuffling into the room, a chintz dressing gown swathed about his spare frame, his feet clad in blue morocco mules. The skin over his cheekbones was parchment-thin, and his cheeks were sunken and hollow. Indeed, the man appeared more in need of a physician than likely to be one himself. And yet his balding forehead bore marks of a gentle dignity.

"Dr. Adam Glencoe?" Gilly asked hesitantly.

The doctor nodded, the porcelain shepherd and shepherdess clutched in his gaunt hands. He regarded Phaedra and her cousin as though they were resurrection men, bringing him a corpse fresh from a violated grave.

"You have the advantage of me, sir," the doctor said, the faintest trace of a Scottish burr in his voice. "I don't wish to give offense. But if I have ever met you or this young lady, my memory—"

"No, sir," Gilly interrupted hastily. "Permit me to introduce

myself. Patrick Gilhooley Fitzhurst at your service, and this—this
is my sister Phaedra Fitzhurst."

Although surprised by Gilly's words, Phaedra was quick to
conceal her startled expression, realizing her cousin's reason for
the lie. The name of Grantham would not be a welcome one to any
friend of the Lethington family.

For what that was worth she thought—for the doctor could
scarce have looked less welcoming than he did at this moment. He
invited them to be seated, although he made no move to do so
himself. She and Gilly perched uncomfortably on the edge of the
threadbare settee.

Gilly cleared his throat. " 'Tis that sorry we are to be intruding
upon your rest, Doctor. But we drove all the way out from the city
to ask you a question regarding those figurines."

At the mention of the statues, Dr. Glencoe set both the shepherd
and shepherdess down upon the tea table with great care, almost
as though loath to release them.

"Aye, the figurines," he repeated. "Might I ask you first how
you came by them?"

Before beginning to speak, Gilly shot Phaedra a sidewise
glance as though warning her not to contradict him. "Our grandda
is a magistrate. Recently he tried the case of a thief who had been
hoarding a great deal of stolen merchandise. Most of it was of
little value, but these pieces of china were so exquisite, we wanted
to see them restored to their rightful owners. My sister made
inquiries amongst the china merchants, where she was told the
artist had been Julianna Lethington."

Here Gilly paused to give Phaedra's hand a squeeze. "Being the
tenderhearted soul that she is, my sister was much moved by the
tale of the tragic deaths of Julianna and her brother James, and
wanted to return the figurines to some member of the Lethington
family."

The full weight of the doctor's scrutiny now fell upon Phaedra.
She blushed, made uncomfortable by Gilly's deception. But the
old man seemed to read something in her eyes which caused his
own expression to soften.

"We were told," Gilly continued, "that you were an intimate
friend of the Lethingtons—"

"Aye, so I was," the doctor interrupted. "Maida . . . that is,
Mrs. Lethington, and her children visited me often enough they
might well have been my own family."

"Then surely you could tell us where we could locate—"

Dr. Glencoe shook his head, cutting Gilly off again. "I am afraid that is impossible." He sighed and looked at Phaedra. She noticed that his eyes were a deep brown and rather kindly, although the age-carved lines in the flesh beneath made him look very tired.

" 'Tis a most generous impulse on your part, Miss Fitzhurst," he said. "But I fear there are no more Lethingtons to receive your gift."

"But—but," Phaedra said, speaking up for the first time since entering the cottage. "I understand that the mother, and the younger brother, Jason, yet lived."

"Aye, I pray that the lad does still live, but not in these parts. He and Maida set sail for Canada many years ago." The doctor bowed his head for a moment, shading his eyes with his hand. "I've heard but once from the boy . . . he wrote to inform me that his mother had not survived the crossing."

It was obvious that their questions were stirring long-buried griefs inside the old man, and Phaedra loathed herself. She exchanged a wretched glance with Gilly and sensed he was thinking the same thing. But Canada . . . Canada had been the destination of the real Armande de LeCroix, a fact far too strange to be merely coincidence.

"And Jason never wrote you again?" Gilly asked the doctor.

"No, nary another word."

"Sure and that's too bad," Gilly said. "I fear my sister will be disappointed, having worked out all sorts of romantic imaginings. We had heard naught but praise of how handsome this Jason is." He added with seeming casualness, "Dark hair and striking blue eyes, isn't that what they said, Phaedra?"

Phaedra nodded, her mouth suddenly gone dry, realizing what Gilly was hinting at. She prayed that the doctor would tell her that Jason was short and blond, but her hopes were dashed when he confirmed, "All the Lethingtons were dark-haired. Though I would have to say Jason was not as handsome as our poor Jamey was."

The old man seemed to unbend completely. He sank down in an armchair opposite them, his eyes misting over as he stared at the figurines. "I daresay you think me a doddering old fool to hear me talk so. As though they had been my own sons. But for a brief time after their father died, they might have been."

"You helped Maida Lethington look after her fatherless little ones, did you?" Gilly prodded gently.

A wry smile tipped the doctor's lips. "Fatherless mayhap, but scarcely little. When Daniel Lethington was carried off by the fever, James was grown to manhood, and Jason nearly so. And Miss Julianna, she was nigh a lady. But Daniel asked me on his deathbed, as his oldest friend, to look out for his family— especially James, who was a bit much for his mother."

The doctor's shoulders sagged. "He was a restless young man, of such dark moods and with such a quick temper. I never understood him. I very much fear that Jason was my favorite. He was a quiet lad who shared my own fondness for books.

"James was ever hankering after adventure, longing to set sail upon the first ship that came to port." The doctor shook his head, as though still mystified by James's vagaries after all these years. "He never was content to be working at the china shop. Daniel finally gave up trying to make a merchant of him and sent the boy up to Oxford."

"Oxford?" Gilly echoed. "That's a bit unusual for a china-maker's son."

Glencoe shrugged. "Oh, Daniel had the money. And the lad was certainly clever enough."

Phaedra stirred restlessly in her seat, suddenly recalling Lord Arthur Danby's drunken insistence that he remembered Armande from their university days. Reluctantly, she asked, "And Jason— did his father send him there, too?"

"No, but he frequently visited his brother." Dr. Glencoe's cheeks puffed with indignation. "I never approved. Oxford is nothing—except the perfect place for young men to learn the finer points of drinking, gaming, and wenching. James was already wild as bedamned. I didn't like the notion of young Jason being dragged into bad company the likes of Arthur Danby and Lord Ewan Grantham."

Phaedra faltered. "Then—then that's how Ewan—I mean Lord Grantham became acquainted with Julianna. Through her brothers."

"No, at least not then. That unfortunate introduction came later, after their father was dead." Glencoe's eyes darkened at the memory. "James was forced to take on the responsibility of the shop and as head of the family. A very poor job he made of it, too. I frequently tried to warn Maida that the lad was not suited to such duties, but she looked upon James with all a mother's indulgence and saw none of his faults."

The elderly doctor relented somewhat, saying grudgingly, "I suppose James tried, but he had no head for business, and the shop began to fail. He was trying to collect on some bad debts when his path crossed with Grantham's again."

"Then James thought to clap up a match between his old friend and sister, did he?" Gilly filled in. He had been squirming for some time, clearly growing impatient for the doctor to reach the significant part of the story.

But Glencoe looked deeply offended by Gilly's suggestion. "No, indeed. James had more regard for his sister than to wish to see her wed to a rascally jackanapes like Lord Ewan. And if you add to that the fact that Ewan's father, Lord Carleton, was the most depraved creature living, I believe James would have locked his sister up before seeing her marry into such a family."

"But I had heard Julianna and Lord Ewan were in love," Phaedra said quietly.

"Love." The doctor snorted. "Infatuation more like—a most tragic infatuation as matters went. For you see, Carleton Grantham was also against the match and he—"

The doctor broke off, a quiver of pain running along his withered jaw. A murmur of pity rose to Phaedra's lips. She was about to assure the old man he needn't say any more, when he continued, the memory seeming fairly wrung from him.

"When Carleton found out that Ewan and Julianna were planning to elope, the black-hearted devil abducted and ravished her."

"Abducted!" Gilly exclaimed. His gaze traveled wonderingly to meet Phaedra's. This was a little different from Hester Searle's version of the story.

"Why was Carleton never arrested?" Phaedra protested.

Glencoe's eyes clouded. "No one ever had a chance, for James got to him first. That temper of his! Not that I fully blamed James for what he had done. But even at his own trial, when he might yet have saved himself, he ranted like a madman, saying there had been a conspiracy to murder his sister. Dear Lord, James was accusing everyone, Carleton Grantham, the son Ewan, some other prominent man named Weylin . . . Poor James was clearly out of his head."

Phaedra could not conceal a start at this mention of her grand-

father, but the doctor was too overcome at the moment to notice
her shock. The old man sought surreptitiously to wipe his eyes.

"The rest of the tale you've likely heard. James was duly
hanged. I brought his body back for burial in the churchyard here.
Maida's heart was quite broken. Between losing both her son and
her daughter, I saw her health fail more each day. She became
thinner, more pale—"

"But what about Jason?" Phaedra asked, feeling somehow that
the younger brother was like a lost shadow in all of these tragic
events.

Was it her imagination, or did Glencoe hesitate slightly before
saying, "I sent him away, to take his mother out of the country. A
mistake on my part. I should have seen at the outset that Maida
was not strong enough to survive the voyage, but she was not
about to be separated from her son, and it seemed the best I could
do for the boy. I feared for his reason. After James was hanged,
he retreated so far into himself, that he terrified me. No grief, no
emotion of any kind, it was as though his heart were encased in
ice."

The doctor's words painted such an accurate picture of Armande that Phaedra had to look away to hide the tears that filled
her eyes.

Glencoe's voice thickened with self-reproach. "Mayhap if I had
been there that night with James, I could have prevented . . ."
He allowed the thought to trail away unspoken, shaking his head.
"Well, 'tis of no avail raking over the past. I have done it often
enough to know there is no profit in it."

He reluctantly inched the figurines across the tea table toward
Phaedra. "I am sorry I cannot be of more help to you, Miss
Fitzhurst. I am sure Jason would have been delighted to have this
work of his sister's returned, but—" The doctor broke off, flinging
wide his hands in a helpless gesture.

"But you are certain there is no way of tracing Jason," Gilly
persisted. "What if he had decided to leave Canada and return to
England?"

"God forbid!" The doctor exclaimed, going pale. "I would
hope not. There is nothing for the lad here but bitterness. I have
always prayed that he started his life anew and put the past behind
him."

Phaedra looked away. She had not the heart to reveal to the old
man her fears that his prayers had gone unanswered. She tensed,

watching from beneath her lashes as Gilly maneuvered himself toward the cabinet.

"I see you possess some fine examples of Julianna's work yourself, Doctor. And bless me! Are those little portraits of the Lethingtons? Such a handsome family."

"Aye, so they were," Glencoe said.

Phaedra shot to her feet, her hands shaking with apprehension. "Gilly, we have taken enough of the doctor's time."

But the doctor had already rose from his seat and shuffled forward to open the cabinet. "Of course, Julianna is not amongst them, since it was her own hand that painted these." Phaedra watched with dread as the old man handed up the ovals to Gilly one by one for his inspection.

Phaedra sank back upon the settee, scarcely realizing how she dug her nails into the faded velvet. Her gaze never left Gilly's face, and she knew immediately from the arrested expression in his eyes that he had found the evidence he sought.

Silently, he held out one of the miniatures to her. For a long moment she refused to take it. Then her trembling fingers closed about the smooth oval of china. Slowly she lowered her gaze to the portrait, wondering at the sudden sharp ache that pierced through her. Had she still been foolish enough to hope it would be the face of a stranger she gazed upon?

But it was Armande de LeCroix looking exactly as he had a few days ago in the meadow, his dark hair tossed by the wind, his blue eyes laughing. Except that the man in the portrait was somewhat younger, an Armande with no shadows brushing his face, caught in all the strength, the arrogance, the innocence of his youth by his sister's loving artistry.

Not Armande, Phaedra reminded herself sadly, but— "Jason Lethington."

She didn't realize she had spoken the name aloud until Dr. Glencoe turned toward her with a look of mild astonishment.

"Oh, no, my dear. You've made a mistake."

When she glanced up at the old man uncomprehendingly, he said, "That is not Jason's portrait you are holding."

"Then—then who?" she stammered.

The old man gave her a sad, patient smile. "That is our James. *James Lethington.*"

Chapter Eighteen

BEFORE THE CURRICLE GILLY HAD HIRED HAD EVEN COME TO A STOP, Phaedra gathered up her skirts, and leaped to the ground. She swayed slightly as her feet hit, but quickly regained her balance and rushed off into the darkness. With only the moon to light her way, she ran blindly through the graveyard behind the small church. Behind her she heard Gilly utter an oath. He hissed her name while he strove to secure the horse's lead reins to the cemetery's iron gate.

But Phaedra was lost to everything except the sensations of shock and horror that rose up in her breast, threatening to suffocate her. With little thought for the sanctity of the dead, she stumbled across the mound of a new-laid grave and made wildly for that corner of the churchyard where Dr. Glencoe claimed he had seen James Lethington laid to rest.

Her heart thundering, she staggered to a halt and stood gasping several moments before she could focus on the weather-worn stones before her. In the moonlight she could just barely make out the simple carvings. A succession of unknown names passed before her eyes until she came to the last and smallest headstone. JAMES LETHINGTON . . . BELOVED SON OF MAIDA AND DANIEL LETHINGTON.

"There!" she half-sobbed. "It isn't true. I knew it wasn't." Her voice bordered on hysteria as she relived again that chilling moment in the doctor's cottage, hearing the old man identify the portrait of the man she loved as that of the murderer James

Lethington. But the doctor's sight must be failing, his words *must be false*—for here was James Lethington's grave before her, the dust long settled over his tormented soul.

She heard Gilly's running footsteps as he came panting up behind her. "Fae—"

"Look for yourself," she said shrilly. "James Lethington is buried beneath six feet of earth. Armande is not . . ."

Gilly forced her around and held her trembling frame close, as though the fierceness of his hug could still her shaking, hold at bay her fears, dispel the nightmare that descended upon her.

"The old man is mad." She muffled the words against his cloak. " 'Tis—'tis impossible."

A long sigh escaped Gilly. "I was as shocked as you, Fae. But as for being impossible—nay, I am afraid it is not."

Phaedra flung back her head, a wild, mirthless laugh tearing from her lips. "Then you are telling me I have fallen in love with a ghost."

"No. James Lethington is very much alive."

She drew away from Gilly, shaking her head. "Ewan saw him hang. Dr. Glencoe brought the body back here for burial."

"Aye, but did you notice the good doctor's reaction after he identified James? You turned white as bed linens. Then when I began to hint we thought we might have seen the man in the portrait, Glencoe hustled us out like we were carriers of the pox. I would wager my last shilling 'twas because the doctor knows James is not dead."

"Then what did he do? Practice some magic arts upon the crowd so that they all simply thought they saw James hang?"

"What I'm thinking happened is a deal worse than that." As the moonlight skimmed Gilly's features, she realized her carefree cousin had never looked so grim. "You've never been to a hanging, Fae. You could not imagine . . . very few snap their necks at once. Most die by slow strangulation."

"I've been regaled with enough of my grandfather's gruesome tales," she cried. "I don't need you to—"

"I am only trying to explain to you that James would not be the first man to survive such an ordeal. I've heard the cases where doctors can detect signs of life even after hanging an hour. They can revive a hanged man."

Phaedra turned away, but she could not shut out the sound of Gilly's voice. "The procedure is known as a bronchotomy. The surgeon makes an incision in the base of the throat, which helps the man start to breathe again."

Phaedra's hands flew to her throat. But it was not her own flesh she was feeling, but rather the memory of Armande's bronzed neck, of running her fingers over that tiny scar. A result of something a friend had done, he had told her.

She shuddered as Gilly continued, remorseless in his logic. "Dr. Glencoe admits he was there at the hanging to recover the body. If James had been yet alive, he could have revived him and spirited him away, and buried anything in that grave—even a coffin weighted with rocks."

Phaedra walked slowly away from Gilly, toward the gravestone of James Lethington. She bent to trace the carved lines with her fingers as though somehow her touch could draw forth the secrets of the grave, raise up the spirit of a dead man to refute Gilly's words. But she heard naught but the wind whispering mournfully through the grass. The coldness of the stone seemed to seep through her like the chill of death itself.

Gilly settled her cloak more snugly about her, then wrapped his arm around her waist, drawing her gently away from the headstone. "Come, Fae. Lingering here will change nothing. 'Tis time I was taking you home."

She laughed bitterly to herself, and wanted to ask him where he thought that was. But she said nothing, permitting Gilly to lead her back to the curricle.

They rode away from Hampstead in silence, the sleepy village already lost in the hush of night. Gilly, ever alert to the dangers of traveling after dark, kept a brace of loaded pistols at the ready. Phaedra sat numbly beside him, with no fear of highwaymen. Her terrors were the conjurings of her own mind, phantom memories of a summer that would never come again, an illusion born of the heat and a too-bright sun. She had stripped away Armande's mask at last, and found not love, but death.

The long, dreary ride back to Heath passed in a blur. The plan had been for her to slip back unseen from the day's outing. Even now Lucy was covering for her, saying that her mistress was in bed, ill from her shock of Hester Searle's death.

But such small deceptions scarce seemed to matter any longer. Wearily Phaedra directed Gilly to drive her up to the Heath's main gates. The sleepy-eyed porter regarded her arrival with some surprise, then shuffled to swing wide the iron bars.

The curricle swept down the length of the gravel drive. Black-heath House was silent and dark at this late hour. The moonlight skating off the stark block of granite, unadorned except for the tall white Corinthian pillars, gave the mansion the look of a Greek temple—cold and forbidding, awaiting its sacrifice.

When Gilly drew the curricle to a halt, he twisted the leather of the reins between his hands, nervous and unsure about permitting her to alight. "I never counted on us returning so late. Oh, Fae—I'm so sorry. Mayhap I should come in with you. We could talk to your grandfather now—"

"No!" Phaedra startled herself with the violence of her outcry. "Grandfather is likely already in bed and—and surely there is no need to disturb him tonight."

Gilly placed his hand soothingly over hers, but his voice was firm as he said, " 'Tis a different situation now, Fae. Your grandfather has a right to know he harbors a murderer under his roof."

"Don't call him that," she whispered brokenly.

"Fae, you cannot still be denying—"

"I'm not denying anything. I'm only asking you for a little more time to think matters through." She clutched at her cousin's fingers, pleading. "Give me just the one more night, Gilly. Then tomorrow, we can do whatever you think necessary."

He held her hand for a long time, obviously uneasy at her proposal. Finally, with great reluctance, he agreed. "I suppose you have been through enough hell for one day. But you take great care. And for the love of God, stay away from de LeCroix."

That was an easy pledge to make. Phaedra was now afraid to face Armande, knowing what she did, terrified to look into his eyes, and see the eyes of James Lethington staring back at her. Yet she still bridled. "He would never hurt me, Gilly."

"Perhaps I don't believe he would, either," was her cousin's last admonishment, "but all the same, you keep your door locked."

Alighting from the curricle, he saw her safely back up the lane to the house, not parting from her until she slipped in through the front door.

Despite the fact that it was not yet midnight, the Heath seemed oppressively silent, as still and lifeless as a yawning grave. None of the footmen was in attendance, nor did she see any of the other servants as she stepped cautiously into the front hall. Without Hester's grim presence, the household had already grown a bit lax.

She supposed she should count herself fortunate that someone had remembered to leave an oil lamp burning upon the hall table.

She found a candle end in one of the drawers and touched it to a lamp's wick to light her own way up to bed. She should have been grateful to find no one abroad, for her return would go unremarked. But the house's relentless silence preyed upon nerves already stretched taut from the shock she had received at Glencoe's cottage.

The candle trembled in her grasp as she glided through the hall. 'Twas like being swallowed up in a cavern; as the stone walls loomed above her, the candle flame sparked glints of illumination upon the collection of medieval weaponry. She averted her eyes, trying to avoid the sight of wicked curving hooks and sharp blades.

Phaedra felt her heartbeat quicken. She loathed the hall even in the daytime. Why now, of all nights, was she lingering here instead of bolting up to the security of her bedchamber? Mayhap she sought to prove to herself that she was not afraid. Sometime in the hours between now and dawn she would have to come to terms with the truth of Armande's identity as James Lethington. Mayhap that was best done here in the hall, where it had all begun seven years ago—the chain of tragedy that reached out from the past to threaten her.

Drawing in a deep breath, she forced her feet past that one part of the hall she had always avoided. The suit of armor stood cloaked in shadow, the lifeless man of iron menacing her with the weapon in its upraised gauntlet. Mocking eyes seemed to regard her through the slits in the plumed helmet, the lower joining of the visor appearing curved into a taunting smile.

She attempted to confront the worst of her fears, picturing Armande's face distorted with the fury to kill, his strong, supple fingers replacing that fist of tarnished iron, grasping the mace. Her heart rebelled, refusing to allow such an image to linger even in the darkest recesses of her thoughts.

"So you have returned at last."

The familiar silken voice sliced at Phaedra out of the darkness, terrifying her with its sudden proximity, like a razor stroked too close to her flesh.

She cried out, whirling to look behind her, stumbling and clattering against the armor. The candle dropped from her hand and rolled across the floor, sending wild arcs of light through the chamber. She caught a glimpse of the hard, pallid angles of Armande's face set beneath his thick mane of dark hair, his eyes like blue flame, the wavering shadow of his hard-muscled frame falling across her as the candle spun away.

She cowered against the suit of armor, unable to speak. Miraculously the candle did not snuff itself out, but came to rest against the wall, dripping wax upon the stone floor.

Armande turned aside long enough to retrieve it. Then he held the taper so that the light fell fully across her face. She flung her hand before her eyes in a defensive gesture.

"I am sorry if I frightened you," he said dryly. "You needn't tremble so. There are no windows here."

His sarcastic reference to her suspicions regarding Hester's death did nothing to calm Phaedra's racing heart. Armande's lips curved in a bitter half-smile, his frozen look not quite concealing some darker emotion that raged within him. His wintry eyes never left her face as he snuffed out the candle, the smoke curling in wisps between them, the hall entombed in darkness except for the glow of the oil lamp by the door.

Yet Phaedra inched away from the lamplight toward the marble stairway, the concealing blackness of the landing above them. "I—I wasn't expecting anyone to be awake," she said.

With one deft stride, Armande placed himself in front of her. He made no move to touch her, but the broad width of his shoulders straining beneath the immaculate shirt of white linen formed an impassable barrier between her and the stairs.

"I looked into your room this morning, but you were gone," he said. "I have been watching for your return all day. I believe you have something that belongs to me."

The accusation was couched in the softest of accents, yet Phaedra's keen ears detected the anger beneath. Unable to meet his stare, she lowered her eyes to the cravat knotted with precision about his neck, the lace-trimmed linen concealing that familiar small scar.

She moistened her lips and stammered. "I—I don't understand."

He took a step closer, the movement rife with an impatience barely held in check. "The figurine is missing from the wooden chest in my room. It was taken either by your hand or your cousin's. I don't care who took it. I want it returned."

Phaedra's hands fluttered to the joining of her cloak, but she abandoned any further attempt to deceive him. Fumbling beneath the mantle's dark folds, she produced the small parcel from one of the voluminous pockets. Silently she handed Armande the shepherd without unwrapping it. He pocketed it, his mouth pinching into a tight white line. After a moment's hesitation, Phaedra drew forth the shepherdess. Slowly she peeled away the cotton batting. She raised the diminutive statue so that it was outlined by the lamp's glow.

She heard the quick intake of Armande's breath. He stared for long moments, the lines of anguish deepening about his eyes revealing the painful memories that seared through him. In constricted tones he said, "And how did you come by that?"

"I found it a long time ago in my garret. I didn't know the significance of it until I saw yours." Rather clumsily she held out the statue. "Take it. By rights it belongs to you."

He made no move to accept it, his gaze raking her, the lean planes of his face flushing dark with suspicion and uncertainty.

She retreated a step, essaying a shaky laugh that was but a whisper away from a sob. "You were right about me all along. I never know when to stop asking questions. Today I asked one too many." She swallowed. "I—I went to see a doctor named Glencoe."

The name seemed to thud between them with all the force of a hammer's blow. When she fell silent, Armande prodded harshly, "And? What then?"

"I know everything, Armande," she said, struggling to keep her voice level. "Or—or perhaps I should call you James."

"You may call me anything you damn well please!"

The sudden release of his anger caused Phaedra to shrink back further. Yet she pleaded, clinging desperately to one last hope. "If you told me that none of it were true, even now I would believe you."

"Would you?" He laughed almost savagely. "Nay, I won't put your faith in me to such a strain." He advanced upon her, his fine-chiseled features twisting into a furious sneer. "That is exactly who I am, my dear. Old Lethe, the legendary murderer of Blackheath Hall. A walking corpse with bloodstained hands. I wonder you dare to be down here alone with me."

With each step he took, Phaedra stumbled backward until she was pinned against the cold, rough stone of the wall.

"Except that you don't dare, do you?" he bit out. "You've been waiting for your chance to escape up those stairs, terrified that I mean to throttle you at any moment."

She shook her head, trying to deny it, but her breath came out in a frightened sob.

"Damn you, Phaedra. 'Tis you who are killing me." He yanked her into his arms, trapping her ruthlessly against the hardness of his body so that she could scarcely breathe or cry out. The shepherdess, still clutched in her hand, all but broke apart between her gripping fingers as she struggled to be free.

James pressed hot, savage kisses along the column of her throat, his words choked with the embittered fury of despair. "How oft have I held you in my arms, loved you in a way I never have loved any other, and still you could think that I would—"

Scarcely thinking what she did, Phaedra drove her foot hard against his instep. In that brief second he relaxed his grip enough for her to claw her way out of his arms. Tears streaming down her cheeks, she backed away toward the stairs.

"Phaedra!" He raged her name, sending it echoing off the rafters. He stretched his hand toward her in a gesture that was half a demand, half a plea.

She pressed her hand to her trembling lips. Looking into his tormented eyes, she could see how her fears tore him apart, and she hated herself. She sensed that he was deliberately seeking to terrorize her—daring her, nay begging her, to fight back, to do anything but shrink from him.

But she could not give him the reassurance he sought with such desperation. Instead of her hand, she placed the shepherdess in his open palm. "Please, Armande . . . James," she gasped. "Let me go. Tomorrow, when 'tis light—"

She broke off, flinching away from him as he uttered a vicious oath and hurled the figurine against the opposite wall. The sound of the delicate china sharding into a myriad of pieces shattered what remained of Phaedra's control.

Sobbing, she spun about and hurled herself up the darkness of the stairs, stumbling on the hem of her gown, nearly pitching forward onto her face. She expected at any moment to feel James's hands close upon her, dragging her back.

She was about halfway up the long, curving stair before she realized he was not coming after her. She slowed, taking one more uncertain step. The hall had resumed its unnatural silence, the only sound her ragged breathing.

Phaedra turned, risking one glance back at the chamber below her. By the spot where the figurine had shattered, James stood frozen, a lonely silhouette in the soft glow pooling from the lamp. She watched the last vestiges of anger drain from him, his face taking on the blank despair of a man blinded, left forever to grope alone in the darkness.

His hands balled into fists, and he buried his eyes against them, sinking down until he knelt amidst the glistening fragments of china.

Phaedra's fear vanished, a dull ache taking possession of her heart. Damning herself for a fool, she rushed back down the stairs and crossed the hall to his side. His powerful frame was wracked with such tremors that she hesitated to touch him. Such grief in a man of James's iron control seemed almost too private a thing to be witnessed even by her eyes.

Gently, she caressed his bowed head, her trembling fingers snagging in the strands of dark hair. She felt him stiffen, then he lowered his hands, to look up at her. He wrapped his arms about her waist, burying his face in the softness beneath her breasts. Phaedra clasped her hands behind his neck, her own tears glistening upon his hair as she kissed the top of his head. She held him thus for a long time, offering him wordless comfort. When at last she could speak, the only words she could utter were "I'm sorry." How foolish, how inadequate, that sounded in the face of all that he had suffered!

He pulled gently away from her. Resting one hand heavily upon her shoulder, he struggled to his feet. She could almost feel him regathering his strength and pride as he rose.

He cupped her face between his hands. The smile tugging at his lips was so achingly sad that Phaedra had to battle against a fresh flood of tears.

" 'Tis I who should apologize to you," he said. "You have now seen the worst of James Lethington's infamous temper. A condition I thought I had cured in myself long ago."

Although he brushed aside the last traces of her tears, his eyes clouded with bitterness. "When I was young . . ." He spoke as though that had been many, many ages ago. "I was nearly consumed with ambition, dreams. I was going to make my mark upon the world, leave behind a name to echo through time."

He laughed softly, the sound lacking in all mirth. "Little did I realize the name of James Lethington would be used to terrify little girls."

His fingers trailed along her skin, tracing the curve of her cheek, his gaze softened with tenderness. She caught his hand and pressed her lips against the warm hollow of his palm.

"This particular little girl is a fool," she whispered. "Can you ever forgive me?" She tried to find the words to explain to him what she scarcely understood herself, that even loving him as she did, she could yet be afraid. " 'Tis only that I felt bewildered, stunned. In all my wildest imaginings about your past, I never thought that—that . . ."

"The dead could return to walk the earth?" He meant the words to sound mocking, but his voice cracked.

"My feelings for Ewan betrayed me once, made me a victim," she continued. "But what I felt for him was mere infatuation, not one particle of the love I bear for you. I have never been so vulnerable in my life as I have been with you. I think that is, more than anything, why I was so terrified when you . . ."

Her words trailed off as she spread her hands in a helpless gesture. "But you have always been so strong, so self-contained. I daresay you do not understand what it is to be afraid."

"Aye, but I do. There is one fear that is my constant torment."

When she regarded him questioningly, the haunted look in his eyes pierced her to the core of her soul."

"The fear of losing you."

He gathered her up in his arms, straining her close to the region of his heart. "Phaedra," he murmured against her hair. "I should have told you the truth long ago, but that fear kept me silent. I was terrified that once you had heard my real name, once you knew I was a condemned murderer, that you would flee from me in horror. Is it too late for me to explain? Will you listen to me now?"

Before she had the chance to assent, they were both startled by the creak of a door, the sound of a footfall behind them. In a movement that was almost reflexive, they drew quickly apart. Phaedra turned to see the footman Peter come straggling belatedly into the hall, bearing a candlestick in his upraised hand. Although he appeared somewhat surprised to see Phaedra and her house-guest standing alone in the dimly lit chamber, the young man appeared far more anxious to cover up his own dereliction of duty. His features flushed as he sought furtively to redo the uppermost button of his breeches.

"Lady Phaedra. My lord," he stammered. "I am sorry. I was away from my post for but a moment. Then I thought I heard a noise."

"I dropped a piece of china." James's voice was wooden as he thus described the destruction of a most cherished treasure. Whatever self-reproach he felt, he concealed it beneath a gruff command to Peter to see that the fragments were swept away. He took the candlestick from the footman, saying, "I will see her ladyship safely upstairs."

Leaving the abashed footman still trying to offer excuses for his absence, Phaedra followed James silently up the stairs. At the second-floor landing, he turned to her, saying, "You never gave me your answer, my lady. May the accused be permitted to speak in his own defense?"

Although he attempted to make the question sound light, almost indifferent, she sensed with what anxiety he awaited her answer. Silently, she slipped her hand into his.

James set the candlestick down upon the windowsill in his bedchamber. The flame reflected back in the night-darkened pane, an ignis fatuus, a foolish fire, hovering just beyond the glass. The moon was hidden behind the clouds, rendering the sky a sea of blackness. It was the most lonely part of night, when darkness threatens to stretch on forever, the rose-gold of dawn never to come again.

While Phaedra settled herself into a stiff-backed chair, James paced before her, for all the world as though he were a prisoner in the dock preparing to mount one final, desperate defense for his life. The candle flickered, its illumination darting upward, casting James's hard-sculpted features half in light, half in shadow. Watching him was like gazing upon the souls of two men trapped within the taut silhouette of his lithe frame.

It was Armande de LeCroix's well-modulated voice that spoke to her, as icily controlled as ever; but the fire in the blue eyes and the angry set to the mouth were the features of James Lethington.

"It's a long story, Phaedra, and my faith not one I care to . . . to bring again to life."

Phaedra nodded and said gently, "I am ready to listen."

His words came hesitantly at first, then more confidently as James delved deeper into his tale, weaving a spell about Phaedra until she felt carried back into the past, transported by the anguished recounting of his memories.

Through James's eyes, she saw, in more detail, much of the story that had already become somewhat familiar to her—the restless young man longing for adventure, yearning to pursue some intangible dream far beyond the staid confines of his family's china shop. Then came the death of his beloved father, forcing him to assume the responsibilities of the business as well as to look after his gentle mother and sister and his quiet younger brother, Jason. Phaedra heard James's bitterness at being entrapped in a role to which he was so ill-suited, his guilt and despair as the shop began to fail, his anger and apprehension when he realized the growing attraction between Julianna and Ewan Grantham. She could feel his determination to keep his impressionable sister away from the weak man whom he held in contempt.

"You see, my dear, Ewan's father had already begun arranging his marriage to a rich man's granddaughter, the beautiful Miss Phaedra Weylin, yet residing in Ireland." Here James paused to give Phaedra a rueful, tender smile. The smile abruptly vanished as he continued, "Ewan had not the courage to defy his father openly, but he wanted Julianna to elope with him. My sister Anne loved all of us far too well to deceive her family in such a manner. Before the elopement could take place, she confessed everything to us."

James sighed. "I reacted too harshly. I cursed Ewan, forbade her to ever see him again. Anne dissolved into tears and fled to her room. That was the last time I ever saw her.

"When I came upstairs from the shop for tea, I found her gone. No," he said as though anticipating the question Phaedra had been about to voice. "She hadn't left to elope with Ewan. She had only gone, with my mother's permission, to tell him good-bye. I was angry, and would have gone after her at once; but my mother said, 'Let be, Jamey. She loves the lad, but Anne is a sensible girl. She only wants to see him one last time, bid him farewell, and give him that little shepherdess she made. We can always design something else for the Emperor.'"

James interlaced his hands, his fingers tightening. "I wasn't concerned about the damned Emperor's commission. I was worried about my sister, but I allowed my mother to dissuade me. I waited for her return until the sun went down. When I saw the darkness gathering outside and she still hadn't come back, I went after Ewan Grantham."

James's shoulder stiffened, and the high contours of his cheek-bones pulled blade-sharp with tension. His eyes were twin flames as he rounded the darkest bend of this journey back into his past.

"I tracked Ewan down to his lodgings, and we nigh had a set-to there and then. He was as furious as I, ranting that I had kept Julianna away from their rendezvous. That was when I realized he hadn't seen my sister all day, either. A feeling of dread began to churn in my stomach. Then Ewan turned pale. He was obviously afraid. 'If it was not you who detained Julianna,' he said to me, 'then it must have been . . . my father.'

"Ewan didn't want to explain any more than that, but he finally told me his father had made threats of what he would do to Julianna if Ewan did not give her up."

"That sounds most likely," Phaedra interrupted softly. "From what I have heard, Carleton Grantham was badly in debt. He needed my grandfather's money desperately, and his son's marriage to me was the guarantee he would get it."

James nodded. "And Lord Carleton was not the sort of man to hold any particular regard for human life. When I thought that Julianna might have been in his hands . . ." James shuddered. "I forced Ewan at once to tell me where his father was. He said that Lord Carleton had gone out to the Heath to go over marriage settlements with Sawyer Weylin. As usual, Ewan lacked the courage to confront his father himself. So I went alone."

James's voice dropped so low it was nigh inaudible. He closed his eyes. Phaedra reached out to him in a comforting gesture, but when he opened his eyes, she shrank back. His gaze fired with a hatred that seared her own soul, although she knew his rage was not directed at her, but at some shadowy figure from the past only James could see.

His voice sounded almost leaden as he resumed. "I had no difficulty gaining entrance to the Heath. The place was strangely empty, not a servant in sight, no one except for *him*. Lord Carleton," James spat the name with loathing. "When I confronted him, he, at first sneered at me, denied knowing about my sister. Then I saw Julianna's cloak dropped in a heap by the stairs. It was torn as though in a struggle. Carleton . . . the damned devil just laughed in my face.

"He told me that aye, he did now recall 'entertaining' my sister, could understand why his son Ewan found the pretty little whore so fascinating. I—I should have held my temper, should have found out exactly what he had done with Julianna, but something just seemed to explode inside me." James's hands clenched into fists, a savage light coming into his eyes even now at the memory. "I could have ripped him apart with my bare hands. I went for his throat, but he seized a pike from the wall and rushed me with it. I managed to deflect the tip and grappled with him, sending him flying back—"

Phaedra was scarcely aware of her own tension, that she sat upon the very edge of her seat, gripping the arm rails until James paused to wipe at the perspiration beading his brow.

"Dear God, Phaedra, after all these years I am still not certain how it happened. That damned mace was set on the wall in those days. Mayhap when Carleton grabbed the pike, he somehow loosened the mountings. I only know that when he crashed back, the mace came down and . . . He died almost instantly."

Phaedra stirred uneasily. This was far different from any account of Carleton Grantham's death she had ever heard before. With his uncanny perception, James sensed her feelings at once.

"Aye, you are right to look so doubting, my dear," he said. "An accident so bizarre surpasses all belief. I realized that myself at once. But before I could react, your grandfather came upon the scene. He clubbed me over the head with his cane. Next morning, I awoke in Newgate. I tried to render my account of the death, but already it was too late. Ewan Grantham had sworn that he saw me murder his father in cold blood."

Phaedra had half-dreaded to hear that it was her grandfather who had borne witness against James. Greatly astonished to hear that it had been Ewan, she protested, "But you said that Ewan was not even there. Why would he tell such lies?"

James raked his fingers through his dark hair, the gesture rife with frustration and helplessness. "To this day, I don't know for certain. Maybe he believed that I had killed his father and would come after him if given a chance. I probably would have, for at that point Julianna's cloak had been found by the river and everyone was saying she had killed herself. But Ewan seemed so frightened that I wondered if he had learned more about her death than he was telling."

James's shoulders sagged, a weary sigh escaping him. "Of course, no one believed my version of the event. Not even Dr.

Glencoe, not even my own mother. My temper was legend, my account of the accident far too strange for belief." James's gaze shifted toward her, bitter with accusation. "Just as you don't believe me now."

Phaedra ached to assure him that she did, but the words that escaped her lips sounded faint even to her own ears. He looked quickly away from her.

"To make a tedious story short," he continued dully, "I was convicted of murder and hanged."

He gave a mirthless bark of laughter. "And that is probably the strangest part of my whole tale. You see, I had never been to a hanging. 'Twas not a diversion my father ever felt suited for his family. If I had been a little more experienced in such matters I might not be here now."

When Phaedra shot him a look of troubled bewilderment, he explained dryly, "If you want your neck to snap quickly, you have to take a small leap into the air as the flooring drops away. Otherwise you just . . . dangle."

James's hand moved involuntarily to his collar. "The rope tightened, digging into my flesh, pressing on my throat, crushing . . . cutting off my air." His eyes glazed with the memory. Phaedra clutched her hands in her lap to still their trembling. She was so caught up in the pain and horror of what he described, 'twas as though she could feel the rope constricting about her own neck, tearing at her own life. She doubted James realized that his own breath now came faster, and his fingers unconsciously yanked at his cravat, ripping it away from his neck.

"I—I couldn't seem to breathe—couldn't seem to die, either," he rasped. "I don't know how long I fought for my life. It felt like eternity. The crowd blurred before my eyes. The last thing I saw was Ewan's face. My last thought was that, if I had to come back from hell itself, I would find a way to make him tell the truth."

James's powerful fingers massaged his neck. He drew in a steadying breath before he was able to speak calmly once more. "When I next regained consciousness, I was not in heaven or hell, but Dr. Glencoe's cottage. My throat swathed in bandages, I felt like I had swallowed fire, but I was alive—if you want to call it that.

"As recompense for saving me . . ." James could not quite keep the bitter sneer from his words. "Glencoe wanted me to take my mother and brother and go away. I was in no further danger from the law, because a man who survives hanging is generally pardoned. But the old man feared the vindictiveness of Ewan Grantham. Mayhap he feared my own vindictiveness even more. I wanted to get at the truth of Julianna's death, and if there were any besides Lord Carleton who had had a hand in it, I wanted them to pay. But for my mother's sake, and for Jason's, I was persuaded to go. We salvaged what few belongings we could from the shop, and set sail for Canada.

"My mother was a gentle woman, Phaedra, far too gentle. Losing Julianna, the grinding days of my trial, witnessing my execution and return from the dead, having to flee our home . . . 'twas all too much for her. She fell ill on the voyage. I believed she might have recovered if she had had the will. As it was, Jason and I could do naught but watch her slip away . . ."

His words trailed to silence. James turned from Phaedra to stare out the window as through his story were done. Her own heart weighted with the sharing of his grief, the horror he had survived, it was some moments before Phaedra could speak herself.

"But now, after seven years, you have come back," she said almost timidly.

He bowed his head in ironic acknowledgment.

"Why?" she breathed, half-knowing the answer to her question, half-hoping to hear she was wrong.

"I would have thought that would be patently obvious, my dear." He swiveled to face her, his eyes narrowed to shards of ice.

"I've come back to learn the truth of sister's death, and to crush those responsible for destroying my family."

"Carleton Grantham is dead. So is Ewan."

"Aye," James said, his soft voice chilling her. "But Sawyer Weylin is very much alive."

Chapter Nineteen

PHAEDRA BOLTED UP FROM HER CHAIR, FEELING THE COLOR FLOOD into her cheeks. "Not Sawyer Weylin," she cried. "'Tis *my grandfather* that you threaten."

"You have no need to remind me of that," James said tersely. "It is a fact that I have cursed in my own heart more than once."

She stretched out her hands to him in a gesture of appeal. "I understand your hating Ewan, wanting revenge against him, but—"

"Ewan's dead." The savage regret in James's voice caused her to recoil from him.

"So you've transferred your fury to my grandfather." She lowered her eyes. "And—and mayhap to me, as well."

"No! Never would I hurt you. You must believe that. Damn it, Phaedra. You are more a victim of Weylin's schemings than anyone. Did he not sell you to the devil in marriage?"

"But what has my grandfather ever done to you?"

"He was part of it all—the scheming that destroyed my family. Curse him!" James hissed. "Can you not see that?"

Phaedra shook her head in vehement denial.

"He must have witnessed what took place between me and Carleton that night. Yet he made it look as though he had stopped me in the act of murder. Weylin never appeared at my trial, but he allowed Ewan to come forth and tell his lies. He very likely was the one who persuaded Ewan to speak."

"But—but," she faltered. "My grandfather would have had no reason to—"

"Wouldn't he?" James's voice grated harsh against her ears. "If he knew all about Lord Carleton's plans to abduct my sister, it would have been in Sawyer Weylin's interest to silence any questions regarding her disappearance. And to do that, Weylin had to silence me."

Phaedra opened her lips, wanting to deny it, but no sound came. She knew her grandfather to be ruthless, but he held to his own code of gruff honesty. And yet balanced against that was his obsession with raising his family into the ranks of the aristocracy, securing a title for his heirs. Would the wily old man have gone so far as to see a young girl destroyed, an innocent man hanged, if he could thus further that goal? The mere suspicion of such a thing was enough to make Phaedra press her hand to her mouth, nearly sick with despair.

Yet the concern that clutched at her heart was not so much for her grandfather as it was for James. When she saw the hatred burning in his eyes, she scarcely recognized the man she loved. It was as though flames of vengeance flared up inside him, threatening to consume his very soul.

She touched the rigid curve of his cheek, her caress holding both pity and fear. "And you've spent the last seven years of your life plotting this—to be avenged upon a weak fool like Ewan and a gout-ridden old man?"

"No." A bitter, fleeting smile touched James's lips, but not his eyes. "I spent the last seven years trapping fur and getting rich, trying to bury the past as my brother did. But I am not cut from the same cloth as Jason. I could not forget, though God knows I tried." He resumed his restless pacing as though the emotions churning inside him no longer enabled him to remain still. "The hatred I felt kept festering within me until finally Armande said—"

"Armande?" she echoed, startled.

"My trapping partner, the most noble Marquis de Varnais. A bandy-legged little Frenchman who wouldn't be caught dead in these satins and silks." James gave the lace at his wrist a contemptuous flick. "He despises his title as much as your grandfather covets it."

"So you stole his identity," she accused.

"Not stole. He loaned it. A most practical man, the marquis. He said I should return in disguise, learn the truth of my sister's death, kill my enemies, and be done with it, then get on with my life." The matter of fact way James said this chilled Phaedra's heart. He continued, "I suppose I was fortunate Ewan was already dead. The rest of the world appears to have forgotten James Lethington, but he would have recognized me. That only left your grandfather. With him, I took a great risk by appearing as the marquis. But Weylin had only ever set eyes upon me once, on the night of the murder, and I suppose he did not expect to see a dead man rise up to haunt him.

"'Twas an easy matter to arrange chance meetings at his coffeehouse, flatter him with the attentions of that great nobleman, the Marquis de Varnais, and thus insinuate myself into his confidence."

"And what have you learned?" Phaedra asked. "Have you any definite proof connecting my grandfather to your sister's death?"

"No," James admitted, "but I have seen the ruthless manner in which your grandfather deals with other unfortunates. Remember the Wilkins family? I know now that he would have been capable of helping Carleton to dispose of my sister."

"Oh, James," Phaedra cried. "On the basis of only suspicion, you would—would kill my grandfather?"

She thought that if she had been possessed of the strength, she would have seized James by the shoulders, tried to shake this madness from him. She blazed, "Are you so eager then to stand trial for murder a second time?"

"I've learned to be a little more subtle," James said through clenched teeth. "I have been going through Weylin's business records, his dealings with parliament, seeking something, anything, that could ruin him, but leave him alive to suffer as I have done."

"And what on earth do you expect to—" She broke off, going cold at the memory surfacing in her mind. "My God," she faltered. "You've already found the way, haven't you? And I gave it to you—the morning I told you I was Robin Goodfellow."

"Yes, curse you!" James stalked furiously toward the windows. After what they had both been through in these hours, Phaedra expected to see some sign of dawn lightening the sky. But the night stretched on, unrelentingly black.

James paced back, muttering savagely, "Weylin's own granddaughter the writer of revolutionary essays, loaded with information she gleaned from him. The scandal alone would have brought him down. He'd have lost his place in parliament and—" James's voice choked with bitterness. "The very thing I'd been looking for! And I cannot use it, because of you!"

"I am sorry to be such a hindrance to your plans," she said brittlely. "How unfortunate that I ever returned from Bath."

James swore softly. "Damn it, Phaedra! You know I never meant that. But surely you must see what a cursed irony it is. I find the one woman capable of gifting me with love, with the desire to do more than just exist—and she is also the one obstacle to settling this score, to finally knowing peace."

"I only see one thing—that you will never find peace this way." She planted herself in front of him to stop his pacing. Catching his face between her hands, she pleaded, "James, I beg of you. Let it go. Leave my grandfather alone."

He forced her hands down, his voice accusing as he said, "I didn't know you harbored such great affection for the old man that you would desire so much to save him."

"It is not him I want to save, but you. If you could but see your face when you talk of this vengeance. You grow so cold, but your eyes burn as though you were consumed with fever." She averted her gaze. "It frightens me to look upon you."

Her words appeared to have no effect. He paced away from her, his facial muscles pulled taut, his eyes stormy as he retreated into that dark realm where she had no way to reach his thoughts. The sufferings he had endured were enough to have broken most men. It was a testimony to his strength of will that he had survived without descending into madness.

Phaedra loved him far too well to see him hover now on the brink and make no effort to draw him back. In desperation, she followed after him, catching at his sleeve. He did not shake her off, but he seemed more distant and unreachable than the night she had first met him.

She lowered her voice, trying to infuse more softness and patience into her tone. "James, you have been grievously injured by my grandfather. I admit that, though I still cannot believe he had any responsibility for Julianna's death. Some recompense is indeed owed you. I simply wish that you could bring yourself to extract a—a more gentle form of retribution."

He turned to stare at her, the set of his mouth hard and discouraging. "What do you mean?"

She was not altogether sure herself, but an idea was forming in her mind. Now it took on a crystal clarity that both frightened her and caused her pulse to race with undreamed-of hopes.

"C—could not having taken his granddaughter away from him be payment enough?"

His granite expression relaxed somewhat, but a deep frown crossed his brow. "I am still not certain what you are suggesting."

"I am asking you to leave London, forget why you came here, leave my grandfather undisturbed. In return, I will go away with you." She made the offer with a defiance that barely masked her fear of his rejection.

James regarded her a moment in blank, uncomprehending silence. Then he said slowly. "You are offering to come back with me . . . to—to Canada?"

"Aye, to Canada, to wherever you choose. To hell itself if that is where you lead me."

His eyes raked her face almost as though he dared not credit what he was hearing. "You trust me enough to abandon everything—your own dreams of being independent—to put your very life into my keeping?"

"Aye. I *love* you enough, even for that." She managed to keep her voice steady, although she quailed inwardly, certain that in another moment he would smile with scorn, laugh at her. But the light that broke over his face took her breath away. He looked like a prisoner emerging from his chains in the dark, glimpsing the sun for the first time in years.

"Phaedra!" He choked her name, crushing her in his arms, sweeping her off her feet.

"Then—then 'twould be enough for you?" she breathed.

"Enough!" A sound escaped him, somewhere between a laugh and a groan. "It would be a dream. I should have to tread softly for fear of waking." He drew back to look at her, a shadow of doubt momentarily darkening the glow in his eyes. "You truly mean it? You would do this out of love for me and not some sort of sacrifice to spare that obscene old—"

She cut him off by touching her lips to his. "I would come for no other reason than that I should perish without you."

"You realize that the home I could offer you would be nothing like this?" James gestured, indicating the gilded magnificence of the bedchamber. "Canada is an untamed land, and there is the war in the American colonies. Although we have not been much disturbed by it yet, there is always the chance—"

Phaedra kissed him again to silence him. "I should not mind any of that if I was with you." She gave a shaky laugh. "Indeed, I might regard it as a challenge to convince your Canadian friends they are supporting the wrong side in the war."

James stared down at her for a moment, clutching her to him as though she were an armful of mist he expected to vanish at any moment. Then he kissed her with such infinite tenderness, Phaedra tasted upon his lips all the poignancy of his longing, all the wistfulness of his dreams too long denied.

He held her, kissed her as though he would never let her go. He was consumed with the feverish joy of a man whose very soul had been parched and who had found the wellspring of life at last.

When he drew back, it seemed to Phaedra as though their hearts touched in the meeting of their eyes. He swept her off her feet, cradling her high against him, carrying her to the bed to set tender seal upon the pact they had just made.

As often as James had made love to her this summer, Phaedra had experienced nothing like the passion that coursed between them now. Before there had been a desperate edge that had sparked almost a ferocity into James's loving. This time he undressed her so slowly, with such great care, Phaedra nigh cried out with longing for his caress.

Even after he stretched out naked beside her, the warm, strong contours of his muscular frame straining against her, James yet prolonged the moment of their joining. He kissed and stroked, his hands molding her curves with trembling worship as though she offered him a great gift, one that he scarcely dared to accept.

Phaedra banded her arms about him, her lips brushing the scar upon his throat, the only visible mark of all that he had suffered. She sought to draw out that pain from him as much as she did to fan the flames of his desire.

He pressed her back into the downy softness of the pillows, burying his lips against her hair, his breath warm as he murmured, "Tell me again. Say it—that you will be mine."

"Aye, yours," she whispered. "Yours forever."

A soft moan escaped her when he at last eased himself inside her. He moved slowly, bathing them both in tender fire. Phaedra became lost in the rhythm as though she already followed James upon that sea of forbidden dreams—upon wild, dark waves that, when they crested, left them both spent upon some faraway shore.

Long after their passion had faded into warm afterglow, James continued to hold her close, molding her flesh to his. He clung to her, claiming her with a possessiveness that both filled her with joy and frightened her. He could not seem to relax the tension cording his strong fingers, as if he feared that by releasing her, ceasing to touch her, she would draw away from him and change her mind.

"You will never want for anything, never regret your choice. I swear it." His voice was a fierce whisper in the darkness.

"Hush, love." Phaedra burrowed deeper against James's shoulder, wishing he had not spoken of regrets. But it was not hers that she feared so much as his. What if her love was not enough? What if the time came when his desire for her was overcome by the desire to be avenged?

Nay, her love would be enough. She would make it so.

It took James several days to arrange for their passage from England. By the night they were scheduled to depart, Phaedra felt as though her nerves were as brittle as glass, stretched too thin by the blower's art, ready to shatter at the slightest touch.

On the day of the elopement, she alternated between the desire to brim with laughter and to burst into tears. As the sun slowly set, bathing her bedchamber window in hues of rose and amber, Phaedra fidgeted, scarcely able to stand still long enough for Lucy to mend the flounce of her white satin petticoat.

"Only a moment longer, milady," her harried maid pleaded, taking several more quick stitches. "There. 'Tis done." Lucy smoothed the petticoats down over the whalebone hoops billowing out around Phaedra. Then she helped her don a robe à l'anglaise of green pomona silk.

"You will look such a picture, milady," Lucy crooned. "So beautiful. I declare—just like a bride."

Phaedra started, shooting a wary glance at Lucy. If the girl were not so blithely imperceptive, Phaedra might have feared she had guessed something of the planned elopement.

Glancing at herself in the mirror, she supposed she could see what had occasioned Lucy's remark. She certainly looked pale enough to be a skittish maiden upon her wedding day. A hectic flush mounted high into her cheeks, the glittering green of her eyes enhanced by the matching shade of the gown.

As Lucy dressed her hair, Phaedra tried to calm the flutters in her stomach by mentally rehearsing James's plan. They were to attend a performance of Handel's opera, *Rinaldo*, at Covent Garden Theatre in the company of her grandfather. Phaedra was to pretend to be overcome by the heat, feeling faint. Knowing full well that her grandfather would never bestir himself, it would be left to James to take her out of the gallery for a breath of air. From there, they would simply vanish into the night, bundling into a closed carriage James had hired and make for Portsmouth. By dawn tomorrow, they would have caught the tide, and England's shoreline would be fast receding in the mist.

A simple plan. What could possibly go wrong? All the same, Phaedra's hands trembled as she drew on her gloves. Beset by all manner of qualms, she wondered what her grandfather would do when the theater chandeliers were lit and neither she nor James had returned. Would he have them pursued or simply sit back chuckling, still deluding himself she had run off with the Marquis de Varnais? If he did somehow glean the truth, Phaedra hated to think he would experience his shock in such a public place.

Although she fought against the notion, she could not help wondering if James had deliberately planned it that way. Had it ever occurred to him that mayhap he had indeed found the perfect revenge against Sawyer Weylin? The spiriting away of his only granddaughter would smash the old man's hope of realizing his most cherished dream—that of acquiring a title for his family. With Phaedra gone, he would have no family, and the broken old man would end his days alone.

Despite all that he had done, Phaedra felt a stab of pity for her grandfather. But she despised herself for even suspecting that James had ever considered such things when he had accepted her offer to go away with him.

No, she told herself firmly. The joy that suffused James's face of late came not from the anticipation of dealing a crushing blow to his old enemy, but from the knowledge that they would spend the rest of their lives together.

Lucy at last finished arranging a tiny spray of silk roses upon the crown of Phaedra's upswept hair. Only one long red-gold curl was left to trail over the creamy expanse of her shoulder.

" 'Tis not the fashion," Lucy said, looking pleased with her handiwork all the same. "But ever so much more becoming."

Phaedra regarded her own reflection for a moment before turning to stare at Lucy. How loyal the plain girl had always been, obeying her every command without question, even lying at times to cover for her. On a sudden impulse, Phaedra enveloped the tall, lanky frame of her maid in a quick hug.

"I don't know how I would have gotten on without you, Lucy," she said hoarsely. "You have served me well."

The maid looked astonished, but she blushed with pleasure. "Why, th—thank you, milady. I hope I continue to do so for many more years."

"Aye." Phaedra quickly averted her face. "There is no need for you to wait up for me this evening."

Or ever again, she added silently. The thought saddened her, despite her joy at the prospect before her. Lucy bade her a good evening and slipped out. Phaedra gave herself a brisk shake.

She would forget all of these qualms when she stood with James upon the deck of the ship, feeling his strong arms about her, his lips warming her. 'Twas only when she was left alone for too long that she was beset by doubts and hints of depression.

She tried to subdue her nervous tremors by taking a practical survey of her belongings. James had already spirited away one small trunk, all that she could take away with her, except whatever items she might fit into her purse.

Phaedra lifted the lid of her jewel case, studying the contents. Most of the sparkling gems meant little to her. Even the diamond aigrette earrings and the emerald brooch were but part of the image she had been expected to maintain as Lady Grantham. But she hesitated over the strand of pearls her grandfather had so recently given her.

Their luster seemed somehow dulled now, as she thought of the torment on James's face, and of how her grandfather's silence had helped see him hanged.

As though some of James's bitterness crept into her own soul, she rejected the pearls, dropping them back into the box. The only object she removed was an oval gold locket.

The locket was extremely plain. Its beauty for Phaedra lay in her memory of the giver. Two days before she had set sail from Ireland to become Ewan Grantham's bride, Gilly had tossed the locket into her lap, saying, with one of his teasing grins, "And you can rest easy wearing it, darlin'. 'Tis even paid for."

Phaedra's hand shook as she fumbled with the catch, opening the locket to reveal the hollow emptiness. Her eyes clouded with tears. "Damn you, Patrick Gilhooley Fitzhurst. Why did you never think to put a likeness of yourself inside?"

She clicked the locket closed, telling herself it didn't matter. She would carry the image of unruly black curls and laughing green eyes forever in her heart. It was the most painful part of her leavetaking—not being able to bid Gilly farewell. She had forestalled him with great difficulty these past few days, sending him notes begging him not to come to the Heath until she sent for him. She had even gone so far as to lie, writing that James Lethington had left the Heath, simply disappeared, assuring Gilly that all was well with her.

She feared seeing her cousin, knowing she might break down and reveal her plans. She could well imagine what Gilly's reaction would be. He would attempt to kill James rather than let her go off with a man he deemed dangerous.

Her only choice was to slip away like this, leaving behind a letter for Gilly, pleading with him to understand and not to fear for her, ending with the prayer that, God willing, they would some-how meet again one day.

Phaedra wiped at her eyes, then fastened the locket about her neck. She took one last glance about her bedchamber, but she felt no regrets that she had now spent her last night here. She had never truly known happiness in this room or any other of the elegant chambers of Sawyer Weylin's mansion. Only one part of the house had ever held any charm for her.

Lighting a candle, Phaedra rustled out of her bedchamber to take one final peek into her garret. She had not been up there since the day she had discovered Hester dead. As she mounted the narrow stairs, she tensed with apprehension. But she need not have worried. The candle's soft glow revealed her little sanctuary to be undisturbed even by the ghosts of the past. The dust gathered silently upon the jumbled assortment of furniture, which meant nothing to anyone save herself.

Phaedra walked immediately over to the bookshelf, running her fingers ruefully over the stiff leather spines. It was impossible to take the volumes with her. How ironic, she thought, that once more she must lose her treasured books—and this time because of the very man who had restored them to her.

Her gaze roved about the garret with a kind of bittersweet nostalgia. She found herself remembering all the dreams she had woven up here, her plans for independence, the desire to be free, never to place herself in the power of any man again.

Of course, she told herself hastily, that had all been long before she had fallen so desperately in love with James. A mocking voice inside her strove to remind her that she had once fancied herself wildly devoted to Ewan Grantham.

But it was far different this time, she assured herself. It had to be; the risks were so much greater. She was flinging herself into a void, with only this man's love to sustain her. She had to trust him.

Thus resolved, Phaedra had but one more task to perform before she quit the Heath forever. Briskly she walked over to the oak desk and unlocked it. She intended to make sure all copies of her Robin Goodfellow writings were burned. But as Phaedra groped inside the desk, an unreasoning feeling of panic settled over her. They were gone—the drafts she had bound up so neatly with the black ribbon.

Frantically, she rifled through the drawer, coming up with nothing but blank sheets of parchment and yellowed issues of the *Gazetteer*. Phaedra straightened, willing herself to be calm and think.

The last she had seen of the papers had been the day she had showed them to James. He had flung them back at her. She had gathered up the parchment in great distress. And then . . .

She pressed her fingertips to her temples in frustration, her mind drawing a blank. She simply couldn't remember. She thought she had brought the papers back up here, stuffed them into the desk. Phaedra rummaged through the drawer one more time, but with no result. She supposed she might have temporarily placed the drafts in her dressing table.

Snatching up the candle, she raced down to her bedchamber, but although she fairly tore the room apart, she turned up no sign of the missing papers. When Lucy came upstairs for the second time to report that Sawyer Weylin was growing impatient, Phaedra reluctantly had to abandon her search.

But as she flung her cloak over her arm, she fretted, "What could have happened to those accursed things?"

A thought occurred to her. Not a thought so much as a name—James. But she would not allow herself to pursue the fear. Instead she tried to tell herself that it truly did not matter. She was leaving London and her days as Robin Goodfellow far behind. If the papers came to light after the departure, she could rest assured her grandfather would be quick to destroy them.

Still striving to stifle her uneasiness, Phaedra descended the main stair to find her grandfather awaiting her in the hall below. James had not yet come down either, and the old man was fuming. Leaning upon his cane, Sawyer Weylin hobbled past the suits of armor, his elaborately curled white wig and purple satin waistcoat straining over his huge middle, making a strange contrast to those lean men of iron.

Phaedra tensed at the sight of him. Ever since hearing James's story, it had been difficult for her to bear being in the same room with Sawyer Weylin. She had adjured James to forget the past, but discovered she had a hard time doing so herself.

Each time she regarded the stubborn set of her grandfather's thick lips, the shrewd eyes set beneath heavy lids, she felt repulsed, unable to think of aught save the misery her grandfather had brought to both herself and James. How different things might have been if Weylin's first concern had been for his granddaughter's happiness! But he had thrown it all away, for the dream of enabling a great-grandchild to wear a coronet.

Phaedra feared that her face revealed some of what she felt. Her grandfather had seemed uneasy in her presence of late, and had grown more belligerent than ever. After growling his usual dissatisfaction with her unpowdered hair, he barked, "Why the deuce do you keep staring at me in that addle-witted fashion? Sometimes I think you've not been right in the head since the death of that Searle woman."

"Hester's violent death came as a shock to me," Phaedra said quietly, lowering her eyes. "Despite the fact that I never liked her. She was a most unpleasant woman."

"But a demned efficient housekeeper. I shall ne'er come by another so cheaply."

Phaedra choked back a bitter laugh. Hester's presence at the Heath had proved far more costly than her grandfather could ever imagine. The woman's death had forced Phaedra to open her eyes, to seek answers about "Armande." Those answers had led to her plans for this night. But thinking of the manner of Hester's death,

Phaedra shuddered. She supposed that was one mystery that must remain unsolved, although it would continue to haunt her long after she had left this place.

Phaedra's eyes traveled unwillingly toward the iron-spiked mace. There was more than one matter she should be content to let rest, but she could not seem to do so. She would never see her grandfather again after tonight, never have the chance to demand an accounting of his exact part in James's tragedy.

She said slowly, "Did you ever hear how Hester used to terrify cook's children with the story of James Lethington?"

Her grandfather appeared absorbed in consulting his pocket watch, shaking the timepiece as though it had stopped running. He grunted, "Fool woman would've done better to tend to her dusting 'stead o' blatherin' about what was none of her concern."

"But I often have wondered about the murder myself," Phaedra continued, studying her grandfather through her thick lashes. "Ewan sometimes spoke of it, of how he testified at Lethington's trial. But something never quite rang true. Do you suppose Ewan truly did witness his uncle's death?"

Weylin's florid countenance seemed to darken a shade. "'Course he did." Then after a lengthy pause, he added, "And even if he hadn't, it would scarce have mattered."

"Scarce have mattered!" Phaedra trembled with outrage, tortured by a vision of the rope crushing James's neck. "When a man's very life was at stake!"

"Lethington was guilty. I saw enough myself to be sure of that."

"Truly, Grandfather? Exactly how much did you see?"

But he feigned not to have heard her bitter question. He stumped over to the bottom of the stair, peering upward. "Where the deuce is Armande? The man takes his blasted time about everything. Why hasn't he proposed to you by now?"

Phaedra refused to allow herself to be diverted. "From what I heard, James Lethington might have had a reason for attacking Ewan's uncle. Carleton Grantham abducted his sister. Did you ever hear anything about that, Grandfather?"

His only reply was a grunt.

Phaedra persisted, "Julianna must have been a great inconvenience. Ewan always said he would have married her instead of me if she had not died."

Her grandfather dragged forth a handkerchief to mop at his

brow. "Ewan was a fool. From the way your marriage to him turned out, without even a son to inherit the title, I might as well have let him indulge his folly and marry some poor china-maker's chit."

Phaedra sucked in her breath. "*You* might as well have let Ewan marry Julianna? Pray tell me, Grandfather, what you did to prevent it."

Never had Phaedra seen such an expression upon her grandfather's face. His eyes shifted about as though he scarcely knew where to look. He appeared almost guilty. "Why—why, nothing," Weylin blustered. "Except to offer Ewan Grantham enough money to make sure he forgot about the Lethington girl. 'Twas the wench's own idea to run off and kill herself."

In that moment, Phaedra had a sick feeling that all of James's suspicions were correct. Her grandfather *did* know more of what had happened to Julianna Lethington than he ever would tell. But before she could ask anything further, James descended the stairs.

He looked magnificent, his powerful thighs molded by a pair of satin breeches, his rich burgundy frock coat showing off to perfection the power of his broad chest and shoulders. Phaedra was disturbed to see that he had powdered his hair. It was as though upon this final night as the Marquis de Varnais, he was determined to play the role to the hilt.

But he was not quite bringing it off. There was a high color in his face that belied the marquis's cool indifference, a suppressed excitement in his movements. Phaedra thought it fortunate that her grandfather had never really obtained a good view of James Lethington, or surely he would have recognized him in Armande tonight.

When his gaze met Phaedra's, she forgot all her doubts. She read nothing upon James's face but the glow of a man deeply in love, about to realize his heart's desire. Yet when his eyes shifted to her grandfather, her uneasiness returned.

James's mouth hardened with a contempt he was no longer at any pains to conceal. "Ah, *Monsieur* Weylin, garbed in all the splendor of your customary good taste, I see."

Even her thick-skinned grandfather could not possibly mistake the sneer behind James's words. Bewildered by his guest's change in manner, he sought to reply; Phaedra hastened to interpose herself in between the two men.

"We'd best hurry. I do detest arriving after the performance has begun." She handed James her cloak with a nervous smile. He stared hard at her grandfather a moment longer, then gazed down upon her with a gentle smile.

"Aye." He eased the cloak about her shoulders with great tenderness, even daring to press a furtive kiss behind her ear.

"Soon, my love," he breathed. "Very soon, 'twill all be over."

She thought that a most strange way of expressing their departure, but she nodded in agreement. She felt relieved when they left the house, James supporting her arm, her grandfather trailing after them. The air was so thick with tension and seething emotion; she wondered if the vast dark night itself could contain it all.

The carriage ride into the city passed by in a haze. She remembered naught of it but the warmth of James's hand clutching hers in the darkness. And yet she could not seem to draw any comfort from his strength. His fingers were never still, constantly caressing her palm as though it were the only outlet he could find for his restless anticipation.

The carriage set them down in the square outside Covent Garden Theatre, The "Market of Venus," the magistrate Sir John Fielding had once referred to it. The painted ladies of the night certainly did seem to outnumber those attending the opera.

Most of the *haut ton* no longer lived in London, preferring to spend the autumn hunting season at their country estates. And opera had lost much of its popularity since the days when the great Handel had been the director at Covent Garden Theatre.

Phaedra did not know whether to feel relieved or sorry not to be caught up in a press of people. A large crowd might have made their plans that much easier. As it was, she scarcely saw anyone that she knew—until she and James were about to step beneath the theater's portico. Then a familiar figure melted out of the shadows.

"Sure and this is a surprise. Fancy encountering you here, my dearest coz."

Phaedra's heart slammed against her ribs. She stared up into Gilly's unsmiling face, torn between the joy of seeing him one last time and a sickening sensation of dread.

Gilly's eyes darkened with reproach, then narrowed as he shifted his gaze toward James. "And if it isn't himself, his most noble lardship, the Marquis de Varnais. *Still* taking in the pleasures of London, I see."

Phaedra scarcely dared to glance at James's expression as he acknowledged Gilly's presence with a stiff nod.

"Gilly," Phaedra started to plead, scarcely knowing what her cousin might be prepared to do or say next, when her grandfather huffed up to join them.

"Eh! Fitzhurst, you here? Never knew you Irish had a fancy for opera."

"Oh, I would never miss an opportunity to hear the English acaterwauling." Gilly's hard gaze never wavered from Phaedra and James. "Would it be too imposing of me to include myself in this charming little party?"

Phaedra felt James's grip tighten possessively on her elbow as he spoke. "I am sure you would find a far better seat in the pits."

Gilly's jaw tightened. "I don't think so. I'm thinking I might be missing a great deal by not being up in the gallery."

Sawyer Weylin pressed past them all impatiently. "Well, come along to my box then and cease nattering about it before we miss the first act."

Gilly shot James a defiant stare and squared his shoulders. He insisted upon walking behind them, as though he intended not to let her or James out of his sight.

"James," Phaedra whispered. "What are we going to do?"

"Exactly as we planned," was his cool reply. He gave her hand a reassuring squeeze. "There is no need to worry about your cousin. Everything will be all right."

But it wouldn't be. She swallowed hard. James did not know Gilly as she did. He would not be so easily hoodwinked as her grandfather. Already she feared Gilly had read far too much of her intention upon her face.

Jut as they were about to enter the box, Gilly managed to yank her aside and hiss in her ear. "You wrote to me that Lethington had gone. Now just what the devil are you about?"

"Attending the opera," she said with a weak, nervous laugh.

Gilly's fingers crushed so hard about her wrist, she nearly cried out. "Aye, a cozy entertainment, this," he said angrily. "Just you, Jamey-boy, and his next intended victim."

"Don't!" she shrilled, then lowered her voice. "James is not going to hurt anyone. I—I have seen to that. You must trust me, Gilly."

"Trust you, bedamned. You lied to me, Fae, and 'tis plain as a pikestaff, you're far too besotted to know what you are doing anymore. When I accidentally met up with that Burnell fellow and he told me you were coming to the theater tonight, I could scarce credit my ears—"

"Gilly, please." Phaedra noticed James observing their tête-à-tête from the doorway. "I will explain everything to you—after the show."

The lie tasted bitter upon her lips, but it satisfied Gilly for the moment. They took their seats upon the benches in the box, James forestalling Gilly's efforts to sit beside her. From the grim looks that passed between the two men, Phaedra almost feared a scuffle. But Gilly grudgingly removed himself to sit directly behind her. He lit a candle to follow the book of the opera, then swore when James turned and snuffed it.

"'Tis a practice I would not encourage," James said levelly. "The dangers of fire, you know."

The savageness of Gilly's glowering countenance seemed inescapable. Phaedra was relieved when the lights in the theater's glass chandeliers were extinguished. But she saw nothing of the performance, and the shrill voice of the soprano served only to grate upon her nerves.

In their box, the members of the little party were all but shadowy figures in the dark. Yet Phaedra could sense Gilly's watchfulness and James's determination. Dear God, this was never going to work. Gilly would never believe her excuse of feeling faint. She had never swooned in her life. And even if he did believe her, he was bound to follow her and James out of the box. Her grandfather nodded off as he usually did at the theater, but she didn't have to look to know that Gilly's eyes were not trained upon the stage.

They were deep into the second act, when Phaedra felt James's touch upon her hand, giving her the signal. She tried to ignore it, but the pressure of James's hand became more insistent. She half-rose, starting to speak, then sank back down in despair.

She could sense James's growing impatience, but before any of them could react, the door to their box was flung violently open. Much to Phaedra's astonishment, Jonathan rushed in. She had never seen the somber man in such a state. Pale and wild-eyed, he seized her grandfather by the front of his coat, shaking him awake.

"Sawyer—Sawyer, for the love of God, you must leave."

Her grandfather snorted, rubbing his eyes. "Eh, what? But the opera—'tis not over."

He tried to push Jonathan's hands away, but the man would not release him. "Sawyer, you must leave London without delay and hide."

"What the devil's amiss?" Gilly said.

"Burnell's gone completely mad," Weylin groused, almost at the same time as Jonathan blurted out, "Jessym's been arrested."

Phaedra went cold. She avoided meeting Gilly's eyes.

"Jessym?" her grandfather huffed. "That scoundrel of a publisher? Why, 'tis nothing to me."

But everything to me, Phaedra thought. She tried to shrink against James, seeking the support of his arm about her. But he seemed to have gone suddenly stiff.

Jonathan wrung his hands. "Blast it, Sawyer, don't you understand? Jessym has been taken before the magistrates. To save himself from imprisonment, he has attempted to strike some sort of a bargain by offering them proof."

"Proof of what?" her grandfather asked impatiently.

"The proof that you, Sawyer Weylin, are Robin Goodfellow."

Chapter Twenty

SOMEWHERE IN THE DISTANCE, PHAEDRA HEARD A RICH BARITONE filling the theater with haunting notes of despair. But the tragedy unfolding on the stage below seemed remote, lost in the impact of Jonathan's dramatic statement. Sawyer Weylin began to bluster, "Why, I'll see Jessym hanged. The lying rogue."

But Phaedra shot to her feet, cutting him off. "What sort of proof could Jessym have possibly produced against my grandfather?"

Jonathan gave her a pleading glance, as though begging her not to interfere. "I believe Jessym had packets of original drafts with Weylin's seal upon them."

Phaedra placed a hand to her brow. The theater had begun to rock around her. Her missing drafts with her grandfather's seal on them? Nay, this was madness. She glanced at Gilly to gauge his reaction and found him staring hard at James.

Her stomach tensed. James's facial muscles had gone rigid, a strange light glowing in the blue eyes set beneath the hard slash of his brows . . . a light of—triumph?

"James." His name escaped her lips in a despairing whisper. But he didn't seem to hear her. He was lost to her, as she had always feared he would be, swept away by the dark currents of his revenge.

She bowed her head, trying to still her trembling. What a fool she had been, to ever think she could stay his hand! It was all painfully obvious now. He had taken her drafts, forged the seal, and then given them to Jessym, even while he had made arrangements for their elopement. Her love had not been enough for him.

Lost in her misery, Phaedra was only dimly aware of Jonathan dragging her grandfather out the door of the box. Weylin protested furiously enough to draw the attention of the entire theater.

"I'll not skulk off anywhere. Demnation, I'm an innocent man."

What vicious satisfaction her grandfather's declaration must be giving James, Phaedra thought unhappily.

"But Weylin," Jonathan said. "If you had but seen the crowds gathered outside the bailey. Many are still angered by that article Goodfellow wrote about the Catholics."

"By God, I'll roast the lot of them, starting with Jessym and his impertinent forgeries—" The rest of Weylin's angry words were lost as Jonathan managed to hustle him into the hall.

"Not forgeries, Grandfather," Phaedra said grimly as she started to go after him.

But Gilly barred her path, scowling. "Hold your tongue, Fae."

"Aye, your cousin is right." Phaedra heard James's steely whisper near her ear. She felt him grip her arm. "This is scarcely a prudent time for confessions."

She whipped around to face him, her eyes blazing with tears. "And did you truly expect me to stand by and let my grandfather pay for what I have done? Or maybe you thought we'd be long gone before he was ever arrested."

He frowned, his eyes darkening as he studied her with uncertainty. "My only interest is in protecting you, Phaedra."

"You're only interest is in destroying my grandfather. And you took my papers to do it, didn't you?"

Anger flared in his eyes with a pain that matched her own. "Why do you ask me, when you obviously already know?"

She spun away from him. Shoving past Gilly, she stormed out of the box.

She heard James hard after her. "Damn it, Phaedra, I love you. That is all that should matter." He caught her roughly, jerking her around to crush her in his arms. "You are leaving with me now, just as you promised."

"Take your hands off her." Phaedra heard Gilly's menacing growl, but she had already wrenched herself free.

"Nay," she said to James. "Our pact is ended, but it was you who broke it, not me."

"Then you are choosing to sacrifice our love to that—"

"What choice did I ever have?" she choked. "You made it for me!"

Tears spilling down her face, she ran blindly toward the stairs that led to the foyer below. As she half-stumbled down the carpet-covered length, she was aware of someone plunging after her. It was not James, but Gilly.

He caught up with her at the bottom of the stairs. His face looked pale but determined as he tried to soothe her. "Easy, Fae. I'll not be letting you do anything rash. We have but to keep our heads, and we'll see our way clear of this mess. No one will go to prison."

But she refused to listen to him. What odds did it make if she found herself flung into Newgate? It didn't matter to her now. Nothing did. Choking back another sob, she ran out of the theater into the streets beyond.

Her grandfather and Jonathan stood beneath the portico, still arguing. Their raised voices drew more than a few curious eyes in their direction, linkboys lingering with their lanterns to escort theatergoers through the dark streets, a few ragged beggars, lightskirts offering some burly sailors an evening's entertainment.

"You can take a hackney cab," Jonathan was saying to her grandfather, "and hide at my house until—"

"Demned if I will. I'm not some cowardly criminal, skulking away in the dark." He thumped his chest, raging so half the street could hear. "Blast it all, I am Sawyer Weylin, a respectable man of property. And I am not the flea-bitten writer who calls himself Robin Goodfellow."

"For the love of God, Sawyer," Jonathan said. "Keep your voice down."

Dashing away her tears, Phaedra pressed forward. "Grandfather, there is something I must tell you—"

Jonathan elbowed her aside. "Phaedra, leave this to me."

She glared at him, sick of the "protection" of men. But her grandfather had already hobbled away from the portico and into the street, bellowing at the top of his lungs, "So where is Ridley with my demned coach? I'll go to Newgate and throttle Jessym this very night."

For the first time Phaedra became aware of the mutterings borne to her upon the night breeze. Where the gathering mob had come from, she could not have said. One moment the pavement had been filled only with innocent onlookers; in the next, the shadows had spawned a threatening cluster of some dozen angry faces. The grumblings got louder until she made out snatches of words. "Sawyer Weylin . . . hear him say so . . . Robin Good-fellow."

Apprehension knotted Phaedra. Somehow she and Jonathan had to get her grandfather away from here.

But one coarse voice swelled above the rest. "Aye, he is Goodfellow. I heard Jessym say it, not three hours past." One of the sailors, a burly half-drunk fellow, shoved his way forward. The rest of the crowd surged after him into the street until they stood but yards from Sawyer Weylin, cursing and pointing accusing fingers.

"That's the one as wants to raise up the Catholics to murder us all."

Phaedra tried to rush to her grandfather's side but was stopped by Gilly and Jonathan, who attempted to hustle her back inside the theater.

"Jacobite!" "Scoundrel!" "Go live in Ireland 'mongst your papist friends."

Despite the crowd's taunts, all yet might have been well if Sawyer Weylin had ignored them. But he responded with characteristic aggression, brandishing his cane as he always did when infuriated, and shouting back, "Don't dare call me a Jacobite, you gutter scum. I'll have the streets swept of the lot of you."

A sailor rushed forward, catching at Weylin's cane, and the two men grappled for possession of it.

"Grandfather!" Phaedra wrenched herself free. She heard her cousin mutter, "Glory in heaven." As she raced forward, she sensed Gilly running by her side down the stone steps of the portico, but neither of them was swift enough to reach the street in time.

The sailor wrenched the cane away from Weylin and cracked it with bone-shattering force upon the old man's skull. As Weylin staggered back, Phaedra caught him, but she could not support his tottering weight. He crashed to his knees, his wig askew, the blood flowing down his face.

Phaedra saw Gilly's fist smash into the sailor's jaw, but after that the scene descended into a violent whirl of madness. As Phaedra tried to stem the blood gushing from Weylin's head, the rest of the crowd crushed forward. Gilly seemed swallowed up in a press of struggling bodies and a flurry of fists.

It was all Phaedra could do to keep her grandfather from pitching forward onto his face when rough hands drew her back. A male face, distorted with an ugly sneer, pressed close, the reek of his fetid breath sickening her. "Eh—this must be one o' those Irish whores I've heard tell of."

Phaedra struck out blindly, leveling her fist at the man's eyes. A bellow of rage followed, and a hand smacked hard against her cheek, making her dizzy with fear and pain. She struggled against the hands she felt trying to thrust her downward, tearing at the sleeve of her gown.

But she was released so suddenly, she fell back upon the pavement. She scarcely had time to comprehend what had happened when a whisper of steel flashed past her line of vision. The man who had assaulted her reeled back, clutching his bloodied shoulder and yelping with pain.

She gazed upward to see James's hard-muscled frame providing a barrier between her and the madness erupting on all sides of her. His eyes narrowed to deadly slits, his face a mask of granite, he swept his sword in a protective arc, ready to cut down the next man who approached.

He spared her not so much as a glance, barking a command over his shoulder. "Get her out of here." She did not know to whom he spoke until she felt Jonathan trying to help her up.

But she pulled away, staring wildly about her. She could not find Gilly. Her grandfather lay sprawled on the street near the curb, his coarse features ashen beneath the smearing of blood.

Phaedra crept to Weylin's side just as Ridley drew up with the carriage. In the midst of such mayhem, Phaedra scarcely knew how they managed it, but somehow she, Jonathan, and the footmen hefted her grandfather's inert bulk onto the floor of the coach. She looked frantically about for some sign of James and Gilly, and she saw them at last by the rear of the carriage, providing a protective shield for her grandfather's escape, the dark-haired Irishman with fists upraised, and the silk-clad James, the glint of his sword as lethal as his expression.

Before Phaedra could protest, Jonathan thrust her into the carriage after her grandfather. "No!" she cried out. "We can't leave—" But her words were lost as Jonathan vaulted in after her.

Gilly and James vanished from view as Jonathan slammed the door and the coach lurched forward into the night.

As her unconscious grandfather was carried into Jonathan Burnell's house, Phaedra refused to follow. "Damn it, Jonathan. We've got to go back."

"Please, Phaedra." He caught her by the wrist, pulling her toward the door of his town house. "Didn't I tell you that I saw the marquis and Mr. Fitzhurst escaping just as we drove away? Your cousin grabbed up a horse and pulled Varnais up after him. Don't you believe me?"

"Aye, but . . ." Phaedra still turned her gaze to peer down the street, praying to see Gilly and James materialize out of the darkness. How she wished she had seen them ride off herself. She would not breathe easy until she was sure they were safe.

Feeling helpless, she followed Jonathan into the house. While the doctor was summoned to attend Sawyer Weylin, Phaedra was ushered into one of the spare bedchambers. She washed away the blood that spattered her hands and changed into a drab gown provided for her by Jonathan's elderly cousin. She was overcome with guilt. In the next room lay her grandfather, unconscious— mayhap dying—and yet she could think only of Gilly and James.

She had all but decided she had to go back to Covent Garden to search for them, even if she had to steal one of Jonathan's horses to do it, when she heard a commotion down below. The banging of the front door heralded someone's arrival.

Her heart constricted with both fear and hope. She raced to the front door, thrusting aside Jonathan's elderly manservant. Phaedra choked back a cry of relief as Gilly staggered across the threshold, but her relief quickly turned to alarm when she realized he was supporting James.

"Don't be so damned stubborn, man," Gilly said, gritting his teeth with the strain of his efforts. "Lean on me before I am obliged to carry you."

"James." She spoke his name softly, her voice constricting. But it was her cousin who glanced up at her, his face caked with dirt and blood. They might have been two old friends, staggering home after a drunken spree, if James's face had not been so deathly pale.

"Gilly. What . . ." she faltered.

"Now don't start to fret, Fae. We did just grand until his

lardship broke his sword. Quite a dab with his fists, he is. If it hadn't been for that blasted sailor pulling a knife—"

"Knife!" she cried out as James's legs threatened to buckle beneath him. She strove to support him on the other side, but he managed to regain his balance and thrust her aside. The sting of his rejection was lost in fear as she saw the blood soaking his shoulder.

Tersely she summoned Jonathan's manservant, and they managed to get James up to the spare bedchamber. The room was austere, as sparsely furnished as all the other rooms in Jonathan's house.

As James was eased onto the bed, his head sagged back against the pillow. He appeared to have lost consciousness, and his face was so drained of color that Phaedra was paralyzed with dread. But she forced herself into action, her fingers working the buttons of his shirt. As she tried to ease the fabric away from his shoulder, his eyes fluttered open. He regarded her through an agony-filled haze, then muttered to Gilly, "Get her out of here."

He tried to sit up, but Gilly forced him back to the pillows. "Steady, man. You're better off with her care than that of some doctors' I've known."

James ground his teeth as she finished peeling the shirt away from the wound, exposing an ugly jagged gash.

Gilly pursed his lips. "He'll be needing a bit of stitching, I'm thinking."

Phaedra nodded, scarcely able to speak past the lump in her throat. "See if the doctor has finished with my grandfather."

As Gilly left the room, Phaedra sought to apply pressure to the wound to stop the bleeding. Although James no longer tried to move, she felt his eyes upon her, their clear blue depths beclouded with pain. When his lips parted in an effort to speak, she hushed him.

"Don't try to talk. It will be all right." She wished she could believe so herself. He had lost so much blood.

"Phaedra." He managed to whisper the one word, making it sound so sad, so full of regret, she felt as though a knife had been thrust into her own breast.

It seemed an eternity before Gilly returned with the harried surgeon.

The short, bustling man shoved her aside, but Phaedra continued to hover over James until she was satisfied as to the man's skill. The doctor knew his trade, and he stitched the wound with a brisk efficiency. From time to time, as James flinched with pain, Phaedra felt the sting herself. His face had drained as white as the bed sheets, his fine-chiseled features so rock hard he might indeed have been carved from ice.

Phaedra pressed her hand to her lips, unable even to utter words of prayer. When the doctor had finished, he stepped away from the bed, rolling down his sleeves and snapping out commands. "Keep him quiet. Watch for signs of infection, and he'll do. He's young. He bears a far better chance of recovery than the old man."

With a guilty flush, Phaedra tore her eyes from James. "Aye, my grandfather. How—how is he?"

"Still unconscious. He suffers from shock as much as the blow to the head." The doctor shook his head, giving the impression that he bore not much hope for Weylin's recovery.

The rest of the night passed with agonizing slowness for Phaedra, who was torn between her fears for the man she loved and her guilt over the pass to which her writings had brought her grandfather. She paced from one bedside to the other, where both men lay deathly still.

Despite his bulk, her grandfather looked somehow shrunken upon the pillows, as though he had aged years. But the timeworn lines of pain and grief upon James's brow appeared smoothed, making him look younger. Phaedra had heard that it was often thus with those who were about to . . .

Morning's light found her with eyes raw from unshed tears, her senses giddy from exhaustion. When Gilly discovered her upon her knees, being sick into the chamber pot, he led her firmly to bed.

"Enough of this, Fae," he said sternly, "or you will soon be the one needing the doctor. I will watch over Lethington. And Jonathan has hardly left your grandfather's side. You've got to sleep."

She tried to protest, but she had no notion how exhausted she was until Gilly forced her back into the pillows. She consented to a few moments' rest merely to appease Gilly, never intending to close her eyes.

But the next she knew, the soft shadows of evening were drifting into the room. She heard someone moving about beyond the bed-curtains and sat up with a frightened start. But it was only Gilly, bringing her a cup of tea.

Gratefully, she gulped down the honey-sweetened brew, then started to fling aside the covers to rise. "How could you have let me sleep so long?" she asked reproachfully.

"Because you needed it," he said, gently restraining her. "You don't have to dash off in such a fret. Your grandfather's improving. He's even got a bit of his color back. And as for Lethington, he's resting easy as a babe in his mother's arms."

Phaedra murmured a prayer of relief, although she could not be content until she saw James for herself. Yet Gilly refused to let her go until she attempted to choke down some toast. She ate without tasting, for the first time noticing how haggard Gilly looked himself. Deep rings had settled beneath his green eyes, and a purple bruise swelled his cheek. She touched his face. "I am so sorry, Gilly. I hadn't thought— No one has been looking after you."

"No one has to." He gave a soft laugh. "I came out of this fray far better than usual. See?" He leaned forward, indicating his eye. "For once no black eye, although . . ." He grinned widely, revealing a tooth missing in the back. "I think I swallowed the blasted thing."

"You never really explained how you and James escaped."

"Well, after your grandda's coach hied away, I think everyone kind of forgot what the riot had been about. Most were just fighting for the pure fun of it." Gilly's half-guilty expression revealed that he had not been above such feelings himself. "We were doing just fine until that scurvy sailor stuck his knife into Lethington. By that time, the constables had arrived, and the old fools only added to the confusion. I snatched someone's horse and—"

He broke off with a grimace of disgust, "And would you believe that damn fool James didn't want to take it? And himself dripping blood all over the road? These English with their law-abiding notions are so cursed impractical."

He concluded cheerfully, "Now I expect we'll both be strung up for horse—" Gilly looked away with an embarrassed flush. "Um . . . sorry, Fae. A poor jest."

" 'Tis all right," she said, giving her cousin a fierce hug. "I promise I won't be turning the pair of you rogues in." But when she became serious and tried to thank Gilly for what he had done for James, he would have none of it.

"I could scarce let him die in the street, even knowing—"

Gilly's eyes fixed upon her, his gaze growing stern. "And now, mayhap you wouldn't mind telling me what sort of mischief you were about last night?"

Although she could not meet his eyes, Phaedra made no attempt to lie. "I was going to run away with James."

She heard Gilly suck in his breath. "I won't even begin to tell you what I think of you just fixing to disappear without one word to me—"

"Please, Gilly." She stopped him, unable to bear the raw hurt that laced his voice. "I am sorry. Don't be scolding me or upsetting yourself. I am going nowhere." She added in hollowed accents of despair, " 'Tis finished now."

She walked away from him to stare out at the night, fast mantling the rooftops of the city. "I am more likely to find myself standing in the dock than on the deck of a ship. When they come to arrest my grandfather—"

"No!" Gilly came up behind her to grip her shoulders. "You're not making any foolish confessions, even if I have to lock you up myself. I know you are feeling guilty. Let that be your punishment. Jonathan has seen to a temporary stay of the orders since—since it seems most unlikely the old man will ever rise from his bed again."

Phaedra buried her face in her hands, her words thickened with tears. "James has destroyed my grandfather. And I helped."

"I don't know as how you think 'tis your fault or his. If the old man had slunk quietly away until this was sorted out, he would yet be unharmed."

Gilly tried to pull her into his arms, but she shoved away from him. She was beyond any sort of comfort now.

"My Goodfellow papers," she said. "I believe that James took them and gave them to Jessym to incriminate my grandfather."

Haltingly, Phaedra told Gilly all that had transpired since he had left her at the Heath. She related James's version of the murder and his suspicions that Sawyer Weylin had participated in a conspiracy, first to destroy Julianna, then silence James; and how she had tried to stop James from seeking vengeance, an effort that had obviously failed.

"I only thought to save James," she concluded miserably. "But I was years too late."

A heavy silence settled over the room. At last Gilly stroked his fingers along her temple. "If it is any comfort at all to you, Fae,

I do believe James loves you. I watched him through the night. He even speaks your name in his sleep." Gilly flinched at the memory. "I hope to never hear such cries of despair again, not even after I descend into hell—which I likely will, someday."

"I realize he loves me, Gilly," she said wearily. "But his hatred is stronger. Mayhap it is as well our elopement was thwarted. I can see now I was making a bitter mistake."

"What a blasted tangle." Gilly rubbed the back of his neck. "But mayhap there is yet some way that you and James can—"

She shook her head. "No. Whatever happens, I will stay and take care of my grandfather. I owe him that much. He is the one who needs me the most."

Gilly looked as though he did not entirely agree with her, but he kept his lips sealed.

Phaedra left him, tiptoeing across the hall to slip softly into James's room. Gilly was right. James's color was improved, and he was sound asleep. But she would never have described it as resting easy. Even in sleep, his brow appeared pinched with some pained remembrance. She touched his forehead, longing to soothe away the tension. But he stirred restlessly, turning away from her. Fearful of waking him, she retreated quietly from the room.

With a heavy heart, she went next to where her grandfather lay in Jonathan's room. Jonathan, ever faithful in his vigil, had fallen asleep in a wing-backed chair. Phaedra skirted silently past him to the bedside. As she looked down at the old man, remorse tore at her heart.

His bald head was swathed in bandages, his once-ruddy features ashen. Phaedra expected to find him asleep and was startled to see him staring up at her. His eyes were dulled, and she glimpsed no recognition in their depths. His coarse lips strained to form a word.

"Wh—wh . . ."

As she bent closer, she realized he was asking for a drink. She fetched a small quantity of wine in a glass. Raising his head, she held the goblet to his lips. He sipped, choked, but managed to swallow some of the liquid. It appeared to help. As she eased him back onto the pillow, his eyes cleared. Frowning, he focused upon her.

"Dy—dying," he said.

"Nay, Grandfather," she whispered.

But he managed to lift one hand, indicating that she should be silent, the old gesture still rife with his impatience.

"Tell someone in—in case. Someone must know."

She tucked the sheets more snugly about him. "You will have plenty of time to tell me later."

"No! Must tell now."

He was becoming agitated; Phaedra saw she would have to humor him.

"Other—other day you were asking me . . ." His voice trailed off.

Phaedra waited patiently for him to continue, but when he did, the words he gasped took her by surprise.

"Leth—Lethington girl."

"Julianna?" Phaedra tensed. When he lapsed into silence, she prodded, "Is it something to do with her death?"

His jowls quivered as he moved his head in a barely perceptible shake.

"Julianna Lethington," he repeated in a hoarse whisper, his words rasping through the still chamber. "She's alive. I know where she is."

Chapter Twenty-one

PHAEDRA TOUCHED A HAND TO HER GRANDFATHER'S CHEEK, FEARING to find him feverish. But his beard-stubbled flesh felt cool. She could only suppose the blow had addled the old man's wits.

"You mean you know where Julianna is buried," she said.

Weylin caught her wrist with surprising strength, pulling her closer. "Not buried. Alive. Girl is alive." Then he released her, closing his eyes as though the effort had been too much for him. It was all Phaedra could do not to shake him. "Grandfather?"

At her sharp whisper, his eye fluttered open, the depths clouding with torment. "Never meant to hurt . . . Carleton said we would only abduct girl . . . keep away until Ewan married you." Tears glinted in the old man's eyes as he paused for breath.

"Should not have trusted Carleton alone with girl . . . Ravished her. I . . . tried to stop. Too late. Girl broken, mad . . . no memory. Carleton wanted to kill . . . but I locked her in the garret."

"The garret," Phaedra repeated, scarcely able to believe what she was hearing. So that was how the shepherdess had come to be left there! Julianna must have dropped it during her imprisonment. All the while James had engaged in his life and death struggle with Lord Carleton, his sister had been much closer than he ever realized.

"And then, Grandfather?" she asked. "You obviously did not keep her in the attic forever. Where is Julianna now?"

Her grandfather's eyes hazed. She feared he meant to drift into unconsciousness without telling her anything more.

Phaedra caught his shoulders roughly. "Where? Damn you!"

Weylin made a feeble effort to shrink away from her, but at last, he said, "Found woman to care for her . . . cottage in Yorkshire. Made sure girl want for nothing."

Nothing but her mind, Phaedra thought savagely, and the family whose love might have restored her. Phaedra nigh forgot that her grandfather lay wounded and broken himself as she reproached him, "And all these years, you've never told anyone—never tried to reunite her with her family!"

"No family left. Caught brother James after he had murdered Carleton . . . Wild lad. Afraid of his questions. Vengeance. I . . . I bullied Ewan into testifying. Made sure Lethington hanged. Mother and other brother disappeared."

Weylin closed his eyes as though he could also shut out Phaedra's anger and his own guilty conscience. "After I'm gone . . . you see money paid. Take care of that girl until she dies."

"Then tell me where she is," Phaedra hissed. "The name of the woman looking after her."

"Mrs.—Mrs. Link." Her grandfather was tiring. Phaedra had to lean forward to catch his words. He mumbled the woman's address and heaved a great sigh. As though he had eased himself of a vast burden, he fell back to sleep.

Aye, and so he had, Phaedra thought as she straightened. She felt the full weight of that burden upon her own shoulders. What was she going to do now? James would have to be told. And yet, how she dreaded his reaction!

To discover that his cherished sister had been alive all these years, her mind broken, taken care of by a stranger. Phaedra was certain it would only add more fuel to the fires of hatred that already burned in his heart. She had to fight back a selfish impulse not to tell him. But it would do no harm to wait until he was stronger.

During the next days, she avoided James's room, contenting herself with Gilly's reports of his progress. She sensed her cousin relaxing and his grudging admiration of James. He had begun to like the man in spite of himself.

It caused Phaedra some pain that James never once asked for her, but she supposed he also realized that their separation was for the best. But a week after the disaster at the theater, she decided she could put it off no longer. James had to know the truth about Julianna.

As she approached his room, her heart thudding with the anticipation of seeing him again, she found the door ajar.

Gilly had just entered, bearing a breakfast tray. He was now clumsily attempting to arrange James's pillows so that he could sit up and eat.

"If you could just be shifting yourself a bit," Gilly said testily. "It would make things a damned sight easier."

James winced as he complied. His muscular frame was swathed beneath the folds of a white nightshirt. The face she remembered, possessed of such lean strength and bronzed by the sun was now wan and hollowed by suffering. Phaedra had to swallow back a lump that formed in her throat.

"You make a cursed rough nursemaid, Fitzhurst," he growled at Gilly.

"And you are a damned surly patient, de LeCroix . . . Lethington." Gilly pummeled the pillows so hard that Phaedra expected to see feathers fly about the room. "Whatever the devil I'm supposed to be after calling you."

"You can always try *your lardship*," James said with a dry smile, perfectly imitating Gilly's accent.

Phaedra knocked lightly and stepped into the room. James's smile fled immediately. For an instant an expression flared in his eyes, a raw hunger and despair. It quickly vanished as he hooded his gaze.

As Phaedra hovered awkwardly just inside the door, her own heart strained toward him. She steeled herself, bidding him a brisk good morning.

"Ah, Fae," Gilly said cheerfully. "You're just in time to witness a battle the likes of which hasn't been seen since Culloden. I'm about to force a bit of breakfast down his lardship's stubborn throat."

Phaedra forced an overbright smile to her lips. "Oh, is he being difficult?" Her gaze flicked nervously to James. "How are you feeling this morning?"

"Tired," he said dully.

His rigid expression was not encouraging, but she cleared her throat and said to her cousin, "Gilly, I wonder if you could let me have a few moments alone with James."

She saw James tense. A brief hope flickered in his eyes, then
uickly died.

Gilly frowned at first before shrugging. "Ah, well, I never have
een one for insisting upon the proprieties." He angled a glance at
ames. "I suppose 'tis safe enough, considering the man's
veakened condition." But there was more of banter in Gilly's
omment than any intended insult.

"I trust your lardship will call me to fetch away the tray. I am
ecoming so good at this, I may seek out a post as butler."

"No one would ever trust you with the keys to the wine cellar,"
ames retorted.

Gilly merely grinned. On his way past Phaedra, he gave her an
ncouraging wink and squeezed her arm. After Gilly had gone, an
neasy silence settled over the room.

Phaedra avoided any proximity to the bed. She had no idea how
o begin. She sensed a listlessness about James that disturbed her.
Even when playing the role of the impassive marquis, a steely
ension had always coiled within him, leaving her in no doubt of
he passions pulsing beneath. Now he seemed empty. It was as
hough while his body healed, his soul continued to waste away.
Exactly as she'd always feared.

And yet it was he who first broke the silence. Slightly raising
imself, he said, "Phaedra?"

"Aye?" She tried to keep the nearly breathless eagerness from
er voice.

He sank back immediately. "Never mind," he muttered. "I
row tired of protesting my innocence." After a pause, he added,
"How is your grandfather?"

"I doubt he'll live to see another winter."

James passed his hand across his eyes in a weary gesture. "I
ould say I was sorry. But I am tired of lying, as well."

She studied his face, looking for some sign of regret that she
new she would never find. "Why didn't you just vanish from the
heater that night? Why did you rescue him again?"

"You know damn well I came to save you," he said. "Just as
hat time at the supper party, I was only trying to prevent that fool
Wilkins from committing a hanging offense."

"Which he did, anyway."

"No." A taut smile of satisfaction pulled at the corners of
ames's mouth. "Wilkins was transported. He and his wife are far
way from London by now, which we should have been, too,

if—" He broke off the accusation he had been about to make, as if it were not worth the effort.

Phaedra drew nearer in spite of herself. She fidgeted nervously with the end of the counterpane. "What will you do?" she asked. "When you are well, I mean."

"No, I don't know what you mean," he snapped.

"Your plans for—for the future."

"Plans. I haven't got any. I had no notion that when you persuaded me to let go of the past, you meant to turn your back on me and rob me of my future happiness as well."

Phaedra's eyes flashed to his with an expression of reproach. How dare he accuse her of such a thing! It was he who had kept on with his quest for vengeance, destroying any chance of a happy life together that they might have had. But she swallowed her anger. All recriminations now seemed both pointless and unavailing.

She drew in a quick breath. "I have something to tell you. Something that will affect whatever you decide to do. I have been talking to my grandfather—about his part in what happened seven years ago."

"That must have been an exercise in futility."

Ignoring his cynical comment, she continued, "He spoke of your sister. Your—your suspicions were correct. He took a greater part in her abduction than I ever wanted to believe."

James said harshly, "That comes as no surprise to me."

"I am afraid something that he told me will." She saw no way to ease the shock, but plunged breathlessly on, revealing to him what her grandfather had said about Julianna. By the time she had done, James's face was ashen, his eyes burning in a manner that terrified her.

She tried to mitigate her grandfather's sins by adding, "He—he made certain she was well cared for—"

But James was no longer listening. He flung aside the counterpane. His lips set into a thin, bloodless line as he struggled to stand.

"What are you doing?" Phaedra gasped. "Do you want to tear open your wound?"

She tried to force him back into bed, but it would have been easier to move a block of granite. He pushed her aside.

"Where are my clothes?" He took a few unsteady steps and Phaedra thought she read murder in his eyes.

"Please!" She thrust herself in front of him. "My grandfather is already injured. Nothing more that you can do will change—"

"To the devil with him. I'm going after Anne."

Phaedra's eyes widened with dismay. "You cannot possibly. Not all the way to Yorkshire. You'll be dead before you get there."

But James had managed to make his way to the wardrobe. Pawing through the drawers, he located some garments, which had been fetched by one of the footmen from the Heath several days ago. James pulled out a pair of breeches and a shirt, his jaw grim with determination.

She fled to the door, calling for Gilly.

By the time her cousin arrived, James had already painfully struggled out of the nightshirt and into his breeches. His face was as white as the bandage that bound his shoulder.

"What the deuce!" Gilly said.

Phaedra quickly explained, but she did not receive the support from her cousin that she had expected. His brows drew together in a furious scowl.

"Well, I cannot say as I blame the man. If it were my sister, I would be off like a shot myself."

"Gilly! You can see he's in no condition to ride anywhere."

She glanced to where James was pulling on his shirt, his features contorted with pain. Phaedra started to rush to his aid, then stopped. She would be damned if she lifted one finger to help him with this madness.

"In any case," Gilly said, "I don't know how you think I'd be after stopping the man, short of brute force."

"I don't advise you to try it, Fitzhurst," James growled, his fingers fumbling with the buttons.

Phaedra glanced from one man to the other. James's face was set; Gilly's was equally obstinate. Her shoulders slumped with momentary despair, then she turned to her cousin.

"If you won't stop him, I want you to go with him."

"I don't need a blasted nurse," James said as he located his boots.

"Don't fret," Gilly flung back. "You're not getting one." He looked at Phaedra. "Are you mad, Fae? Do you think I'd be after leaving you to tend a sick old man and with that Goodfellow business still hanging fire in the courts?"

"It will be all right," she insisted. "I will have Jonathan to help me."

The skeptical look that passed between James and Gilly showed clearly what both thought of Jonathan's capabilities.

"Pay her no heed," James said. "I will manage quite well on my own."

"No, you won't!" Phaedra stomped her foot, impatient with all these arrogant male heroics and stupidity. "Gilly, please . . . after all my grandfather has done, I feel that I owe—"

"You don't owe me a damned thing." James cursed savagely as he painfully thrust his foot into a boot.

But Phaedra clutched at Gilly's arm, giving him that melting look she knew he could not resist. "He'll never make it alone," Phaedra whispered. "He'll break open that wound and bleed to death somewhere on the road."

Gilly exuded a deep sigh. "I suppose the journey would take but a fortnight at most." His eyes traveled ruefully toward James. "But it will not be easy. His lardship doesn't take too kindly to the notion of my company."

"You can go or stay. 'Tis all the same to me." James jammed his heel into the other boot. "But don't expect any gratitude. I will likely curse you every league of the way."

"I have been cursed frequently, Englishman," Gilly said. "In more tongues than you are master of."

When she saw Gilly relenting, Phaedra gave him an impulsive hug. While James gathered up the rest of his belongings, Gilly treated her to a stern lecture. "While I am gone, you keep to yourself and out of mischief. No matter what happens, I don't want you making any noble gestures. No heroic confessions, coz."

"Oh, of course not," Phaedra said, avoiding meeting Gilly's eye. She knew she would do whatever she deemed necessary.

"Make her promise." Although he had never so much as glanced around, Phaedra was startled by both James's perception and his strained command.

When her vague pledges of good conduct did not satisfy Gilly either, she snapped, "Oh, very well, I swear it in blood. I will keep silent. I hope that satisfies the pair of you."

Gilly grinned. "Then be off with you while I change my own clothes. I am not so free and easy before the ladies as Jamey lad. My extreme modesty, you know."

James glared at Gilly, a heated blush overtaking his pale cheeks.

It was a bare half-hour later when Phaedra trailed after the two men to the small stable yard at the back of Jonathan's house. The grooms had fetched both Nemesis and Gilly's sorrel.

After bestowing upon her a brisk hug, Gilly mounted his horse. Phaedra was relieved to see that James was looking stronger, although still quite strained. She wanted to help him up into the saddle, but knew he would resent the gesture. His expression nigh caused her heart to break.

She saw no trace of warmth in his face—no trace of the man she'd known. His mouth appeared so hardened she doubted if he would ever smile again. Ever since she had given him the news of his sister, all fragments of youthfulness had disappeared. Suddenly Phaedra envisioned him as an aging, embittered man, ever trapped by angry resentment. She had tried to break those chains for him, but now she saw that she had only attempted the impossible.

It was so ironic. Both of them had sought a freedom—he from memories, she from dependence upon any man. But he would never know his freedom, and she didn't want hers.

As he reached for Nemesis's reins, he paused, his gaze drawn back to her against his will. "It would seem," he said, "that this is farewell."

She nodded numbly. "I wish you . . ." What was there for her to wish him? She doubted he would find any happiness in his reunion with his sister, a broken woman, so mad she would not even know him. "I wish you peace, James Lethington," she finished sadly.

He vaulted into the saddle, his eyes empty, his voice hard. "I won't find it. Not this side of the grave." Without waiting to see if Gilly followed, he reined Nemesis about and was gone.

A fortnight passed. Sawyer Weylin improved enough for Phaedra to consider moving him back to Blackheath. Jonathan, however, argued vehemently against it.

"Your grandfather will never again be strong enough to leave his bed. 'Twill be entirely too much for you to cope with that vast house and an invalid."

"But we have burdened you with our presence here long enough," Phaedra protested.

"Never!" Jonathan pressed a fervent kiss against her hand. "It has been the greatest happiness of my life to have you safe beneath my roof."

Phaedra disengaged her hand. "I want my grandfather to spend his last days in his own house." She did not add that she had another reason, equally compelling. The look in Jonathan's eye had waxed far too passionate of late. She had no desire to give the man false hope. She herself had known too much of that kind of pain to inflict it upon Jonathan.

Although Jonathan continued to resist the notion, Phaedra prevailed in the end, and her grandfather was conveyed back to his cherished Heath. September had come, but the summer did not slowly dissolve into fall; it died. The summer—Phaedra's season of fire and love, had snatched away all its greenery and warmth and fled. The chill of autumn blighted the Heath's gardens; brittle leaves and withered stalks now stood where the roses had bloomed. To Phaedra it was like watching the promise of life itself dying, the passing of dreams that were to never come again.

She began to fear that returning to the Heath had been a mistake. It did not give her grandfather the ease that she had hoped, and his condition seemed to worsen with each passing day. He spoke less and slept more, and the right side of his body was paralyzed. In spite of Weylin's dreadful crime, and the pain the old man's ambitions had brought both herself and James, Phaedra could not help pitying him.

Never before had she realized how much her grandfather's presence had filled the Heath. It was as though the ostentatious, overlarge rooms had been scaled to match his enormous bulk and blustery temperament. Now he was but a sunken shadow of himself, and the vast house seemed like a suit of clothes that no longer fit.

At least the cool winds of autumn had eased tempers somewhat. For a long time, Phaedra had gone in dread of another attack upon her grandfather. Despite her promise to James and Gilly, she had been fully prepared to confess that she was Robin Goodfellow. But the Londoners were quick to find new interests, and the *Gazetteer* and Goodfellow were both forgotten in the heat of new political matters. The king and his ministers were now being harried by the prospect that France would almost certainly sign a treaty with the American colonists. Jessym had paid a fine and been duly released.

Phaedra was astonished with what indifference she received the news of colonial affairs. Once she would have been ecstatic to hear of the treaty with France, certain that with such aid the colonists would be bound to emerge victorious. In a burst of enthusiasm, she would have reached for her quill to applaud France's intervention. But now she regarded all such political tidings with indifference. The struggle for liberty being waged across the sea seemed but a small matter compared with her own heartbreak.

Because no housekeeper had been engaged to replace Hester Searle, Phaedra filled her own days by directing the servants' activities at the Heath. She found herself increasingly grateful for such mundane tasks, and she had neither the heart nor the mind for greater exertion. Listlessness had taken possession of her. She was frequently ill, especially upon rising in the morning.

At first she had supposed her fatigue was merely so much stress, finally taking its toll upon her. But when she studied her body in the mirror, she was forced to admit that the tenderness of her breasts and the slight thickening of her waist were not caused by any illness.

She could no longer delude herself. She was with child.

After her initial shock, she experienced a rush of anger at the perversity of fate. How oft she had longed for a child! The prospect of knowing a mother's joy had been the only reason she had ever tolerated those brief, humiliating couplings with Ewan. And now she was carrying the child of the man she loved, yet the knowledge filled her with sorrow and dread.

How would James react when she told him? Phaedra doubted that she would ever know, for she had a feeling that when he found his sister, he would never return. Two weeks had stretched into a month with still no word from him or Gilly. She wondered why at least her cousin had not returned. Surely it could not be taking this long to locate Julianna. Phaedra suppressed a secret dread that they had found the girl in worse condition than anyone could possibly have imagined.

Turning away from the mirror, Phaedra dressed herself, feeling more depressed than ever. She went down to her grandfather's study. She felt an intruder there, but someone had to keep track of the accounts and see that the bills were paid.

Shortly after returning to the Heath, she had taken on the task. It was not so difficult, considering her grandfather's meticulous accounting. She had even located a private ledger in which he had recorded with great detail, every sum, every item he had sent to Mrs. Link for the care of Julianna Lethington.

After Phaedra finished toting up the reckonings of the household expenses, she proceeded to clean out the center drawer. Jonathan had very kindly offered to take charge of all matters dealing with Weylin's many investments, an offer she had gratefully accepted.

But as she stacked up record book after record book, she felt somehow saddened. Was this all that her grandfather had to show for his life? It all seemed so impersonal, those cold stacks of ledgers with the entries made in his crabbed handwriting.

She had come to the bottom of the pile when she felt something cold and hard in the back of the drawer. She drew forth two objects, realizing with some surprise that she held small miniature portraits in gilt frames.

The first of these represented a young woman whose features bore such striking resemblance to Phaedra's father, she did not doubt that she gazed upon a likeness of her grandmother. Corinda Weylin had deep, cornflower-blue eyes, just like George Weylin. But the hair wisping about her sweet face was a soft brown, not the red-gold Phaedra once had guessed.

She set that portrait aside. It was the other that most intrigued and puzzled her. She studied the stocky young man with the belligerent tilt of his chin, almost as though suggesting he had scant time for this nonsense of posing for the artist. It took a few moments for her to recognize her grandfather's features in the stubborn set of the lips and heavy eyelids. Most startling of all was the hair—the thatch of red-gold hair that waved back from his brow.

Phaedra fingered a lock of her own fiery curls, a tremulous smile curving her lips. All those times that he had groused at her about the color of her hair! Her lips parted to laugh, but to her surprise a heavy sob escaped her instead. She bowed her forehead against her arm, her flood of tears wetting the scarred oak surface of the desk.

Lost in the release of her pent-up emotion, Phaedra did not realize she was no longer alone until she felt a light touch upon her hair.

"Phaedra?"

She jerked upright to meet Jonathan's concerned gaze. Wiping hastily at her eyes, she hiccuped and said "Oh, J—Jonathan. You startled me."

"I knocked, but I fear you didn't hear me."

"I but laid my head down on the desk to rest a bit and—and . . ."

She allowed her voice to trail off, realizing how ridiculous it was to try to deceive him when she knew her face must be splotched and red with weeping.

"My dear!" Jonathan regarded her with deep, mournful eyes as he brushed away the last of the moisture from her cheek. "I should never have let you return to this gloomy house. You are never happy here."

"I—I am all right," she said, drawing back from his touch. "I was only feeling a bit depressed about Grandfather, that is all."

"Aye, my poor old friend. It saddens me to see him thus, too." Yet Jonathan's gaunt features assumed a look more anxious than melancholy. "I—hope you have never blamed me for what happened that night. For not permitting you to tell Sawyer the truth about Robin Goodfellow."

"Of course not," she said wearily. She rose from the desk. "I have gathered together the ledgers that you need. Here they are."

But Jonathan's eyes never wavered from their discomfiting stare. "My dear, you do not look at all well. I must insist upon your seeing my physician."

"'Twould do no good. I fear I am past all curing."

She regretted the bitter words when she saw Jonathan pale with alarm. She started to pass off her comment as but a foolish jest, but she could not seem to speak past the lump in her throat. Her shoulders sagged. She felt so desperately alone. Added to the strain of worrying, of wondering about James, and of trying to care for her grandfather, she was now burdened with another dread secret. She feared she would go mad if she did not confide in someone.

"The truth is, I am in a great deal of trouble," she whispered. "It seems—that is, I fear . . . I am with child."

Jonathan's face registered shock but no censure. He was struck dumb for a few minutes, her own misery mirrored in his dark eyes. She dreaded that he would demand to know who the father was, but Jonathan had far too much delicacy for that.

"Are you certain?" he asked.

She nodded. God help her, she did not know how, but she was absolutely certain.

His fingers laced together in a nervous gesture. He asked anxiously, "You are going to marry the father?"

Phaedra was rather astonished that that should be his first thought. "No," she said dully. "There is little likelihood of that. He's gone."

Jonathan exuded a deep sigh. His sallow face flushed as he caught her hands in a tight grip. He startled her by bursting out with, "Marry me, Phaedra! I have adored you ever since—"

"Hush, Jonathan," she begged, trying to stem the flow of words they would both regret on some calmer day in the future.

He dragged one of her hands to his lips, then the other, kissing them with a passion Phaedra had never imagined the man capable of. His eyes glowed with such yearning that for one weak moment, Phaedra was tempted. She was so tired of struggling alone. At least she knew Jonathan would ever be kind to her and the babe. But her heart rejected the notion. She knew what it was like to marry without love.

She pulled away from him. "Nay, Jonathan," she said as gently as she could. "'Twould not do. You are most kind and I thank you, but—"

"Phaedra, please."

"No!" She evaded his attempts to recapture her hands. "You will only add to my distress if you continue to press me."

For the barest instant his eyes gleamed wildly, and she thought he meant to force her into his arms. But the high color in his cheeks ebbed and he lowered his eyes, his hands dropping limply to his sides.

"Then what will you do?" he asked hoarsely.

"I don't know. When Grandfather—" She paused, unable to bring herself to say *is dead*. "When he no longer needs me, I shall probably have Gilly take me back to Ireland. No one would know the truth about the babe there."

"Ireland!" Jonathan's echoing of the word was so bleak, she might have been suggesting a voyage to the outer reaches of the Arctic. She began to regret her moment of weakness, that she had ever told him about the babe.

"You will drive yourself to distraction if you keep worrying about me," she said, trying for a lighter note. "You know I am forever in some sort of scrape."

"So you are." His voice held a touch of asperity. He forced his lips into a smile that Phaedra found strangely disquieting. "But I shall find some way to help you, just as I always do."

Although Phaedra thanked him for his concern, she was grateful when he said no more. Wearing a heavy frown, he took his leave, appearing so agitated that he did not even pay a visit to her grandfather before departing.

As soon as Jonathan's coach vanished down the drive, Phaedra felt once more the depression of loneliness. This day seemed far drearier and twice as long as all the wearying days before it. That evening as she sat dining in solitary state, she left her food untouched again. Instead she glanced at the ceiling and thought of the old man in the chamber above, dying by slow degrees. She felt as though the same were happening to her. The very walls hemming about her seemed to reek of death. She could bear it no longer. Flinging down her napkin, she fetched her cloak and set out for a walk upon the grounds.

The days faded into night much earlier now, and the sky was already misting into the royal purple of twilight. The moon rose, a pale silver in the gathering darkness.

A bitter wind whipped the ends of Phaedra's cloak, making her glad of its heavy folds. She supposed she should turn back, but the house behind her looked dark and uninviting, like a hearth whose fire had burnt to naught but cold stone and ashes.

She kept on with her aimless wandering until she found herself drawing near the region of the pond. The bushes rustled, the dried leaves hissing at her like snakes in the presence of an intruder. As she pressed past the brush into the clearing, the loud crackle of a twig made her pause for a moment, listening. But she supposed it was naught but some animal, mayhap one of the groom's dogs who had escaped being locked up for the night.

She glided silently toward the man-made pond. In the evening's dim light, it was but an expanse of darkness, marked by one knifelike shimmer of light from the moon above. How different it all was from the hot summer day when the sunlight had dappled the waters. Then it had been a silvery mirror, reflecting herself and James upon the bank, entwined in each other's arms. Then their love had been bright in all its first flush of passion.

Yet how fleeting and ephemeral that love had proved, just like the ripples upon the water, going cold and still with the dying of the wind.

Phaedra inched her way to the very brink of the pond, peering down into its depths. It was as black and fathomless as the River Styx, the legendary boundary that separated the souls of the living from the souls of the dead.

Phaedra's bleak thoughts wandered to all the tales she had heard, of the hopeless people who had sought oblivion by flinging themselves into a river. 'Twas said that the Thames in London nigh claimed as many lives as fever or the pox.

She could not understand that. The Thames was so vast, impersonal. How much better to end one's life in the familiar depths of . . .

Phaedra shuddered, taking a step back from the pond's edge. What nonsense was she thinking? She felt her spirit rebel, stirring inside her like a bird with a broken wing that yet struggles toward the sky.

To even think of killing herself was a sin. She now had more than Phaedra Grantham to consider. Her hand moved gently over the region of her abdomen. Aye, she was now custodian of another life, a life that, despite everything, was the creation of love. Hers and James. She could not . . .

Her thoughts broke off as she heard another sharp snap behind her. But this time her heart thudded uncomfortably. Surely that sound had not been caused by an animal. It sounded more like a stealthy footfall. She remembered once how James had stolen upon her here. An absurd hope welled within her. She spun about with his name on her lips.

But it changed to a cry of terror. The shadows themselves seemed to have taken on life and assumed the form of a cloaked phantom. Before she could move to flee, two hands gripped her shoulders and gave her a rough shove.

Phaedra fell backward, her arms flailing through the air, her body breaking the surface of the pond with a harsh slap. As the dark waters closed over her, their chilling depths sent a shock through her entire system.

Cold . . . she had never felt such numbing cold. The water soaked quickly through her gown, the lengths of her cloak tangling about her legs, weighting her down. She had not had time to catch her breath, and the water choked her.

In those first few terrifying moments, she forgot everything Gilly had ever taught her. Paralyzed with panic and the icy cold, she floundered, her frantic movements only serving to drag her down. She broke the surface once, then immediately sank again before she could scarcely draw air into her tortured lungs.

She was drowning, dying, her arms and legs becoming numb. Her struggles grew weaker and weaker, the pain in her chest unbearable. Images of her life shifted through her mind, the last one of a bronzed sun-god, his dark, windswept hair, his mouth sweet as fire. So warm, all of him—except for those cold blue eyes, so cold . . . so very cold.

Phaedra surrendered, letting blackness take her.

Chapter Twenty-two

PHAEDRA SHIVERED, DRAWING UP THE ENDS OF A RAGGED BLANKET to ward off the chill. Such intense cold could spring only from the regions of death itself. She feared to open her eyes, knowing she would confront the darkness of her grave. Yet they fluttered open of their own accord.

She was confronted not with the blackness she had dreaded, but hazy gray. The mist settled, becoming solid, stone walls that were narrow and confining. She longed to sink back into the peace of oblivion, but her mind fought her, already striving to regain its bearings.

She must have been dreaming—how long, she could not say. Dreaming of the summer she had spent with James, that season of fire that had blazed far too bright, leading her astray like a will-o'-the-wisp until she was lost in . . .

Phaedra frowned. Exactly where was she? Her eyes roved over the room, which was little better than a cell. Her gaze finally came to rest upon the iron grate that barred the window of her door. Reality slammed upon her as though the door itself had just banged closed.

Bedlam. She was a prisoner in Bedlam.

With a groan, Phaedra rolled over, then flinched. Every muscle in her body was raw and aching, and most of the soreness settled in her midsection. She tried to sit up, bracing herself with her hand. She stared at that hand, scarce recognizing it as hers; the skin was nigh transparent, stretched taut over her fingers.

Her effort to rise left her dizzy so that she had to lie still, both trying to forget and trying to remember. She had been here in Bedlam since the night she had plunged into the pond. How long ago had that been? Two weeks? Three? A month? She was not sure.

She knew she had been rescued, miraculously, by one of the grooms at the Heath—or so she had been told. But her behavior had been wild. She had been brought to Bedlam by order of the local magistrate and confined amongst the mad for attempting suicide. No one, not even Jonathan, had believed her tale of being pushed. But it was all most strange. She had always thought that one could not be admitted to the hospital without the recommendation of one of the patrons.

Each day she had paced the floor, waiting for someone to help her, to obtain her release. Aye, that much she recalled quite clearly. It was the day that she had collapsed in her cell that was fuzzy in her mind.

She tensed her eyes with the effort to remember. Visitors. That disgusting old hag, her gaoler Belda had been displaying her to visitors again . . . the foolish Lord Arthur Danby and his simpering mistress, Charmelle. Then Jonathan had come with the dire news he could not have her released. When he had gone, she had tried for the sake of her babe to eat—

The stew! Poisoned! Phaedra drew in her breath with a sharp gasp. How could she have forgotten the pain that had wracked her, nigh ripping her apart. Her stomach yet burned with the reminder.

She opened her eyes, and this time she managed to sit up, clutching her abdomen. She felt so weak, as if her very life had been drained—

Her fingers froze, the realization creeping over her. She ran her hands over the region of her womb, slowly at first, then more urgently, praying for just one butterfly whispering of life there. But she felt nothing except an aching emptiness. Her lips parted, a shriek of denial echoing off the indifferent walls of her cell.

Belda's bewhiskered chin appeared at the grating. "Stop that infernal racket. What ails ye?"

"My—my babe," Phaedra wailed, desperately seeking some assurance that it could not be true.

But Belda's smug smile confirmed her fears. "Aborted," she said, "And a good thing, too. There are enough bastards to fill the world."

An inhuman scream tore past Phaedra's throat, a sound she scarcely recognized as her own. She tried to lunge to her feet, wanting to fling herself at the bars and claw out the old woman's hateful eyes. But she tottered and fell back upon the bed, a prisoner of her own weakness.

Belda shrank back from the window, muttering, "And the wench would have us believe she isn't mad." But Phaedra scarcely heard the woman's retreat as she buried her face in the pillow and wept.

The sobs that wracked her frame seemed as if they would never end. But when her tears ceased at last, she felt nothing. Her soul was as empty as her womb. With the miscarriage of her child, she seemed to have lost her once indomitable spirit as well.

She again ceased to count the hours. Limp as a waxen doll, she somehow swallowed the food that Belda periodically forced down her throat. But as the days passed, she somehow regained strength; it was as though her body had turned traitor, surviving in spite of her will to die.

One morning as Phaedra stared listlessly at the walls, Belda came in and flung a gown at her. "Put this on."

Phaedra allowed the garmet to drop to the floor.

"I said put it on, you fool." Belda snatched up the dress and shook it at her. "Don't you understand? Yer gettin out today."

Phaedra turned her face to the wall. "Leave me alone."

But Belda seized her and rent the shift from her back. "I've stood enough of your nonsense. I'll be mighty pleased to see the last of you, my fine lady, and that's the truth."

Belda roughly dragged the gown over Phaedra's head. Phaedra experienced enough annoyance at the feel of the woman's hands upon her to thrust Belda's fingers away and straighten the garment herself.

"Why they are letting you go beats all fire out of me," Belda said. "As if one inmate escaping wasn't bad enough, they have to go setting another one loose."

Although Phaedra evinced not the slighted interest, Belda continued to rant, "That lunatic who thought she was Marie Antoinette vanished only days ago. I don't know how she managed it. One of the visitors must have helped her. Sometimes I'm not certain where the maddest ones are—locked in here or out there on the streets."

Still shaking her head and grumbling to herself, Belda went out of the cell. It occurred to Phaedra that she had not even bothered to ask who was coming for her. It could not be her grandfather. He might even be dead by now, for all she knew.

A slight stir of hope moved inside her, the first genuine feeling to penetrate the numbing cocoon she had wrapped herself in. James. Could it be possible that he had returned and somehow—

The hope was immediately dashed when the cell door opened to admit Jonathan. His sallow features were suffused with color, the flush in his cheeks appearing to be more than merely the result of the brisk autumn air. There was a hectic gleam of triumph in his eyes.

He clasped Phaedra's hands between his own. "I have come to take you home, my dearest one."

She regarded him dully, but Jonathan did not seem to notice her lack of gratitude. He produced a cloak, which he wrapped about her shoulders, his fingers clumsy and trembling. "Come. Let me take you out of this dreadful place."

Although she was not quite steady on her feet, Phaedra resisted his offers to carry her. When he escorted her through Bedlam's main gallery, the scene that had once so horrified her no longer seemed real. All the slack mouths, the blank stares, the emaciated arms straining against chains, gesturing toward the visitors like performing monkeys—it was like gazing upon one of Hogarth's disturbing sketches of London's dark side. Phaedra remembered what Belda had said about Marie and experienced a brief surge of satisfaction. She was glad that Marie had escaped. Wherever the poor creature had gone, it would have to be better than remaining here.

Phaedra felt exhausted by the time they emerged into the street, and she permitted Jonathan to lift her into his waiting carriage. She sank back against the squabs. In the early days of her confinement at Bedlam, she had longed for nothing so much as the sight of the sky, the feel of the sun upon her face. Now she shrank from the light like a wounded animal.

As they rumbled away from Bedlam's walls, Phaedra felt grateful for Jonathan's silence. He had made no mention of the loss of her babe. But then, he had ever been a man of great sensitivity and consideration. He appeared content to sit opposite her, gazing at her with a feverish glow of happiness in his eyes. She wished she could demonstrate more thankfulness for his rescue, feel something besides this leaden despair that weighted her soul.

The progress of the carriage seemed painfully slow. After some time, Phaedra roused herself enough to glance out the window. Frowning, she realized the coach's dilatory movement was owing to the fact they were heading into the city's crush of traffic, not away from it.

"Jonathan, this is not the way to the Heath."

"I know that. I am taking you to my home instead." He could not quite meet her eyes. Phaedra thought she understood why.

"My grandfather died while I was in Bedlam. Didn't he?" she asked.

"N—no." Jonathan's hands fluttered in a nervous gesture. "But there is naught more that can be done for him. 'Tis you that need taking care of now, and I mean to do it—as I have always done."

Phaedra started to voice a weary protest, but hesitated. The way Jonathan looked at her made her uneasy. Such a strange stare. And yet, the expression was somehow not unfamiliar to her.

He reached across to pat her hand. "You were never happy at the Heath. Sawyer was so wretchedly careless of you. So much evil in the world, and he never protected you. First Lord Ewan, then that Searle woman and—and worst of all, that cursed marquis."

It disturbed Phaedra to hear Jonathan couple James's name with those other two, although she did not know what caused the shiver to course up her spine. Then the thought struck her. Ewan and Hester were dead. But James . . .

Somewhere in the numbness that was her heart she felt the first knife stroke of fear. "Jonathan, have—have you heard some tidings of the marquis?"

"Aye, he is back in London," came the colorless reply.

Back! The knife stroke became a piercing stab. James had been in London, while she lay trapped in Bedlam, near death, losing their child.

"And he made no effort to come for me?" she faltered.

"There is nothing to fear my dear. I am the only one who knows where you are."

Phaedra could not understand why Jonathan's calm statement raised prickles along the back of her neck.

"Jonathan!" Her voice was strangely sharp as she said his

name. She supposed that as always he was attempting in his muddled way to help. "But I have to see Jam—the marquis."

"Eventually." Jonathan caressed her fingers. "I will have him out to the house."

Phaedra found nothing in Jonathan's words or touch that was reassuring. An unreasoning fear grew steadily inside her, although she tried to quell it. Nay, nothing was wrong. This was Jonathan, her quiet, solemn friend. He seemed to have been part of the background of her life forever, as solid and unthreatening as her desk or books.

And yet when he kissed her hand, the feel of his lips lingering upon her flesh caused her to shrink away from him. When the carriage was forced to halt because of the press of traffic, she inched toward the door.

"It is kind of you to want to care for me, Jonathan. But I need some time alone. I will take a hackney back to the Heath."

She reached for the handle, but he was too quick for her. He caught her wrists, pinning her back against the seat. Although weakened by her recent ordeal, Phaedra yet had no notion that Jonathan could be so strong. Her lips parted to cry out, but he pressed one hand over her mouth, fairly suffocating her.

"You must be quiet, my dear," he soothed. "Too much excitement is bad for you . . . and I will never let anything bad happen to you again.

Phaedra's heart thudded as she felt the coach lurch into movement once more. Feeling too stunned to move or struggle, she stared up at Jonathan, past the skeletal tension of his fingers crushed against her face. How could she ever have been so blind? After all her weeks amongst the madness of Bedlam, she should have recognized at once that look of the damned roiling in her friend's dark eyes.

Phaedra strove to maintain an outward semblance of calm as she was led through the silent house, guided by the inexorable touch of Jonathan's hand upon her elbow. Where was everyone? She saw no sign of any servants or the elderly cousin whom she had hoped would help her gently subdue Jonathan. She regretted not having appealed to the coachman or anyone in the street. But it was too late to correct that error in judgment now.

Jonathan gave her a nudge and forced her into a room of his house she had never seen before. Here the oil lamps were aglow even in the daytime, revealing a chamber far different from the austere decor of the rest of the house. In the center was a bed with a canopy and gauzy, delicate curtains. It looked like a fairy queen's bower, all pristine white lace and ribbons with a pale blush of pink. A gilt dressing table was laid out with all that a feminine heart could desire—perfumes, ivory-handled fans, and a jewel box so laden with sparkling gems the lid did not quite close. Wardrobe doors had been left flung open to draw attention to a rainbow array of gowns.

Jonathan twisted his fingers, his eyes pathetically eager, like a child offering a bouquet of wildflowers. Phaedra rubbed her arms, averting her gaze so that he should not see how sick at heart she was. She noted the initials engraved on the silver handle of a brush with a flourishing scroll. *P B*

At first, it made no sense. Then the significance hit her with a jolt. *P B Phaedra Burnell*—exactly what her own monogram would be, if she were Jonathan's bride. She gazed at the elaborate room, the work of many months of planning, dreamings spun out in Jonathan's mind, until the thread worn so thin had wrenched apart with a quiet snap.

She stared at her old friend with pitying eyes and fought the urge to sink down upon the bed and weep for him. She would be no use to either of them if she succumbed to hysterics.

He hovered far too close to her. "Do you like it?"

" 'Tis—'tis beautiful," she managed to choke.

"I have been arranging it all for over a year now."

"But Jonathan," she could not refrain from protesting, "over a year ago, I was still wed to Ewan."

His soft smile chilled her. Apprehension whispered eerily along her flesh like the brushing of moth wings.

"There was no difficulty about that," he said. "Ewan was ever reckless when he rode, cruel to his horses, cruel to everyone. After you told me what he had done to your books, I couldn't let him torment you any longer. I had to do something."

"But his death was an accident," she said hoarsely.

"Not precisely, my dear. Oh, his death was his own fault. But I met him out upon his estate and suggested the direction in which we should ride. When we got to the stone wall, I simply had to rein in. He was so reckless the way he took his jumps. The plow was ready and waiting. It was almost all his own doing."

Jonathan spoke as though it were the most reasonable thing in the world. Phaedra ran a hand over her eyes. This was a nightmare, and she couldn't seem to wake.

"Everything would have been all right then." Jonathan sighed and regarded her with mild reproach. "Except by that time, you had started that Robin Goodfellow business. I hated it. I knew it be only a matter of time before that old woman found you out."

"Old woman? What old woman?" she asked, wondering if this was but more of Jonathan's madness.

"That Searle woman, of course. She was always prying. Dreadful creature. I told Sawyer never to employ her."

But her grandfather had paid no heed. No one had ever paid heed to Jonathan, least of all herself. Perhaps, Phaedra thought sadly, that was what had reduced him to this. Feeling her legs ready to give out, she sank down upon the chair at the dressing table. Dreading what he might say next, she yet felt it far safer to keep him talking, clinging to the desperate hope that someone— perhaps one of Jonathan's servants—might return to the house to help her.

"So Hester knew about my writing?" Phaedra was astonished that her voice could sound so calm. They might have been conversing over the tea table, as they had so many times before.

"Aye, Hester found your drafts, and she wanted money to keep silent. She knew better than to approach Sawyer, but being aware of my fondness for you, she came to me instead."

Memory rushed back to Phaedra. Hester's conversation in the garden that night, the unseen man. It had been Jonathan, and not James, that she conspired with. Phaedra's fingers fidgeted with the ivory handle of a fan; the gesture, she hoped, would conceal how nervous she was. "So then you planned to kill her, too?"

Jonathan looked hurt. "I didn't plan it, Phaedra. I was very reasonable and paid her what she asked. But the wretch was too greedy. Even as I placed the money in her hands, she was already sniggering, saying this would do for a start. I knew I never would be able to trust her or rest easy again. It was her own fault.

"We were in the kitchen. When she turned away from me, I had to do something to stop the greedy witch. There were logs stacked by the hearth. One of them was just right."

Phaedra shuddered at how pathetically proud of himself Jonathan sounded. "I never acted so quickly in my whole life. But then I realized I had to make it appear more like suicide or an accident.

So I carried her up to the garret and thrust her body out the window."

Phaedra glanced quickly away from him. It was like peering into the dark, twisted corners of someone else's soul. She trembled when he rested his hand upon her shoulder.

"I felt so relieved when you gave up that writing. The worst part of it all was when those riots began and I overheard Jessym at the coffeehouse, threatening how he would expose Robin Goodfellow if he had to—to save his own miserable hide."

The grim thought crossed Phaedra's mind that Jessym was lucky to find himself still alive. It was a wonder that Jonathan hadn't . . . Suddenly another realization clicked in place with painful clarity.

She gazed up at Jonathan. "You! It was you who took my papers, forged grandfather's seal, and gave them to Jessym."

Her accusation agitated him. "Short of killing Jessym, there was nothing else I could do. I hated to shift the blame to Sawyer, but he is nothing next to your happiness. I would destroy anyone who threatened your safety."

Phaedra slunk out of the chair and backed away from him. The vehemence in his words frightened her. She paced toward the window and shifted the curtain aside, hoping to see help in the streets below. But as she drew back the material, she found the glass boarded over, the wood covered with a landscape scene painted in pastels. She was as much a prisoner here as she had been in Bedlam—only now she had a madman for her gaoler. Phaedra clutched her hands together resisting an hysterical urge to beat against the boards.

Jonathan stalked toward her, pleading, "Don't turn away from me, Phaedra. You must see that I have done all this for your good. I never meant to hurt you. The most difficult of all was helping to rid you of that babe."

Phaedra's veins turned to ice. She felt her face drain of all color. "Jonathan . . ."

But he didn't seem to hear her faint plea to make an end of all these horrible confessions, to tell her it was but a bad dream, to become her calm, dependable friend again.

"I thought the cold water of the pond would be enough. The shock should have made you miscarry. I knew you swam far too well to drown, and of course I was right there, to protect you." He shook his head mournfully. "But it didn't work. And then I was afraid that when you recovered, you would go back to Ireland, just as you had said. It was then that I thought it might be best to have you looked after, until I could think of something else."

With a chill, Phaedra dredged up a memory. Jonathan had always loved to boast about his patronage to various charities, and Sawyer Weylin had chaffed him about throwing away good money. Bedlam. It must be one of Jonathan's good causes.

"You—you are a patron of Bedlam?"

"Indeed I am. I have always been most generous, so that it was not difficult at all to arrange your stay there. I kept praying that somehow you would yet miscarry by natural means. But in the end, to protect you from that sinful child, I had no choice but to put the tansy root into your stew."

Phaedra bit down hard upon her knuckle, drawing blood. Yet she felt no rage against the man who had destroyed her child, only horror of his twisted logic, of a mind diseased past all healing.

She cowered back when he advanced upon her, but he only stroked her cheek. It was like a caress from the grave. Her friend Jonathan was dead, and now some demented stranger was using his gentle voice and soft eyes to terrify her.

"You must put everything behind you now, Phaedra. You are safe. No one will find you here."

No, she thought wildly. That couldn't be true. James. Hadn't Jonathan said earlier that James was looking for her? Her lashes swept down to conceal that hope, but with the cunning of madness, Jonathan seemed to read her mind.

"No one," he repeated. "Not even the Marquis de Varnais. I will see to that."

Her heart gave a wild thud. She could scarcely speak for the fear strangling her. "What are you going to do?"

"You must not worry." He brushed a kiss against her mouth, and she fought the urge to scrub her hand across her lips. "You must rest now, my dear. You are looking quite fatigued."

As Jonathan turned to go, Phaedra had a wild impulse to dart past him, but she knew she would never make it to the door. She must remain calm. James's life could depend upon it. Jonathan was clearly planning something, and James would not be on his guard against the gentle-seeming man—any more than Hester or Ewan had been.

She raced after Jonathan and caught his arm. "J-Jonathan. Let me . . . let me help you to destroy the marquis."

He patted her hand with an indulgent smile. "I could not do that. It would be far too distressful for you."

"No, I hate him!" The shrillness of fear in her voice made her words sound genuine. "He seduced and abandoned me. I will never know peace—never be happy unless you grant me this."

Jonathan's brow furrowed. Her heart plummeted in despair. She would never fool him. Then he nodded gravely and said, "Very well, my dear. I will come for you when it is time."

"Jonathan," she pleaded, but he was already leaving, locking the door behind him.

Phaedra could no longer keep her frenzy at bay. She rattled the handle, but quickly realized the futility of it. Racing over to the window, she pounded against the wood, then attempted to pry free the boards. Hopeless. Jonathan had obviously taken care to leave nothing in the chamber—not even fire irons—that she could use to smash her way to freedom.

Phaedra spun way from the boarded-up window and began rummaging through the drawers of the dressing table. Surely she could at least find a hairpin and attempt to pick the lock on the door. But it seemed Jonathan had even considered that possibility, for her search turned up nothing.

He had done a most thorough job of sealing her off from the world. There was no way out, no one to hear her. Her only choice was to wait—if she could keep from going mad herself before Jonathan returned. What if he changed his mind and simply went ahead . . . No. She refused to consider that grim possibility.

Instead she spent her time in the useless pursuit of re-examining the past, entertaining guilt-ridden thoughts of how much she had had to do with Jonathan's broken mind. Had she given him the wrong impression when she had risked her life to nurse him through the pox? Had she been too kind to him over the years, or mayhap not kind enough? Would it have made it better or worse if she had . . .

Phaedra sank her head into her hands. She did not see how it could possibly be any worse. The time dragged by until she wanted to scream. She had no notion of how many hours passed before the click of the lock announced Jonathan's return.

As Phaedra raised her head to look at him, she caught a glimpse of herself in the mirror. Her face was ghostly pale, her hair wildly disheveled. Jonathan, by comparison, looked perfectly ordinary, his neckcloth arranged somberly, his demeanor calm. Anyone might be forgiven for supposing that *she* was the mad one.

" 'Tis time, my dear," Jonathan said solemnly. He extended his arm in a courtly gesture to escort her downstairs. Phaedra wanted to shrink from him, but her recent terrors had left her so light-headed that she was obliged to accept Jonathan's support.

He led her to the small parlor below. The rest of the house was dark and silent, but here a small fire glowed on the hearth. The candles were ordered in such grim array that the room had a funereal look.

"The marquis will be here soon," Jonathan said. "I told him I had tidings of you."

Phaedra concealed her shudder. She could not formulate her own plans until she knew what Jonathan meant to do. He drew her over to the sideboard and indicated a large crystal pitcher, filled with what appeared to be water.

"Pure vitriolic acid," he said. "I have diluted a small portion and added it to this."

Jonathan held aloft a full wine decanter for her inspection. "Rascally merchants do it all the time to improve the body and color of inferior products. There is a little more here than is customary. His lordship will perish from careless drinking of clumsily adulterated wine."

Phaedra's gaze flicked with horror to the crystal decanter. The burgundy liquid sparkled a rich red. Never had death been put in a more inviting form.

Jonathan arranged the decanter and the glasses neatly upon the tea table, then tugged her by the hand. "You will wait in the next room behind the door. You can see everything from there. You shall have your vengeance soon, Phaedra."

His eyes glazed over as he said, " 'Twill be a most hideous painful death, but no more than the marquis deserves. Then nothing will stand between us, my love."

As Jonathan reached up to stroke her cheek, Phaedra could no longer conceal her revulsion. She felt relieved when he permitted her to slip past him into the dining room. She hoped he would close the door; then she might be able to escape through one of the long windows and warn James before he reached the house. But whether Jonathan simply reveled in gazing upon her or he did not yet completely trust her, Phaedra was unsure. Whatever his reason, he kept her within sight during the strained half-hour of waiting that followed.

Her jarred nerves shook when finally there came a thundering summons at the front door. Jonathan's features suffused with an expression of suppressed excitement as he held one finger to his lips. Warning Phaedra to remain silent, he closed her in the dining room. She could hear his footfalls fade as he stalked toward the front door.

Phaedra whirled about frantically, but she knew it was already too late. By the time she escaped through one of the windows and raced around to the front, James would already be inside the house.

Indeed she could already hear Jonathan returning. Cautiously, Phaedra inched open the door and peered into the parlor.

Jonathan addressed a shadowy figure beyond his shoulder. "Come and warm yourself at the fire. I will fetch you a glass of wine."

James swept in, impatiently stripping off his gloves. Phaedra's heart constricted with a mingling of joy and fear at the sight of the familiar hard angles of his face, the waves of dark hair, the cool blue eyes that were so blessedly sane.

With a choked cry, she flung open the salon door and ran to him. She had but a glimpse of his astonishment as she hurled herself into his arms.

"Phaedra, thank God," he said. "I have been going out of my mind searching for you."

She sagged against the welcoming strength of his chest, gasping out words that were barely comprehensible. "James, take care. Jonathan . . . he's mad. He—"

But James was given no chance to make sense of her words before Jonathan's mournful tones broke in. "You shouldn't have done that, Phaedra. You have made it all so much more difficult."

Without releasing her, James turned and she felt him start. Phaedra looked up in time to see Jonathan raising a sword. The tip glinted, but its shine was no more lethal than the fanatical light in Jonathan's eyes.

With incredible calm, James eased Phaedra away from him. His voice reasoned gently, "You'd best put that down, Mr. Burnell."

Jonathan advanced, his eyes blazing. Phaedra knew he would try to run James through where he stood. She flung her body protectively in front of James.

James hurled her aside, hissing in her ear, "Run!" A split-second later, Jonathan thrust at him, but James was too quick. He sidestepped the blow, recovered and backed toward the mantel. Phaedra watched, terrified. Why didn't James draw his own weapon? Her gaze flicked to where his sword should have been, the sickening realization sweeping over her. He was unarmed.

She moved desperately, catching at Jonathan's arm, but he shoved her roughly and knocked her into the tea table. She fell, bringing the table down with her. The glasses shattered and the poisoned wine stained the carpet bloodred.

James was forced farther back as Jonathan came on, brandishing the sword. "Villain!" Jonathan half sobbed. "You—you hurt Phaedra once, but you'll never touch her again. I will protect her as—as I always have done."

He lunged wildly, but James again eluded him. As Phaedra struggled to her feet, she saw that James had managed to move away from the fireplace into the center of the room.

"Easy, Jonathan," he soothed. "All we need do is be calm and talk this over."

Jonathan lunged again, this time catching the end of James's cloak with the sword. James dove toward the sideboard. In desperation, he snatched up the thick crystal pitcher and dashed its contents over Jonathan's face.

Letting out an inhuman scream, Jonathan dropped the sword. He clutched madly at his eyes and fell to his knees, writhing like a soul in torment.

"Wh—What?" James glanced toward Phaedra, his eyes clouded with confusion and horror.

"Acid," Phaedra said, pointing numbly to the pitcher James still held in his hand. "It was acid."

With a savage oath, James flung the pitcher aside. He leaped at Jonathan and pinned him to the ground, trying to restrain the older man from tearing at his own flesh.

"Water! Fetch water!" James commanded. Phaedra stood frozen. "Move!" he bellowed.

She bolted from the room.

Hours later the parlor yet bore signs of the struggle. The poisoned wine had left a large red stain on the rug, and no one had bothered to upright the tea table. James perched upon the edge of the settee. He buried his face in his hands as they waited for some word from the grim scene upstairs, where the doctor was attending Jonathan.

Phaedra crowded close to James, curling one arm about his rigid shoulders. The room was silent, except for the fire crackling upon the hearth.

"Blind," James muttered at last. "He's going to be God-cursed blind."

Phaedra stroked back the dark strands of hair that fell across his brow. "It was not your fault. You had no way of knowing. It was Jonathan himself who placed the acid in that pitcher, not you."

"The poor bastard was mad. I only wanted to stop him, not—" James broke off and pulled away from her. He rose to his feet, rejecting her efforts at consolation.

A lump formed in Phaedra's throat as she stared at him. This was the man she had once thought of as cold-blooded. Nay, a lack of feeling had never been James Lethington's problem. The man felt far too much.

When a sound came from the hall beyond, both she and James tensed, anticipating the return of the doctor.

"Jamey?" someone called, in a lilting Irish accent. The parlor door opened, and a tousled head of dark curls poked inside the room.

"James? Where the deuce have you been, man? I've been waiting forever."

Gilly halted abruptly as his gaze fell upon Phaedra. "Fae!" He bounded into the room with a joy-filled growl and swept her up into his arms, nearly crushing her. The roguish green eyes moistened as he choked, "Damn it, Fae. I thought you'd been carried off by the banshee this time for sure."

She started to assure him she was very much alive when he gave her an angry shake. "What the devil do you mean vanishing that way, frightening the life out of everyone? Where have you been?"

Phaedra drew back, wiping at her tears. "It is a long story," she said. And she wasn't sure she would ever have the heart to tell it.

Gilly's eyes darted shrewdly from her to James's haggard face. He uprighted the overturned tea table. "And what in blazes has been happening here? Where's Jonathan?"

But he didn't wait for an answer, shrugging. "Well, I suppose it will keep for a few more minutes. I have to fetch Julianna in from the carriage."

"Julianna!" Phaedra started. In light of the disastrous events of the past few hours, she had forgotten James's mission to find his sister. But before she could say anything more, James glowered at Gilly.

"Why the devil did you bring her here?"

"I could scarcely be after leaving her alone, could I? What with you haring off and not sending me a blessed word."

James turned aside with an impatient gesture. "I suppose you'd best bring her in," he conceded with bad grace.

As Gilly left the room, Phaedra gazed at James. "So you did find . . . how was . . . I mean, how is she?"

"You will see for yourself in a moment."

The bitterness in his voice told Phaedra all she needed to know. Dread clutched at her as she awaited Gilly's return.

When he stepped back into the parlor, a timid wraith of a girl clung to his arm, her blond hair and ravaged blue eyes all but swallowed up by the hood of her cape.

Phaedra's greeting died upon her lips. She blinked and stared as though seeing a ghost.

"Fae," Gilly said solemnly, "may I present Miss Julianna Lethington."

But Phaedra swept past her startled cousin to ease back the girl's hood to peer closer at the white face, trembling with uncertainty.

"Dear God," Phaedra breathed. "Marie."

Chapter Twenty-three

THE FIRE BLAZED IN THE HEARTH, SENDING WARMTH CRACKLING AT the far end of the music gallery. Candle shine spilled a soft glow upon the spinet and the couple who sat there. Gilly's remarkably gentle tenor voice crooned a ballad to the girl seated beside him, who shyly ducked her head. The girl Phaedra had known as Marie Antoniette.

Since Phaedra had last glimpsed the girl in Bedlam's satanic halls, Julianna's appearance was altered. Her hair was neatly brushed, and she wore a pretty gown. But her frame was still too thin, and there yet lurked a lost, childlike quality to her eyes. Phaedra had the impression that Julianna still sometimes dreamed she was the Queen of France.

Phaedra tucked the ends of her shawl more securely about her. She and James lingered in the cool shadow at the end of the gallery, watching the other couple. Phaedra sat in one of the massive armchairs while James paced before her. He directed a heavy frown toward the spinet. Phaedra had sensed no diminution of the sharp tension in him since their return to the Heath yesterday. She was uncertain whether it stemmed from his feelings toward the old man upstairs, who clung tenaciously to life, although he no longer moved or spoke; or if it sprung from the sight of his sister, who didn't even know him.

Julianna did remember at times that she had a brother James. But she made it painfully clear she could not connect that fiery young man with the tall stranger whose hard features seemed to frighten her.

Gilly stopped singing long enough to guide Julianna's fingers over the keys. James pursed his lips, then resumed what he had been saying to Phaedra before he had become distracted. "When Gilly and I arrived at the cottage, there was no sign of Julianna or Mrs. Link. We eventually found out the woman had died a year ago. Her rascally nephew had been pocketing the money your grandfather sent all that time. He told us some taradiddle about other relatives having taken Julianna north to Scotland."

He sighed. "It was a long, wearisome search before Gilly and I discovered that my sister had actually been despatched to hell."

James's words were such an accurate description of Bedlam that Phaedra did not trust herself to reply. She was stung as a moment of painful recollections shot through her.

James must have noticed, for his grim features softened. He started to reach for her hand but stopped himself abruptly, fairly flinging himself away from her. He resumed his pacing, continuing to frown at Gilly and Julianna.

"Bedlam was . . ." Phaedra broke off, then faltered, "I hate to think of Jonathan in that dreadful place."

"He won't be sent there, I promise you. He will be looked after in his own home."

Phaedra knew that James had been to see Jonathan after the doctor had left, but she'd scarcely dared to ask after him. "Is there any chance that he will ever . . . recover?"

"No!" James's brusqueness did little to conceal his own sense of guilt. "Neither his eyesight nor his sanity. When I left him, he was lost in his own world, talking as though you were there by his side."

Phaedra's lips trembled.

"He appeared strangely happy," James said. "Mayhap more so than the rest of us, who must perforce remain in touch with reality. I sometimes feel that I would have been better off mad or dead than ever have lived to see—"

He broke off, his eyes fixing darkly upon his sister once more. "Anne never was a clever girl, but always gentle and loving. Her genius was in her hands, her ability to breathe life into porcelain. Not only has she lost that talent, but . . ." His voice thickened with anguish. "Christ! She doesn't even know who I am."

Phaedra swallowed hard, wishing she could think of the words

to comfort him. But James was already composing himself as
Julianna rose from the spinet. The girl shrank back as Gilly led her
across the room. She seemed to be forever clutching at his sleeve,
but Gilly showed no signs of impatience. Phaedra had never seen
her teasing cousin quite so gentle.

"Gilly says 'tis time that I went up to sleep." Despite her
manner of childlike obedience, Julianna's eyes were clear. It was
one of her better times. At least she knew who she was. She
curtsied to Phaedra. "Good night, milady."

The girl prepared to skitter away when Gilly stopped her. He
gave an almost imperceptible nod in James's direction. Only at
Gilly's urging, did Julianna approach her grim-faced brother.
Beneath James's stony facade, Phaedra could see the hurt lashing
in his eyes.

" 'Night, sir," Julianna said in a breathless whisper and bolted
out the gallery's door. Gilly offered James a rueful smile and
prepared to follow her, when James bit out, "I need to talk to
you." His gaze slid to include Phaedra. "Both of you."

Raising his brows questioningly, Gilly acquiesced. He summoned Lucy and sent her to look after Julianna, then returned to
sprawl upon the chair next to Phaedra's. Phaedra nervously
fingered the ends of her shawl. She was uncertain of what was
coming next, but the rigid set of James's face assured her it was
not going to be pleasant.

"Tomorrow I intend to take my sister away from here," he
announced. "It is not fitting that either one of us should continue
under Sawyer Weylin's roof."

Phaedra said nothing. She had been expecting this. She gripped
her hands quietly in her lap. It was Gilly who protested. Sitting
bolt upright, he asked, "But where will you go? 'Tis far too late
in the year for you to think of embarking for Canada."

"I had thought of taking Julianna to Dr. Glencoe's. I fancy we
would not be unwelcome there."

Gilly relaxed. "Ah, Hampstead? 'Tis not so dreadfully far. I
could still ride over and—"

"No, you couldn't," James said. "I must ask you to stay away
from my sister."

Stunned, Gilly turned white; pain flashed in his green eyes.
Phaedra leaped to her feet, glaring at James.

"How dare you speak as though Gilly means more than kindness by Julianna! Are you implying that my cousin would take advantage—"

"Nay, Phaedra, 'tis all right." Gilly rose and placed a restraining hand upon her arm. "You cannot be blaming the man. I understand, even if you don't. Very few would want a papist, an Irishman besides, to come calling upon his sister."

"Damn it. That has nothing to do with it." James's hard look wavered as he regarded Gilly with an expression of gratitude and brotherly affection. His lips twisted into a half smile as he said, "You are a damned fine man, Patrick Gilhooley Fitzhurst. Under other circumstances, I would have been happy to—" James raked his hand through his hair with a weary sigh. "As matters now stand, the idea of any man courting my sister is absurd."

"I don't quite follow that," Gilly said stubbornly. "She has recovered remarkably since we took her away from that place."

"Open your eyes, man. She will never be what she once was."

"I don't know what she *was*," Gilly said. "I only see what she is now, a gentle lady whose spirits need time for mending."

"Gilly, for her sake as well as yours, don't be cherishing any false hope. Her mind can drift away at anytime. She would never be able to love you as a wife should."

"Her needing me would be enough," he said, an unaccustomed touch of bitterness shading his green eyes. " 'Twould be more than anyone has ever done before."

James flung up his hands in exasperation. He glanced at Phaedra as though appealing to her to reason with her cousin. But she could not bring herself to do so. She had been deprived of much hope herself; she would never attempt to snatch away Gilly's.

Gilly abandoned his belligerence and assumed a more coaxing tone. "Don't be after looking so grim, James. I'm not saying I expect to wed her tomorrow, next month or even next year. I only want to be her friend until she grows strong enough to accept more."

"You could be waiting the rest of your life," James said.

Gilly gave him a light poke on the arm, saying with a half-smile, "You'd never think it to look at me, but I can be a very stubborn man."

He turned to go, but before he reached the door, James called after him a grim warning. "I will be taking my sister along with me on that ship to Canada next spring."

Gilly's saucy grin in no way diminished the obstinate jut of his chin. "That won't be disturbing me at all. I don't suffer from seasickness."

Phaedra hid her smile as he whisked out the door. James continued to look like a thundercloud, then he let go with a laugh compounded of anger and reluctant admiration.

"Your cousin is a far bolder fool than I," James complained to Phaedra.

"His folly is one of his most endearing traits," Phaedra said softly. With Gilly's departure, the vast music gallery seemed too quiet.

Her eyes met James's and a deep consciousness seemed to rush between them. Suddenly, they were left alone, with all that they had shared, the pain of all that could never be.

They broke eye contact simultaneously. Phaedra shook out her skirts and said, " 'Tis late. I suppose I should be retiring, too."

James nodded. He didn't even attempt to stay her. They might well have been strangers, not two people who had shared the greatest intimacy a man and woman could know. For a moment, Phaedra hesitated, realizing she had never told James about the life they had created. But the babe was lost in that same desperate darkness that had consumed their love. There was no point in inflicting any more pain upon him. Let it be her own private grief.

She started to turn away, when she felt a touch upon her shoulder so tentative, it seemed far too slight to bridge the gulf of misunderstanding between them.

His voice constricted as he said, "You—you have not told me what your plans are, what you intend to do now."

She shrugged. "I shall stay with Grandfather until—until he no longer needs me."

She saw James compress his lips and read the condemnation in his eyes. "How touching," he said. "Mayhap I should abduct young girls and send innocent men to the gallows. I didn't know it could inspire such loyalty."

Phaedra flinched before his harsh words. "I know I should likely despise my grandfather as much as you do, considering all that he has done," she said. "But I cannot."

In halting phrases, she explained to James some of Sawyer Weylin's background—the dire poverty and the tragic circumstances that had led to the death of his young wife.

"I think Grandfather simply grew too hard. He learned to

substitute ambition for love, which is a great pity." Phaedra's voice dropped to a whisper. "For I could have loved him if he had ever given me the chance. James, my grandfather is not an evil man like Carleton Grantham was. I don't expect you to ever forgive him, but for your own sake, please—"

James's flinty tones interrupted her. "I am planning no more acts of vengeance, if that is what you are afraid of."

"No, I didn't mean . . ." She drew in a deep breath. "And I am sorry that I ever accused you of being the one who used those papers against my grandfather." She raised her hand in a helpless gesture. "But I was hurting too much to be reasonable. I felt you had rejected all that I offered you, that you didn't understand exactly how much that was."

She continued in a small voice, "I never thought I would trust any man again after Ewan. To put my life entirely in your hands was not that easy—"

"It was not easy for me, either," he broke in passionately, "to set aside the anger that had occupied the whole of my waking thoughts these past seven years. God, Phaedra, I did try!"

"Mayhap neither of us tried hard enough," she said.

James reached out to capture her hand. His voice was husky. "Is it so impossible that we should try again?"

She gazed up at him, her breath catching at the depth of love she found blazing in his eyes, the desperate yearning. Before she could answer him, the gallery door opened.

Lucy thrust her head inside, her voice a frightened squeak. "Lady Phaedra, you must come upstairs at once. Your grandfather! He's surely about to die."

Phaedra had no need to disengage her hand from James's. He had already withdrawn.

As Phaedra walked alone to Sawyer Weylin's bedside, the lamplight fell across a face withered past recognition. And yet Phaedra thought Lucy must be mistaken. Her grandfather appeared more alert than he had for many a day. He was even trying to speak.

"Grandfather." She caught his hand, the once-plump flesh seeming to sag over his bones. His hand already felt cold.

"That you, girl?"

She could barely understand his ragged whisper. "Aye, 'tis Phaedra."

His glazed eyes roved past her. "Who's that?"

His question made little sense to her until she realized that James had slipped in silently behind her. Even now Phaedra felt an impulse to form a protective shield between him and the old man. She wanted to beg James to go, not to lower himself by triumphing now. But although James's gaze was fixed upon Weylin, his blue eyes devoid of pity, she saw no hate burning there, either.

"Good evening, *Monsieur* Weylin," he said, using the French accent Phaedra had not heard for many a day. "It is I, Armande."

Her grandfather pursed his lips forming the word "marquis" with a kind of satisfaction in producing the sound.

Phaedra could not let this farce continue, not at her grandfather's deathbed.

"James, please go," she whispered.

But he didn't move, never taking his eyes from her grandfather. A struggle seemed to wage within James, then he said, "There is something I need to ask you, sir."

No, not now, Phaedra cried silently. It was far too late to be seeking any answers now. But James's next words were so unexpected, she nearly sagged against the bed.

"I want permission to marry your granddaughter."

Phaedra could not believe what she was hearing. She doubted her grandfather comprehended, either. The old man's breathing was becoming more labored.

"I want to make her my wife," James said. "The Marchioness of Varnais."

For a second, her grandfather's eyes flew open wide, a trace of his old gleam appearing. He tried to repeat the title but he could not manage the sounds. With the words still on his lips, his eyes closed.

The silence that followed seemed to stretch out forever. Phaedra knew the exact moment when her grandfather drifted into his final sleep. His coarse features had never known such restfulness in life.

Phaedra realized she was clutching James's hand. Their eyes met. "Thank you," she said, "for letting him believe . . ."

"I didn't do it for him," James said hoarsely. "I did it for you."

She was well aware of that, but it was enough. With a muffled sob, Phaedra flung herself into his arms.

* * *

They were married on a cold day in February, the simple ceremony witnessed only by Julianna and Gilly. The service was performed by a fresh-faced young curate who had never heard of James Lethington.

As they left the church, Gilly roguishly remarked to Phaedra, "The fellow had not the least notion he was marrying you to a dead man."

The four of them gathered in the Green Salon afterward. Gilly leaped up on a stool and proposed a toast. "To James and Phaedra: A long, happy married life, and a quiver full of children."

His boisterous good wishes were echoed softly by Julianna. Gilly crowded forward to kiss the bride. As he planted a rough buss upon her cheek, Phaedra was pleased to see Julianna daring to embrace her brother.

When his sister timidly presented James with a wedding gift, Phaedra noted an expression of barely veiled triumph upon Gilly's face.

James slowly undid the wrappings. His hands trembled as he unveiled a bird molded of clay. The execution was crude, and yet there was promise of something more, some life stirring in those outstretched wings. Phaedra saw James swallow hard. With some difficulty he murmured his thanks and pressed a tender kiss upon Julianna's brow.

"Come, Julie," Gilly said, linking an arm about her waist. "As the French would say, I'm thinking we are quite de trop." But before Gilly could leave, James clasped his hand in a hard grasp. From the look the two men exchanged, Phaedra could tell an understanding had been reached.

When they were alone, Phaedra glided over to her husband's side. He was yet examining the bird, a smile teasing his lips as he glanced up to look at Phaedra. He indicated the outstretched wings. "It looks as though he is straining to be free. He rather reminds me of you."

Phaedra shook her head, taking the bird and setting it down. All the freedom that she wanted stood only a heartbeat away. James caught her hand and pressed a tender kiss to the simple gold band encircling her finger.

"Are you disappointed," he asked softly, "to be the plain Mrs. Lethington, and no longer 'milady'?"

There was only one response to such a foolish question. Phaedra flung her arms about his neck and pressed her mouth to his. James returned the kiss, imbuing it with all the fire and passion of his spirit.

With a long, blissful sigh, Phaedra nestled her head against his shoulder. James held her thus for a long time, both of them watching the snow fall past the Green Salon's long French windows, the heavy white flakes enveloping the world in a hushed softness.

" 'Tis strange," Phaedra murmured, "but I have always hated winter. It always chilled me to the bone. I never realized how beautiful it could be."

"The winters are far harsher in Canada," James said. He added hesitantly, "I have made the arrangements for us to embark next spring, but if you truly did not wish—"

But Phaedra pressed her hand to his lips, hushing him. "I would follow you to the end of the world." A tremulous smile curved her lips. "Even if I freeze to death."

"Nay love." James kissed her fingertips, his blue eyes aflame with love. He swept her up into his warm strong arms to carry her to their bridal bed. "I promise you," he said huskily, "that you will never feel cold again."